HOW TO QUIET A VAMPIRE

Writings from an Unbound Europe

■ □ ■ □ ■

BORISLAV PEKIĆ

HOW TO QUIET
A VAMPIRE

A SOTIE

Translated from the Serbian
by Stephen M. Dickey and Bogdan Rakić

NORTHWESTERN UNIVERSITY PRESS

EVANSTON, ILLINOIS

Northwestern University Press
Evanston, Illinois 60208-4170

Printed in the United States of America

10 9 8 7 6 5 4 3 2

ISBN 0-8101-1719-3 (cloth)
ISBN 0-8101-1720-7 (paper)

Library of Congress Cataloging-in-Publication data are available
from the Library of Congress.

The paper used in this publication meets the minimum requirements of the American
National Standard for Information Sciences—Permanence of Paper for Printed Library
Materials, ANSI z39.48-1992.

■ □ ■ □ ■

CONTENTS

■ □ ■ □ ■

TRANSLATORS' FOREWORD

Borislav Pekić was born on 4 February 1930, in Podgorica, Montenegro, in a well-to-do middle-class family. His father, Vojislav, was a high-ranking state official who also worked for the police—a somewhat ironic twist, considering his son's life-long problem with this institution. Pekić's mother, Ljubica, née Petrović, an outwardly energetic and rational high school teacher of mathematics, had a strong inclination for painting. During Pekić's childhood, the family frequently moved, following Vojislav's professional reassignments to Novi Bečej, Mrkonjić Grad, Knin, and Cetinje. It was in Cetinje that eleven-year-old Borislav first showed his rebellious nature and had the first of his many unpleasant encounters with the police: he was briefly detained during the anti-German demonstrations of 27 March 1941. The Pekićes spent the years of the German occupation at Ljubica's estate in Bavanište in the Vojvodina. This was where Borislav again got in trouble with the police: in an adolescent patriotic outburst, during a soccer game, he called a German player "a kraut swine." The family moved to Belgrade in 1944, after Marshal Tito's partisans liberated the city with Russian help and established a communist government. As young Borislav noted, the ideological change spoiled the taste of victory for him: "That year I was deprived of one of the happiest of all human feelings—the feeling of being liberated, victorious, and triumphant—and I realized how poignant it is to be defeated in victory."

Pekić's problems with the communist regime culminated in November 1948, when the police arrested him as a member of the Association of Democratic Youth of Yugoslavia, a well-organized, rather large anticommunist group, which, in his words, raised necessary funds "using both Robin Hood's and Lenin's methods."

Pekić was in charge of ideology, propaganda, and the work of a secret printing shop. One of the group's escapades, in which a few typewriters and mimeographs were stolen from a government office, brought charges of "terrorism and armed rebellion" against him. The indictment also included "espionage on behalf of one or more foreign powers." Pekić originally got eight years in jail, but the prosecution lodged a complaint and he was sentenced to fifteen years.

Pekić's imprisonment decisively affected his life, ideas, and subsequent writing career. After five years, he was released on probation, but the rough treatment that he received during the pretrial investigation in Belgrade and in the Sremska Mitrovica and Niš prisons undermined his health, and he fell ill with tuberculosis. He also began to write in prison, although he insisted that his first attempts "at creativity" dated back to his elementary school days in Knin, when he wrote a diary urged by his mother's wish to improve his handwriting. The reasons behind the prison diary were naturally quite different, as were the tools that he used: on one occasion, he scratched his observations on pieces of toilet tissue with the tooth of a comb.

After he left prison, Pekić studied psychology at the University of Belgrade. In the early 1960s he began to work as a screenwriter. He was finally able to make some money, but, as he put it, this "improved his games of poker rather than his standard of living." At the same time, Pekić was working on several of his future novels. The first of them, *Vreme čuda* (translated in English as *The Time of Miracles,* 1965), came out when he was already thirty-five. Seven months prior to its publication, Pekić went to the hospital, diagnosed with an extremely serious case of tuberculosis. After his release, he soon discovered that the short period of his relative affluence was over. In search of material security, he became the editor of the influential literary review *Književne novine,* in 1968. Yugoslavia's tempestuous political events of that year helped him find an appropriate ending for his second novel *Hodočašće Arsenija Njegovana* (translated in English as *The Houses of Belgrade,* 1970) and further complicated his relationships with the authorities. He used the Belgrade University students' march on the city in June 1968 as a symbolic illustration of a farcical repetition of revolutionary history that eventually kills his novel's hero; at the same time, the authorities accused him of being the students' ardent supporter, although he did not share their radical Marxist ideology in the least. Consequently, when he decided to leave Yugoslavia and move to England in 1970, he was refused a passport and had to wait for a year before he could join his wife and daughter abroad.

In the 1970s Pekić distinguished himself as one of the best Serbian contemporary dramatists. He always insisted, however, that he was a theatrical dilettante who began to write plays only because he felt "a psychological need for political involvement and action" but eventually "chose theater rather than open rebellion." The end of this decade was marked by the publication of the first in a series of seven books that fully established Pekić as one of the most important Serbian authors. In 1978, after more than two decades of planning, researching, sketching, and developing, the first volume of *Zlatno runo* (The Golden Fleece, vols. 1–7, 1978–86) appeared.

At the age of fifty, Pekić—who insisted that his life took different turns "at the beginning of each new decade"—became somewhat dissatisfied with his work. He claimed that his previous novels had brought him "nothing but disappointments," primarily because they dealt with "inherited models" of human history. Therefore, he decided to project his new vision into the future and thus avoid the restrictions of the "historical models" with which he had inevitably to deal in his earlier works. As a result, during the 1980s he produced three novels—*Besnilo* (Rabies, 1983), *1999* (1984), and *Atlantida* (Atlantis, 1988)—each following the antiutopian tradition in its own way. In the late 1980s, after the one-party political system had collapsed in Yugoslavia, Pekić finally returned to Belgrade and once again became involved in politics as one of the prominent members of the Democratic Party. In another uncanny twist of irony, exactly fifty years after his first clash with the police in Cetinje in 1941, he again was beaten by security forces, in 1991, during demonstrations organized in Belgrade by the united opposition against the ruling Socialists of Slobodan Milošević. And the following year he again developed problems with his lungs; unfortunately, this time the problems proved fatal, and he died of cancer in London on 2 July 1992, active both as a writer and as a public figure almost until his last day.

Although Pekić refused to be actively involved with a group of Yugoslav dissidents during his self-imposed exile in London, the communist authorities at home still considered him a persona non grata, and in 1973 the publishing house Nolit canceled the publication of three of his works—*Kako upokojiti vampira* (*How to Quiet a Vampire*) among them—that had already been accepted and paid for. Nonetheless, as soon as the book appeared a few years later, in 1977, the Association of Yugoslav Publishers recognized *How to Quiet a Vampire* as the best novel of the year.

Based on Pekić's own prison experiences and his firsthand understanding of police methods at work—as well as his thorough knowledge of the long tradition of European philosophical thought—*How to Quiet a Vampire* offers an insight into the mechanisms of the logic and psychology of modern totalitarianism. It tells the story of the former SS officer Konrad Rutkowski, now a professor of medieval history at the University of Heidelberg, who returns to a coastal town of D. in Yugoslavia where he served as a Gestapo agent twenty-two years before, during the Second World War. Rutkowski returns to the scene of his past crimes, spurred by the ambivalent urge both to justify and renounce his Nazi past. His painful inner deliberations are described in twenty-six letters to his brother-in-law. Rutkowski tries to reach a moral compromise with his own past, exploiting some of the major currents of European philosophy. Thus, the self-styled editor of his manuscript, Borislav Pekić, loosely connected the individual letters to some of the best-known and most influential works of European thinkers: Plato, St. Augustine, Descartes, Locke, Kant, Hegel, Marx, Nietzsche, Freud, Wittgenstein. The editor considered this necessary in order to show that Rutkowski and his ideology and the logic do not represent an aberration from the traditions of European philosophical thought, but rather its continuation and logical development: Rutkowski's thought was simply the result of a "logical radicalization" of that European philosophical tradition.

Written at the peak of the Communist era in Yugoslavia and allegedly dealing with German Nazism, *How to Quiet a Vampire* simultaneously looks back to the 1940s and sums up the political reality of Yugoslavia in the 1970s. In view of the upsurge of new forms of dogmatism in the Balkans (and elsewhere) during the 1990s, the novel has certainly not lost its topicality—it remains one of the most chilling accounts of the psychology of the "captive mind" in contemporary European literature. But the real meaning of this sometimes harsh satire is much more subtle: the glaring horrors of the "practice" of totalitarian ideologies are associated with more obscure threats implicit in some of the "theories" of the seemingly benign tradition of European rational thought. In this regard, its message parallels the reappraisal of recent Western culture (especially with respect to the Holocaust) suggested by George Steiner's *In Bluebeard's Castle* (notably, both were written more or less simultaneously in the early 1970s). Thus, exposing totalitarianism as well as challenging accepted Western philosophical tradition, *How to Quiet a Vampire* is a warning to a world that is well aware of what has transpired in the past but apparently unwilling to believe that some of it can happen again—and in the most unexpected intellectual, cultural, and political surroundings at that. In this respect, the novel is clearly distinguished from most other literary accounts of modern repressive systems. Pekić claimed that his intention was to show that "fascism or a similar form of totalitarian oppression could show up at our doorstep once again, and this time submerge us in its floodwaters once and for all." But he also indicated that there is no discrete boundary separating the intellectual tradition of which Europe is so proud from some of its more recent aberrant political ideologies. In this way, *How to Quiet a Vampire* is one of the most important literary works to question the ethical validity of a large part of the history of rational thought in the Western world as well as the role of intellectuals in it.

—Bogdan Rakić

Borislav Pekić's *How to Quiet a Vampire* presents considerable challenges to a translator. They begin with the title itself. The verb in the original, *upokojiti,* while containing the root *-pokoj-* "quiet" as well as "rest," has in fact a particular meaning: to perform the ritual killing of a vampire, laying it to rest forever (including the well known task of driving a hawthorn stake through the heart). There is no verb in English that has these particular connotations. Therefore, we decided on "to quiet," which serves as an adequate translation on a metaphorical level if not on a technical one.

A trickier set of issues lies in the threefold linguistic interface of a translation into English of this novel, written in Serbian, which at the same time includes considerable amounts of Nazi German terminology and concepts. One problem is the translation of the peculiar Germanicized SS ranks occurring directly or indirectly throughout the text. Pekić sometimes gives these ranks in the original German (e.g., *Obersturmführer*) and sometimes in Serbian translation (e.g., *poručnik* "second lieutenant"). We have opted to render these ranks consistently in the original German, primarily because of problems stemming from the way superiors were and are addressed in the German and Yugoslav armies on the one hand and in the United States army on the other (which we will not waste space explicating) and also because these ranks have been often kept in the original in the literature and films of Eastern European countries (e.g., Poland). The result is that the original German terms appear more frequently in the translation than in the original. The inclusion of little-known foreign language material is, however, very much in the spirit of Pekić's writing in general. These ranks, as well as other recurrent German language terms and various abbreviations, have been translated and defined in a glossary at the end of the novel. With this, we offer the reader one last compromise in Pekić's Rutkowski case—our translation, a compromise between the Serbian original and nothing at all.

■ □ ■ □ ■

HOW TO QUIET A VAMPIRE

To Danilo Kiš

EDITOR'S PREFACE

This book contains twenty-six letters and two postscripts written by Konrad A. Rutkowski, Ph.D., professor of medieval history at the University of Heidelberg, addressed to Hilmar Wagner, assistant professor of twentieth-century history.

The role of the editor was determined by the nature of the manuscript, which alternates between a personal confession, a historico-philosophical essay, and a narrative. The editor, however, resisted the temptation to interfere with the text and give any one of these elements primacy. As a consequence, his role necessarily remained minor. Nevertheless, its extent should be defined.

First, even during the translation from the German original, technical adaptations were made for the Serbian reader. The original German is retained only in places (in letter 12) where vital literary considerations required such an approach.

No factual changes were made in the manuscript other than the substitution of certain names of individual persons and places with fictional names or initials. The intention was to avoid any misunderstandings that might arise from any emotional damage to those who participated in or witnessed the events portrayed. In this regard, it should be kept in mind that these letters present the view of the history of the Second World War and the historiographic ideas of one of its educated participants, whose mental condition, unfortunately, occasionally leaves something to be desired.

The titles given to the letters were, obviously, added by the editor and may be justified as a vain burst of artistic imagination. They are, however, based on the spirit of each individual letter. The bitter polemic led by Professor Rutkowski against the European intellectual tradition (though he proudly considered himself to be an organic part of it), in which he ascribes to it an inordinate share of the blame for his own personal tragedy as well as the catastrophic demise of Germany, gave me an excuse to associate each letter with one of the European philosophical schools and to title each one of them after a masterpiece of human thought from a different epoch. As the titles reflect the content of each letter—sometimes obviously and sometimes only indirectly—associations are occasionally created that might lead to the erroneous conclusion that the editor agrees with the author and adds his own jibes to the serious arguments of the latter. May these lines eliminate the possibility of any such misunderstanding: The editor is a devoted admirer of the European philosophical tradition, even when it, via Pythagoras, recommends that we renounce the pleasure of eating beans for the sake of a more fruitful life.

(The *Meditations* of letter 1 belong to M. Aurelius; *Matter and Memory* of letter 2, to H. Bergson; *Thus Spake Zarathustra* of letter 3, to Nietzsche; *Principles of Nature and Grace* of letter 4, to Leibnitz; *A Discourse on Method* of letter 5, to Descartes; *Introduction to Psychoanalysis* of letter 6, to Freud; *The World as Will and Imagination* of letter 7, to Schopenhauer; *The Meaning of History* of letter 8, to Berdyaev; *The Phenomenology of the Spirit* of letter 9, to Hegel; *Ecce Homo* of letter 10, again to Nietzsche; *Essays on Human Nature* of letter 11, to Locke; *The Decline of the West* of letter 12, to Spengler; *Phaedon; or, of the Soul* of letter 13, to Plato; *Logical Investigations* of letter 14, to Husserl; *Praise of Folly* of letter 15, to Erasmus; *The Apology* of letter 16, once more to Plato; *A Debate on Human Nature* of letter 17, to Hume; *Sic et non* of letter 18, to Abelard; *Reason and Existence* of letter 19, to Jaspers; *Being and Time* of letter 20, to Heidegger; *Being and Nothingness* of letter 21, to Sartre; *Creative Evolution* of letter 22, once more to Bergson; *Civitates Dei* of letter 23, to St. Augustine; *The Rebellious Man* of letter 24, to Camus; *The Poverty of Philosophy* of letter 25, to Marx; *Beyond Good and Evil* of letter 26, a final time to Nietzsche; *A Critique of Pure Reason* of postscript 1, to Kant; and the *Tractatus Logico-Philosophicus* of postscript 2, to Wittgenstein.)

The book's title, however, was inspired by the editor's conviction that Professor Rutkowski's reflections are the colossal attempt of a guilty conscience to find a modus vivendi with its own past, either by atoning for it or by silencing it.

While working on the manuscript, the editor attempted to verify certain facts by interviewing witnesses as well as consulting documents in the archives of the municipality of D., the archive of the Belgrade office of the IV D section of the Geheime Staatspolizei, and the central archive of the Gestapo headquarters on Prinz Albrechtstrasse in Berlin. The results of these investigations are presented at the end of the book in the form of notes.

In addition to sporadic comments by the editor, these footnotes present the expert findings of three respected German psychiatrists (Drs. Schick, Holtmannhäuser, and Birnbaum), who were requested to ascertain the state of Rutkowski's mental health on the basis of his correspondence. Although in agreement that he had a severe mental disorder, they could not reach a unified conclusion regarding any aspect of his illness. They differed in their views on the type of illness and on the cause and time of its development; there was even a serious debate about the possibility that this was not a case of insanity, but rather of an atypical case of psychopathy. It is difficult to avoid the impression that they confused a puzzle that was already in and of itself quite complex. But inasmuch as this confusion, in addition to serving as a warning, represents an almost organic part of the Rutkowski case, the editor has included it in this book, in a somewhat abbreviated form.

At several points in the last six letters the text has been *reconstructed,* as it was, because of extraordinary circumstances, illegible or incomplete.

No other alterations were made. The editor, in fact, believes in the principle—the object of so much ridicule nowadays—according to which the task of a storyteller is not to create or destroy myths, but *to tell a story.*

And for the story I am indebted to Professor Hilmar Wagner of the University of Heidelberg. It was through his kindness that I obtained this manuscript (which he apparently never read) as well as the permission to publish it, as the author died in an automobile accident during his trip home on 6 October 1965, in circumstances that have never been clarified. I am also indebted to Mrs. Sabina Schrägmüller, Rutkowski's widow, presently married to Mr.

Schrägmüller, the former chief of police in Magdeburg and now a federal official in the Bundesrepublik. I am likewise grateful to the following: the municipal government of D.; the members of the psychiatric team (even if it seems that their contribution did more harm than good); and, finally, those who gave me access to various closed archives relevant to this case.

I would also like to express my gratitude to the authors of numerous published studies that have enabled me not only to better understand the problems addressed in Konrad Rutkowski's letters and to annotate them with endnotes, but also to begin to comprehend such unusual personages as SS Standartenführer Heinrich Steinbrecher, and even Professor Rutkowski while still an SS Obersturmführer. The realization that they developed from one current of the standard European philosophical tradition and that the "molecular structure" of their thought was merely a logical radicalization of that current was stunning and exciting. For those interested in checking the validity of Dr. Rutkowski's conclusions, I can make the following suggestions for further reading:

Adolf Hitler, *Mein Kampf; Organisationsbuch der NSDAP;* Jaques Delarue, *A History of the Gestapo* (1966); *Trials of War Criminals before the Nuremburg Military Tribunals:* I –XI (1951–53); Erich von dem Bach-Zelewski, *Leben eines SS Generals* (1946); N. Baynes, *The Speeches of Adolf Hitler,* 1942; Edward Crankshaw, *The Gestapo, Instrument of Tyranny* (1956); Rudolf Diel, *Lucifer ante Portas* (1949); Gunter D'Alquen, *Die SS* (1939); W. Frischauer, *Himmler* (1953); P. Hausser, *Waffen SS im Einsatz* (1959); E. Kogan, *Der SS Staat* (1947); E. Kogan, *The Theory and Practise of Hell* (1951); H. Arendt, *The Origins of Totalitarianism* (1959); K. Patel, *Ein Beitrag zur Soziologie des Nationalsozialismus* (1954); Gerald Reitlinger, *The SS* (1956); G. Reitlinger, *The Final Solution* (1953); J. F. Steiner, *Treblinka* (1967); Evelyn Le Chêne, *Mauthausen* (1971); F. Friedman, *Oswięçim* (1946); R. Hilberg, *The Destruction of the European Jews* (1961); R. Conquest, *The Great Terror* (1968); Weissberg-Cybulski, *Conspiracy of Silence* (1953); A. Koestler, *Darkness at Noon;* A. London, *The Confession* (1969); T. Mann, *Doktor Faustus;* L. Feuchtwanger, *Josephus;* G. Grass, *Die Blechtrommel;* R. Howe, *The Story of Scotland Yard* (1965); F. Stead, *The Police of Paris* (1957); Bruce Smith, Jr., *Police Systems in the United States* (1960); B. Whitaker,

The Police (1964); J. Coutman, *Police* (1959); E. Freund, *Police Power* (1904); J. Wilson, *Varieties of Police Behavior* (1968); E. Lavine, *The Third Degree* (1930); Charles Franklin, *The Third Degree* (1970); H. Gross, *Criminal Investigation* (1962); Leon Radzinowicz, *Ideology and Crime* (1966); G. R. Scott, *The History of Torture Throughout the Ages* (1940); H. C. Lea, *A History of the Inquisition of the Middle Ages* I, II, III (1889); A. Turberville, *Medieval History and the Inquisition* (1920); St. Ignatius Loyola, *Autobiography* (English edition, 1956); R. Harvey, *Ignatius Loyola* (1936); *Orleans Manuscript for the Trial of Joan of Arc* (English edition, 1956); Even D'Estrange, *Witch Hunting and Witch Trials* (1929); D'Estrange, *Witchcraft and Demonianism* (1933); Goldsmith, *Confessions of Witches under Torture* (1886); T. Lowe, *The History of the Devil* (1929); J. Sprenger and H. Krämer, *Malleus Maleficarum* (1494; English edition, 1928); L. Ruff, *The Brain-Washing Machine* (1959); J. A. C. Brown, *Techniques of Persuasion* (1963); T. Reik, *The Compulsion to Confession;* E. Kinkead, *Why They Collaborated;* W. Sargant, *Battle for the Mind;* Mills, *The Power Elite;* E. O. Mönkenmöller, *Psychologie und Psychopathologie* (1930); D. Jeftić, *Sudska psihijatrija* (1951); K. Birnbaum, *Kriminal-Psychopathologie* (1931); B. Hart, *Psychology of Insanity* (1946); Kann, *Die psychopathische Personlichkeit* (1928); K. Horney, *The Neurotic Personality of Our Time;* R.E. Money-Kyrle, *Psychoanalysis and Politics;* H. D. Laswell, *Psychopathology and Politics;* K. Wittgenstein, *Tractatus Logico-Philosophicus;* Nietzsche, *Thus Spake Zarathustra;* Nietzsche, *The Will to Power.* . . .

And all I must do now is answer one question: Why are the private letters of an SS Obersturmführer being published thirty years after the war, when it would seem that the issues they address are no longer significant or relevant? The fact that Prof. Rutkowski served in the RSHA, whose Section IV was known throughout Europe under the ominous abbreviation *Gestapo,* would not in and of itself suffice as a justification. We have abundant documentation of its activities. What distinguishes Konrad Rutkowski's story from the quagmire of the numerous volumes of other testimonies is his unflinching personal attitude toward the subject, his fanatical attempt to draw profound philosophical consequences from it, as well as his rather extravagant manner of acting on those consequences. In addition to the "external" histories of the Gestapo, efforts enumerating its actions and methods, we now finally have one that we might, without great reservation, call "*internal.*" Not only because—for a change—it is the criminal and not the victim who is speaking on the subject, or because it is the organization of individual operations and not their consequences that are described, but because the central and dominant position of the narrative is occupied by a *conscious awareness of it.* A new awareness that observes the old mind-set in past actions, and on the basis of this newly acquired picture endeavors to determine its own possible role in the future. Professor Rutkowski did not succeed in resolving his conflict with the past in the manner that he hoped. Rather, it seems that, in his attempt to erase his old mind-set, he renewed it in a still darker version. The evolution of the professor's thoughts, as it were, shows in slow motion the birth of a totalitarian mind-set, paradoxically from a conflict with totalitarianism, and its consequences for the world and an individual's personal life. And it is precisely this evolution (despite its psychopathic foundation, or precisely as a result of it) that should reveal one of the ways in which fascism or a similar form of totalitarian oppression could show up at our doorstep once again, and this time submerge us in its floodwaters once and for all. This is not meant to dismiss the vital importance of other factors (social or economic, for instance) or as an attempt to reduce real history to a biography of the mind. It is merely intended to reveal that inner, intellectual and psychological motive, which we are inclined to neglect as we observe history on the street, anonymous history lacking names, faces, and origins.

Borislav Pekić
London, August 1976

Geschrieben steht: "Im Anfang war das Wort!"
Hier stock ich schon! Wer hilft mir weiter fort?
Ich kann das Wort so hoch unmöglich schätzen,
Ich muß es anders übersetzen,
Wenn ich vom Geiste recht erleuchtet bin.
Geschrieben steht: Im Anfang war der Sinn.
Bedenkt wohl die erste Zeile,
Daß deine Feder sich nicht übereile!
Ist es der Sinn, der alles wirkt und schafft?
Es sollte stehn: Im Anfang war die Kraft!
Doch, auch indem ich dieses niederschreibe,
Schon warnt mich was, daß ich dabie nicht bleibe.
Mir hilft der Geist! auf einmal seh ich Rat
Und schreibe getrost: Im Anfang war die Tat!

"In the beginning was the *Word*": why, now
I'm stuck already! I must change that; how?
Is then "the *word*" so great and high a thing?
There is some other rendering,
Which with the spirit's guidance I must find.
We read: "In the beginning was the *Mind*."
Before you write this first phrase, think again;
Good sense eludes the overhasty pen.
Does "*mind*" set worlds on their creative course?
It means: "In the beginning was the *Force*."
So it should be—but as I write this too,
Some instinct warns me that it will not do.
The spirit speaks! I see how it must read,
And boldly write: "In the beginning was the *Deed!*"

—Goethe, *Faust*

Part I

Professor Konrad Rutkowski's Letters

■ □ ■ □ ■

LETTER 1

WHY PROFESSOR KONRAD RUTKOWSKI VACATIONED IN THE TOWN OF D., OR *MEDITATIONS*

The Mediterranean Coast, 12 Sept. 1965

My dear Hilmar,

You'll probably be surprised by these letters from a proselyte who could never take up the pen in service of anything more recent than the Counterreformation without considerable spiritual effort. I hope they will find their justification in the unnatural (were I not the offspring of an austere, rationalist tradition I'd say *supernatural*) quality of the events in question. And the fact that I personally "helped those events along" eliminates any doubt about my competence to report on them.

So here I am, Hilmar, in the pit of history. Misled by the pseudodivine indifference of scholarship, we believed that it had been dug for others, and that the task of the historian consisted only in scrupulously labeling and measuring it.

So here I am then, as the people say, in deep shit.

Konrad Rutkowski, Ph.D., professor of medieval history at the University of Heidelberg—*nota bene* the healthy offspring of our clerical herd sitting at the place of honor at the historical dining table—has been irretrievably thrown from the security of our scholarly watchtower, which we considered to be an untouchable fiefdom and which gave you (and until recently, I fear, me as well) an excuse for a bourgeois life of inhumane indifference and irresponsibility.

And for god's sake, don't try to slip away between points *A, B,* and *C* of one of Hilmar's famous notes! Or to hide behind a convoluted reference from one of the multicolored index cards with which you've lined your thin intellectual skin. The things that make for excitement at our conferences have no value as evidence in this "pit of history." Therefore, I'll give you a friendly piece of advice: If you're going to try to disqualify me on the basis of my admission that I have a personal interest in this affair, as you do with all eyewitnesses whose contrary statements frustrate your wise conclusions, hanging a deadweight of footnotes around their necks—you can toss that worthless little arrow away. Because the real topic of these letters is not the Indian summer of 1965 and some boy-scout vacation adventure of mine, but the wartime September of 1943. Although the people, the city and even my spiritual condition have hardly changed at all, the twenty-two-year interval, filled with my convalescence, studies, university career, and for a while now your sister Sabina (despite your silent disapproval), has nevertheless ensured my wartime memories a position of *armed neutrality,* if nothing else. A position, by the way, merciless enough to let this case, which I'm hastening to tell to you in a few letters, be objectively reproduced in the spirit of our profession, but, fortunately, kind enough to allow us to draw from it far-reaching instructions for future historical scholarship. If, of course, there will be any after all this.

Indeed, dear Hilmar, it happened that, since this morning, spurred by the ceremonious removal of a canvas from a giant granite monument, my thoughts have flooded out of the old rut of my bourgeois habits and rushed through uncharted mental wildernesses, in a direction no known rudder can steer.

I'm not inviting you to follow me around across the blank spaces of that geographic map. Even if the amazing secret of Adam the municipal file clerk (the subject of what follows) did capture your heart, if you succeeded in unlocking it with me, you wouldn't gain anything from that discovery. As for losses, I don't believe you're mature enough for them. It isn't worthwhile for a historian of our glorious present day to draw morals from the object of his research, because he has neither the time to turn them into reality, nor the power to ensure their application in the future. You, Hilmar, existing alongside your subject, the history of the twentieth century, side by side with its dates, chimeras and delusions, you have no use—neither professional nor personal—for even the wisest conclusion. And I fear the future you're courting has no use for it either. As always, the future will want to cultivate newer delusions of its own; and the fact that they'll indeed be ours and as old as the world itself won't keep any of our great-grandchildren from taking pride in them and wiping their asses in the meantime with your jeremiadesque warnings and bits of advice.

One more thing. Overcome your thief's habit, otherwise known as the *exchange of scholarly information,* and don't try to pull a bone out of this story for yourself, some meager footnote for your DOCUMENTARY HISTORY OF THE NATIONAL SOCIALIST GERMAN WORKERS' PARTY, and to cram Konrad Rutkowski into the three pages of bibliography that end every scholarly study and resemble a police register of burgled and robbed businesses.

Please limit yourself to understanding, and, if possible, not ridiculing my conclusions.

I can already see you frowning and wondering why that idiot Konrad, if his discovery really has any historical significance, doesn't write a scholarly paper instead of bothering you with his private confessions. Well, Hilmar, here's why:

The fear that the weird circumstances of the postwar—not to admit right away the *posthumous*—life of Adam S. Trpković, the municipal file clerk of the Mediterranean city of D., will be maliciously interpreted and that his incredible story (a chronicle of death and postmortem transfiguration, a story, I repeat, not of Adam but of what happened to his otherwise unimportant personage in what's known as the Second World War) will be ascribed a parabolic, universal significance that it doesn't deserve—this fear forces me to hide the truth about him from the public in the deepest gutter of memory, in a world of perpetual imprisonment where our true essence is left to rot. It is a regrettable circumstance that in this particular case

I am, by experience and conscious choice, not a storyteller but a *scholar*—to emphasize my real roots with this dead expression— whose current research interests are focused, as you know, on the relations between the Curia Romana and the Slavic Wislans, who adopted the Christian Gospel in its legitimate Western European interpretation as early as the tenth century and thus became the basic purpose of our ethnic, spiritual, political, and military *Drang nach Osten*. This circumstance has only strengthened my fears of the public and the misfortune that befalls any being that, lacking the gregarious instincts that have ensured the primacy of the community from the time of our ancestral cave dwellers and provided its loyal members with a comfortable security in exchange for freedom, ventures to challenge its unpredictable behavior.

On the other hand, I could no longer keep quiet either. So I've opted for a compromise—that old, cunning rat gnawing at all great heroic acts. I've decided to tell a story, which is nothing other than the chronology of the devastating effects of such heroism on our lives. That's the reason why I'm writing private letters when you would be publishing a paper that would win you, in addition to scholarly acclaim, a reputation among the most ardent opponents of our turn eastward, those, indeed, who insist that the term "turn" be replaced with the traditional Germanic term "thrust."

Therefore, I ask that you not bandy my discovery about while I'm alive. Afterward you may do whatever you like and whatever your—most often misguided—inspiration tells you to do.

Let me get back to myself. I do promise you that these letters will, in spite of their confessional tone, not be the story of a scholar who's lost confidence in his work, in the purpose of historiography and perhaps history itself, but the story of a provincial scrivener who stumbled into that history like an unsuspecting person falls into a pit dug for others, and who unexpectedly found his purpose and reckoning there.

However, as I am lost when it comes to anything beyond reliable and incontestable facts—because up to now it has been my hope, and this hope alone has redeemed my work, that by studying history I'll come to know the immutable realities of our distant past and not its phantom, protean appearances—the inadequacy of these lines is unavoidable and we must learn to live with it. I'll never be sure that I've stressed this aggravating circumstance enough, both as an excuse for my lack of skill as a storyteller and as an explanation of the inexcusable revulsion I feel for the loathsome person comprising the content of my confession. I'll add as a consolation that this humiliatingly unprofessional excuse, so alien to my monographs, wouldn't be necessary had not the aforementioned Adam (although an isolated and neglected topic of my wartime experience, buried with a few sentimental honors in the mass grave of my memories of the Geheime Staatspolizei) throughout his unjust imprisonment strove to break into the world of Prince Mieszko, which had been conjured up for the prince's coronation in the seventh chapter of my current book, and to proclaim his own misfortune *Urbi et Orbi*. Not as a reproach or a request for compensation—the impeccable clerk must have known that the administration would compensate him in full—and still less as a call to rebellion, but most likely in the simple hope that his bad luck would be joined by similar misfortunes all over the world, so that when united they would form a brotherhood that wouldn't lack a single kind of suffering, a single form of poverty, a single example of deprivation. In short, they would form a MODEL SOCIETY which in its perfection, definitiveness, and immutability would appear to be the best of all possible worlds: natural and not exceptional, inevitable and not accidental, necessary and not superfluous.

Don't think that Adam's resurrection wasn't natural. It really was. It's in vain that we want misfortunes to be outcast, rejected, refuted. Futile is our wish for adhesion, the mother of chaos, to reign in the world of evil, in the world of the Sorrel Horse. Misfortunes—and here is one more, perhaps the most unbearable—exhibit a mutual magnetic attraction, complement and complete one another like days spent in prison (days that are identical like twins), which move from east to west with deathwatch discipline, from evening's renewed hopes, ambitions, and plans to the sobriety and discouragement of morning. Among misfortunes there holds a cumulative principle, cohesion rules—the mother of order and orderliness. And the short breathers, slipped like a cuckoo's egg in between the evil we've experienced and the evil that awaits us, are announced to us like a crude bait, whose purpose is to keep us in tolerable condition in the name of a still darker torment. This was why my miserable file clerk yearned to join me. Because, Hilmar, I was an unhappy man, no matter how little the gilded aura of my public life pointed to this fact. Adam rushed at me as a ravenous vampire descends on blood. The hawthorn stake of shame, with which I hammered him fast deep down in my subconscious, was not, even according to the magic formulas, enough to quiet him. It only immobilized him. And when, through my inattention, the stake was pulled from his heart, Adam came to collect.

When we decided to spend our vacation on the Mediterranean, your sister Sabina's thriftiness, her northern Altmark habit of getting the most for her money—in our case as much sun as possible—met with wholehearted support from my secret plan to make a pilgrimage to all the locations of my wartime service. While we were choosing our vacation spot, hunched over geographic maps and tourist brochures, I suggested that we set up camp in the town of D. I swear I did this without any noticeable mediation by Adam Trpković, except in the extremely condensed form of a stream of prisoners that flowed through the basement of the Sonderkommando der Geheimen Staatspolizei in D., where I was forced to work with much bitterness and inner resistance, as you know. Only this morning did I determine that it was Adam and no one else who dragged me out here, though I still don't know why: to take a cruel revenge or to teach me that *real history*, which I apparently didn't have a sense for.

Why fool ourselves, Hilmar? Even the best among us never get beyond a more or less conscientious reconstruction of historical facts. But historical facts are the oysters from which time has already extracted its pearls. Despite an abundance of material, we're unable to restore their living innards; we have only the dry, dead shells, leaving beyond our knowledge and perception everything that *really* happened under those enigmatic ciphers of the past, no matter if it assumed the cruelest forms of suffering, tribulation, and death. However, it is those innards, as I realize only now, that comprise the only relevant content of a *real history*, which will never be written down.

Hilmar, do you see how much hesitation and disapproval there is in my description of the file clerk's vampirization and his satanic efforts to intrude on my peace of mind and work? Indeed, I intended to finish editing my book on the birth of the Polish state in the Oder and Vistula river basins during the reign of our Oton I. But evidently nothing will come of this. For something like that you need a conception of history as a material in a hard, aggregate state. Adam's transfiguration demonstrated that the true aggregate state of history is *gaseous,* resembling smoke, which constantly changes form. And when we finally succeed in discerning it, it leaves in our consciousness hardly a single droplet of truth. And under such conditions, what sense is there to even the most conscientious historiography?

Sadly, this isn't the only reason for my idiosyncratic approach to Adam. It might sound sacrilegious, Hilmar, but I can't stand unhappy people. The realization that I number among them does nothing to dispel that animosity. On the contrary, it almost seems to provide more lethal ammunition. (Don't you think that unhappiness has something ugly, renegade, rebellious, sinful, if not *demonic* about it?) Of course, I'm not indifferent to the suffering of others. I did, after all, receive a Christian upbringing firsthand, so to speak, from my grandfather, the spiritual shepherd of a small evangelical community in southern Banat. But my manifestation of this sensitivity is fairly exclusive. In the presence of suffering I feel a slight intolerance, a nervous indisposition toward the afflicted, instead of sympathizing with him in his misfortune and feeling anger at his tormentors.

Don't try to be witty at my expense, as is your repulsive habit, and to maintain that I joined the police to ensure legitimacy (and perhaps a higher meaning) for that unchristian aspect of my character. I was forced into the Gestapo, because of my extraordinary memory and knowledge of the local language, of which I have proof in my correspondence with the Berlin Central Office at Prinz Albrechtstrasse 8 concerning my transfer to the front.

It's time to mention another one of my qualities, because it had a decisive influence on my attitude toward Adam Trpković both during his first life—that is, in 1943—and now, during his second, phantom life. This quality, I should say, is nothing other than the active, albeit unseen flip side of my disgust for misfortune and those it afflicts: just as I lose my temper when I encounter suffering (and I know the comparison is inappropriate), I'm seized by unbridled rage at an otherwise impeccable Latin sentence that contains a shamelessly glaring grammatical or orthographic error. But—and this, take note, is the strange thing with me—my rage is not directed at the real culprit for the slip, the printer, author, or copyist, but at the phrase itself, as if it were guilty for the monstrosity it has acquired. In such cases, I take a rough eraser or a special little knife, similar to a nail file, and erase, scratch, or scrape the mistake from the paper like a scab from skin. I thus return the clumsy freak of the original idea to its virgin appearance. All the books I use are pockmarked throughout with my corrections, and it is only a lack of time and perhaps a fear of embarrassment that keeps me from sneaking from library to library like the raging Spirit of Errata and bringing my reformational mania to its full implementation, taking any and all published books, encyclopedias, dictionaries, handbooks, textbooks, newspapers and brochures, letters (public and private), annals, memoirs, enactments, petitions, charters, proclamations, manifestos, announcements and declarations, forms and formulas (including mathematical ones, naturally), decrees, laws and minutes, recipes, price lists, records, inscriptions and transcripts, and even the obscenities on the walls of public toilets, and by careful scientific reconstruction restoring to them their only possible, divine appearance.[1] By reminding you that everything which surrounds me is too full of signs of my craze for happier, more harmonious and effective forms, of my painstaking work on objects which the incompetence or negligence of their creators left in the unhappy state of half-completion, I've presented all the relevant aspects of my attitude toward the file clerk's unusual case. I'll let you, as an experienced historical hack, find the appropriate term for my craving for perfection; I personally think it's a primal manifestation of that same reformational desire with which a higher intellect rocks, reams, and turns this world upside down every twenty years.

As for the significance of the revelations I experienced in D. for my research and even my life, I'll tell you about that when I'm sure what it is; in the meantime, let's see how they can contribute to our story. Probably in the same way, I assume, as the awareness that you are dead drunk helps you walk straight ahead and not come crashing down in the first ditch that appears in your path. Owing to the realization that I've brought the congenital illness of the intelligentsia to its logical conclusion—to the erroneous assumption that WORDS REMEDY DEEDS—I'll at least on this occasion manage to refrain from well-intentioned interventions that make of our history a pleasant fairy tale good for lulling one's conscience to sleep. I'll tell you about Adam Trpković, the municipal file clerk and copyist in D., the official secretary and keeper of the Holy Protocol, *in summa* a state official of the former Kingdom of Yugoslavia, from the lowest and last gutter of the payroll, *sine ira et studio*, without intolerance or sympathy, although at the time of our last meeting in mid-September 1943 I suffered from both sentiments equally. (We were just in the process of replacing the carabinieri on the Yugoslav Adriatic coast. The former Italian zone of occupation was exposed to attacks by the communist bandits—as we called them then—or our generous hosts—as we prefer to address them now.)

In any case, dear Hilmar, all this would be superfluous, both the confessions (which are unpleasant even when made to one's best friend) and the subversive inner resistance (with which I am approaching an episode of *modern history*, something for which I have neither the inclination nor experience that you have), and I'd be leisurely editing my MONOGRAPH ON THE ROYAL CITY OF CRACOW, slightly unnerved by the murmur of the water and the illusion that our pensione, with me at the desk and your sister in bed in the next room, is drifting like an unanchored ship on impenetrable black seas, if only memories did not have lives of their own, lives entirely parasitic, like mildew, but still in some sense independent and not subject to our commands. We are, indeed, sometimes capable of summoning them. In return, we're not in a position to repel at will those that haunt us on their own. Our memories wait in the misty ambushes of the past like faceless, bloodthirsty warriors whose intentions we cannot fathom and whose intrusions we cannot halt. And the memory of Adam Trpković was of their same intrusive nature. So how could I have known what was in store for me?

And yet, I did have some presentiment. Yesterday, at around 5 o'clock in the afternoon, as soon as we entered D. and especially when we pulled up in front of our pensione, in which I was shocked to recognize the onetime *Sonderkommando der Gestapo,* I felt as if I'd been tricked, or as if I were just then awaking from a deception, which, in the end, is the very same thing. Hilmar, that was the humiliating bitterness we feel when we're roused from a reality we view as ours and inseparable from us, and—finding ourselves in a completely different, most often ugly, world—we realize that we've been living for years in a useless dream, that our life has been pure illusion, that what seems to us to be an evil dream is the true, flesh-and-blood, overlooked reality, from which we fled faintheartedly, and that it is the living, painful, and convoluted material of a history that will never be written.

So, my dear Hilmar, a sense of foreboding was my initial state of mind when we drove out onto the beautiful overlook above D., exhausted from the drive through Bosnia-Herzegovina, dirty and depressed, and saw the old Renaissance town laid out below as if on the gray wrinkled palm of an old man, its stone shapes jutting into the blue of the sea. In the next letter I'll write about that feeling and, with it as a sign of warning, begin the history of the miserable life, brutal death, miraculous ascension, and glorious transfiguration of the municipal file clerk Adam Trpković.

In the meantime, stay healthy.

Your somewhat frightened KONRAD.

P.S. As Sabina knows nothing of these letters, she will not sign them, and I ask you not to mention them in your correspondence with her. I have neither the time nor desire to discuss my wartime memories with anyone. You should understand this to mean that, for the time being, any response and especially advice on your part is completely unnecessary.

■ □ ■ □ ■

LETTER 2

PARALLEL TRAVELS, OR
MATTER AND MEMORY

The Mediterranean Coast, 13 Sept. 1965

Dear Hilmar,

The town of D. is a picturesque Mediterranean resort offering an abundance of poorly preserved archaeological sites from the late Roman period, as well as considerably better-preserved testimonies to its inhabitants' skill at Renaissance architecture dating from the time of the unstable, often barely recognized Venetian and domestic (Slavic) condominium. Let's attribute this destruction of history less to southern slovenliness than to the natural consequences of acclimatizing oneself to one's surroundings: what appears to a chance visitor to be extraordinary and—all chained off, guarded, and marked with multilingual signs—worthy of admiration, appears to a local as a part of his everyday routine and thus cannot count on special treatment. When you wash your underwear at a fountain of Michelangelan beauty, you cannot worship Michelangelo or attach mysterious and holy significance to a Roman emperor who cooled his feet in it. In all other respects, the town would remind you of a noisy Calabrian agglomeration. The heat, a certain dilution of color, and an absence of shadows are the features that first strike a foreigner. Followed, of course, by those animalistic southern smells.

We descended a steep road that Roman legions had also used to reach to the seashore, and drove off toward the Miramare pensione, a stocky two-storied building of cut stone, with a musical name but a sinful past, the pitiful dates of which I will acquaint you with when I describe how its interior looked in September 1943—once I have, by some obscene coincidence or Adam's postmortem intrigues, received as a room my old investigative office, which in 1965 is now a quite comfortable two-room suite.

For the time being I drove around the town, and the realization that I would be spending my vacation in a mausoleum amid the corpses of my police memories was still far away. Nevertheless, I responded to Sabina's lively remarks with a gloomy silence. When I let a word or two slip out, it had nothing to do with what she was saying. It was as if we were driving through two different towns, built on the same space but kept completely separate by differing depths of perception: Sabina's eyes saw only her D., a town in 1965, whereas my eyes saw only my old D., the town I passed through in 1943. While your sister was getting excited about the bas-relief on the town hall, I was listening beyond the stone masks of the bustling parapets to the scrambling activity of our military garrison. Her "sweet bungalow" was for me an open area overgrown with weeds, where the soldiers of the *Brandenburg* Regiment played soccer. Sabina's "shady promenade" was where Konrad's machine-gun nests were positioned, their muzzles overlooking the sea. Sabina's "cute square" was in Konrad's town a gallows.

Thus, the town I was driving in wasn't the town your sister was passing through, and so any meaningful exchange of impressions was disallowed in advance. As soon as we entered the homey protection of the pensione's rooms, this discrepancy was aggravated considerably by my feeling that I was again in the offices of the Gestapo and eventually resulted in a bitter argument on account of my insensitivity, sagacious dryness, and even thriftlessness, because I wouldn't take everything I was paying for. But as this disagreement will continue up until the end of our stay in D., let the description of Sabina's entry into the town end here, and let me return to my entry, the *real and true one.*

When I entered D., dearest Hilmar, I was in the third staff car of the first motorized column of the *Brandenburg* Regiment. We arrived from central and western Bosnia after smashing our hosts near Mrkonjić Grad, and Jajce and on the Dinarian massif—without my direct participation, of course—and in the majority of the coastal areas that came under control of the partisans after the news spread that the Italians had finally done their traditional duty as allies and left us in the lurch. (The town of D. itself, however, had never been in communist hands. The garrison of the *Marka* Division had been caught in an attempt to break through to the west and had been disarmed, so that the situation in the town when we arrived is best described as anarchy.) When we arrived, we were more or less on our own. That is to say, surrounded by a patient scorn, which now in 1965 is suppressed by certain interests and which then in the autumn of 1943 was stifled by fear. Our reputation was one of cruel and effective conquerors, and I don't think it was exaggerated. At least not as far as cruelty was concerned. With respect to effectiveness, the fact that I'm not writing this letter from our Dalmatian protectorate has a considerably devaluing effect. In any case, that change of masters must have seemed rather conspicuous, sudden and worrying to the locals, as if a mild Italian summer had been replaced without warning by a severe German winter.

In the lead car, surrounded by a motorcycle escort, was the regimental staff; in the second was the communications command with its operational orderlies, and in the third, as I said, were those of us from the Geheime Staatspolizei. The administration brought up the rear.

Do I even need to say that a certain distance was kept between our car and the other staff cars, in spite of all wartime regulations? Thus, the column resembled a giant message in Morse code, in which our signal was typed at the end by mistake. You were in the war. You know what everyone thought of us. You'll understand the insulting significance of the irregular distancing of our car from the others. Given the requirements of the service, we were allowed to enter the town first. We were also obligated to do that by a special army order. Nevertheless, this isolated position of mock honor in the column served to let us know that the German Army had nothing to do with us or our obscure police activities.

I sat in the back seat in the black uniform of an SS Obersturmführer of the Geheime Staatspolizei and in the capacity of wing adjutant of the Sonderkommando staff, which meant—to boil things down—the spiritual and physical runner of SS Standarten-führer Heinrich Steinbrecher, the commander of the mobile executive unit, which was otherwise stationed in Belgrade. He was standing beside me, ramrod stiff, resting his left hand on the back of the driver's seat while the gestures of his right accompanied his procedural conclusions about an unknown town where he had to take his measures.

Let me first introduce my superior to you by highlighting his most negative qualities. It's through them that we learn a person's character best. And besides, I fear Steinbrecher didn't have any positive ones, *cum reservatione:* Prussian steadfastness in conduct and conviction. However, because this was of the most loathsome sectarian and partisan cast, I wonder whether it's appropriate to stress his staunchness as one of the lighter sides of his dark character. To be brief, SS Standartenführer Heinrich Steinbrecher, the commander of our Sonderkommando, twice received the Iron Cross for nonmilitary accomplishments in territories under military occupation and was a hardened National Socialist. And if he were more hardened in anything else, if there were anything for which in a moment of crisis he was prepared to sacrifice his ideology, his fatherland, his immortal soul, and even himself—that was the supremacy of the spirit of universal and omnipotent police control; he was its unwavering believer and incorruptible high priest. Thus, in the final account (and it took me a while to figure this out) he was not even a National Socialist. Or, to find a compromise, he was a National Socialist only due to the geographic circumstances of his birth and only inasmuch as national socialism and police control, which state strategy supported as two harmonious and complementary principles both professionally and ideologically, didn't end up in a provisional conflict as a result of party tactics.

Do you remember Inspector Javert from Hugo's *Les Miserables?* Steinbrecher was his Germanic version. He even met a similar end. To jump ahead a little, he killed himself when news of von Stauffenberg's plot against the Führer broke,[2] but not, as you might naively suspect, because he was involved in the conspiracy, but rather because he, because of his unprofessional intellectual weakness for an insignificant Obersturmführer (need I even tell you who that was?), allowed one of the conspirators to slip away. And—pay attention, Hilmar—one of the *virtual* conspirators at that, because I didn't even know of von Stauffenberg's plot, let alone participate in it. I can prove this most convincingly today, when von Stauffenberg's conspirators stand in high historical esteem, by stating openly that I wouldn't have participated in their stupid venture even if I had known about it.

(Forgive this brief intrusion into your favorite area. I'll be clear. If history doesn't manage to exhaust the possibilities of the direction it's taken, if it's forcibly prevented from unleashing everything, even its most monstrous forces, sooner or later it'll return to seek out its curtailed rights, its insane continuation. Had Adolf Hitler been killed, had the natural course of history been upset and halted on 20 July 1944, and had the main artery of the Germanic vampire—that eternal, astral twin of the Germanic national sentiment—been severed in the "Gaster Barracks," we would, my dear Hilmar, have yet another national socialism today, or we'd at least have to defend ourselves from it. Hitler wouldn't have been defeated, rather his certain victory would have been thwarted. Hitler wouldn't have violated the military and civil oath that he'd given to the nation, rather he would have been prevented from fulfilling it by a new "Versailles," a new betrayal. The vampire within us would once again have had an alibi, our national pride would have gained one more Versailles scapegoat, and we, like immature schoolchildren, would have had to repeat our entire national tragedy from the beginning. Moreover, it's senseless to attempt to crush an order that is based on a consistent ideology. To disappear, it must completely exhaust the last bit of its historical energy. It must die like an old man whose sinful life has exhausted his reproductive energy and even his instinct for the survival of the species.)

The *perpetuum mobile* of our police outpost, the seventh wonder of professional conscience, possessed one more defining form. Honestly, I don't know whether it enhanced or impaired his consummate quality—his fanatical devotion to the profession. I believe that his habit of psychological experimentation with the prisoners (anticipating the glorious contribution of our concentration camps to medicine) had practical benefits in the short run; with his hyenic methods he ensured the appearance of scientific precision, and at his zenith the appearance of a certain inverted, satanic poetry. In the long run, however, from a broader perspective from which one would evaluate the Standartenführer's entire professional life, I'm convinced that this meditative component of his character was his secret undoing. In brief, his penchant for analyses and their logical consequences led him to suicide.

Neither in his appearance nor in his mind did Heinrich Steinbrecher correspond to the popular image of a policeman—the magical symbiosis of a computer, a Renaissance villain, and an Olympic medal winner. Mentally, of course, he was a kind of intellectual machine, but he had nothing of a Renaissance mixture of saint and devil. And above all, that impeccable machine was housed in a rather unsightly body. He was short and small-boned and had a wiry build. He had dark skin, dark, graying hair, and a sharp, narrow face that pulsated like cooling lava. Tireless, unpredictable, effeminate hands and legs like bent springs, quick and elastic. In short: a jester, a black jester from a jack-in-the-box. And if you've gotten the impression that this tireless sentry of our Aryan world domination had indeed a subversively Semitic appearance, you're right. With a beard and a black cloak he'd have fit right in at the Wailing Wall.

I must add one more color to the portrait. I'm afraid that some of his actions might give you the misapprehension that he was cruel. No one was less cruel than he. Whenever Standartenführer Steinbrecher was occasionally forced to resort to violence, it took his heart away, as if he were admitting his ineptness at eliciting the truth from a prisoner by means of a delicate mental game, an unseen assault on one's senses and instincts that surpassed in its power even the most perfect torture. At the Standartenführer's performances—let's characterize his interrogations accurately—the chances for success at the outset were divided fairly between the players who were given the questions and the players who had the answers to them. The playing field was level. Steinbrecher didn't care for suspects who began their great arias of confession and repentance as soon as they entered the room, without the intervention of the conductor. He considered them at the very least professionally inappropriate, not only with respect to him, Steinbrecher, as an opponent, but also to the conspiratorial roles they had assumed. The prisoner's professional duty was to keep silent; the investigator's was to force him to talk. Any deviation from this situation was an unforgivable violation of the holiest laws of nature, on which the institutions of both Crime and Punishment were based. Policemen and Conspirators were, in his view, two sides of the same process and had to be of the best stock in order for the conflict between those two antagonistic yet kindred wills to be considered worthy of effort, and victory interpreted as the perfection of the investigator's discipline.

(One wonders if, in spite of the extraordinary successes in the area of the elimination of state enemies, Steinbrecher should have been ashamed in the face of the astonishing results of his Russian colleagues? I don't think so. Especially since we know that his police task was considerably more difficult and complicated. After all, his competitors in the east were dealing with their friends, not their enemies. One and the same apparatus of "prelogical thought" was ingrained in both the prisoner and the investigator, and through ritual code words, terms such as Revolution, Party, Working Class, or Stalin, a direct inner link was established between them, an emotional pontoon over which there would later be a smooth flow of information and confessions. Because both they and their prisoners had been molded by the same dogma, the investigators sometimes felt that they were investigating themselves, as if they were confronting their own doubts and wrestling with the echoes of their own heretical thoughts. That was what gave them the strength to endure. In their patients they were curing their very own illnesses. And on the other side of the table, the prisoner felt the same dichotomy. The man sitting opposite him was not some unknown policeman, but his very self, his own conscience, the whole of his betrayed life. That conscience spoke a kindred language, had the same way of thinking, and strove toward the same goals. So why resist? Why be ill when the illness in no way distinguishes you from the healthy? Half the battle—victory or defeat, depending on how you viewed the investigation—was already contained here. Heated exchanges on party dogmas could now yield to the routine. But Standartenführer Steinbrecher and all of us in the Gestapo were facing an enemy in the true sense of the word, a counterpart whose brain—what we were really dealing with—functioned according to principles that were completely different from those that governed ours. Most of us were never quite able to cope with this. For most of my colleagues, whose imaginations had dried out over the flame of Rosenberg's *Myth of the Twentieth Century,* the only means of coercion were the traditional pizzle whips, needles pressed under fingernails, and presumably a few cigarette butts pressed into the skin. The war had not given us time to apply the more refined Oriental techniques. Obsessed with an insane pragmatics, the West disposed neither of the Confucian patience of the East nor of an inclination for sadistic abstractions. And the patents of Europe's marauding imagination from the catacombs under the palace of Prince Mieszko Piastowicz were not mobile enough to keep up with the speed of the developments on the battlefield, and seemed anachronistic anyway, like the equipment of a provincial circus. And we did all that with results that couldn't compare to the successes of Standartenführer Steinbrecher, attained by will and pure reason. Therefore, I think I have the right, at least with regard to the quality of the investigative process, to rank the successes of my former commander above all others.)

It seems I must unfortunately end this morning's letter on that parenthetical remark. Your sister is calling me. And although I can't bear the sun, anything is better than sitting in a Gestapo office. I hope I'll be able to write the next letter as soon as tonight. Because, as you've already gotten a glimpse of Standartenführer Steinbrecher, I want you to hear him as soon as possible. But until then—

Sincerely yours,

KONRAD

■ □ ■ □ ■

LETTER 3

SS STANDARTENFÜHRER HEINRICH STEINBRECHER, OR *THUS SPAKE ZARATHUSTRA*

The Mediterranean Coast, 13 Sept. 1965

Dear Hilmar,

Standartenführer Steinbrecher is standing in the staff car, like a captain on the bridge of a destroyer sailing into battle. His assistant adjutant, Untersturmführer Haag, is sitting beside the driver. But where is his adjutant, Obersturmführer Rutkowski, and what is he doing?

Lacking the martial spirit of those around him, my dear Hilmar, he sits cowering miserably in the back seat, like a threatened hedgehog.

Why is he acting like this—why is he doing it?

So that, by taking up the least amount of space in this traveling wartime circus, he can vent his inner discord.

But doesn't he feel like a victor?

Not in the least, damn it! Not in the least.

So what does he feel?

Shame. Shame and terror.

And what does he think he'll accomplish with this demonstrative withdrawal into the fold of his seat?

He thinks he'll let the soldiers and the locals (whose hidden presence he senses behind the narrow slits of their shutters and the opaque windows of the cafés) know that he, Obersturmführer Konrad Rutkowski—despite his funereal uniform and the cuneiform, lightning-bolt insignia on it—according to his deepest and most genuine convictions, does not belong in this spectral column, which the roads have covered with a layer of yellowish, pollen-like dust. Rather, he's been attached to it by force, drawn into it by the whims of wartime organization, owing first and foremost to the chance composition of his blood (which should have been Slavic and not Germanic in southern Pannonia), and owing second to his extraordinary memory, damn that as well.[3]

I believe that Standartenführer Steinbrecher sensed my disloyalty, although I was careful not to give him even the slightest evidence of it through any careless behavior. I performed my regular duties, perhaps not with Rotkopf's murderous enthusiasm or the Standartenführer's machine-like precision, but still fairly effectively, in accordance with the Manual of Military Service, so there was no cause for me to be reprimanded. My resistance adhered to the most virtuous intellectual traditions. It spent itself completely in the domain of the intellect and in the insistence on formulating itself in its own terms. Thus, it was of no use to anyone for the time being, except that it eased my disgusting investigative work with the awareness that I inwardly despised it and that, in this respect, I was different from every other son of a bitch in the profession. My disloyalty remained a secret from the prisoners, from my colleagues, and to a certain extent from Steinbrecher himself. That is, I hadn't yet informed him of my request for a transfer to the front. That would have been a gesture, a challenge, a declaration of war I wasn't yet mentally ready for.

(And when I finally was ready—to get ahead of myself once more—to the highest degree that an intellectual can assemble good reasons for a bad deed, it turned out that my request wasn't prepared to bear the weight of the Standartenführer's counterarguments, despite my having worked on it with academic zeal and attentiveness. Constantly bearing in mind that I needed Steinbrecher's counter-signature in order for my request to be forwarded to Section IV of the Reichssicherheitshauptamt in Berlin, I labored for weeks on the formulation of my reasons. The problem lay in the rather unconvincing nature of my fighting spirit. If the truth be told, I—in contrast to your patriotic haste—decided to enter the war against the Allies exactly four years after the Great German Reich.

"Don't you think you're just a little late, Rutkowski?" he would ask me a few months later.

"With your permission, Herr Standartenführer, the war hasn't ended yet."

"But in the nick of time you've determined that it can't be won without your personal intervention? Rutkowski, do you think your entry into the war on the side of Germany will radically alter the temporarily shitty situation we find ourselves in now?"

"Of course not."

"So then?"

"I thought that in this situation . . ."

"Which situation? Please, be clear. You're an intellectual, not a stargazer."

"I thought that, in the shitty situation which the Standartenführer spoke of, my place is at the front."

"If I'm not mistaken, I spoke of a *temporarily* shitty situation. As you've deigned to eliminate its temporary nature, am I to understand you as considering our situation to be permanently shitty?"

"Not at all, Herr Standartenführer."

"That's heartening. Otherwise I'd have to have you shot for defeatism. So you don't think we're in a difficult position?"

"No sir, of course I don't think so."

"That's disappointing, Rutkowski. It seems that in the end I'll have to shoot you anyway."

"But why, Herr Standartenführer?"

"For subversive negligence. At a moment when we're retreating on all fronts and our cities are going up in phosphorescent flames, your senseless optimism undermines the German war effort."

And then we'll hear one of his famous lectures:

"By the way, if we're not in a jam, what are you going to do at the front? And Rutkowski, don't you consider *this* the front? Do you think we're here on vacation or something? That the front is only where there's shelling going on? Rutkowski, are you too much of a fool to realize where the decisive battlefield of this war is, where our success or failure will be measured? And do you really think we gain anything by occupying territory, if the people slip away from us? Our strategic goal is to defeat, subjugate, and pacify the population. Territory is merely a space in which this goal is accomplished. The real spoils are *people*. And our front is where they are dealt with, Rutkowski. All the other fronts, with the help of providence, are held only so that we might prevail on ours. It's only with the success of the police that military victories gain their meaning. Defeat on our front renders any other victory meaningless for us. Are we in agreement?"

"Yes, sir."

"In that case, you realize that your request may be interpreted only as a flagrant violation of your oath and desertion, which, as you know, is also . . ."

"Grounds for execution."

"Precisely. It turns out, Rutkowski, that I'd have to kill you either way. Considering your miserable professional performance, God alone knows what keeps me from it.")

Let's rejoin the column, Hilmar, to see what else Standarten-führer Steinbrecher has to tell us. Without lowering his gaze, which is as relentless as a drill press boring into the passing houses, as if he were silently penetrating their walls and exposing groups plotting resistance there in those shaded chambers filled with the fragrance of lemon and orange, he places his free hand on my shoulder: "Rutkowski!"

"Yes, sir?"

"You're a born policeman. Genetically a perfectly organized policeman."

"Do born policemen really exist, sir? Besides you, of course."

Instead of answering, he cautions me:

"Everything exists for us. The foundation of the police is a belief in the impossible. *Credo quia absurdum* is our first dogma. If we don't believe that even the impossible can occur in this world, then what's possible will slip by us as well. Inquire who lives in that house on the left, the one with the frieze."

"Any particular reason?"

"Really, do we need a *reason* for something like that?"

"No, of course not. I only wanted to have some sort of orientation point."

"We're in enemy territory, in a zone of maximum subversive activity. But if the generality of such an orientation point doesn't satisfy your refined disposition, try to find a reason inside the house. By the way, if for a moment you'll stop rummaging around in yourself and your little intellectual indignations, and devote some of your precious attention to our mortal world, you'll notice that it's the only house where the shutters aren't closed."

"And where does that lead us, sir?"

"*Primo:* To the conclusion that this house wants to fool us with an innocent and benign appearance. *Secundo:* That you're an idiot if you didn't notice it."

The column creeps cautiously through the outskirts of the city.

"Rutkowski!"

"Yes, sir?"

"You certainly think I consider you a born policeman because I see you hiding from view, obeying the basic law of police behavior, as you imagine it, of course: camouflage oneself, mimic the environment, remain unnoticed at any price. Correct?"

"Yes, sir," I assert dejectedly. "That's exactly what I had in mind."

"You didn't have anything in mind, Rutkowski. Nothing at all! Because if you had, you'd have known that a good policeman does precisely the opposite. He insists on being noticed. He does everything to elicit a reaction, not to avert one. He knows the real bullshit can never be prevented, only put off. Rutkowski, the police is obligated to be the yeast, and not the retardant of popular fermentation. Only a weak police limits itself to the quelling of insurrections. A good police is their catalyst, fermenting agent, instigator."

"And the very best?"

"They organize and lead them."

"But don't we have enough insurrections, sir?"

"As long as there are potential insurrectionists, we can never have enough insurrections. We even need them. Keeping a revolt under control, only to transform it subsequently into an open insurrection with a powerful fermenting agent, some mass injustice—therein lies the whole of our art, Obersturmführer. In its highest form, of course, it's an insurrection whose leaders are our agents."

SS STANDARTENFÜHRER HEINRICH STEINBRECHER

37

"I dare say that this view is quite original."

"What do you mean—immoral?"

"Something like that."

"Well, why don't you say it, Rutkowski? Why are you annoying me with those goddamned English euphemisms of yours? Or do you think I'm an animal, incapable of telling the difference between morality and immorality?"

"Not at all, Herr Standartenführer. It's only that in this case I thought you're . . ."

"But *this* case is the point, Rutkowski! In your opinion, will a potential insurrectionist rise up sooner or later?"

"I think he would. At least the majority of them."

"So what's immoral about your helping him along? Viewed objectively, our approach is moral. What's immoral is your puritanical, hypocritical refusal to put it into practice. And put number 29, the house with the recessed doorway, on the list for a preventive search. I'll have you know that you've disappointed me."

The column has halted. Somewhere up ahead our motorcycle escort is probing further along our route. I'm bitter, Hilmar. I realize that in Steinbrecher's eyes I'm a guinea pig for him to test the effects of his venomous dialectic. A position not at all better than that of any of his prisoners. My position is even worse. His prisoners, after all, can struggle, try to defend themselves, resist. Despite certain physical limitations, they're free. Their behavior depends only on their will. But I'm not free. My limitations are invisible, deeply rooted, moral. I'm not thinking of my military oath, my national conscience, and all those other prized trinkets of yours that determine my civil duties. I mean the duties of a man, an intelligent being who doesn't align himself with the course of history and who is therefore bound to take some kind of action. And I'm taking it, Hilmar. As much as I'm able, of course, and with the restrictions imposed by my duty not to give myself away. Namely, I'm the only man in the whole damned Sonderkommando who is, according to his human and intellectual conscience, inclined to do anything for our unfortunate prisoners. But my personal willingness to help them is dependent on my ability to remain in a position where I can do so. And even to advance to positions where I can undertake it even more successfully. Theoretically, of course, all the way up to the all-powerful position of SS Reichsführer Heinrich Himmler, where I would be able to do it with the utmost success. This kind of moral agenda requires the meticulous and conscientious performance of all my police duties, even the most unpleasant, and all of them with the clear awareness that this is only a loathsome means for the attainment of a higher goal, that the temporary infliction of torture on people is only a necessary path to their permanent liberation. Who would dare to sacrifice such an agenda only out of pure intellectual vanity? To take a public moral stand and with a rebellious gesture compromise—undoubtedly forever—the possibility of its secret but significantly more humane and useful activity?

The column finally moves forward. Standartenführer Steinbrecher continues his experiment:

"But still, you're a good policeman, Rutkowski. And you'd be even better were you to yield to your natural instincts. Do you know why you're potentially a good policeman, Rutkowski? Because you have a soul. Yes, Rutkowski, a soul."

"In that case, it'd be better for me to be a priest."

"A priest? Why a priest, of all things?"

"Because of my soul, sir. Then I'd be able to do something real with it."

"Nonsense! The police is the only place where you can do something real with a soul. In the church it's just communion decor. What does a priest need a soul for? Priests don't need souls. They've got their holy dogma. A policeman doesn't have a holy dogma. He doesn't have anything. For him a soul is an absolute necessity. A policeman without a soul is a machine without a purpose. A *perpetuum mobile!* A maker of wind! A blower of clouds! But I bet you thought the basic quality of a policeman is soulnessness, didn't you?"

"Insensitivity, to be frank, as one can read in some highly esteemed textbooks."

"Really? What do you think the task of the police is?"

"To learn the truth."

"The truth? My foot! What are we, a bunch of goddamned philosophers or something? We *make* truths, Obersturmführer Rutkowski! We don't learn them, we make them! That's a creative endeavor, not an investigative one. We're artists, my dear sir. And were I to have the joy of seeing even the faintest spark of comprehension in your dead eyes, I'd say *poets*. Yes, those who travel *per aspera ad astra*.

(Do you hear him, Hilmar? Can you imagine him? Can you see through him? No? That's what I expected. Don't worry, there's time, there's time. Only when you've grasped to what infernal depths Standartenführer Steinbrecher understands people *like us,* the dark dialectic of our intellectual retreats, moral alibis and spiritual compromises, only then will you understand him and his diabolic power over me.)

He continues: "And in order to plant a truth in someone's soul, you need above all to penetrate it. Now, how in the hell do you plan on penetrating someone's soul if you don't have one yourself?"

"Hauptsturmführer Rotkopf suggests a pizzle whip."

"Hauptsturmführer Rotkopf's a blockhead. Do you carry a pistol, Rutkowski?"

"Naturally, Herr Standartenführer."

"Nothing in this world is *natural,* Obersturmführer. Especially in our line of work. Because I, for example, don't carry one. So we have pistols but not immortal souls?"

"That's not what I said!"

"Even if you do have a soul, I can't imagine it's in great shape. But your pistol, I assume, is as clean as a baby's asshole?"

"According to the regulations, sir."

"However, since the Manual of Military Service does not anticipate any provisions for the maintenance of the soul, you simply let it rust and thus neglect the most effective weapon an interrogator has at his disposal. Rutkowski, did you know that this is an offense equal to the one committed by a soldier who loses his rifle?"

"Well, I do whatever I can for it, as much as the circumstances allow."

"I might have guessed that. We belong to a fine, noble class of men who care for their souls—develop, refine, and polish them—but when they leave for the office in the morning they dismantle them and lock them in their house safes along with letters from their dear mothers and their secret diaries. So they won't get dirty at work. Or be damaged, god forbid. Thus, we have souls, pure and primally transparent, but don't mix them up with our work. After all, they're not what we're paid for. Assuming that our employer, Reichsführer Himmler, has bought them as well, that would mean we've sold our souls to the devil. Because only the devil is capable of buying one's soul. But we certainly don't think our good old Reichsführer is the devil? Or do we? Or do we actually think that, Rutkowski?"

"Of course we don't, sir."

"Accordingly, we have the right to keep our small, tender souls for personal use, and to show up for work at the Great German Reich like a sack of bones and muscle held together only by a center for motor coordination and a black uniform? And I should add Rotkopf's generous contribution: high blood pressure. Is this the picture you have of your contribution to this Sonderkommando?"

"With your permission, Herr Standartenführer, it's not."

"Then sometime you'll have to explain to me exactly what it is. Because one can hardly tell from your job performance. Now tell the driver to stop. They're giving us some sort of signal. We've probably arrived."

The car stops in front of a squat building, which, twenty-two years later, with some architectural additions and subtractions, would be turned into the pensione we're currently staying in.

"Conduct a search of all the neighboring houses," the Standartenführer orders, "and relocate the inhabitants if necessary. Haag, report to General von Klattern that we've moved into position, but that we have objections concerning our quarters."

"What objections, Herr Standartenführer?" Haag asks.

"Is that really important? Simply objections. Because if we don't have any, they'll soon be stationing us in stables! And don't kiss the Army's ass!"

"Understood, Herr Standartenführer!" Haag declares and blinks. Indeed, he worships the Standartenführer. But he also worships the general. "Don't kiss their asses."

"But don't act like a stiff. I don't want problems with the Army. Find the right mix."

"Understood, sir. Find the right mix."

Haag leaves. The Standartenführer turns to me again: "And we'll take a look around the house. Or do you have other plans? I think we passed by some ruins on our way in."

"Remains from the late Roman period. Caius Aurelius Diocletianus."

"Can you tell me at least as much about the locals?"

"Racially Dinaric, with certain Latin features, primarily in their temperament. They're quite similar to the Italians."

"I've had enough of the goddamned Italians! I'll have nothing more to do with them."

"And you won't, Herr Standartenführer," I say spitefully. "They're only superficially similar."

Steinbrecher stretches agilely. Before him lies an unfamiliar town with unfamiliar people, from whom he'll select his enemies. Oh, he won't wait for the bandits to jump him from their ambushes. He'll jump *them*. He'll drag them from their holes before they realize that, with his arrival in the place of some coiffured Latin ape, things have changed fundamentally.

"I'm ready to get started. And you, Rutkowski?"

"Tired and dirty, Herr Standartenführer."

I realize I've made a mistake. Once again, my moral being could not resist the temptation to play the big shot. I should have swallowed all that, my dear Hilmar, and (in the name of the higher interests which I've been writing to you about and which not only excused but also necessitated my work in the Gestapo) demonstrated a mystical devotion to our bloodthirsty work and a readiness to get down to it right then and there. Instead, out of pure intellectual conceit, I betrayed my conscience with useless, rebellious remarks. Nothing happens, however. Steinbrecher gives me a congenial laugh, takes me by the arm and leads me up the stairs.

"I admit, Obersturmführer, that your historical sense for reality sometimes makes my old-fashioned idealism sound funny. Let's see first what our quartermaster has bestowed upon us, and then we'll find somewhere to wash up."

And this reminds me that it's already late and I myself need to wash up before bed. I'm hopelessly dusty.

In the meantime, good-bye until tomorrow.

Yours,

KONRAD

■ □ ■ □ ■

LETTER 4

HOW STEINBRECHER SPOKE, OR *PRINCIPLES OF NATURE AND GRACE*

The Mediterranean Coast, 14 Sept. 1965

Dear Hilmar,

Your sister is out on the beach, but I excused myself by saying I didn't feel well. So I'll be able to send you my fourth letter in the morning mail. I hope the sunny weather will last long enough for me to finish this report. Rain would have kept Sabina inside, and now I'd be playing cards with her instead of chatting with you. Perhaps you'll reproach me for not showing this preference while we were neighbors. Or you'll remember (you never forget anything) that I avoided you whenever it was technically possible. It's true, I couldn't stand you. But you liked me even less. You'll have to determine the reason for your animosity on your own, should you care to do so. I'm obligated, however, to explain the reasons for mine because, as you'll see, they're connected to my topic in a surprising way.

Until now I've thought that I scorned you only because of your mental conformity and the intellectual arrogance with which you camouflaged it, because of your impudent ambition, for which you were capable of sacrificing your better side, the moral potential of your personality. I'm now convinced, however, that the problem here has nothing to do with your personal and scholarly shortcomings. The events in the town of D. in September 1943 and September 1965 have helped me to gain a true picture of the nature of our relationship (which has nothing to do with any family ties) and the reasons for it, and to assume all the blame myself, except, of course, for your crass interference in Sabina's marriage. That falls to your account.

Because I, my dear friend, didn't hate *your* miserable qualities, *your* selfish lifetime goals, or *your* intellectual dishonesty—in short, the conformist and calculating behavior of a citizen of Germany, a democratic Germany but still Germany, which in 1965, like every other country, still has room and cause for moral rebellion. No— I hated *myself,* a citizen of National Socialist Germany in 1943, who was inwardly opposed to its demonic spirit and planned on taking some action to that end, but nevertheless only served as its slave. And paradoxically, I served it more loyally the more I imagined that I was cunningly and successfully resisting it. This repentant confession—which, however, doesn't change anything in your character—will, I hope, enable us to understand one another better over the course of this correspondence. And the happy circumstance that it is unidirectional and planned as a monologue can only facilitate such an understanding.

The room from which I'm writing to you was in 1943 my investigative office. The smooth, brown desk was a little closer to the barred window than is this walnut secretary, its younger double. Instead of the comfortable, low leather arm chair, there was a simple wooden chair . . . But I'm getting ahead of myself. We're just entering the house. We're climbing the dirty staircase where there are traces of an evacuation. The building in which the carabinieri held court is completely empty. I hear Sturmbannführer Freissner swearing that he can smell brilliantine and cheap pomade. Steinbrecher orders the windows to be opened all the way. The Romanic scent of *Eau de Cologne* and priapic ointments must be aired out as soon as possible and give way to the Germanic odors of iron and leather, the penetrating smell of power and pure will. In the meantime, while the imaginary odor of condoms, those "rubber masks of love," is drifting out to sea, in search of their runaway penises, the Standartenführer meditates on our former allies:

"What kind of a police station is this, Rutkowski? It's nothing but a brothel! *Das ist ein Puff!* Just look at the cells! Are they supposed to be for confinement? They're bordello booths! Caverns of promiscuity! All they need is some red velvet upholstery! But they do have the red lamps! Those fucking Italians, they've got the imagination of prostitutes!"

With puritanical disgust, he touches the wall with the tip of his riding crop, touching the image of a hanging phallus that's been scrawled on it, which, as in an old manuscript, illuminates the initial letter of the name *Dagllione*. The *D* is unnaturally elongated and swollen at the end, ready to discharge the seed of the potent Maresciallo Dagllione into the world and increase its population by a multitude of smaller potent Daglliones, future *carabinieri* with plumes on their caps, each of whom will in his turn procreate into greater numbers of even smaller potent Daglliones, more rooster-plumed carabinieri, until they fill the universe with that birdlike militia, all with the same surname and the same racial qualities.

Then he reads, sounding out the following letter by letter:

Tanto gentile e tanto onesta pare
La donna mia, quand'ella altrui saluta,
Ch'ogni lingua divien tremando muta
E gli occhi non ardiscon di guardare.*

"A sonnet by Dante Aligheri," I said. "Dedicated to his Beatrice."

"Rutkowski, do you think a nation with a language like this could win a single war? Personally, I don't think so. I think it must, by the very nature of its language, lose any war it ever ends up fighting."

Standartenführer Steinbrecher is in his element, in one of his most negative moods. He steps through the empty chambers like a conqueror passing through the palace halls of a vanquished enemy king, his boots squeaking and the metal buckles on his belts clinking. The

---

*"She seems so gentle and honest, / My lady, when she her greeting to others extends, / So that all one's tongue becomes tremulously mute / And one's eyes cannot stop looking."

Visigoth descending from the Alps into the rich valley of the Po to smash the Empire. (But apart from me, all he smashed was a single municipal clerk, and he didn't even smash him completely.)

"Paint all the rooms. Which color? Green, of course. White suggests innocence. No one wants to betray his friends in the virginal ambience of a Protestant church. White distracts us too. It spitefully reminds us of empty records, blank interrogation transcripts, unconvincing reports—failures that you seem to be quite experienced at, Rutkowski. We become hasty and rash. We overlook details. We begin to suffer from an elephantiasis of ideas. We crave great and significant discoveries. But they don't exist. All discoveries, by their very nature, are small and insignificant. We're the ones who make them great.

"And what would you think of another color, Rutkowski? Red, for instance?"

"I don't know, Herr Standartenführer. I don't know what to think about red."

"Do you ever think about anything from the point of view of the Service? Or do you leave the diamonds of your thought at home and come to work with a head full of gravel? You must know whether you like red or not. Because I know. You don't like it, Rutkowski."

"No. I guess I don't, Herr Standartenführer."

"None of you bourgeois intellectuals ever care for red. It's too lively, agile, active. It won't leave anyone alone. It unsettles people, unnerves them. And you don't like to be unnerved, do you, Rutkowski? You want *your peace of mind*—peace of mind in spite of a war, in spite of any goddamned circumstance that might keep you from thinking about your favorite subject: yourself. Well, fine. That could serve as a pleasant theme for some future discussion. For now we'll stick to colors. I admit, I'm not crazy about red myself. Some idiots claim it's practical, because it hides traces of blood. But I don't see the logic here. Why should we hide any traces of blood? That's hypocritical. Are we running a girls' lycée perhaps? Brushed onto the green background of a wall in discreet amounts, touches of blood or any other red substance can work to our benefit. Pay attention, gentlemen! We have other means at our disposal. And one more thing, Rutkowski—I don't want to see any patterns on the walls! Patterns can be counted. Patterns resemble things that people can think about. We can't let the time people spend here pass more quickly for them. Apart from fear, Obersturmführer, time is our most reliable ally. Although we do always have so damned little of it. We're always requested to work quickly. In principle, the army shouldn't be allowed to bite off more than the police can chew. In practice, however, we find ourselves in the position of Buridan's ass, which had only one head and a hundred stacks of hay to choose from. Meanwhile, our glorious Section IV is bombarding us with telegrams. Have you finally uncovered something, Steinbrecher? What kinds of organizations have you infiltrated, Steinbrecher? What kinds of confessions have you extracted? And then: names! As many names as possible! As if a successful conspiracy consists only of a list of names. In point of fact, good conspiracies always consist of a single name only. Everything else is unimportant. All the others are merely minstrels singing someone else's song. If we only learn the right name, our work is done. Isn't it, Rutkowski?"

"Yes, Herr Standartenführer."

"Well not exactly, Obersturmführer, it's not over yet. Why are you always in such a goddamned hurry to jump to conclusions? It's as if you find our work boring. Or should we say *repugnant?* Should we say that? Should we say *repugnant,* Rutkowski?"

I decide to try the chances for my transfer to the front. The Standartenführer's insulting remarks give me a kind of right to that. But strangest of all, Hilmar, is that I'm not pretending to be insulted. I *am* insulted.

"If the Herr Standartenführer isn't satisfied with my work, he can always send me to the front."

"So we can't say that. We can't say you find it *repugnant.* You intellectuals are so damned hard to please. If we praise you, you're insulted that we consider you good at an essentially murderous line of work. If we criticize you, you're insulted that we think you're incompetent. Now where was I?"

"You were talking about the right name, the one that, if we get it, means that we've completed only half of our work."

"The problem is that those prisoners most often have their own view of things, their own truth. A bad policemen limits himself to finding that out and putting it down for the record. Unfortunately, in the majority of cases, this truth is useless. It's inconsistent with ours. And what the hell are we going to do with a truth that says we're wrong? You probably see that we can't change the entire system that serves as the foundation of the German Reich on account of a single truth that's incompatible with it. The only option left to us, then, is to alter the prisoner's truth to fit our needs. Therein lies our whole mission."

"And if in this process it ceases to be true?"

"It wasn't a truth to begin with, Rutkowski. A truth that allows itself to be altered is a pure lie. It's like a prisoner who keeps changing his story during an interrogation. It's unreliable and unstable, and thus there's no harm in disregarding it."

Then the Standartenführer changes the subject. You'll notice this habit, which he acquired during his interrogations, with many policemen. This is why conversations with them always seem like interrogations. (And most of the time they are.)

"What are your thoughts on eyes, Rutkowski?"

"In which sense, Herr Standartenführer?"

"In the police sense, of course. We're not optometrists."

"I must admit I've never thought about them from that angle before."

"So you haven't noticed that they lose their color during the first interrogation? But by the second, it starts coming back; fear contracts the pupils. In the acid solution of fear, one's eyes act like litmus paper. I have my own little theory about eyes."

He has, in fact, one of "his own little theories" about everything. *Sub specie policiae,* of course. Again, I didn't dare to admit to him that I tried not to look in the prisoners' eyes during interrogations. This was why I always preferred to interrogate those who shared my weakness and looked to the side or down at the floor. As long as our gazes didn't meet we could imagine that nothing was going on between us, that the man across the desk was just a chimera, the product of a bad dream, and that the horrible scene, enclosed by the four green walls of the office, was only a passing nightmare. The ones who sought out my gaze were the worst. They wanted to be aware of the hopelessness of their situation at any price. When they looked straight into my eyes, confessing that there would be no confession, I took it to be a signal from the darkest depths of hell, *a call to action,* a summons to something I wasn't ready for, neither according to my professional abilities nor my mental constitution, nor especially my personal choice. This brought me to the point of hysteria and I fear, Hilmar, to demonstrations of the most degrading atavism, the details of which I will omit. Because such rigid behavior on the part of the prisoner completely derailed my plans for mercy. Success in this matter depended on the prisoner's trust in me. Unconditional cooperation provided us both with some hope of getting through this—me morally, him physically. Under favorable conditions (which were fairly infrequent, I might add) we were able to extricate ourselves and survive this mutual misfortune, I with my self-respect and position, and the prisoner without revealing his secret and with a bruise or two. In this apparently unnatural conspiracy between the investigator and the investigated, all that was required was asking the right questions and giving the right answers to them. There had to be some kind of answer. There had to be a confession of some kind of guilt. A crime was an inherent feature of an arrestee. And all I could do was transfer it to a less punishable domain. This, I admit, happened rather seldom. Paralyzed by fear, we both made mistakes. The questions I asked were clumsy and put my ally across the desk in a bind, whereupon he was forced to give clumsy answers that, according to the iron logic of the Transcript, I was forced to follow up on with even more dangerous lead questions and received, of course, even more hopeless answers, until one night we'd reach the desperate realization that we were each only steps away from the very end—he from the gallows, and I from one more mental breakdown.

However, now I won't describe in detail what I felt as I waited, numb with fear and uncertainty, for the door to open and for the anonymous herald of my salvation or downfall to enter the office, cast his first glance at me and speak his first words, tidings of my fate, a *Talita Cumi* or an *Anathema Te;* I'll wait until later, when Adam Trpković is brought to me. Now let's hurry up to hear Steinbrecher's "little theory on the significance of eyes for the psychology of a deposition."

"Last year I had to deal with a blind violinist. He was suspected of passing messages to the bandits as he went playing from café to café."

"Because of an anonymous tip, I assume?"

"No. It was a logical inference. A handicapped person who evokes compassion, with such a wide radius of movement, with unlimited possibilities for contacts—you understand, of course."

I don't understand, but I say nothing.

"But his playing was fantastic. The stroke of his bow was almost ethereal. Schubert. Schumann. E. T. A. Hoffman. Niccolo Paganini. And—don't report me—that Jewish duo, Mendelssohn and Meyerbeer! I know because he played his entire repertoire in my office."

"The messages were, no doubt, coded as musical phrases?"

"Don't be an idiot, Rutkowski. There wasn't anything in the music, only pure beauty. His hands made the coarse horsehair sing. It wasn't singing, but chant, as Homer would say. He'd usually perform after an interrogation. We'd exchange roles. Now he would direct the game. But this isn't what I wanted to talk about. I was thinking of his eyes. Although it had been medically determined that his eyes were dead, they were filled with life, like precious stones: the light of the sky, the reflections of a mirror, the gleam of glass, the flame of a lamp. They'd move, but their movements were false—do you know what I mean, Rutkowski?—phantasmal. They didn't come from within, but resulted from the refraction of light. There was an unbearable sensation when you looked into them, I assure you. My investigation even suffered on account of this. In the end I was forced to cover them with a black blindfold. Funny, isn't it? But logical nevertheless, because what use are eyes if they don't give anything away?"

Hilmar, can you imagine that supernatural scene? The Army Hall on Prince Mihail Square in Belgrade. A granite mausoleum with a broken clock on its tower. Four o'clock in the morning. The offices are empty. All but the most urgent interrogations have been postponed until the following day. The last officials, with the pale, poisonous traces of vigilance on their faces, are plodding down the aseptic corridors and disappearing into the green dawn. The reflector lamps in the interrogation cells go out one by one. Only the light bulbs inside their wire-mesh housings flicker on for a bit, like the wicks in hanging cemetery lamps. All sounds are hushed. The slithering song of pizzle whips has fallen silent. Nothing can be heard except the ethereal delirium of insects around the remaining sources of light. And then, like a dirge sung after a massacre— *Karneval,* opus 9. *Der Maskenball.* A masked phantasmagoria. A fiesta for the dying. Schumann in a fit of madness. From the depths of a deranged soul, through painful tenderness, a lament rises up to God. In the basement, which has just been scrubbed clean of his blood with stiff brushes, the violinist accompanies the composer in his holy orgy, a black blindfold over his eyes. Like a minstrel in the service of someone else's despair, the blind man doesn't forget his own either. The message of the song is that there's no hope. There's no salvation, not even in madness. That's the answer from the heavens. Two artists are addressing the same woman. *Ave Maria,* all in one breath, in a single scream so painful that its final chords become cheerful, roaming the deserted corridors in search of the Virgin Mother. Standartenführer Steinbrecher sits upright. He's unbuttoned his uniform. Only one button, the top one, of course. He won't surrender himself any more than that for art. Dawn thaws his face. Unsettled, he listens to the hopeless dialogue with heaven. Is he doing it as a policeman or a wretch? Is he still in the line of duty or is he himself also trying to come into contact with the loftiest mysteries? Will he also enter into a conspiracy for once?

I ask him what happened to the blind violinist.

"We shot him."

"So he'd been passing messages?"

"No. He was shot as a hostage."

I'll end here. I'm tired. There's no need to miss Steinbrecher. We'll hear him talk some more in the next letter. Until then.

Sincerely,

KONRAD

■ □ ■ □ ■

LETTER 5

HOW STEINBRECHER SPOKE, OR *A DISCOURSE ON METHOD*

The Mediterranean Coast, 14 Sept. 1965

Dear Hilmar,

If we pick up where we left off this morning, the Standartenführer is still taking a look around the former carabinieri barracks. He comments on the discovery of castor oil in the basement: "What can one think of a people whose police employ purgatives for investigative purposes?"

"They give them to deserters as well."

"What kind of lame-brained justification is that? Deserters get a bullet, not castor oil. It's that damned Latin penchant for bad odors. They probably had Il Duce's portrait hanging right here. Fortunately, we won't be hanging up any portraits. Inform our esteemed officers of this. Right now I bet they're all figuring out where we'll hang up the Führer. And be careful, Rutkowski, don't start hoping that you can turn me in for this remark. Ah—don't try to deny it, Obersturmführer! We all want to turn each other in, to catch each other at something. That's natural; it's even healthy. A robust society is founded on mutual suspicion, and on ubiquitous control.[4] Universal espionage. Continual denunciations. That keeps the police in a constant momentum. The police will disappear only when all men have become policemen. I alone, my dear Rutkowski, I'll never let myself get caught. And don't tell me there's nothing I could be arrested for. We all have our weaknesses and doubts. We're all potential enemies. In the final account, each of us would hang— if we were interrogated with any competence at all, it would be the end of every one of us. Especially you. Your performance has been miserable, below the average professional level. Your reports are more full of holes than Emmentaler. All your prisoners end up more or less innocent instead of more or less guilty. For them to become what we need, we have to hand them over to Rotkopf or some similar butcher. And this despite the fact that you do exhibit certain abilities. But it's clear that you exploit them exclusively for private purposes. You use them to lament your own fate. By the waters of Babylon we sat and wept! Am I right? Do you think that as an intellectual you don't belong in the Gestapo? Perhaps you're considering leaving us? Perhaps you feel like playing hero at the front? But Rutkowski, we have enough heroes. What we need are intelligent men who would take the foundation laid by such heroism and build something important. By the way, I wouldn't be surprised if you came to me one of these days with a request for a transfer."

"What would you do?"

"Maybe I'd let you go. But maybe I'd have you shot. Most likely I'd have you shot."

"May I ask why?"

"Don't always be looking for some goddamned reason for everything, Rutkowski. This is war, not a compendium of history. War is irrational. And so is death. We're endeavoring to bring some order into the war, to give it some organization, to lend some sense to it. We from the police, I mean. In light of this, the execution of Obersturmführer Konrad Rutkowski becomes completely logical. The Obersturmführer is insubordinate. The Obersturmführer is irrational. His request for a transfer to the front shows his irrationality clear as day. And what are those of us who are laboring to rationalize the senselessness of this widespread slaughter to do except eliminate this Obersturmführer? Shoot him as an irrational and thus unusable part of the German military organism. Isn't that clear?"

"With the Herr Standartenführer's permission, it's not."

"And why, if I may ask? Because it's your head that's at stake, or because there's something wrong with mine?"

"Because it isn't rational, sir. Obersturmführer Rutkowski would end up a head shorter at the front, too. He'd have to, in accordance with his irrational nature."

"On the contrary, Obersturmführer, the most irrational end to your fate would have to be one that's completely rational. It would be the logically consistent crown of your irrationality and you'd survive the war. Which brings me back to having you shot. In the meantime, note down that the windowpanes are to be replaced with opaque glass. The grills should be just barely visible from inside, as if they were surfacing from the subconscious. Nevertheless, nothing should give the impression that they're provisional or temporary, despite the pitiful amount of time we have at our disposal. If you give the impression that you're in transit, that you're in a hurry, then any prisoner with any brains will assume that you're going to leave him alone if he only perseveres long enough. You can never defeat the prisoner in the battle for time. He always has more time than you do. Fortunately, the time equation can be altered in our favor. How, Rutkowski? How can it be altered?"

"I don't know, Herr Standartenführer."

"Of course you don't. It'd be overdoing it to expect something like that from a policeman. But if I asked you something that was relevant two thousand years ago, you'd certainly know the answer. So let me tell you, Rutkowski: It's altered with the help of the omnipotent coefficient of surprise. Fabricated confessions of co-conspirators, blackmail, propositions that corrupt, unexpected changes in interrogation techniques, arbitrarily severe accusations, arbitrary changes of routine, arbitrary actions that will cloud the prisoner's sense of reality and logical thought. But above all—counterpoint behavior. Blows laced with promises, if you like. And since we're already on the matter of time, I doubt we'll stay here very long. Our real front is Belgrade. This is just a tactical sortie, and I don't believe it'll be particularly interesting. Out here in the middle of nowhere we certainly won't be dealing with intellectuals, but most likely with a bank clerk or an elementary school teacher. In the very best case, with a secondary school teacher. I like working with intellectuals. But the excitement doesn't increase in proportion to the academic title. It adheres to completely different principles. Have you noticed that the profoundest among them are also the most sensitive? Their skin is as thin as tissue paper. They're all nerves. They'll react to the subtlest of ideas. And all those traumas, complexes, frustrations, and inhibitions of theirs! It's simply amazing, if one remembers that most of them are swine! With the insanity morals of a herd of pigs. But on the other hand, they break out in tears when you curse their mothers. Their associations are as complex as the connections in a central telephone exchange. And their childhoods, those dear, unique childhoods of theirs! They adore them even when they were unhappy. As if the rest of us never had childhoods! As if our mothers gave birth to us from their asses! As if we were born in police uniforms with batons in our hands! Once one of those numskulls asked me, 'Were you ever a child, Herr Standartenführer?' And I answered, 'No, I've always been a Gestapo Standartenführer!' *Nota bene,* did you ever know Leonid Njegovan, the attorney?"

"I saw him at receptions at his wife's and at Stefan Njegovan's."

"Then you know what I'm talking about. People who behave as if they were born by parthenogenesis. I'd like to be able to verify that. Unfortunately, the Njegovans have connections all the way up to Berlin: the I.G. Farbenindustrie. Schacht, Gustav Krupp von Bohlen und Holbach, and so forth. Our economic giants. Those who nourish our war machine. And Rutkowski, it seems that you too are an intellectual?"

"I'm not so sure anymore."

"Parthenogenetic, sensitive as an amoeba, inhibited, high-strung, bloated with theories like a turkey, sick with your conscience and principles, eternally in some dilemma, and, of course, you had a beautiful childhood. In a word, a monster. And to top it all off, a historian by trade. A rummager in garbage bins!"

"Historians aren't to blame for people turning history into a garbage bin!" I said sharply, aware the moment I said it that the tone and content of my answer had dangerously overstepped the bounds of my subaltern position. However, my dear Hilmar, even under the threat of the severest consequences there were some pressure points in my view of the world that, when subjected to any rough handling, unleashed a dangerous incapacitation of my self-defense mechanism so absolutely necessary for a soldier in the fight against the Gestapo. One of those pressure points was my academic field. "Historians aren't to blame for the fact that they're left with only garbage to classify."

Instead of calling me back in line and returning me to my subordinate position, which I'd left to make a fleeting and stupid sortie, the Standartenführer admits with surprising nonchalance:

"It seems you're right, Obersturmführer. I'm sorry if I've offended you. I was puzzled by the realization that an officer of the Reich considers his history, including his Führer, to be a trash heap."

I'm stunned. It was no longer a matter of my field, but of my head. Ultimately it was a matter of an anti-Nazi struggle, for which my head was necessary.

"I didn't say that."

"You said that people have made a garbage bin of history."

"Not all people, and not every history!"

"So you weren't thinking of Germans and their history. Naturally, you meant the English, Americans, and Russians, not to mention all the other nations we're at war with."

"Of course, Herr Standartenführer."

"Whereas, I assume, you just as naturally have only the highest opinion of German history?"

"Of course."

"In contrast to intellectuals, whose impudence we've just had the privilege of witnessing, things are quite different with workers. It's not a matter of physical endurance. There's no such thing. No one has physical endurance in the ultimate meaning of the term. Every organism has its Achilles' heel, every soul has a soft underbelly. That's not the catch. The catch is, paradoxically, precisely in the fact that there is no catch. It's in their mental simplicity. They have no alternatives that you could refer to. You can't confuse them by opening up new perspectives, or shake them up by dressing reality up in a new guise. They have no receptors that you might have recourse to. Because they didn't arrive at their convictions with their brains, Rutkowski, or with weak nerves, but on their stomachs, on empty intestines. Through generations of hunger and helplessness in the face of injustice. By a kind of aristocratization of that humiliating feeling and position. That attitude can't be wiped away just like that. You can't defeat their reasoning with any means, including torture. Can you feed all the generations hungering within them? Can you make up for centuries of injustice? You'll say this isn't our goal. Of course it isn't. But you have to find some way to their hearts. And you don't succeed, of course. You're simply helpless in the face of the simplicity of their demands and the logic of their behavior. They're fanaticized with themselves. Things are far better with peasants, thanks to their dependence on the land. The most perfect specimens are all root. No leaves, flowers, fruit. Everything about them has turned into a root. And there's your chance. If you pull them up out of the ground, then you can say you've succeeded. We'll talk about women some other time. What exactly was I talking about? It was certainly something about the impression that should be made on the prisoners. This impression is of major importance. We must provide them with a sensation of the permanence of this situation. Pay attention, Rutkowski. I say permanence, but by no means eternity. Let's not overdo it. Eternity deprives one of hope. The absence of hope tempers people. Instead of clay, you get a mineral that nothing can break. Our door must be left ajar. This can't be a place that no one ever leaves. Releasing a few prisoners undermines the resistance of the others more effectively than any execution. Of course, it goes without saying that those who leave here are no longer their people, but ours. In this manner you break their spirit. When one's spirit is broken, the body surrenders—sincerely and without reservation. Reverse the order and you'll usually be deceived. A broken body doesn't obligate the spirit. On the contrary, it swears the spirit to resistance and vengeance. And in addition there's orderliness: I can't overemphasize the significance of the impression that a sense of orderliness—or even punctiliousness—makes on our clientele. And I don't mean only conscientious administrative practices. I'm also thinking of curial formalities. I want even the most insane complaint of a prisoner to be recorded and acted upon. And its further fate would no longer interest me if by complying with certain demands and strictly keeping certain promises we didn't get them to believe those big promises that, of course, we won't keep. I don't want to see the fringes on the rugs messed up. Or any wrinkles in the curtains. And more than anything I don't want to see unshaven police mugs shambling through the hallways. I won't ask you if you've read Freud! As an intellectual, you'd have to answer that you have, but you'll say you haven't. Certain impressions from childhood predetermine our behavior. That's simplified somewhat, and disregards the fact that Freud was a Jew whose imagination was perverted by his race. A prisoner's impressions starting from the day after his arrest determine his behavior during the investigation. That brings us directly to the significance of the fringes on a rug. Brought in here at three in the morning, bombarded with preliminary questions and preliminary blows, the prisoner has but little time and desire to notice the disorderly condition of those fringes, but in his subconscious it will inform him that slovenliness reigns in this institution. And he'd be an ass not to use that to his own advantage."

So, my dear Hilmar, you see how fringes on a rug, through a kind of inverted logic, acquire the significance of a dominant symbol. Neatly arranged fringes on a rug become part of a holy police ritual, a prerequisite for the power of its magic. The reddish peach fuzz on Hauptsturmführer Rotkopf's chin becomes a decisive impediment to the success of the investigative procedure. Haag's oily collar strengthens the character of the communist bandits in proportion to its oiliness. Muddy bootprints on the curtains in the admission office, which until then I considered to be an illustration of Oberscharführer Max's uncouthness, represent in fact the conspicuous pinnacle of our incompetence, a cartographic symbol pointing to the secret path taken by enemies of the state to escape from our basements unscathed.

Where does he come up with these comparisons?—I wonder as I follow him through the corridors. With what kinds of demonic tools does he forge these satanic generalizations? Because his concept of terror, my dear Hilmar, had all the characteristics of art for art's sake, created to serve nothing other than its own perfection. In the end, the world it painted was a kind of hell that functioned not to administer punishment, but to develop torture as such.

"Rutkowski, are you listening to me or are you dreaming your own parallel thoughts again?"

"Herr Standartenführer, I'm wondering . . ."

"He who wonders and doesn't know the answer is on a perilous path."

"The picture you've been so kind as to develop resembles to a certain extent a heaven of hell, where everything is in its place, but determined by a single virtue—subjugation."

"You're really disappointing me, Rutkowski. Your analogies go no farther than folklore, in the best case no farther than theology, which is probably the fault of your grandfather. Did you write in your application for admission into the Gestapo that he was a pastor?"

"I didn't write an application for admission into the Gestapo, Herr Standartenführer."

"And why is that, Herr Obersturmführer?"

"I don't understand the question. I simply . . ."

"You simply didn't consider us worthy of your services?"

"Not at all!"

"Do you mean you can be proud of what you do here?"

I hesitate, Hilmar, but I don't consider this the place to go into battle either.

"I can be proud of it, Herr Standartenführer, I only fear that it doesn't correspond to my abilities. You once compared our service to . . ."

"My dear fellow, we can't be compared to anything."

"I'm convinced of that. However . . ."

"Those who would forge a new world can't embody the garden of Eden or the Hades of old. We're only now creating our heaven and hell: the hell of individualistic atonement and the heaven of identification with one's community."

But nevertheless, I thought to myself, individualistic atonement reigns in the collectivistic concentration camps, and our Führer, the foremost leader of the heavenly identification with one's community, is the most isolated and most individualistically disposed man in the world.

"But if you really care for hackneyed comparisons, we can't be hell. Hell is a final answer to all earthly questions. So is heaven. No roads lead out of those places. Heaven or hell encompasses everything. Nothing happens, because the same thing is always happening. In our world, however, eternal selection shall reign. All trials will be in permanent resumption and appeal. People will be sent to heaven or hell, but this will not guarantee anything lasting. They'll never be permanently damned or permanently saved.[5] Their status will be subject to constant review. Those in hell will have to struggle to leave, and will only have real prospects for success if they find a sufficiently suitable replacement. Those in heaven will have to devote their time and attention to keep from falling down into hell. Fear will make a hell of heaven, and hope will make a heaven of hell. As a result of the continual intercommunication, the lively exchange between the two modes of existence, the difference between heaven and hell will gradually disappear, and alone our position in that world will determine whether we call it heaven or hell. Personally, I'd call it purgatory. Which brings us to purification, Rutkowski— this whole place smells of pomade. Really, it's as if we're in Sicily! What is this, a mafia headquarters? Get all the furniture outside! I'll leave it to you to choose something to replace it. With a valid requisition order, and within the limits of wartime regulations, of course. Luxury is out of the question, but we need a reasonable degree of working comfort, by all means. The chairs for the prisoners must have backs. You're surprised, aren't you? Indeed, the textbooks recommend an awkward sitting position. The prisoner wants to finish the interrogation as quickly as possible, and since he is aware that it won't end until after a confession, he confesses in proportion to the degree of his discomfort. Bullshit! No one ever confesses because of a stiff butt; a sore ass means an empty head. A prisoner's only thoughts are devoted to his own ass. But we need people who think. We want to ventilate their best ideas, and not hallucinations induced by maltreatment. The duty of the police is not to *produce,* but to *eliminate* enemies. At the same time I understand the logical necessity of enemies. Today it's impossible to organize a strong and healthy state without them: otherwise, everything falls apart. I suspect that enemies are the only bolts holding our machine together. But there's enough of that mortar in the natural state of affairs. It need not be mixed artificially. Only if a state needs illegal organizations of an exceptional profile for the political needs of the day—combined espionage networks, acts of sabotage in certain geographic areas and, in general, an enemy conspiracy that can't be obtained by ordinary cultivation on the ground— only then would I justify the artificial development of the desired situation. But even then one can't act like a sleepwalker; he must be Teutonically rational and pragmatic. We didn't, for example, accuse Minister of Propaganda Goebbels of setting fire to the Reichstag; we accused Thälmann and Dimitrov, our *real* enemies: it was logical for them to have set it on fire, and thus the objection that they didn't becomes purely academic. And Rutkowski, one more thing: I wouldn't mind if pictures of women and children were hung in the offices. Any women with any children, except the Madonna, needless to say; she doesn't evoke any personal associations. What we need to do is change the prisoner's personal attitude toward the situation. We need his emotional engagement, a subcutaneous internal disorder, miniature mental catastrophes, limited tremors of the heart, increased turbulence in his feelings. No, my dear Rutkowski, I'm not as sentimental as I look."

Who on earth said that?

"I'm rational, precisely because I place so much importance on feelings. It's dangerous to neglect the human heart. Humans are not made of ideas, but of a rectum and memories. Ideas are merely rationalizations, most often feelings of the futility of memories. Or of an empty stomach, by all means. Ideas are their revenge against the senselessness and misery of real life. Take communism. It's just a high degree of rationalization of the historical failure of the human race. You bourgeois have a cannibalistic image of communists."

Hilmar, he was telling this to me, one who had consented to wallow, along with him and his brutal doubles, all over Europe in the same bloody and senseless historical quagmire, only so I could help people, even communists, within the limits of my power.

"You, like every petit bourgeois, imagine that there's a little studied and arrogant Marx in every one of them. In the great majority of cases, however, you'll find in the deepest layer of their experience something quite banal, the attachment to a memory of some injustice, to which only a subsequent rationalization—under the name of dialectical materialism—can provide the general significance that we're trying to extract from them. Maybe it will come as a surprise to you, but even the most die-hard communist bandit has a mother, a wife, and daughter, and again, to your surprise, he cares about them like any other normal person. Let him feel his own heart and it'll soon be beating for you. According to my statistical tables, only one in ten politically motivated suspects will start talking while being beaten. Of the remaining nine, considering only those who sign to complete confessions—even for crimes they didn't commit—

four do so out of concern for their loved ones. But the largest number, five of every ten, break under the weight of some moral problem. The table applies only to intellectuals. With workers, however, a noticeable increase of their concern for loved ones at the expense of a concern for morals has been observed, in proportion to their lack of education and intellectual immaturity. You know where the difficulty lies, Rutkowski. You're an intellectual. You yourself, I assume, are inclined to asking questions such as: May I sacrifice OTHERS without their consent? Do I become a murderer if I cause the death of INNOCENTS, for whose good I am allegedly fighting? What's more important, what's more worthy: a man or an idea?—and all that intellectual bullshit. Stimulate them to think in that direction. Organize executions of hostages if you have to; real or imaginary executions—it doesn't matter. The effect is the same. Don't allow them to hide behind luxurious generalizations; don't let them burrow like moles into the warm tunnels of abstraction. Cast them out of their phantom worlds devoid of living people who hurt and suffer; out of their ethereal projections, in which all people, in the incubator of sunny revolutionary ideas, are happy, content, and healthy. Drag them down into the mud of individual responsibility. If, instead of letting them decide the fate of some fictive world, you let them drag the real fates of their friends, brothers, sons, fathers, and their people in general into their statements, then I bet they'll break quicker than under torture. Soon you'll have a capitulation ratio of three to one, instead of one to three. We don't expect any more than that. More than that would be unprofessional. Within reasonable bounds, failures must exist, otherwise we'd lose all our self-respect. You'll put thick carpets everywhere. You'll give the people bast slippers. Like in Moab. It's one of headquarters' few good ideas. You'll ask Hauptsturmführer Rotkopf not to shout like a lunatic. This isn't an asylum for mentally deranged indigents. I want us all to feel like we're in a communal grave. A mass grave. Very isolated and left to depend on one another. Physical coercion should be reduced to a minimum. Don't let Rotkopf determine the minimum—for him it's beating someone to death. And since we're already speaking of him, bring me his dossier. I'll see, maybe we can get rid of him."

Thus, one had to be an extroverted savage like Rotkopf to get a chance for a transfer. But to get such a reputation, one would have to do everything that would preclude a transfer from being a relief to one's conscience.

"In the meantime, contact the municipal authorities. Request a detailed overview of the situation in the area. Don't be satisfied with the same old formula according to which 'fortunately, sirs, nothing ever happens over here.' Fortunately, it most certainly does. Request to see the prewar registers of suspected antistate elements. If they tell you that, according to the regulations in the case of war, the registers were destroyed, don't believe it. The majority of county leaderships did not follow the law on the burning of archives.[6] Balkan negligence, which helps us in this bastardly pandemonium of movements, parties, organizations. Don't take any preventive measures. Do you know Sturmbannführer Schmidt? You don't? After entering Orel, he hung several people as a preventive measure—the first people he encountered. It turned out that they were a ceremonial delegation from the Ukrainian separatists. This is now told as an anecdote. I don't want to be the cause for any anecdotes among the troops. Is that clear Rutkowski?"

"It's clear Herr Standartenführer. Get the registers of suspicious persons from the municipal building. And don't hang any Ukrainian ceremonial delegations."

Standartenführer Steinbrecher laughs. The tension subsides.

"We'll see each other this evening at General von Klattern's quarters. We'll certainly win this war at the dinner table there."

Thus ended the first inspection of what the Standartenführer vividly called my mausoleum. But you won't find out how right or wrong he was in the next letter. Instead, we'll attend a military banquet and hear of our Adam for the first time. In expectation of that monumental meeting, greetings from KONRAD

■ □ ■ □ ■

LETTER 6

A DINNER IN THE MAUSOLEUM, OR
INTRODUCTION TO PSYCHOANALYSIS

The Mediterranean Coast, 15 Sept. 1965

My dear Hilmar,

I wonder whether you're reading these letters at all.[7] I don't imagine you even read the first one. If we forget your dislike for me, you had no reason for doing anything like that. Namely, you couldn't have known what I'm writing about. But when you suspected that these letters might put all the key arguments of your neutral way of life to a serious test, I believe the defense mechanisms of your intellectual alibis were activated, which protect you from any activity that might hinder your scholarly work. I don't blame you. If I were in your position, I'd most likely do the same. It's unpleasant to accept a polite invitation to a dinner party and then find out at the table that you're intended to be the main course. I hope you've nevertheless continued reading. I'm counting on your curiosity, and still more on my secret hope—that you might laugh at my discoveries. I don't care; and I don't expect that in a few tutorial sessions I can defeat a centuries-old moral laziness produced by bad experiences with every real deed. And, finally, I'm not writing these letters for you, but for myself.

Let's do a little chronology. Not of the events in 1943—they're clear. On the evening of the day of our entry into D., after the banquet at General von Klattern's quarters, I made the acquaintance of the municipal file clerk Adam Trpković. Rather, what I'm talking about is the chronology of events in 1965. On the afternoon of the 11th of September, we arrived in D. On the evening of the following day, I wrote you the first letter. By that time an event had already occurred, the unveiling of the monument, which was the whole reason why I began writing to you in the first place. Thus, it's necessary to stop on this journey through the past and to pick up speed in the story on its other, contemporary track. So we won't be going to General von Klattern's dinner party. We'll dine with Sabina on the evening of the 11th, out on the terrace of the pensione, among the flowers, like in a jardiniere on top of a giant mausoleum.

Like a diving board overgrown with tender grapevines, the terrace overhangs a sea permeated by moonlight. Nothing reminds one of the war. The feeling that I'm dining in my very own mausoleum slowly fades, and I'm soon able to make calm comments on Sabina's remarks about her impressions.

Hilmar, I'd already completely given myself over to the calming effect of the quiet Mediterranean evening, saturated with the scents of evergreen shrubs and fish, when she abruptly asked me if I'd already been in this town before.

"Where did you get that idea? Of course I haven't. You know I served in Belgrade."

"But you made trips to the surrounding areas, didn't you?"

"Certainly, but never out this far. This was the Italian-occupied zone."

"Hilmar says we took control of it after the Italian occupation."

"Yes?"

"Hilmar says that was in the fall of 1943."

"Yes, it was, even if Hilmar hadn't said so."

"I thought you might have passed through this area with our troops but not remember it."

"I didn't even pass through this area."

"Then how did you find the way to the pensione?"

"I don't know, I asked someone."

"You didn't ask anyone."

"I must have, Sabina, you just didn't hear. You never hear what I say, you only hear what Hilmar says."

"Is that really important now?"

"Is it really important whether I was in this damned town or not?"

"No," she says sarcastically, "It really isn't. It's only important for you not to swear and act like a swine. Hilmar thinks . . ."

"Hilmar can go to hell!"

"I won't allow my brother to be spoken of like that."

"We're on vacation, really! We can probably allow ourselves a little bit of freedom! Anyway, I'm sorry!"

You, of course, realize that my negative reaction to your name was nothing personal. I'd have been upset had Sabina had the habit of referring to her "dear, departed father" instead of her "dear, clever, and overweight brother." What I found offensive in her manner was its air of subservience, which had manifested itself before in the popular phrase *The Führer has spoken!*, with so many disastrous consequences for our nation. I'll draw your attention, however, to another aspect of the squabble. When I realized that continuing to display a negative attitude toward you would lead to an argument with Sabina, I gave in and made a compromise. In exchange for retreating on the front facing you, I gained a retreat on the issue of whether I had been in D. In and of itself, a move such as this isn't fateful. Anyway, conversations between people are impossible without such trade-offs. Every dialogue presupposes a certain degree of compromise. Dialogue itself is already a compromise. Our acquiescence to hear out others presupposes an anesthetization of our vanity, which guarantees that we will have no benefit from it. However, modeling one's behavior on one's intellectual convention, acting exclusively through and in the form of compromise, means subjecting one's right to life to an unnatural mutilation. And that was my initial mistake, which led me from one compromise to another, eventually ending in these letters as a final compromise between suicide and complete indifference.

Sabina, of course, wasn't convinced, but since she couldn't figure out why I'd lie about any possible stay in D., she didn't try to continue the investigation. I was released on a lack of evidence, which again is only an insulting compromise between an admission of innocence and proof of guilt. In fact, I could have confessed a brief wartime stay in D. to her had I not shuddered at the thought of further questions. Your sister did know that I'd been in the Geheime Staatspolizei in 1943, but believed that I'd performed the function of a clerk, an insignificant persona in the structure of a monstrous legend that shrouded our earthly jobs. And she didn't even look on that with a sympathetic eye.

As you know, Hilmar, Sabina belongs to that slightly annoying and arrogant kind of young proselytes who have somehow discovered that they're obligated to redeem Germany from sins that we committed and they have no connection to except a genealogical one. I must admit that she got on my nerves here as well, trying to atone for me before the locals, in whom she with iconophilic steadfastness saw the victims of our policy of conquest in 1943, while they, the locals, saw in me what I really was in 1965—a tourist on whom they were supposed to make money. As if, while the English were strutting all around in full splendor, she were saying with her entire condescending posture: Well, we're back again, we're courageous enough to confess our sins and we're mature enough to draw the moral lessons from them, the foundations of our future national rebirth. She took upon herself all the vices of the Third Reich, including the acts of mass repression, but nevertheless agreed to share personal responsibility for the "final solution" of the Jewish question with Reichsführer Himmler. That sin was too much even for her novice's enthusiasm. The residents of the gas chambers at 50°3'30" latitude and 19°13'30" longitude ultimately achieved a posthumous revenge: the Germans' souls are still obsessed with them. The fact that the souls in question are— by an inverted, Old Testament principle of historical revenge—not those of the murderers (the murderers are in the meantime boating down the Amazon) is of no significance.

Anyway, why am I telling this to you, Hilmar? You yourself tried on several occasions to explain to her that her spiritual masochism didn't do anyone any good and led nowhere, and, given how they are today, brought only harm to the Germans; that all that barbarian self-torture with memories was a quality of the Slavs; and, finally, that we were all both the victors and the vanquished, victims and murderers, pawns in the very same historical game and, no matter on which side, brothers in misfortune. Let the dead bury the dead!

Beautiful, Hilmar, beautiful! The only solution worthy of a humanist. We're proceeding—or should I say hurtling—into the future as innocent as children! Let's shake off the dust of history from our clothes at the threshold of a new age! Let's await a new insanity stripped of confusing memories of our old insanity. As far as I'm concerned, I can only wish you a nice journey down that road, and that on it you won't find yourself facing once again the same tests that we failed back in 1933 and 1939.

Our discussion was interrupted by a series of explosions above the bay. The detonations scattered colored dust in all directions. The night was transformed into the howling jaw of a wolf. Out of the celluloid depths of the darkness, out above the sea, enormous, watery, brightly colored chrysanthemums bloomed and then dissipated, scattering their flickering seeds on the pale, rocky coast. There was the smell of something burning in the distance.

The obliging waiter informed us that this was the eve of the local holiday celebrating the day of the uprising. He didn't say who the uprising was against out of politeness, but I was convinced that it was against us, the Germans, and that he'd have been more forthright to a table of Frenchmen. I was shaken; it suddenly seemed to me that all uprisings that had ever been organized had been led against us. I maliciously gave myself over to this feeling:

"Who was it against—the uprising?"

He was flustered. He cleaned the crumbs from the table with quick, routine motions.

"Well, against the occupier, sir."

"Which occupier?"

"There were all sorts of them here."

"It wasn't against the Turks, was it?"

"Against the Italians."

Sabina was giving me frantic signals, but I wouldn't give up.

"Only against the Italians?"

"And the Nazis, of course," he said cautiously. He was kind enough to keep my nationality in mind.

"But the Nazis were Germans, weren't they?"

"On the whole, yes," he said, blushing as if he himself were a party functionary. "But other nations had Nazis, too. We even had them. Ours were even more dangerous."

Let me interrupt the portrayal of this conversation to discuss with you one question that's been bothering me for a long time, and to which you, out of your stupid national pride, have devoted almost no attention in your studies. It concerns a difference in the behavior of the Nazis and the communists in the face of the repressive bodies of an ideological foe. Thus, I'm not thinking of the street fights on the eve of elections to the Reichstag, when a party's fighting spirit was most often spurred by the animal instincts of the mass and the sadistic inspirations of individuals among them, but of those hopeless moments when someone, stripped of everything but his pride, found himself in a cold, deep cell, face to face with an omnipotent and merciless enemy. In such circumstances, the behavior of Nazis before hostile authorities was quite striking and contrasted with the impressive energy, brutality, and recklessness that they demonstrated while in power. On the whole, the Nazis didn't hold up well at all in the face of the police, be it that of Versailles or any other—the Americans or Russians after the war. Not a single kind of resistance, not even the most temperate, such as disrespecting a flag or violating supply regulations, was practiced after our capitulation in 1945. Not at all to the degree we experienced in this country. The excuse for the faintheartedness of the German people is well known. It's impossible to deny the role of certain factors in our indifferent behavior. An inborn respect for legal authority; a racial sense of order and organization; a distrust of revolutionary methods and a lack of skill at their employment (although German communists both in Bavaria and Berlin demonstrated quite some skill). Moreover, there's the folkloric myth of the German general staff that no battle may be won without the appropriate uniforms; the practical goals of the Renewal and Reconstruction, so sacred to the citizenry; a Russian policy which spared us from a new Versailles and made of us the greatest consumers of aid in world economic history; a repudiation of Hitler's dictatorship (though the very same people had given it its mandate). Then, there's the sense of complete helplessness before an animosity of monumental proportions that people have for us as the culprits for the war; and, finally, an apathy induced by a catastrophe unprecedented in our national history. All these factors acted together to render us incapable of offering any resistance. You mentioned some of them in the chapter entitled "Plan Werewolf" of your (in my opinion quite mediocre) COLLAPSE OF THE THIRD REICH. I only mention them as ostensible reasons for our behavior and for the difference between it and the way other nations met us, especially those with powerful communist minorities. My view—that the roots of this difference lie in the fact that communism originates in the stomach, a *real* human need for a better life, whereas Nazism originated in the brain, a *fictitious, intellectual* need for a higher order in which the individual's will for power harmonizes with the gregarious impulses of the people—is another topic and cannot be the subject of this letter.

And now I'll continue chatting with the waiter.

"Against us? Against me?"

He was really in trouble:

"Oh, not at all sir! Not against you!"

"But why not? I was also in the war."

"Konrad!" Sabina begged me.

"I don't even think I need to tell you that I, as an upstanding German, was on the German side."

"Who knows where you were, sir. We only rose up against the ones who were here."

He evidently wanted to save me at any price. He owed this much to his hospitality.

"But what if I was right here? Right here in D.?"

He broke. He'd done everything in his power. He'd generously thrown a rope to me. I refused to use it. I could go to hell.

"Well, then we naturally rose up against you, too. In fact, we rebelled way back in 1941, but tomorrow we're celebrating an event that took place three years later, in 1943."

I remembered that date. An execution was carried out on the main square. Hauptsturmführer Freissner photographed the scene. I made a copy later; it's the only photograph in my war album. If you find yourself engrossed in this story, you can find it among my papers in the upper left drawer of my desk.

The waiter also added that on the next day a monument was to be unveiled on the hill above the town to commemorate the event. The monument was to a local hero.

"You have to see it, sir."

The thought didn't cross my mind. I saw no reason to honor a man who had gained his glorious title shooting at me.

"Of course we'll go and see it," Sabina said. Her feeling of shame for Mauthausen, Auschwitz, Majdanek, Buchenwald, and Dachau was in full swing.

"It's more than ten meters in height. It's life-size."

That was too much even for Sabina:

"Don't you mean larger than life?"

"Yes, that's what I meant to say, ma'am."

Strictly speaking, the waiter was right. Hilmar, that really was the actual size of this hero. Those ten meters were now his actual size, the dimensions of his legend. He was finally proportional to the tales of his deeds, as great as the glory that erected him. But the more than eight meters' difference between his height in flesh and blood and the copy in syenitic granite represents the ant's work of national conscience and patriotic imagination that to such a great extent inhabit the pedestals of all peoples of the world.

When the waiter withdrew, Sabina blew up:

"How could you behave like that, for the love of god?!"

"How did I behave?"

"Crassly. As if at the very least you're sorry that we lost the war."

Sabina never raised such an issue with you, Hilmar, did she? But she should have. You were the right man for such stupid questions. Since in your historical works it's never entirely clear whether we lost the war because we championed an unjust cause or because the combined effect of our propaganda, tanks, and police beatings was unable to turn it into a just one. In other words, it's never clear to what extent the weaknesses of our motives augmented the mistakes of our leadership.

"In any case, you should've shown more respect. These people have a right to their memories of the war, more than you do to yours."

"I don't have any memories of the war."

And that's true, Hilmar. I'd given up my memories of the war in exchange for an uncertain expiation. A partial forgiveness that was never even issued. I'd fought secretly and unsuccessfully against my own country, and it was practically irrelevant that it had stood for the colors of anathema. And this feeling of mine, this recollection of my hypocrisy will not let me guzzle beer on equal footing with you and your army buddies and shout *die alten Kameraden!* when our defeat is celebrated, or should we say—mourned. On the other hand, since my contribution to the struggle against Nazism wasn't spectacular (What am I saying? It hardly even existed!), and since I sank to ever lower moral, spiritual and mental depths in that isolated, troubadour's pseudocombat, which was more an intellectual phantasmagoria than real action, I had no right to adopt our enemies' memories of the war and consequently to guzzle beer with them and shout *die alten Kameraden!* I was a has-been warrior, left by his penchant for compromise out in no-man's land, along with the remnants of barbed-wire obstacles, rusted shell fragments, and anonymous bones.

"Anyway," I continued, "the memories of the war that I do have are completely Steinbrecherized."

"What's that stupid expression supposed to mean?" she asked me, and I'm sure you're wondering as well.

We'd used this term, which by the way was my invention, to describe everything that had any official connection to Standartenführer Steinbrecher. For example, a prisoner who passed through his hands was *Steinbrecherized* in the first degree, firsthand. Since we, as the Standartenführer's co-workers, were already Steinbrecherized ourselves, our prisoners could be considered to be Steinbrecherized secondhand. Any living being, any object, any situation under the supervision of the Standartenführer's authority was Steinbrecherized, as were many other beings, objects, and situations that came into prolonged contact with him, sooner or later, indirectly. Exceptionally (and this was the sole deviation) I termed prisoners who had been beaten to death *Rotkopfized.*

Sabina was right, Hilmar, completely right. But it was just the fact that she was so damned right that wouldn't allow me to withdraw without winning even the smallest concession, and so I began explaining to her that in principle I shared her opinion regarding the responsibility for the war, but that, again, it was one thing to be a sheltered observer and to condemn the war from a historical perspective, but something entirely different to be living neck-deep in its excrement and to smell the poisonous stench of the earnings of history with one's own nose. But soon, mellowed by red wine, the stifling scent of the southern moonlight and the tremolo of a *barcarole* out on the sea, I began viewing things with more good will. I started to think about the dirty jokes and puns of history that you've devoted your academic life to without ever seeing through them even once—in this case, about a secret process of historical trans-mutation. An ordinary man, the champion of all our mediocrity, the cannon and ballot fodder of our industrial machinery, becomes a hero—in the majority of cases a *compulsory* hero. (As war is in and of itself coercion, not even the greatest feats of heroism in it may be viewed as acts of free will in the strict sense of the term.) The per-formance of a heroic deed is often a fight on two fronts: against the enemy and against one's own fear. (By this I don't mean to dimin-ish it, but to rehabilitate the Promethean victory over that fear as the most magnificent but also most often neglected feat.) Immediately after a hero's death, the dimensions of his deed are still modest and human, sometimes even smaller than their actual proportions. But sometime later, in the course of the banal years of peace, when the war is forgotten and the soul of the people overgrows with the weeds of security and affluence, via an elephantiasis of a sprouting legend, an everyday and ordinary act becomes an astounding feat. That innocent man was fodder for future statistics, an incomputable fraction of history. But then history grabbed him by the throat and at one utterly insignificant moment squeezed from him all his power of self-control and all his will to survive; it extracted his life's entire vein of gold from a single pit, and then threw him back into that unmarked grave. But as the result of a metabolic disorder in his descendants' sense of historical reality, that man begins to grow posthumously, under a mound of earth, until he breaks out of the soil like the shoot of a giant plant and transforms himself before his awestruck nation, which is unaware that this is a projection of our ideal *dream of ourselves* onto a colossus of marble, granite, or bronze.

My dear Hilmar, as far as Konrad Rutkowski is concerned, he could consider himself fortunate that your sister wasn't particularly clever in her repentant performances. Otherwise, he'd be forced to show up at the monument with a memorial wreath in his hand. (What about this golden inscription: TO OUR GLORIOUS VICTIMS. *The Gestapo.* How would that be?) Instead, she announced that she was tired, giving me to understand that my behavior did not have an insignificant role in that, and demonstratively withdrew to the bedroom, and I've remained in the salon to add a few important footnotes to my work, which is spread out on the desk.

Yours,

KONRAD

P.S. For atonement to be effective, a sinner must give himself over to it entirely, but this is impossible if he doesn't find a certain satisfaction in it, even if his satisfaction lies in the knowledge that his chances for forgiveness are greater than before, when he sinned. Pleasure is, accordingly, a component of the process of repentance, its *conditio sine qua non*. On the other hand, atonement that's defined by anguish can't be a pleasure, because then it would be its own end. Thus, pleasure simultaneously appears in atonement as a *contradictio in adjecto*. I write this because I'm not sure whether I'm enjoying this confession or am sickened by it.

■ □ ■ □ ■

LETTER 7

AN INHERITED CAPTIVE, OR *THE WORLD AS WILL AND IMAGINATION*

The Mediterranean Coast, 16 Sept. 1965

Dear Hilmar,

I wondered whether I should take you to Generalleutnant Reinhardt von Klattern's dinner party. I know your provincial craving for social gatherings of the distinguished and influential. There's no intellectual experience more thrilling for you than gnawing on a fish's tail across the table from the dean, and the thought that you might one day sit across the table from the chancellor puts you in an almost religious ecstasy. Unfortunately, this garrison revel has no significance either for the story or the history under whose stepmother's wing it takes place. The only justification would be that the grotesque and phantom dimension of this (almost reconciliatory) army and police banquet in the soft underbelly of the new Europe provides the most natural introduction to the supernatural appearance of the municipal file clerk Adam Trpković. It's a kind of satanic choral prelude before Beelzebub's great aria. Thus, I've decided as always to resort to a compromise as a saving measure and to take you along, but only for dessert.

We were drinking coffee and munching on almonds, while the fifth bottle of Georgian cognac went around the table. Under the wise command of Generalleutnant Hoth, in the eastern sector of the Dnieper bend, the front was being consolidated with extraordinary mobility and effectiveness. On the damp white steppe of the division's banquet tablecloth, the emptied glasses of enemy cognac paradoxically represented von Manstein's likewise fairly depleted Army Group "South," while the coffee cups represented Vatutin's First Ukrainian Front.

Grand strategy reigned amid the meager furnishings of the local hotel's dining room, which had been hastily refurbished and decorated. The air was filled with the acrid odor of a pollen of gunpowder, the stench of consecrated blood, and the smell of blazes ignited by the concentrated fire of artillery of all calibers. There was the ghostly clattering of tank tracks. The signals of field telephones streamed through the fiery air. All field glasses were raised and looking toward the sunlit east, where a slant-eyed, Asiatic fate was marching toward us in thick *valenki*. Let the trumpets sound! Let our colors be presented! Let us give the salute! The military mind was in its full destructive swing. Summoned by this midnight spiritual seance, the Spirit of War, the rider of the Apocalypse, was galloping through the hotel's empty hallways.

"Our forces are deployed in a cordon," explains Generalleutnant von Klattern, "without any operational reserves. Will you please hurry up and empty that glass, Rutkowski?! The Bolsheviks have a considerable operational reserve, and are deployed in depth."

"God help us!" whispers Major Zeller, "I hope we'll win this war by dawn."

"What was that, Zeller?" asks von Klattern, leaning over the theater of operations like Hermes over the battlefield of Troy, and knocks over a Russian tank unit.

"God help us with this balance of forces, Herr General."

"Not God, but military spirit, Zeller," von Klattern says, correcting him, "and ninety three divisions, of which barely eighteen are armored and four motorized."

"Not counting our brave allies the Romanians," Zeller adds, "and all those other shitheads."

Von Klattern doesn't consider the Fourth Romanian Army. Indeed, he was strong enough all by himself.

"Against one hundred sixty eight Russian divisions with an unknown number of motorized armored divisions—with my personal gratitude to Major Zeller for not interrupting me again. They have almost double our number of artillery pieces and mortars, and an almost equal number of tanks."

"How does this guy know all that?" Haag turns and asks Captain Müller, who is sitting next to him and with whom he's been competing to foster military cameraderie with the generals, and learns that the general has recently had a consultation with the Führer.

"But the strategic solution," von Klattern continues, "is sought in the area of Keresten, Zhitomir, Bardichev, Vinnytsya. This is obvious, even to Major Zeller, although he's pretending to be asleep. On the first of January, Hube and the First Armored will move to a position forty kilometers away from Bardichev. Müller, move your glass, please. Thank you. In the direction of the almonds. Thank you. The enemy then makes a breakthrough in the direction of the vase with those disgusting flowers—Vinnytsya, that is. Rutkowski, forward with that cup! Thank you. Wait, what are you doing?—I didn't tell you to take L'vov as well."

"We still have plenty of time for that," Zeller points out.

"Major, I think we're also going to have to give you something to do in this war."

His adjutant points to the cognac.

"I'd be happy to take care of the Russian strategic reserves. I'm not in shape today."

We laugh. Zeller is a sugary addition to the bitter salt of our realization that we're losing the war. Standartenführer Steinbrecher is demonstratively contributing little to the overall mood. He sits next to the host and, between two saucers with cookies that have been upgraded to geographic landmarks, commands the Fourth Panzer Army. He's in a very precarious position, which doesn't allow him to have any fun:

"There are *places* where one gets back in shape, Major."

His allusion to the Gestapo cells is inappropriate, especially since it's made to an officer in the presence of his superior, who's qualified to evaluate Zeller's military performance and prescribe remedies for any shortcomings. An icy wind of the underworld swept over the table. Zeller alone inhaled it with pleasure:

"Really, Standartenführer? I thought that's where you lose it."

"Okay, Rutkowski, what's with that enemy?" Von Klattern finds that in the tie situation he can intervene to return our interest to the real war in its tabletop projection. "What was he doing?"

"Advancing toward the vase with the disgusting flowers, Herr General."

"Excellent. Thank you. Steinbrecher, don't be so grumpy and move your glass to the west. Thank you. Hoth's Fourth Panzer Army is holding, but the west flank wavers. We've ended up with a gap with a radius of seventy five kilometers. Make a gap, gentlemen. Thank you. The Russians see a chance; they too have learned something since 1941. A beating is still the best teacher."

"That's right!" Rotkopf blurts out. "A necessary minimum of beating."

Von Klattern gives him a tired look through his monocle: "It seems you know a lot about that, Hauptsturmführer? . . ."

Rotkopf bends over the "Ukrainian steppe" and clicks his heels together under the table:

"Friedrich Wilhelm Rotkopf, SS Hauptsturmführer, Herr General!"

"Then what the hell are you waiting for? You're holding a Russian cup—move it forward! And make it quick, please. I appreciate your patriotism, but this is science. We're analyzing the war. That's right. Enough. Thank you. Rutkowski, please. That's good. Thank you. In the meantime Hoth makes a masterful move and moves his glass— the Fourth Panzer, that is—to a position sixty kilometers from Vinnytsya, along the Polish-Soviet border. The Russian strike is softened. Are you asleep, Steinbrecher?! Move your damned glass, before they envelop your flanks!"

Steinbrecher retreats. Then he empties his glass and asks:

"May I help myself to some of the operational reserve?"

"We don't have any, Standartenführer."

"The Russian reserve will do as well."

The General personally pours the Standartenführer some Georgian cognac. The ice is broken again. The coffee cups tactically disengage from the glasses of cognac—the Germans from the Russians. A cease-fire is declared on the white tablecloth front; such a cease-fire would be so welcome for us in the Ukrainian marshes.

General von Klattern quickly finds out that these somber and unhewn policemen are not such bad guys. Outside of the service, of course, and outside of their predacious obsessions. On the other side, Standartenführer Steinbrecher also realizes that one can have quite a nice conversation with Pomeranian aristocrats, provided they're plastered and can't tell their asses from holes in the ground. Friedrich Wilhelm Rotkopf confides the secrets of his minimal requirements to his distracted neighbor. Sturmbannführer Freissner prepares to take a group picture of the fragile idyll. Haag and Müller are completely confused. Their worship of superior officers has run into the unexpected obstacle of their quantity. And I, my dear Hilmar, I'm daydreaming. With half a bottle of cognac in my belly I'm overcome by a pleasant drowsiness, as after a warm bath. I've cast off my black uniform, although no one can see that, because my behavior is now ruled by the hypocritical laws of compromise: only my empty body represents me at the table, whereas my spirit has made its escape. I dream free, un-Steinbrecherized dreams from my childhood. I'm ten years old again, in a village called Bavanište. (So you can orient yourself: somewhere in the southeastern edge of Pannonia.) I'm on a country farm. A wedding is in progress. One of my father's sharecroppers is getting married. In front of a green gate, horses decorated with multicolored ribbons are rearing frantically. The wedding song is being sung before the bridegroom goes off to the village for the bride. My father is the best man. He takes a decorated flask of brandy and toasts the bridegroom's father, Marko, whom—after a half a century of harmonious coexistence—he, bewitched with nationalist atavism, would chase like a dog along the Deliblatska sands only to be buried by that same Marko one rainy October morning in 1944 in the horse cemetery. And I'm watching the whole scene from the cellar, lying under a barrel, the spigot of which is dripping intoxicating apple cider onto my tongue.

"Herr Obersturmführer!"

A voice, sharp like the crack of a gunshot reverberating through hills, dispels the wedding, and cuts off the intoxicating cider of my memories. The compromise has been betrayed. I'm once more all there at the table. The orderlies have cleared it and now it resembles a decontaminated and emptied battlefield where black and yellowish pools of blood are drying. The relations along the green-black demarcation line between the guests and hosts are again on the razor's edge. It seems that in my absence the Standartenführer made sure to make a disparaging remark about Manstein, the general's classmate and patron, because von Klattern, raising high the standard of the regular army, had declared that he'd rather be damned than allow such gendarme thinking to give arrogant lectures on strategy and tactics to his schoolmates, and at his own dining table at that.

My dear Hilmar, that was when the municipal clerk Adam Trpković first announced himself.

"Herr Oberthturmführer!" said Hauptscharführer Max, who had come in from being on duty in the barracks. He had a lisp, substituting any difficult letter with *th;* he thought this was simpler than struggling with them. "We've got a pthithoner."

"You've got a what?"

"A pthithoner, thir. With an umbthella."

"Don't be an idiot, Max! What damned prisoner and with what damned umbthella? Are you crazy? Who gave you permission to make arrests?"

"We didn't make any, Herr Oberthturmführer."

"Then how the hell did you get him? How did you end up with a prisoner if you didn't arrest him?"

"We just did, thir. It thounds thtupid, but we did. We've got him. It'd be betht if you'd come and check it out."

Max's intervention is a welcome break for everyone. A temporary quiet sweeps over the table. From the head of the table Rotkopf yells:

"What's going on, Rutkowski?"

I spontaneously decide to avoid answering. That's the only way to keep the initiative and clear up the misunderstanding with Max's prisoner before he gets definitively stuck in the ducts of the police machinery. I turn to Steinbrecher:

"It's a matter of an insignificant technical problem, Herr Standartenführer." And Hilmar, it really was a technical glitch. Genuine, serious prisoners were pure trouble, but this one of Max's, if there even was one, was just bad luck, a mistake, an illusion. Because, where the hell did a prisoner with an umbrella come from so suddenly in the middle of the night? What kind of prisoner isn't arrested, but just appears all of the sudden like the genie out of Aladdin's lamp?

"I'll have to request your permission to leave for half an hour."

Permission granted. Haag also gets up, whose loyalty has been tormented all evening long by the dilemma of which brass to kiss up to. Fortunately, Steinbrecher tells him to sit back down. He required all available police forces for the impending clash with the Army.

Well, okay, I thought, if at one in the morning, with a full belly and a foggy brain I have to deal with magical, self-motivated arrestees carrying umbrellas to boot, it would at the very least be practical to use this one innocent inconvenience to avoid others that were much more dangerous. Dark cumulonimbus clouds were hanging over the festive dining table; a thunderstorm was in the air. From over at the head of the table, from atop the world, like ominous insignia of divine power, the wild eyes of the Army glowed through an alcoholic stupor and an incense of tobacco smoke:

"Congratulations, Standartenführer. Your people really don't waste any time."

The police fires off a return salvo: "We don't have a whole lot of it, unlike you, General. Indeed, we're not allowed to consolidate our front every month."

I didn't hear our glorious Wehrmacht's counterattack; I was on the way to meet my fate and Adam Trpković. Hauptscharführer Max explains to me what it's all about.

While they were cleaning out the basement to refurbish it according to the Standartenführer's plans, a man was discovered in a remote chamber of the left wing of the building.

"At firtht we thought we had a thaboteur on our handth. (The wet, feathery lisp was drowning out Max's *s*'s.) Doeth the Herr Oberthturmführer underthtand? Thome jerk left by the bandith to blow up the barrackth. However, a perthonal thearch produced no evidenthe of this. (Finally!—one *s* triumphantly broke out of the feathers. It was at the end of a word and Max's tongue had open access to it from at least one end.) A regithter of items found has been included in the record. The Herr Obersturmführer can go through it if he likes. (Max's *s*'s had begun an apparent counteroffensive. A few of their commandos, one this time in the middle of a word, had succeeded in breaking a fatal encirclement by the lisp.) No evidenthe of explothiveth was found. But above all, the man, whothe clothing wath otherwithe fairly tattered, had an enormouth black umbrella. (The lisp once again closed ranks and rushed at the terrified *s*'s.) But the Herr Oberthturmführer will admit that the commandos (Bravo, Max!), at least according to current practice (it seemed that the lisp had finally lost the battle for the Hauptscharführer's tongue), don't care if they get wet duwing theiw opewations. (Concentrating on his *s*'s, poor Max lost control of his *r*'s, one of the few consonants he got along with well.) And the man we found didn't look like a bandit at all, but we know from pa . . . —from our prior work that lookth can be de . . . —can trick you. (His tactics changed. Instead of a frontal assault on the questionable consonants, the Hauptscharführer was trying to avoid them entirely.) There can be no doubt about that. But maybe a charge with a timed fu . . . fu . . .—a time bomb (In any case, what was originally supposed to be a charge with a timed fuse changed its name) could have been put in the barrackth in the few hourth between the Italian wetweat and the arrival of General von Klattern'th twoopth. (Max resigned himself to signing an unconditional capitulation and an occupation by the lisp.) Therefore, there wathn't any need to do it pwactically under our notheth. What's the Herr Oberthturmführer's opinion? Does he think thith analythith ith cowwect? Does thith satithfy the Herr Oberthturmführer's wequirements in thuch catheth? (More and more of Max's consonants were falling victim to the gloomy lisp). Thewe haven't been many catheth like thith. What pwodutheth wethults ith a one-hour tweat . . . tweat . . . tweatment. (And had the Hauptscharführer continued Steinbrecherizing, every consonant in his whole alphabet would have become one omnipotent, dictatorial lisp.)

So, dear Hilmar, this is as far as we made it—to a list of personal possessions "wegithtered in the pwotocol" and searches that produce no results. And then there were nonexistent traces of booby-trapping, deductions based on the habits of saboteurs, correct and incorrect analyses, and to top it all off the crown jewel of this clinical police vocabulary: one-hour "tweatments." It was obvious that Standartenführer Steinbrecher, like some contagious disease, had invaded every pore of our official beings, and perhaps even our private ones as well. We were thoroughly Steinbrecherized, all of us collectively as a unit and, apart from Rotkopf, who was naturally Rotkopfized, each of us individually as well. For my part, it was clear even then that to normal people, and even to any normal

policeman, obsessed as we were with intellectual anamneses, fool-
ishly prone to analysis as we were, and with one artificial language
on our tongues, we must have looked like an extraordinarily dangerous company of retired university professors who had escaped
from an insane asylum disguised in Gestapo uniforms.

Hauptscharführer Max was a slaughterhouse apprentice from
Schweinfurt, a butcher from a town with an ironic name, and
barely literate. As for the reasons why he was employed with us, skill
in calligraphy wasn't as essential as it was in the position of responsibility occupied by Adam Trpković, whose handwriting had the
charming ornateness of antique illuminated manuscripts. It's not
even important how Max ended up in the police. Such a diluvian
specimen doesn't attract any particular attention in the police service, especially in wartime conditions when there's no time for exaggerated and refined selectivity. There he was. Right here, swaying
beside me with the sluggish gait of a dromedary in the desert.
Imagine a stout face, a stout neck, a stout chest and thick arms; pour
some tomato sauce over that pile of hot meat, sprinkle it with sweat
and you've got Hauptscharführer Max. Provided, of course, that you
give it a lisp and take away its power of reason. He never interrogated the prisoners, though that was certainly his dream, which
from time to time he gave in to unofficially. His duty was to bring
the prisoners from their cells to the offices that had ordered them
and later to lead or carry them, depending on their condition, back
down to the basement. He was in charge of transport, if you will, or
if you'd rather stick closer to his occupation in Schweinfurt—he
took care of the delivery of fresh meat with us as well.

But had he been ordered to do so, in any Gestapo office anywhere
in Europe, except Steinbrecher's here, he would have really interrogated the prisoners, Hilmar. He'd have simply asked them questions. In
the sweat of his massive purple face, he'd have scribbled their answers
in the "pwotocol." If he weren't satisfied with their answers, he would
have beaten them. If success eluded him, he'd have perhaps even
clubbed them to death. Death was simply above the power of Max's
ability to reason, so we can't condemn him if he would have joined
forces with it. In any case, no matter how the Hauptscharführer dealt
with the prisoners, he was unable to "treat" them. This was beyond all
doubt. He could certainly mistreat them for days, but not even for a

minute "give them treatment." But nevertheless, dear Hilmar, under the effects of Steinbrecher's destructive intellectual inductors, the Schweinfurt apprentice rose even to that. And even to a precise use of the third person in his conversations with me.

There's no doubt that we're only the products of our environments, and that the difference between a cannibal and a humanist lies in the kind of training.

Under the pressure of Max's super-Steinbrecherized personality, I recalled Haupststurmführer Rotkopf fondly; he abhorred intellectual euphemisms and, from the leathery angle of his necessary minimum of beatings, he openly proclaimed all the Standarten-führer's roundabout logical methods "professorial airs and pretense, conceived to make certain silken gentlemen feel less thuggish, to keep them from feeling at all like killers, which, in spite of the fine analyses or perhaps owing precisely to them, is what they are. Just executioners, nothing more!" He at least wasn't a hypocrite. Unlike you, he didn't call the Second World War a fateful Anglo-German misunderstanding; he didn't call the repressions in the East the very regrettable excesses of an occupational policy; he didn't call Nazism a natural consequence of the Allies' peace terms. Unlike the London BBC, he wasn't at the moment of the destruction of the Polish state on Sunday, 17 September 1939, broadcasting a tennis match and later singing "We're Gonna Hang Out Our Washing on the Siegfried Line." And, finally, unlike Obersturmführer Konrad Rutkowski, Rotkopf didn't seek an excuse for his work in the police in humanism, or an excuse for the application of milder forms of torture in the avoidance of more severe forms. So much for his epitaph.

But in the meantime, what did Obersturmführer Rutkowski think of the results of Max's treatment? He didn't think anything—the question was rhetorical in nature.

Max had subjected the man to a preliminary interrogation. No, he hadn't personally found him. Rottenführer Hans and Rotten-führer Jochen had discovered him. Yes, the man had been composed. He hadn't resisted. But he'd refused to let go of an umbrella he was holding.

Did the Hauptscharführer examine the umbrella?

Yes, he had. He hadn't turned up anything suspicious. Nor did the man say anything in particular to him. He had difficulty expressing himself. No, Max wouldn't say that he'd refused to give answers. He provided answers about everything that he'd been asked.

And what had he been asked?

About anything and everything. He, Max, thought up the questions personally. He'd had opportunities to hear the Obersturmführer doing that. And even the Standartenführer himself. He knew how to deal with prisoners. The prisoner said he was a file clerk in the D. municipality and that he'd been detained by the Italians, but for what he could only confide to someone higher up than the Hauptscharführer. There was no insistence on an answer. Does the Obersturmführer consider such restraint appropriate according to investigative practice?

Yes, he does.

The man stated that he was innocent and that this had been proven in the course of the proceedings against him. When asked why he'd not been released, the man stated that in the meantime the Italians had withdrawn. The partisans had attacked. The garrison had pulled out under bombardment. And he had simply been forgotten about. When asked why the partisans hadn't freed him, he answered that, according to his best guess, they hadn't even entered D. When asked why he hadn't left the prison on his own, he said that had been impossible, because the main grill separating the basement and its cells from the investigative departments had been locked. His answer was satisfactory. In general, everything else had been satisfactory.

Except, of course, that umbrella.

Yes, except that umbrella. It's a fact that arrestees generally don't keep umbrellas in their cells. Indeed, rain would be an unexpected occurrence inside a German prison. When asked about this, the man interpreted the umbrella as a favor to him on the part of the Italians—he was the municipal file clerk. He'd worked in the municipal administration and they'd known him. They knew he never parted from his umbrella, rain or shine. Is the Herr Obersturmführer satisfied with the way the investigation has been conducted so far?

The Herr Obersturmführer was satisfied. What else could he do, Hilmar? The one holding the pen in his hand today would certainly be more cautious in his conclusions. But between that youthful Obersturmführer who was approaching the former carabinieri barracks, accompanied by the giant Hauptscharführer Max, and this elderly historian who is speaking with you, twenty two years of torturous rehabilitation have passed. And at the time of his nonchalant answer, between that youthful Obersturmführer and his potential fate in the shabby figure of a municipal file clerk there was an iron grill, like a visor in front of the face of an unknown enemy.

We entered the barracks. During the last ten hours it had, in the spirit of the Standartenführer's instructions, undergone considerable changes. Apart from the painting of the interior, its Steinbrecherization was nearly complete. The support mechanism for the Standartenführer's convoluted mental analyses had been provided. On the ground floor some of the walls had already turned green. At places on them melancholy women with children in their arms stared indifferently onto the gleaming polished surfaces of requisitioned desks. Typewriters under black covers, inkwells, calendars, ashtrays, lamps with flexible, snakelike necks, pizzle whips. and other orthopedic accessories for our investigative intelligence had already assumed their best positions. The carpets waited to deprive our prisoners of all hope with the cadet formations of their fringes. From somewhere deep inside the building one could hear the tapping of hammers. Local glasscutters who'd been pressed into service were hurriedly installing window grills into the subconscious. Soon the tragic stage of Steinbrecher's black mass would be set.

"So, Münch?"

Hauptscharführer Münch from the admissions section was standing in front of me at strict attention. Hauptscharführer Max was the body of the admissions section, but Münch was its undying soul.

"A very unusual case, Herr Obersturmführer. Never before recorded in practice, administratively fairly odd. We found that it exceeded our jurisdiction and that it'd be best to inform you."

I was still unsure that my intervention would be necessary. The case seemed to me to be a misunderstanding, pure and simple. But out of caution I wanted to free my hand in advance. I told Münch that the Standartenführer had authorized me to solve the matter as I deemed appropriate.

"Where's the prisoner?"

He was still in the basement. Considering the circumstances, Münch had thought it would be best for the man to stay sitting on an empty box of tangerines, where he'd been found. I needed to hurry with his release. I needed to get him out of there before the fratricidal war at von Klattern's table ended and Steinbrecher, without doubt utterly indisposed but all the more ready for work, returned to the barracks. In the strict sense of the word, I didn't have his expressed permission to solve the matter as I deemed appropriate. Any decision about anything concerning the D. Sonderkommando, and thus about the fate of the man sitting on the box of tangerines, was entirely in the Standartenführer's hands. I simply hoped—without excessive enthusiasm, by the way—that I could interpret the Standartenführer's permission to leave the table as his consent to represent him here.

"From the point of view of the psychology of the statement, I find . . . ," said Münch, beginning the customary Steinbrecheriad.

"You hold your tongue, Hauptscharführer, and leave the psychology of the statement to me."

We go down into the basement and stop in front of an iron grill that resembles the sluices in sewer channels. The lock creaks unbearably. It's obviously not yet been Steinbrecherized.

"I am worried about that umbrella, though. Above all, it's not even any special kind of umbrella. That makes it suspicious to the highest degree. It's only large. Too large for such a short man, if you know what I mean."

I don't shut him up. What can I do, Hilmar? Whenever Steinbrecher started coming out of someone's mouth, nothing could put a stop to it. It was clear that the unfortunate Münch was energetically trying to shut up. His disciplinary nerve was being painfully pinched. He was all flushed from his efforts to reign in the Steinbrecher within himself. But Steinbrecher was gushing out in thicker and thicker streams:

"And then, has the Herr Obersturmführer ever seen a prisoner in solitary confinement with an umbrella in his hands? I don't think so. Our prisons don't leak. Our prisons are unequalled in the world. The prisoners are fully protected from all the elements. As for myself, I've never ever seen a prisoner holding an umbrella. Well, in fact I have, but he wouldn't count. He was out in the open. A group of hostages was being led to be executed in the town of G. An orthodox priest was holding an umbrella, a yellow woman's umbrella. It was raining, but it still seemed strange to me. He was wearing his priest's hat. He was sufficiently protected, but he still opened the umbrella. He fell into the trench with it. Such things shouldn't be allowed to happen in a well-organized state. They're dangerous, very dangerous!"

Münch was right. The umbrella was extremely dangerous. Perhaps more dangerous than its owner. It destroyed the foundations of Steinbrecher's entire production. With its spontaneous impudence, the umbrella simply de-Steinbrecherized life. In the perfectly Steinbrecherized atmosphere, where all things living and dead would quickly become the breathless tools of investigation, where barred gratings from the subconscious, the parade march of carpet fringes and the sedative green of the walls would join with the Standartenführer's dialectics and Rotkopf's pizzle whips to snuff out the divine soul in people, the man with the umbrella had quite an unusual effect—like an erroneous color on a painter's canvas, like a glaring typographical error in a minuscule manuscript. Even the circumstances of his discovery mocked all good police protocol. Instead of being kicked awake with jackboots, pulled out of bed by his hair and brought in to the barracks, he was found in the basement of our own house, sitting on a box of tangerines and holding an umbrella. He was sitting on an unusual throne, with an unusual scepter between his legs. (Hilmar, do you remember that on the occasion of the inspection of the barracks I compared Steinbrecher to a Visigoth riding down into the valley of the Po to conquer the Empire? Had the Standartenführer and this man met then, I'd have had to compare the latter, because of the power of an ironic coincidence, to a Roman senator sitting on his senatorial throne with the signum of his power, awaiting Alarich.)

Every born policeman would have felt Münch's uneasiness about the umbrella. That was a horror at the possibility of something significant in the case remaining unexplained, no matter if all the other mysteries had been solved. And the fact that the umbrella caught me off guard, and that I looked upon it, at the beginning at least, with sympathy, as on an ally in the struggle against Steinbrecher's order, was not so much a testimony to its harmlessness as it was to my professional shortcomings. *Sometimes I think,* the Standartenführer would often say, *that even an average police dog could outdo you in drawing conclusions.* I can't think of anything I might say to counter this criticism.

But now let's leave Münch to worry, Adam Trpković to await me sitting on a box of tangerines, and SS Obersturmführer Konrad Rutkowski with his hand on the door of his cell, let's leave the year 1943 in the spellbound motionlessness of wax figures pierced with voodoo needles, and we'll return, my dear Hilmar, again to the year 1965, to be with your sister—the weather's beautiful and she's already waiting in the foyer, armed with penitent symbols—and we will go to the unveiling of a monument of sienna granite.

KONRAD

■ □ ■ □ ■

LETTER 8

A GRANITE LEGEND, OR *THE*
MEANING OF HISTORY

The Mediterranean Coast, 16 Sept. 1965

Dear Hilmar,

Our story resembles a railway: its invisible rails lead in the same direction, but the rail on the left was laid twenty years after the one on the right. All those years the track was unusable and the tale could not take its form. I had to return to D. before the spindle of fate would begin unwinding backwards from the head of the cradle, thus laying the other rail so the track of the story could follow both. And for the story to run evenly, it's again necessary for the crossties to be laid so that they simultaneously encompass both periods of time, 1943 and 1965. Only in their coalescence does the story gain any meaning. Memories provide a content for reflections, and reflections a purpose for memories. Hence the pause in front of Adam's cell and our return to the pensione, with the intention of leaving for the unveiling of the monument more or less prepared.

What I have in mind more than anything is an attempt to explain to you the peculiar way in which the file clerk Adam Trpković turned our second meeting into another crossroads in my life.

Inheriting something from their vanished reality, memories return to us in a manner characteristic of that very reality. Memories of people return coolly like the personalities that fill them or lively and loudly if chaos corresponds more to the vulgar nature of the model. There are memories, Hilmar, that will break your heart just as mercilessly as the event they astrally renew. There are those of timid origin, which would never appear if you didn't wish it. And there are those that nothing save a lobotomy can prevent from destroying your life. Anyway, you know all this, all this is *locus communis*. What you don't know is that it wasn't in any of the afore-mentioned ways that Adam made his return.

He simply burrowed into me like a parasite. He *infected* me like a tropical fever, whose incubation lacks acute symptoms and doesn't allow an opportunity for any kind of preventive treatment. The fact that I'd refused to think about my police past for twenty-two years hadn't been any kind of real preventive. That would have been like someone protecting himself from rabies only by avoiding being bit-ten by dogs. That was a compromise with the illness, in which it agreed not to infect you on the condition that you don't happen upon any—even the smallest—of its germs. The decision to vaca-tion in D. led me to the heart of the contaminated area of my past. The condition was broken, the compromise rejected, to be replaced (as you'll find out) in the good old intellectual habit by something even worse—these hypocritical letters.

The mild irritation that had always defined my attitude toward those who suffer—under a veneer of Christian behavior—preceded Adam's renewed arrival. And that happened on the very first night of our stay in D., when your sister and I had parted so grumpily— she to seek peace in sleep and I to seek it in the finest of yarns about a historical spectacle a thousand years old. If I add to this that he appeared at first in the guise of an invisible addition to the Renaissance square the room looked out on, I'll have sufficiently defined the treachery of Adam's invasion into my thoughts, which were absorbed in the spreading of the evangelical truth among the Slavs west of the Dnieper.

Independently of the hint of his presence in material phenome-na, among which he had once dragged his inevitable umbrella behind him, inasmuch as he himself was surfacing more and more out of a confusion of memories just as the corpse of a victim surfaces in traitorous slime, and inasmuch as his case took on the contours of loathsome facts, my irritation yielded to extreme dissatisfaction. I felt deceived by my own conscience, in the same way that I'd been deceived by the Allied investigators who assured me that my persistent struggle against the Gestapo would completely vitiate the incriminating fact that I had led it wearing the uniform of an SS Obersturmführer in one of its Sonderkommandos. I atoned for my sin while still committing it, and my right to bury the past was indisputable. My trip to D. was accordingly not a penitent pilgrimage, but a proud visit to a place of combat and glory.

Adam spoiled everything. Adam rejected the compromise and decided to return as a vampire.

The opening movement of that vampirization was the unveiling of a monument. But I shouldn't get ahead of myself.

At the crack of dawn, columns of locals in their Sunday best and peasants dressed in picturesque folk costumes, whose gowns and caps wouldn't have looked out of place on the contemporaries of my Mieszko, were already swarming past. Even if we hadn't had any intention of joining them, we wouldn't have been able to sleep because of the songs, the racket, and the traffic. Sabina was very upset. Her feeling of responsibility for the Second World War had been complicated by the trouble she had in choosing a dress that would express the true state of affairs and the Germans' attitude toward their dark history. She finally decided on an austere and modest blue suit.

(Hilmar, I admit I treated your sister indecently in this critical matter, purely out of a desire for revenge. Asked for my opinion—I myself adamantly refused to wear a tie and took part in the festivities in a short-sleeve shirt—I answered that she couldn't have chosen a more appropriate outfit. Owing to Sabina's ignorance of history and the fact that she'd never seen the uniforms of the members of our auxiliary women's services, that history pulled one more of its pranks. In point of fact, that "austere and modest blue suit," with its metal buttons and sporty pockets, brought to the monument a Blitzmädel in regulation uniform, in full martial splendor.)

We joined the procession and ascended the hill. The heat was unbearable. Sabina, however, wouldn't agree to go by car. That wouldn't have been fair to the locals. The locals, of course, went by car. But they could afford that. They weren't responsible for a world war. Abusing their innocence, they drove past in their cars, waving and blanketing us in a layer of yellow dust. Schoolchildren, walking in double file, waved banners and bunches of wildflowers. Once in a while, an open truck would pass us, crammed full with people, wreaths, posters with slogans, and flags. For a while we walked alongside a regiment of workers from some firm; later we trudged next to a group of youths carrying party and state banners. We were passed by a group of nuns—a flock of dignified black penguins, and then several bicyclists pushing their bicycles. I tried to dispel my bad mood by imagining that somewhere in the distance, ahead of us at the front of the procession, there was a mysterious piper dancing, all clad in black. The legendary magical flutist who would lead us, joyous and charmed, straight into an abyss, an abyss that would once and for all reconcile my unbearable wartime memories with the survivors who were transmitting them like a disease.

Finally, completely exhausted, we reached a clearing, hidden behind a sharp curve in the road, and saw the monument on a plateau covered with reddish gravel. Hilmar, it was truly grandiose. Perhaps it's better if I tell how it would be when the canvas tarpaulin was removed from it, and when it no longer looked like a cumbersome armchair covered with a white slipcover before its giant owners left on a trip.

The plateau was crowded with people. From a bird's-eye view, this formless monument must have looked like God on the sixth day. The Creator, dissatisfied, rejected and cursed his first, beginner's attempt at the world, and now on the top of a Balkan hill he's at work making a better one. The formless heap at his feet is white clay, the mixture from which the first specimens of the new world have begun to form, still stuck together at the sides. At the base of the monument a provisional podium rose up, assembled from brightly painted boards and decorated with colorful crepe paper. The sky was filled with the martial music of Genesis played on brass instruments: Josephat's trumpets sounded amid the thunderous beating of drums.

We stood in the scant shadows of some olive trees, a little off to one side, apart, alone, like leftover specimens from the first world, chosen to demonstrate its failure. But maybe that's what we were:

samples that were allowed to survive solely to ensure comparisons to their own detriment.

Fortunately, the monument would be visible from there as well. It was built to be seen from kilometers away all around. And I, parenthetically, imagined the heroism that would be worthy of it. The bravery, zeal, and sacrifice of one man could hardly be worthy of it. That required the unified efforts of a whole people—their joint heroic feat. However, monuments aren't erected to honor the people. If a people built a monument to themselves, that would be an arrogant act of disregard for international considerations. It would be an open act of scorn for other peoples and races. Thus, they resort to an artistic synthesis. In most cases, the individuals to whom monuments are erected really were heroes. But they have names and surnames, *curriculum vitae,* and even their little weaknesses, which provide them with personalities and distinguish them from their drab surroundings—surroundings that they nevertheless represent. The general and the individual find in art a common language at last.

In the meantime, the music stopped. It yielded to ceremonial speeches. From one I learned, despite the bursts of applause, that beneath the white tarpaulin was a man to whom many of those present owed their lives, a man whose hands (while they had still been flesh and blood, and not granite) had once held the fates of most of those who were honoring him today. His extraordinary conduct in the face of the enemy—so the speaker said—had best expressed the tradition of freedom in the area of D. This was followed by a recount of the ancient battles of this people, which the monument couldn't take part in, as they had occurred in the mists of centuries past. Finally, it came to the Germans. The vocabulary became picturesque, and the historical images (accurate, by the way) lively and bloody. I was glad that Sabina couldn't understand the speech; the procedure for penitence would have turned out to be more difficult than she'd foreseen.

So instead of going to the beach, we had to climb five kilometers uphill at a temperature of 40°C to learn what a swine I'd been. From a historical point of view, that's exactly what I was. As a historical model of an officer of the Geheime Staatspolizei, I'd been everything that institution was as a whole. But as Konrad Rutkowski I'd been only what I'd *done with my own hands.*

(This was what I thought at the unveiling of the monument. Today, my dear Hilmar, I think THAT I NEVER ACTUALLY WAS WHAT I DID AND CAUSED, BUT ALWAYS ONLY WHAT I DIDN'T DO OR CAUSE. In other words, I think I was always negatively defined by what I failed to do, what I avoided doing, and, finally, what I gave up doing at the last moment out of my soul's pathetic adaptability to compromise and the laziness of my mind. But I'll save this for later.) The speaker had in the meantime decided to say a few words about the occasion for the celebration. It turned out that the man had been in prison. Whose, I couldn't figure out. And then that, while in captivity, he'd been subjected to inhuman torture by the occupier's police. Whose, wasn't yet clear to me. And finally, that he'd withstood all the torture and, instead of betraying his comrades, he'd spit into his executioners' faces. But it wasn't said exactly into whose face.

"Whose face was it that he spit into?" I asked a young man who was standing not far from me, chewing on his own tongue.

"One of the occupiers'. Who else?"

There was no sense in getting into a discussion with those people about the date of the heroic feat, which was insignificant for them, but of the utmost importance for me. Because if the aforementioned arrest and torture occurred during the first three years of our Balkan campaign, then the bespittled face undoubtedly belonged to Maresciallo Dagllione, whose priapic initials on the wall of the carabinieri barracks had promised a microbial birthrate to his whoring nation. But if all this had occurred later, then I knew who the monument was supposed to be to. And I knew the bespittled face only too well. I myself was present at that so-called historic spitting and will describe it when the time comes. Rotkopf—here's a little advance—after a split second devoted to the deadly realization that he'd been degraded in his authority as an unlimited ruler, with a lightning motion, like the reflex of a skunk, raised the rubber truncheon, which was still sticky with blood, and rubbed his cheek with it. The spit wasn't wiped away, but rubbed deep into the skin of his face like a medicinal balm. It was incorporated forever into his being under the auspices of Satan.

The worker was obviously one of those subjects who weren't tied in a mental knot. One of those wretches who arrive at their convictions not by means of frazzled nerves, but by an empty rectum and generations of dull helplessness. He wasn't equipped with a receptor for the subtle messages Steinbrecher was sending to his subconscious by the unruffled fringes on the carpets, and couldn't be broken by any means of coercion. Throughout his internment he'd refused even to give his name. As he apparently wasn't from these parts, there was no way of finding it out. He squatted, handcuffed to the radiator, and watched us. His very light eyes were bloodshot, and radiated a vampirish, warm red. He looked at us not with reproach and hatred, but indifferently. He'd been beyond our reach from the very beginning of the investigation. And now he even shook off his body, which was hanging against the damp wall, bloody and wracked with pain. Rotkopf began beating him once more, rhythmically and methodically, striking his joints and his scrotum, his eyes and his belly. The black trunk convulsed galvanically in the quiet of that basement, which by the grace of immeasurable suffering had suddenly become the heart of an accursed world. Somewhere outside there was the screeching of an automobile's brakes. A dog started howling at the moon, and I, standing in the corner, needed all my mental energy to keep from rushing at the Hauptsturmführer and strangling him, and thus ruining with one senseless act any chances I had of really helping any of those wretches. Fortunately, Hilmar, I restrained myself. My mission lent me the strength to go even further, but I won't write about that now. And when everything was over, when the worker lost consciousness, when the torture had lost any purpose, I went to the toilet to puke my guts out.

Hilmar, I've helped you to gain an impression of what a Steinbrecherized person is like. Now the time has come for you, there over the toilet bowl, to make the acquaintance of one Rutkowskified being.

And since you met him in one of his most moral versions, we can continue with the story. We can observe the stout, sweaty speaker, assisted by some clumsy guards, laboring to untangle the steel wire from the canvas tarpaulin. We can at last breath in a little of the breeze that has blown in from the glittering high sea to air out that overheated crowd if only for a moment, for the mystical moment of the Apparition.

Then we're illuminated by a flash of divine, porphyrous granite-lightning that strikes from the white tarpaulin as it's removed, and find ourselves before the powerful figure of a man who is no different from us save in his dimensions, but before whom we are forced, owing to the artistic genius of his creator, to stop, bow our heads and say: *Ecce homo!*

Of course, I thought: The worker!—Rotkopf's worker. The man whose lips wouldn't even let go of his own name. Only his conduct in the face of the police was worthy of such a monument. Only in his superhuman resistance, which one couldn't picture in one's wildest fantasies, was there enough greatness for the national consciousness to consent to recognize its equal.

And so that this is completely clear, take photograph B (it's in the same place as photograph A), place it next to this letter, and look at it while you read the following lines.

You can see its dimensions yourself. The photograph was taken a few days afterward, and Sabina is standing next to the pedestal, which will help you imagine its size. Since it's a color photograph taken in good light, you can easily see what it looks like. The porphyrous statue is enveloped in a mild glow with a steel-blue hue, a transparent nimbus as at the ascent or descent of the gods, victors, avengers, the deliverers of final justice. Don't be disturbed by the fact that he's not holding a scale or riding a black horse. He's riding it—it's just invisible. And he's measuring us, only we don't notice. He's calling the dead and the innocent to rise up for the Judgment, only we don't hear it. The third seal has been broken and we hear the Beast saying: COME AND SEE, AND BEHOLD, A BLACK HORSE, AND HE THAT SAT ON IT HAD A PAIR OF BALANCES IN HIS HAND.

The trial of SS Obersturmführer Konrad Rutkowski was opened, without he himself being notified until late in the evening.

At dinner I was just explaining to Sabina the difference between the pragmatic, artistic, and historiographic approaches to a fact of the past, and she was energetically opposing me, trying to demonstrate her intellectual independence from me, as was her habit, when our friend the waiter came up to us. The one who had so kindly spared me from his uprising the evening before.

"Have you seen him, sir?"

"Who?"

"Our Adam Trpković."

"Who?!"

"You were at the unveiling of the monument, sir. Weren't you?"

"Yes, we were. Of course."

"So then you saw our Adam. What a head he had on his shoulders! A real scholar! He always had his nose in a book!"

"Don't be stupid, man. You know I couldn't have seen him. You must know he's already been dead for twenty-two years."

"Of course I know, sir. Who in D. wouldn't know that?! That's why we erected a monument to him. I knew how heavy it is, but I forgot. I'm not good with numbers. It's not good for work, but I get by somehow."

"What, you think *that thing up there* represents Adam Trpković?"

The waiter looked at me with astonishment. He found foreigners to be quite amusing sometimes.

"Of course. The whole city knows it. And it says so on the plaque."

"That's impossible."

Now Sabina intervened. She suspected that I was drunk—which, to a certain degree, I indeed was—and that I was using that condition as an alibi for the mistreatment of the locals and for continuing the war that I'd lost in 1945.

"Why would that be impossible? And what do you know about it, anyway?"

"I know it's impossible. If that were really Adam Trpković, he'd also be carrying an umbrella."

"Konrad!" your sister shrieked.

"What kind of umbrella, sir?"

"An ordinary men's umbrella, like people carry around here. Only a little larger."

The waiter withdrew discreetly:

"It'd be better if I brought you your food, sir."

Sabina was livid.

"You're drunk. You're acting like a pig. I guess you can think of them what you will, but you have no right to mock them in their own homes."

"I'm not mocking anyone, Sabina. I'm only saying that if it's him, they forgot his umbrella. That's the truth. But if it is him, then I really don't know what to think."

"No one cares what you think. It's none of your business."

"I'm a historian, Sabina. This is of great concern to me. Because if that's Adam Trpković, I might as well close up shop."

Sabina stood up and tried to pull me up out of my chair.

"No one touched his umbrella. Not Maresciallo Dagllione with his big member, who smuggled tangerines. Not Hans and Jochen, who found him. Not Max, who pweliminawily quethtioned him, or Münch, who entered him into the record under number 1. Not even Standartenführer Steinbrecher! Not even he, who was Steinbrecherized down to his last capillary, touched Adam's umbrella. . . ."

"Let's go, for the love of God!" Sabina begged me.

"But these guys took it away from him! Do you understand that, Sabina? The first thing they did was take away his umbrella, which held the key to everything, and then they put him up in the wrong place. So how do you think all this damned history gets written, anyway?"

When I woke up, it was nearly midnight. The window was open and the sky in it resembled a silver shield with a black, spear-like silhouette of a church steeple in the middle. Moonlight hung in the room like a spider's web. Sabina was sleeping in the next bed. I lit a cigarette, got up, and put on my bathrobe. My head was completely clear. I went into the parlor, walking through the door next to which so often a prisoner had been standing with his face to the wall before Max led him into the office. The realization that Adam Trpković sat enthroned high above the city, symbolizing the qualities in whose name I too had thought and acted throughout the course of the war, was no longer as oppressive as it had been earlier that evening. Occasional lapses in our ideas about the past don't have to mean that historiography as a discipline is a failure. Historiography, like everything else in this imperfect world, is a compromise—a compromise between the truth of history and human needs. But so is history itself. It's a hybrid, a compromise. Local delusions shouldn't serve as the basis for universal truths. Where would that lead us? We'd have to believe that the German border radio station at Gleiwitz was, after all, attacked by the Poles; that the communists set fire to the Reichstag; that the interned Jews were nevertheless treated decently. We'd have to subject the Nuremberg verdicts to revision and assess them as largely unjust. (Something that you, my dear Hilmar, are already doing ever so delicately.) The whole of German history would appear quite different. Sabina wouldn't be ashamed, and you wouldn't have to correct her in underhanded footnotes. All our views on European events in this century, especially those between 1918 and 1945, would be radically altered. It would force us to realize that the reports of Stalin's unbridled terror were exaggerated and the numbers of his victims fabricated. In the new version of history, the Christians burn Rome, the women in Salem are witches, and the Knights Templars sorcerers. If you try to envision that history, in which everything is turned on its head and whose events are turned inside out like gloves—a history in which the Jews in fact ritually devour Christian children, in which Danton was paid by the aristocrats and Trotsky was supported by our intelligence service, where Dreyfus also worked for us, where the most extravagant interpretations and the most imaginative frauds finally pay off, you'll see clearly that the beatification of Adam Trpković would have to be considered an isolated lapse by local historians and not a universally valid principle.

But before I completely abandoned the case of the monument, I couldn't—and I still can't—resist the temptation to imagine a world integrally contradictory in its images of itself, a world in which vices are legalized and virtues outlawed as subversive, lies proclaimed to be the truth in all areas of life and thought, and every truth declared a lie; a hell on earth accepted as a heaven on earth; a world whose historiography has as its sole task the revision of all history in accordance with the new views, so it could be said that that's how things have always been, from time immemorial.

Then I sat down at the desk and began to work.

That was when Adam Trpković made his second appearance.

I'll leave that for tomorrow. Today I'm much too tired for such an undertaking. It'd be convoluted and self-contradictory. And you'd make ill use of that. You'd strip my story of its credibility and accuse me of drunken hallucinations, if not something worse.

So have patience until tomorrow.

Yours,

KONRAD

■ □ ■ □ ■

LETTER 9

THE SECOND LIFE OF ADAM
TRPKOVIĆ, OR *THE*
PHENOMENOLOGY OF THE SPIRIT

The Mediterranean Coast, 17 Sept. 1965

Dear Hilmar,

As you know, I stepped into the parlor around midnight on the night of the 13th of September. As I walked past the desk, I turned on the lamp. I didn't pay attention to whether it illuminated anything other than my manuscript. No, I didn't look around the room. I had no reason to do so. To be honest, I avoided it. The parlor already reminded me of the Gestapo office too much for me to enjoy being in it. I went straight to the window, which, unlike the bedroom facing the sea, looked out on the square. Yes, the window was open. I took a deep breath of air. My head was clear of all but the last traces of alcohol, ready to think reasonably and without bias about the unearned, posthumous glory of Adam Trpković. The previous letter told you what that head thought about Adam's glory and about history and historiography, as well as about a few other things.

I didn't sense anything odd in the room, nor did I feel odd myself—unless you consider it strange that a man in an almost tropically warm night was cold. The air felt chilly to me. I closed the window. It seemed, however, that the source of the cold was inside the room, because it didn't get any warmer. I decided it was a matter of a temporary fever caused by my intoxication.

Although the corners of the parlor were in darkness, the middle of the room was bathed in pleasant, clear moonlight, broken only by the circular beam of the electric lamp on the table.

I was planning on using an as yet neglected fact to round off the description of the day's events, in which, during the eighth chapter of my monograph THE ROYAL AND CAPITAL CITY OF CRACOW, Prince Mieszko Piastowicz had for the first time tasted the Eucharist, the flesh and blood of the Polish people. In the center of the muted polish of the walnut desk, the lamp's mild glow traced an ellipse, the one field of light in the dark universe of that room. In that angelic aureole the paper was waiting, empty, blank, submissive. I grabbed my pen with a lazy—what one might call a lustful—gesture. But at the moment of that fecund encounter at the electric crossing gate between light and dark, like in a dim section of a scene of the Grand Guignol, the municipal clerk Adam Trpković appeared. Mieszko, dragging his scepter like a mace, withdrew into the shelter of the centuries, crestfallen, not yet having attained union with Christ, still damned. The Poles reverted to idolatry. History lost all sense. What remained in that desolate world was the accursed scrivener with the oily eyes (which, in spite of the pince-nez with the metal rims, had been losing their sight), dressed in the shabby coat of a municipal file clerk, from which the brass insignia of his position had been torn away, and in long white underwear. The ideal symbol of a disagreement with history, his hand gripped the handle of an enormous umbrella, the clumsy kind that you see only here in the south.

This astral apparition[8]—what else could it be?—was preceded by a deep, otherworldly, commanding voice:

"I've been expecting you, Obersturmführer."

Horror lifted me out of my chair and then dropped me back down into it: through the flickering disc of light, teeming with blinded gnats, I caught sight of the indistinct contours of a man who was sitting on a leather ottoman in one corner of the room, his chin resting on the handle of an umbrella. My perspective created the ghastly impression that the gnats and mayflies were flying out of his dead mouth and swarming around his corpse. At first, I didn't recognize his face. But that wasn't even necessary. I recognized the umbrella, and the way he carried it when Max would bring him in for interrogation. There could be no doubt, Hilmar, the man sitting in front of me was Adam Trpković.

"Who are you and how did you get in here?" I asked as soon as I caught my breath.

"You haven't changed much, Obersturmführer. You look just as bewildered as the first time we met. That happened only some ten meters below where we are right now."

"If you don't tell me who you are and how you made your way in here, I'll call the police!"

"But *you are* the police, Rutkowski—or have they sent you into retirement already? It wouldn't surprise me. Considering your meager results, including my case, it's a miracle you stuck around for so long."

"Are you trying to make a fool of me?"

"My help would be completely unnecessary for something like that, Rutkowski. I never had a particularly high opinion of you. Not even then, when I was a scribbling wretch at the very bottom of the pay scale, without the right to any kind of opinion, not even when my only freedom, the whole purpose of my existence, consisted solely in my calligraphic recording of the thoughts of others. Even in wartime conditions, which as a rule sharpen one's wits, you displayed an astonishing degree of confusion in your behavior, an inconsistency in your actions, and a lack of moral orientation. Don't interrupt me, Rutkowski. There's no point. An intellectual who squandered fifty years in convoluted mental dilemmas and rotten compromises with life can't, at a few moments like this, expect to be able to think of something smart and do it. You always find the most vacuous things to worry about. You haven't changed in that respect, either. At one time you thought it important not to harm a prisoner who was going to be killed the next day. And today what you're most concerned about is how I came in. I came in through the door, Obersturmführer! I availed myself of a compromise between the wall and the air, if that formulation is more appealing to you. The door was open, of course. You were drunk as a skunk, and all your wife could think about was getting you to sleep as quickly as possible and putting a stop to your babbling. However, I move about in other ways as well. I fly or simply materialize on the spot, if you understand what I mean. And about who I am, you know that better than anyone else."

"There's no doubt," I said, "that you resemble a person whom I had the misfortune of knowing in my time, but there's no *natural* way that you could be him. First of all, you dispose of more than ten primordial words in your vocabulary, and second of all, that person was executed way back in 1943."

"Let's be precise—he was hanged."

"That's right—hanged."

"Are you sure?"

"I was present at the execution."

"What do you mean by that?"

"That I saw him die."

"That doesn't necessarily mean very much if you remember that Christ was executed, but it's nevertheless claimed that he's not dead."

"So you're comparing yourself to Christ?"

"Listen, Rutkowski, the fact that we don't belong to the same world doesn't give you the right to insult me. Forget your police manners and your pizzle whips."

"I meant that as a compliment."

"In *my* world that isn't a compliment at all. In *my* world that's the worst insult you can inflict on someone."

"And you expect me to believe that?"

"Think logically, Rutkowski. You saw me die, and later you see me sitting on this ottoman. What conclusion does that lead one to?"

"That the execution was staged. Standartenführer Steinbrecher had already played similar tricks. A jerk like you could only be of use to him alive."

"You're right in principle. Unfortunately, Standartenführer Steinbrecher wasn't of that opinion, and I was killed. I won't request that you put your hand through my heart to convince you of my incorporeity. I'll appeal to your reason. Anyway, you said yourself that my presence in your parlor is beyond the realm of *natural* possibility. For once, you've been served by your instincts, for a change."

"I don't believe in *supernatural* possibilities."

"Who does? The supernatural doesn't exist. The supernatural is only a concept for what you don't understand. Even where I live there are things that seem supernatural in comparison to ordinary conditions. But in contrast to you, we're aware that it's an illusion. One's perspective, Obersturmführer, can move mountains. The sole difficulty lies in shifting one's perspective."

"I'm content with my perspective."

"I'm familiar with that point of view. Every perspective is good as long as it feeds us and keeps us warm. On the other hand, you're an intellectual. You dispose of a healthy ability to reason. How can you deny the existence of something you consent to talk to? Obersturmführer, I fear that this time you won't be able to slip by with one of your famous compromises."

"I'm not counting on a compromise. I'll close my eyes, and when I open them again you'll be gone."

"Don't get your hopes up, Obersturmführer. I'm aware that you intellectuals have gotten used to eliminating evil by closing your eyes to it. Or in the worst case, you explain it as an inevitable condition for the attainment of some higher goal. Like the egg that has to be broken if one wants an omelet. The fact that you're not getting an omelet, even if you're well on your way to breaking all the eggs, doesn't disturb you, of course. The principle is sound. The eggs are the problem. The eggs are always bad, and you can't make an omelet with rotten eggs. But right now I'm not interested in your culinary philosophy, so don't try to bore me with it. Have you been up there?"

"Up where?"

"On the hill, dammit to hell!"

"Yes."

"Did you see the monument?"

"So you know that they've erected a monument to you?"

"You bet I do. What do you think of me? That's my official area, and I don't carry out my duties in the shabby manner that you do. I was conscientious in my work way back when I was a clerk. My cursive flourishes were famed all over."

"I heard, although they reminded many of nooses."

"Don't grab the snake by its fangs, Obersturmführer. Your remark belongs to the argument between the hangman and the rope about who strangled the victim. I suggest a compromise. I suggest we assume that the victim died from a lack of oxygen in his blood. That's the only explanation that no one can object to. So, you've seen the monument?"

"Yes."

"Does it look like me?"

"No. It's only a symbol. Of course, without the umbrella it's a weak one."

"That's the last thing I need. By the way, the monument is what brings me to you. But it would be more honest to say that I brought you to D. because of it. That's what this is all about. . . ."

"Wait, I still haven't agreed that you exist."

"Don't be tiresome, Rutkowski. In the Gestapo you were also constantly rejecting something, disagreeing with something, refusing to consent to something, but you nevertheless conducted yourself as if you did agree, and all the while, allegedly because of a conspiracy, acted sometimes even worse than those colleagues of yours who didn't worry about moral difficulties and who honestly consented to everything. Anyway, I have no intention of hindering you in your harmless intellectual tricks. I don't care whether you agree that I exist, as long as you talk with me this nicely. That's a completely acceptable compromise for me. Far better than if you acknowledged my existence but refused to talk with me."

"That's exactly what I intend to do."

"I don't think so."

"Why?"

"Because you're vain."

"I don't understand what you're getting at."

"If you refused to talk to me, it would mean that you're afraid of me. That you see in me the first signs of a mental disorder, which you can subdue only by refusing any kind of interaction with me."

"Nonsense. By the very act of talking to you I admit that I'm crazy."

"No, Rutkowski. You're just a realist. By that you acknowledge a reality that you are incapable of changing. What that reality is like doesn't matter, as long as it's unchangeable. In 1943 it didn't matter either. And you also accepted that reality in 1943."

"In order to change it, not to protect it."

"Exactly, Obersturmführer. I was a witness. I was sent up to the gallows in that refined manner."

"I couldn't say that I regret it. Given what I've heard about you in the meantime. . . ."

"But as always, this was a matter of a misunderstanding. We simply didn't understand each other, Rutkowski. For you I wasn't Adam Trpković, but one of your numerous moral dilemmas. You wanted to save me at any price. The tragedy was that you wanted to do so *because of yourself* and your idea of yourself, and not because of me. I was a statistical necessity for you, but not at all a human one. I was only an episode that would raise the curve of your morality one more exponential degree. However, I had no understanding for such complications. I wasn't an intellectual. I was a loyal citizen in all possible respects, right until that damned wind started up, which made me hold onto the umbrella, so I neglected to salute the fucking Italian flag. I was even content in the prison until you came to make me the battlefield of your glorious struggle against fascism."

No, Hilmar, Adam Trpković wasn't an intellectual. Anything but. However, during our conversation, which occurred under the extreme suspicion that I was dreaming or hallucinating, I detected something in his bearing, in his way of speaking and even in his way of thinking that was utterly different from even my most favorable memories. Now I knew what was the matter. He was now speaking like an educated man. He displayed dialectic powers that were incompatible with Adam while he was alive. His manner had become authoritative. A cynical, aggressive, and uncompromising mind. He reminded me strongly of someone, but I couldn't figure out who at all.

"I see you're married."

"Yes."

"Does your wife know about your police past?"

"Of course she does."

"So she knows everything? About D. too?"

"She doesn't know about D."

"And why, Obersturmführer? Why didn't you tell her about that?"

"What business is it of yours, Trpković?"

"So you do recognize me?"

"I'll act like I do."

"Fine. That's the way you are, the way you were back during the war. As for your wife, I can understand that. Although our thirst for blood is constantly on the rise, there still aren't very many women who would share their bed with a murderer without some hesitation."

"I wasn't a murderer, and you know that, Trpković."

"Maybe. In your soul. Intimately. Privately, so to speak. For your own consumption."

"Don't tell me you expected me to offer open resistance."

"Why not, Obersturmführer? That was expected from others, for example. Some others lost their lives, and at the very least their honor, when they didn't fulfill those expectations. You were an educated man. You had access to information. Your moral mechanism was completely intact. And you didn't even have the justification that you were a real Nazi. Because if you'd been a real Nazi, then one could say that you were deluded. There was hope that sooner or later you would snap out of the spell cast on you by Reichminister Goebbels' propaganda and the opportunity, under the aegis of a national myth, to give free reign to your bad impulses. But you weren't one of hell's right-hand men. You were just a collaborator, due to your mental cowardice. Consequently, there can be no pardon for you."

"I find this reasoning monstrous. It means that anyone who doesn't run to the aid of a victim—whatever the reason—is a greater criminal than the one who does the killing."

"The one who does the killing commits only one crime, the crime of murder. Anyone who fails to intervene commits two: he both kills his neighbor and is also indifferent toward his death. Your grandfather was a pastor. You know the Christian dogmas. You know that indifference is the gravest of mortal sins."

"I wasn't indifferent. And further, you're the last person who has a right to reproach me for anything."

"I'm not reproaching you, Rutkowski. On the contrary, I'm only considering the issue from the human standpoint. We're quite satisfied with you, Obersturmführer. Given the mental difficulties with which you struggled in order to subdue the natural evil within you and which your superiors didn't know about, your sins were quite satisfactory. It would have been overdoing it to expect such an intellectual to run around with a knife in his teeth slaughtering anyone he ran into. Especially during the forties. And especially with his own hands, without the brokerage of primitive worshipers of the intellect. Today the situation is considerably improved. We catch terrific minds planting time bombs on baby carriages. The intelligentsia has obviously woken from its languor and reached straight for a pistol. We've removed any doubt as to the ability of the intelligentsia to destroy the Christian world. To avail myself of a Spanish formulation, we think it's the best fifth column we've ever had."

"Who are you?"

"You mean you can't guess, Obersturmführer?"

"I don't believe in hell."

"That's obvious. Otherwise you wouldn't have done what you did. Our main hope lies precisely in the fact that people don't believe in us. Had you believed in the existence of hell, you'd have fought against evil, out of fear if nothing else. The way things are, you contented yourself with indignation and some completely innocent act of intervention once in a while."

"It's easy to shoot at the enemy, Trpković. It's much harder to sneak up on him from behind and bury a knife in his heart."

"One's heart is unfortunately always located in the front, Obersturmführer. The enemy's is too, though you think he doesn't have one at all. But for the sake of our conversation, let's assume you're right. You remained in the Gestapo in order to hamper its criminal activities, right?"

"Yes."

"So did you hamper it?"

"Don't be unjust, man! How could one man, a grain of dust, stop the most perfect police machinery in the world?"

"So what did you achieve? Replacing needles under the fingernails with beatings?

"I refuse to go into the details."

"Of course. You're an intellectual. You're only interested in the overall scheme. The details are unimportant. They even get in the way. But, since in reality the overall scheme doesn't mean anything, and since everything consists of details, I must insist on an answer."

"By what right? I've been rehabilitated. I'm no longer the subject of a criminal investigation."

"But criminal proceedings are always being undertaken. Obersturmführer, there are always criminal proceedings being undertaken somewhere: movements are monitored, data are compiled into dossiers, information is collected. You're the focus of someone's attention; you're always being watched. You're the eternal subject of police surveillance. Whether there's going to be a trial or not is of no importance at all. The criminal proceedings are what's important. What's important is that the information about you necessary for such a trial is available at any time."

"I think I've already heard that theory somewhere before."

"It's very possible. Our devices are primarily of earthly origin. All the residents of our numerous domains were people once. There are also policemen among them. They are as a rule now vampires."

"And the intellectuals?"

"A brotherhood of were-creatures, mainly. Werewolves, were-snakes, were-ants. You already know how that goes—according to character. The transformation reflects the nature of the given mind, what a person would be if circumstances allowed. A lycanthropic business, very similar to men of your mold. At night, in the moonlight, you devour what you care for during the day, in the sunlight. In the meantime, you argue about the nature of hell and endeavor to reform it according to the model of your failures on earth. What's wrong, Rutkowski? Do you have some objection?"

I didn't have any objections, Hilmar. I had a vague sense that nothing of what the municipal file clerk (or to put it better, the municipal file clerk's ghost) was saying was unfamiliar to me, and that I'd already had the opportunity to detest those ideas once before.

"I didn't imagine our conversation like this. You deceived me, Trpković. You don't act like someone who needs help, but like an agent provocateur, whose task is to draw me into some lawless activity, and then to meet me at the scene of the crime with the police. I already know about those obscure tricks, Trpković. I know about them as a former policeman and as a current historian."

"Don't be vain, Obersturmführer. Don't attribute greater significance to yourself than your own historiography does. Take your brother-in-law, for example—Herr Doktor Hilmar Wagner. You're an exclusively statistical element of history. You're a number. Your place is either in a footnote or in a tabular overview at the end of a book. You wouldn't make for a single honest paragraph in a work that tries to determine the reasons why this world is going to hell. In order for you to figure in at all, in spite of all your considerable intellectual and mental qualities, you have to be added to thousands of petty spiritual monsters. And as such a wretch, you don't concern me. I'm here on my own business. And as I can see that my presence unnerves you, and is even driving you insane, I'll tell you immediately why I'm here and what's expected of you."

"And what *is* expected of me?"

"To act like a human and tell the truth at least once in your accursed life."

"Tell the truth about what?"

"About me. After all, you at least know how each of the prisoners held up under your investigations."

"I know about one man whose conduct was amazing. I expected the monument to be dedicated to him."

"I know who you're thinking of. That idiot worker who didn't even tell you his name in spite of the most severe torture. Fine. They can have him. Let them glorify *him*."

"Trpković, perhaps you're not as big of a jerk as you act like after all."

"On what basis have you drawn that offensive conclusion?"

"Based on the fact that you're bothered by unearned laurels."

"Nonsense! I'm not bothered by their undeservedness, but by their definition. Where I live, virtues such as self-sacrifice, loyalty, patriotism, mercy, forgiveness, love, and devotion don't sell well at all. How do you think they view a man down there who's honored with a monument up here while he's laboring to perfect all the opposite qualities in order to get ahead with them. Because I, my dear Rutkowski, don't wish to be a file clerk at the bottom of the pay scale in every possible world. Do you understand me?"

"But don't they know—how should I put it—*down there* in hell that your glory is phony? That it arose only due to a misunderstanding?"

THE SECOND LIFE OF ADAM TRPKOVIĆ

"I'm not going to go into whether where I live is hell or not. That's a purely academic question. For me hell is any world where I'm a file clerk of the lowest class, with no prospects for advancement. What I'd like for you to understand is that we down there aren't helped by knowing the truth about something if you up here don't know it. We have certain historical obligations, a mission determined by providence, goals that have priority over everything else. You were a member of the Party, you know what that means. As our final goal is general evil, the monument on the hill contradicts it because it glorifies an antagonistic quality. Isn't that funny? Humiliating? Offensive? Therefore, we want to destroy it through you."

"Don't tell me you want me to try to destroy it?!"

"God, Rutkowski, where's that glorious scholarly intellect of yours? So it seems figurative meanings don't exist for you? Or metaphors? Parabolas? Symbols? The implicit? Associations? I simply can't understand on the basis of what inner material you've built up so many inhibitions, if even ordinary grammatical finesses present obstacles to you. Of course you're not going to destroy it! You'll simply change the plaque. You'll effect a change in the nomination. I think you can accommodate us that much. After all, you're somewhat obligated."

"To hell?"

"Well, as a member of the NSDAP, the SS, and the Gestapo. . . ."

"Okay, okay, stop pestering me. What do I need to do?"

"Well, the ideal solution would be if it were really erected to me, but as an eminent good-for-nothing. Unfortunately, such a monument is still impossible. Black masses, satanic circles, ritual sacrifices, obsessions—they're still a rarity. The repugnance at mass slaughters is powerful despite the intellect that tries to find reasonable justifications for them. Murder is a punishable offense. Deceit is something that men aren't yet proud of. Lies are avoided whenever one can get by with the truth. Hatred is not a dignified emotion. The enjoyment of another's suffering is treated as an illness in hospitals. Selfishness is kept secret. Indifference must be hidden under a clever intellectual roof. The situation doesn't yet allow the ideal solution. We'll be satisfied if you manage to remove my name from the monument. So?"

"I'll do it."

"Very good. You'll go to the municipal building and report everything you know about me. You won't hide anything. Give free reign to your imagination. Exaggerate. Exaggeration never hurts. That's also what Dr. Goebbels thought. His lack of success only means he didn't exaggerate enough. You'll inform me about each phase of your action, in a manner to be determined later. This time try not to be clumsy and bumbling. Don't complicate things, as is your habit. Proceed straight toward your goal and be persistent. I don't believe they'll cause any problems, but who knows? Honest people are so unpredictable. Have you ever wondered why an honest deed is unpredictable? Because it's not done on impulse, Rutkowski, because it's not natural or spontaneous. Evil operates naturally. We're never surprised by evil. We're only surprised if it doesn't occur. Think about it, Rutkowski. Perhaps you'll realize in time whose side the future is on. And don't doze off, for crying out loud! Snap out of it for once and wake up. Stop living with half your strength. Because you're sleeping now, Rutkowski. You'd be in a deep sleep if my words weren't keeping you awake."

At last I remembered. That tone, that temperament, that arrogant way of thinking. That devilish dialectic. Hilmar, that was how Steinbrecher used to talk!

But there was no longer anyone in the room to confirm my suspicion. It was warm again. The air regained its softness. The gnats swarmed in the beam of the electric lamp. I didn't know how much time had passed. I pushed Adam Trpković's visit out of my thoughts. I took the pen and tried to work.

Hilmar, I couldn't any more. And from then on, with greater and greater malevolence, I tried to conjure up the pale apparitions of early Polish noblemen, who in their stiff garments and even stiffer historical dates rested like puppets in metal boxes. History, which until then I'd written about with enthusiasm and a certain degree of public success, suddenly seemed out of place and fabricated. I know I shouldn't have thought like that. It's unprofessional to declare an isolated case to be the rule, the model, the symbol of the falsity of our ideas about the past, and to declare historiography a pseudo-science dealing exclusively with illusions and phantoms. Anyway, a scholar should consider the smallest trifle from his own discipline to be more important that the greatest of phenomena from any other discipline, including life itself.

But that didn't happen here. And with that fainthearted confirmation I'll end this letter. Goodbye.

KONRAD

■ □ ■ □ ■

LETTER 10

THE MUNICIPAL FILE CLERK IN PERSON, OR *ECCE HOMO*

The Mediterranean Coast, 18 Sept. 1965

Dear Hilmar,

You saw how the municipal file clerk Adam Trpković, by some oversight of historiography (although in our case only a local one), became a hero. Then you attended the midnight séance, where you learned how Adam reacted to that honor. What remains is for you to meet him in his earthly version. Now is the best opportunity for that. Do you remember that in my seventh letter I'd stopped outside his cell and put my hand on the bolt of the door? Let's pull it back and step into the cell.

How different everything seemed then, dear Hilmar! When they presented him to me, he was barely one hundred seventy centimeters tall, but now he's grown to a height of ten meters, not including the pedestal. He had the sclerotic skin of a bureaucratic champion, a slave to pen and ink. But look at him now—he glistens like oiled steel, his body diffuses a godly nimbus, in which, as in some heroic aura, his multiton limbs reign mightily. He wore a pince-nez—he doesn't have that any more. He was dressed in a tattered jacket—he doesn't have that either. Now he keeps a vigil above the city in the impenetrable maillot of a visitor from another planet. Grand, mysterious like a legend. When I met him, he was sitting on an overturned box, across which the word TANGERINES was written in pitch, with an umbrella between his legs. Now he was standing on a three-meter high pedestal, which bore his name etched in golden letters and which was covered with bunches of fragrant wildflowers.

Which of all these versions was the real Adam? The metal colossus on the hill, the spiteful demon who visited me a few nights ago and obligated me to collaborate, or the wretch whom I'm approaching just now?

Descriptions aren't my strong suit. My ability to remember numbers and words is extraordinary. The appearance of an object, unfortunately, doesn't find in my spirit a pliable amalgam receptive to impressions. But, there's nothing I can do:

He was sitting on an overturned box, which had the word TANGERINES written across it in black letters. He rose when I entered. I think that was more likely an impulse of old-fashioned respectfulness than fear. He was of medium height, not taller than one hundred seventy centimeters, but his clerk's stoop made him seem shorter. On his nose he had a pince-nez with a metal frame, which was bound by a ribbon to a button of his threadbare municipal clerk's jacket. Under the jacket one could just see a collarless hemp shirt. He was holding on to his pants with one hand. The other was clutching his umbrella. He was motionless. His only movements were devoted to his glasses. Whenever they fell down, he cleaned the dust off them with his right hand and returned them to the bridge of his nose.

"So, Trpković . . . ," I began.

"That's me," he said.

"Trpković is your name?"

"Adam B. Trpković, municipal file clerk eighth class, at your service, sir."

"And a prisoner of the caribinieri?"

"Yes, sir."

"On what charge? Why were you arrested?"

"Because of the umbrella."

"Because of the umbrella?"

"Yes, sir."

"This umbrella?"

"This one. They charged me with disrespecting the flag. And the umbrella was to blame for this. The flag was hanging over the entrance to the city hall. They required us to salute it, with our hand—like this."

"And you refused?"

"God forbid! How would I do that? And why? Everyone coming from that direction walked by and saluted it. Some people's arms even fell asleep. They passed by on purpose only to extend their palm. I saw that and remembered it. I have a list."

"What list?"

"A list of those who saluted it when they didn't *have* to."

"For the partisans?"

"What partisans?! I have nothing to do with them."

"Why the lists, then?"

"For no reason, sir. I just made them, out of habit. My hand did it on its own, it's used to writing things down. Ever since I can remember, I've been entering and keeping track of things. Adam, enter this. Adam, make a note of that. Record this, reply to that. I've always had to be working with some kind of list, and it's always numbered, too. You can't have a list if it's not numbered. The names have to have something to hold on to. The Italians even put me on a list, though they thought it was a hassle. The Maresciallo himself put me on it. *There you go, damn you,* he said, *fifty-five slash forty-three.* Fifty-five is my number, and forty-three is the year I was arrested. And you've put me on a list, too—number one for the same year. So that's what's been going on."

"Fine, Trpković. So why didn't you salute the flag?"

"Well, I always did salute it. Only that one time I didn't. It was raining that day and the sirocco was blowing, so hard it tore roofing tiles away. I had to take care of my umbrella. You can see for yourself how big it is. It would have blown away if I hadn't held onto it with both hands. That's what happened."

"And that's the only reason you were arrested?"

"They wouldn't have laid a hand on me if some bunch of idiots hadn't torn down one of those flags on the waterfront and burned it at the market. The Italians wanted to see if I had anything to do with that. Maresciallo Dagllione said something about some sort of vertical and horizontal—what do you call 'em. . . ."

"Correlations?"

"That's right. He wanted to see if I was some sort of—I can't remember what it's called. . . ."

The potent Maresciallo Dagllione, I thought, must be one of Steinbrecher's apprentices.

"But I'm not, honestly. I'm a familiar face, and loyal. My very profession means I don't belong to anybody. Except the record, of course. I'm a recording clerk who records everything and belongs to nobody."

Just like good historians, I thought. They can't belong to anyone either, not to anything except history.

"And then things got messy. There was even shooting. Later the Italians fled, and forgot about me. Who am I to them? Why should they worry about me?"

"Why didn't you leave on your own?"

"The bars didn't allow it."

"Did you yell for help?"

"Why should I yell? I knew somebody would come down sooner or later. Everybody needs prisons. That's what they always check out first. This is the only place where a person can't get lost."

What do you say to this logic, Hilmar? I find it instructive. I find that in its laconic form it sums up the defensive wisdom of a people as a helpless object of history.

"How did you keep from starving?"

"The tangerines, sir. They kept their contraband here in the basement. That's how I survived."

The case was clear; the man was innocent. Disrespecting the Italian flag, in light of Badoglio's treacherous truce, could only please us. There wasn't anything suspicious about this wretch. Nothing dangerous. Nothing incomprehensible.

Except, of course, the umbrella.

My position, intellectually speaking, was similar to that of a scientist who knows his invention will cause immeasurable suffering, but is nevertheless unable to renounce it. That was how I had to explain the presence of the umbrella. How did it get in? What was a humongous, black umbrella bound with a rubber band doing in a German prison?

Although my brain had inevitably been Steinbrecherized, I could understand the completely human urge that turned a policeman into a black marketeer. Likewise, I could also find an explanation for the Balkan passivity (which, to be sure, was labeled an expression of folk wisdom a little while ago) with which Adam accepted his isolation, not trying to do anything at all about it. I could likewise find reasons for the carabinieri's oversensitivity. All that eluded me was that damned umbrella; it was the only thing that resisted reason.

Was that because my mind had been irrevocably Steinbrecherized, forever stripped of the vital capability of comprehending aberrations, irregularities, and disorder as integral components of the natural and healthy order of things, as the polymer essence of life? Or was it because my mind had been infected with Steinbrecherism as a worldview and my brain had become only a cog in the machine of the rationalization of history? A petty logical monster pinned between the bone screws of the Standartenführer's demonic generalizations? A beast vampirically taught to devour the real, pure, and natural life? An UMBRELLA-EATER? An UMBRELLIVORE? An UMBRELLICIDE? The destroyer of all the magic umbrellas of our life? The mortal enemy of that glorious poetry in black, declaimed to the silken sky? The mortal enemy even of the reason to live—for a normal person to do nothing but open and close his umbrella, collapsing and spreading it out in spite of the climactic conditions, forsaking family and country, God and Devil, everything for the sake of his magnificent construction, that graceful dream-tent of his? And why only when it's raining? Why ever only out of doors? Why not in a room while chatting pleasantly by the fireplace? In bed above a woman one is making love to? Over a child being born? And why not die under it? Why not open it anywhere one gets the urge? On any occasion at all! With or without any reason at all! In pure mockery of rancid human reason! In a rebellion against order! In a revolt against the languor of habits! Out of the shame of hopes betrayed! Spurred by a revulsion at all prohibitions, restrictions, denials! Against all the Steinbrechers and all Steinbrecherization! To change the world by umbrella! A revolution, a fundamental change!

"Fine, Trpković," I said calmly, "that all sounds convincing. I can't say I don't believe you, either. I'm pretty sure we'll get your case cleared up before the night is through. (That was Obersturmführer Rutkowski speaking.) Unfortunately, there's a detail in your story that I don't understand. A little piece that doesn't fit. (This was

Steinbrecher making himself heard in me. Nothing was ever sufficiently clear to him. There was always room for subsequent questioning. For a continuation and widening of the investigation. For surprising turns and leads. For new efforts.) I'm not saying it's important or particularly decisive, or that it can delay your release in any way. (That was me again.) But it can't remain unexplained. (The Standartenführer again.) Tell me first of all how that umbrella got in here to begin with."

"I brought it in, sir."

"I know, damn its wooden handle! I'm sure you didn't receive it as a gift from the chief of police. I'm asking why they allowed you to bring it into the prison."

Some invisible movement knocked his pince-nez off his nose; it was now swinging back and forth on its velvet ribbon. His gaze was empty. He wiped the lenses with his hand and put it back on his nose.

"Well, why shouldn't they let me, sir? It's an umbrella, not a rifle. An ordinary men's umbrella, just a little larger than usual."

The fact that it ended up in one of the cells, under a strict regimen of solitary confinement, didn't bother Adam Trpković. The Standartenführer was shouting inside me, but I spoke calmly:

"Good, Trpković, just don't get upset." The admonition was superfluous. The clerk wasn't getting upset, but sat leaning on the handle of the umbrella, as against the slender neck of a dragon with wooden scales, watching me through the shaded lenses of his glasses. I was the one who was getting upset. "It really isn't a rifle. Its appearance . . . And one couldn't say that at all, although. . . . (The Standartenführer tried fiercely to make himself heard with his famous 'although,' but was rebuffed.) There's no doubt that it's an ordinary men's umbrella. Perhaps a little too large, but still an umbrella. And so far everything's fine. However, there are certain regulations in existence. Let's examine them rationally. As a government official you know that all things in the world are covered by regulations. Everything is encoded in one way or another. We Germans didn't invent this. God himself began with laws. The first thing out of his mouth was a prohibition: where you can go, where you can't. What's allowed and what's not. What's permitted, what's not permitted. What's permitted in certain circumstances, and what's forbidden in all circumstances. This is particularly true of special regimens. For example, I don't see any laces in your shoes. Where are your laces, Trpković?"

"They took them."

"There you go. They took them, of course: regulation such-and-such. Calmly, please. We'll get what we're after. Do you smoke? No. That's smart. However, I'll have a cigarette. I see you don't have a belt, either. You're holding up your pants with your hands. Why?"

"They took it."

"Of course they did. What else? What's allowed, what's not. And what of your personal belongings do you have?"

"Nothing."

"Everything was taken from you?"

"Yes, sir. Signore Maresciallo said that everything would be returned to me when I was released, and now I don't know who to talk to about this."

"So, laces are taken out, belts are removed, all sharp objects are confiscated, even pocket handkerchiefs so no one will suffocate himself. We care for people, as one gentleman would say, who I sincerely hope you won't have the occasion to meet. At least in terms of written regulations, I don't believe Italian prisons are more liberal than anybody else's. And now we're back where we started, at the first question: Why the umbrella?"

"I don't know, sir."

"Did you ask them to let you keep it?"

"No, sir. I had it hooked over my arm, like this. I always carried it like this when it wasn't raining. I also had it when they brought me in. Nobody said anything to me, and that's it."

"Do you find that normal?"

"I don't know, sir," he said. "I never think. I only record other people's thoughts. And anything else they tell me to write down. In calligraphic script, with flourishes on the initials."

My dear Hilmar, that's how the Steinbrecher in me was defeated by an ordinary men's umbrella, which in the hands of a master of calligraphic flourishes became a banner of liberation, able to take under its black, motherly wing all the damned, all the outcasts who rebelled against order, customs, laws, dogmas, and even common sense if it was backing these things up. Thanks to my temporary autonomy from Steinbrecher, gained apparently through the secret intervention of the umbrella, I sensed that it was something more than the eccentric habit of a provincial scrivener. Of course, I didn't yet know the whole truth. I hadn't yet glimpsed the splendid poetry of rebellion in its black, silken sky or a tender canopy of dreams in its metal ribs and spreaders. But one thing was clear to me: the umbrella was a time bomb planted under the roof beam of Steinbrecher's cosmos. It recommended itself to me as an ally. It offered to be a lever in my liberation. In spite of the clerk's claims and what I could see with my own eyes, it was no longer an ordinary men's umbrella but a—likewise male, albeit completely extraordinary—*symbol of resistance* against the violence of all the restrictions that my person was being subjected to both internally and externally. The umbrella became a kind of intellectual orthopedic prosthesis in my war against Nazism.

I needed to hurry with Adam's release. The Standartenführer could return at any moment. In a beastly mood because of the argument with our glorious army—who knew what might seem suspicious to him in this unusual case? Once set into motion, the police machinery wouldn't stop without inflicting some harm on the municipal file clerk.

Unfortunately, certain obstacles appeared. They consisted of the REGULATIONS FOR THE ORGANIZATION OF THE INTERNAL SERVICE SECTION: ADMINISTRATION, and were emitted from the registration office via Hauptscharführer Münch:

The subject was entered into the registration protocol, under number 1 for the year 1943. Indeed, a special dossier had been opened for D. The Herr Obersturmführer can verify that himself. Accordingly, the subject has in administrative terms flawlessly entered through the ENTRANCE column. In order for Münch to lead him out through the EXIT column, his case must necessarily be resolved in one way or another. The Herr Obersturmführer will understand. In this respect, the regulations are quite explicit. Regardless even of *that* umbrella. Even if the subject in question had no umbrella at all. One enters through the ENTRANCE column, and exits through the EXIT column when the appropriate order has been issued by Standartenführer Steinbrecher or his legal representative. Can the Obersturmführer claim to be his legal representative?

Why not?

Because he doesn't have it stated clearly in writing. Something like that has to be in written form. (I remember that he used this wonderful old expression, which we find only in musty old record books in the corner of some attic. Steinbrecher must have been dozing within the Hauptscharführer.) For this a valid delegation of authority is required. (Only for a short time, of course. Steinbrecher awoke and replaced the poetic and even somewhat irrational *written form* with the dry, rational *delegation of authority*.) The Herr Obersturmführer will understand.

The invocation of the Standartenführer's implicit delegation of authority was rejected with indignation. The Herr Obersturmführer will understand. Nothing happens in the administration implicitly. Ambiguities and arbitrary decisions aren't permitted in the administration. Nothing can be taken for granted. Everything must be in black and white. No one can expect him, Münch, to commit a violation of his office, if not a forgery, merely on the wave of a hand, which the Herr Obersturmführer completely subjectively understood as some delegation of authority. As for him, Hauptscharführer Münch, the most that he can see in the Standartenführer's gesture is consent for the Herr Obersturmführer to question the prisoner *preliminarily*, and in no case to make any independent decisions.

I attacked from the rear. I suggested to Münch that he simply tear up the first page of the register for D. He looked at me with horror in his eyes. His utter inability to comprehend that something so blasphemous could be uttered at all—which meant that it hadn't—was the only reason I had to thank him for not reporting me on then and there. Then I tried with logic. Time, with its brass face on the wall, was passing quickly.

"Münch," I said, "You're a smart man and an experienced administrator, but you're constantly babbling about some *prisoner*. But Münch, I don't see any *prisoner* here!"

The Hauptscharführer was confused.

"What do you mean by that, sir?"

"That we don't have any kind of prisoner here. Not with all the ENTRANCE and EXIT columns on earth."

But isn't the Herr Obersturmführer just coming from seeing him? Didn't he just preliminarily interrogate him? And wasn't he even surprised by the umbrella? Didn't he just a few moments ago demand for him to be released? And in that respect didn't he make a few suggestions that he, Münch, didn't completely understand (thank god!) and which were aimed at liquidating the case in a manner absolutely unacceptable from the administrative point of view?

"I was downstairs," I said, "That's true. And I spoke with a man who was found in the basement, but I didn't question him—use your head, Münch—because we don't have any prisoners *yet*. We've only just arrived, we haven't even really got our things unpacked, everything smells of paint, and you're jabbering to me about some sort of prisoner! Are you really an idiot? I appreciate your administrative take on life, but do you really think that if you only have a person in custody, then you *automatically* get a prisoner too? Prisoners don't come in on their own, Hauptscharführer. They're arrested. And before that, they have to do something to get themselves arrested, though I admit that this last condition isn't obligatory. Before that, they're people. Only when they're arrested do they become prisoners. And Hauptscharführer, there are no arrests without warrants. Without an arrest warrant a prisoner remains a person, despite the fact that as such he's worth nothing at all to you. So now show me the warrant for the arrest of the municipal clerk Adam Trpković, pursuant to which you have had the kindness to bring the man and his umbrella through your fucking ENTRANCE column, and I'll leave you alone. In fact, I'll probably go get plastered. The warrant, Münch, so I can screw off!"

No, Münch didn't have a warrant. He was suffering—as an administrator will on behalf of the Administration. To each his own form of suffering. Newton would in all likelihood have suffered if on a second try the apple hadn't fallen to the ground. Plato would have been anguished by the realization that even among slaves there are intelligent people capable of running the ideal state. Caesar would have been deeply disappointed by the news that the Rubicon wasn't a stream but a sea. Mussolini considered the Italian people to be his private punishment. Hilmar, you'd die, I think, were it not for the existence of historical trivialities, such as the existence of Roman Catholic symbols on the robes of the Polish noblemen, which you use to avoid writing about what really matters. Personally, I'd suffer immeasurably if it were proven to me that my whole elaborate resistance to Nazism were merely the projection of an ill conscience, a compromise between ACTION and INACTION. Münch's suffering was caused by a shortcoming of the Administration.

"My dear Münch, you don't have a valid ENTRANCE. You smuggled that man into our prison without authorization. You arbitrarily entered him in the Register. And who knows for what reasons? Yes, Münch, who knows why?"

That was a primitive trick. Something from the antediluvian period of police arts. Hinting to a prisoner that some otherwise completely natural action of his had a secret significance, that it was committed for who knows what purposes, that his lapse was malevolent and even organized (most often from abroad), meant bypassing the bulwarks of apologies erected around his negligence and attacking his undefended criminal intent. This maneuver never fails to produce a tumult in the prisoner's soul, which has already been reconciled to negligence but is completely unprepared to acknowledge a criminal act therein. In order to acquit himself of the charge of criminal intent, the prisoner enthusiastically admits to negligence (which also carries a sentence). However, the investigator doesn't think that this was merely a matter of criminal *intent,* a spontaneous act against the most sacred interests of the state, but rather that the crime was paid for. The prisoner thinks that he has to drive this terrible thought out of the investigator's head at any price. And this isn't achieved with a simple denial. Denials achieve nothing with the police. Only silence or confessions can achieve something. Complete silence or a partial confession. However, there are no partial confessions. The prisoner realizes this as soon as he succeeds in buying a withdrawal of the charge of working for a foreign power with the admission that he acted with intent and on his own initiative. But once an investigation establishes the general extent of the offense and leaves the tiresome domain of a possible motive, the possibilities of establishing guilt are practically inexhaustible. In the area of sabotage, for instance, if someone has confessed to rigging a military motorcycle so it'll have engine trouble, it's no trouble at all to get him to sign a transcript containing a statement that he planted a bomb in the Reichstag. In this he has only wisely and successfully averted the considerably more dangerous charge that he has planted a bomb in the Reich Chancellery. An automobile was cleverly bought off with a motorcycle (after all, what can you get with a single miserable bike?), a garage with an automobile (which is nothing to get excited about, right?), a railway junction with a garage, the Führer's train with a railway junction (which, in comparison with the train, suddenly becomes only an insignificant bundle of rails), the Reich Chancellery with the Führer's train (because there are nevertheless fewer people in the latter). But what about the Reichstag? The Reichstag has disappeared. The Reichstag was only an auxiliary alternative. The investigator and the suspect part with the feeling that they've each gotten the most out of the situation. The investigator usually doesn't change his mind. The prisoner doesn't begin to have any doubts until he feels the rope around his neck.

(Hilmar, do you know what I'm afraid of? That these letters will fall into the hands of the police. Oh, I'm not afraid for myself. There is nothing in them that could incriminate me, no motorcycle which could, by gradually adding elements to the offense, be transformed into the Reich Chancellery. I fear the police could use them as a compendium.)

Münch turned pale. He looked unhappy, but not defeated.

"I can explain!" he whimpered.

"No, Münch! You can't explain a flagrant *excess* in your books. That much I know about bookkeeping."

"But Herr Obersturmführer. . . ."

"I know that a surfeit and a deficit each demonstrate an inexactness in your job performance equally clearly. And that, from an administrative point of view, one prisoner *too many* isn't any less dangerous that one prisoner *too few.*"

"Herr Obersturmführer, allow me to put your mind at ease in this regard," Münch said. The color had returned to his face, and he was smiling victoriously. "I took such objections into consideration and explained the subject in an official note." He opened the register and ran his finger along one of the pages. "Let's see what it says here in the NOTES column. It says that we happened *to come across him.* That obviates the requirement for a warrant. We took over custody of the subject. He was received into our custody, together with the furniture and fittings. Flawless, isn't it?"

And it was, Hilmar, it was. The Steinbrecher in Konrad Rutkowski was obviously not the equal of his double in Hauptschar-führer Münch. I withdrew when a frightened Haag brought news of a happily avoided scandal at General von Klattern's banquet and the Standartenführer's decision not to do us the favor of a visit tonight. Now it didn't matter. As far as Adam, myself, and our renegade umbrella were concerned, he could come right on over. In the meantime, despite my opposition, the municipal file clerk of D. had become an inseparable part of our organism, although his passage through the ENTRANCE column had not even been completely flawless. Were it not for the NOTE, he would have been at liberty. The NOTE had helped him to bypass the irritating administrative obstacles and the lack of an arrest warrant. The inventory of the executive of the Geheime Staatspolizei Sonderkommando in D. established in the register that evening read as follows:

11 walnut desks, 1 with iron fittings;
24 chairs with backs;
7 chairs without backs;
11 roll-top chests;
1 municipal file clerk with 1 men's umbrella.

And now I'll have to go swimming for a little while, for the sake of camouflage. Were it not for this monograph of mine, I have no idea how I could justify my constant absence from the beach to Sabina. As it is, I'm aided by her ambition for her husband to become a genius, which wouldn't be possible without the publication of my book on the royal and capital city of Cracow. Be well and at home with every convenient untruth in this whorish world.

Yours,

KONRAD

■ □ ■ □ ■

LETTER 11

GUSTAV FRÖHLICH, THE SPY FROM MANNHEIM, OR *ESSAYS ON HUMAN REASON*

The Mediterranean Coast, 19 Sept. 1965

Dear Hilmar,

"What's this we're hearing, Rutkowski?" asked Standartenführer Steinbrecher when I submitted my report to him the next morning. He was sitting behind his massive desk with the iron fittings and measuring me with his gleaming eyes, which were full of savage promises. The bars outside the milky glass window vaguely crisscrossed the sky. The fringes of the carpet marched in Teutonic lockstep across the polished floor. On the green wall, which was soft as a freshly mowed lawn, there hung a picture from which a woman stared at the scene with a bovine gaze. In less than twenty-four hours, the building had been Steinbrecherized to the last detail. "You wanted to release our first prisoner? Münch says you were quite determined. You even referred to some delegated authority. Implicit, to be sure. However, I didn't delegate any authority to anyone. And what's an implicit delegation of authority anyway? Authority is either delegated or not. And everyone knows what a valid delegation of authority is. Since when is a mechanical wave of the hand an official order? This isn't an auction, Rutkowski. We're not collectors of antique furniture, who close a deal by wiggling their ears and eyebrows."

I didn't say anything, reconciled as I was to my role as his intellectual punching bag filled with straw and despair.

"I simply didn't know what to do with myself! That von Klattern is such an asshole! He and his *reducing the front in order to balance forces,* or *disengagement from the enemy with minimal complications,* or *elastic defense,* or *sacrificing territory for a gain in concentration.* What a bunch of shit! All those gentlemen should be brought over here and handed over to Rotkopf! Then the idea of withdrawing would never enter their minds, despite the *extremely unfavorable balance of forces in the number of artillery pieces, aggravated by a chronic shortage of mortars.* And you should keep your eye on that fellow Zeller, he's a painful little nail. In the strictest confidentiality, of course. They might accuse us of undermining the army's authority. But, by the way—what army? It was an army while it was winning. Losers aren't an army, just a damned band of deserters. I hope you agree, Rutkowski. You're indeed so discreet in declaring your personal loyalties and friendships, you're so noble and reserved. At the table yesterday you didn't once consider it necessary to intervene. You yawned as they insulted your comrades. And those comrades of ours, the holy jackasses! Haag looked like he'd just been lobotomized. Rotkopf was a drunken swine, his reflexes were totally gone. He could have done some good only if we'd gotten into a fistfight. Freissner acquitted himself well, I won't complain—at least when he wasn't taking pictures. I had to take on the whole officer corps all by myself. What's wrong, Rutkowski? Do you have worms? If you're sick, go to the aid station. What did you say? Not a thing. So much the better. Settle down for once. Have a seat. Don't stand there like a monument to human innocence. We know at least what the score is with innocence in this world. You can pour us each a cognac. It's in the cupboard, to the left. Have a smoke if you like. This is a working meeting, not a military drill. We're carrying out the general-staff analysis of the police. A little better than the Herr General, because we're not doing it *after* we get a licking. Where did you get this cognac? It smells like toilet soap. Thus, we don't require quadrangles, scale-models, map scales and all that other orthopedic shit they use to prove it possible to win a battle that's been lost in the meantime. We've got it all in our hearts and minds. Have you read the reports from the ground? Two average guerrilla raids on the transport vehicles of the Brandenburg Regiment. A factory backup with symptoms of sabotage. Quite nice results for the first twenty-four hours. It's obvious that the bandits have left their people in the city. That's why we need lists of communists. We've already talked about that; it was your assignment. But you don't have to say a thing. They've been burned. And the copies, too, of course. These inefficient, negligent, sloppy peoples always show thoroughness in the wrong places. If they were so conscientious they wouldn't surrender in less than two weeks. They're like a soccer team that keeps kicking the ball around after the time has run out and the other team has left for the locker room. The most dangerous of them are on those damned lists. However, logical thought—your weak point—leads us to the assumption that the majority of documented communists are already in the woods. As soon as they've ended up in the police files, they have nothing more to seek in the city. Do you consider my conclusion valid? You do. Completely valid? You're absolutely sure? Well, then you're a fool, Rutkowski. German pedantry has made our police texts the most instructive in the world. That's correct. But in order to have command of some police situation, you need to have something more than knowledge. That's why the Central Office has tried to recruit our most intelligent specimens.[9] I regret to confirm that in this regard your choice is completely mistaken. My assumption would hold only if the lists hadn't been destroyed. The destruction of the lists made the normal distribution of their cadres possible. They're also here somewhere, not far from us. They're preparing to disrupt the southern flank of our supply lines. And if they manage that, how do you plan on getting your ass out of the Balkans? Maybe you're counting on providence? Unfortunately, only one man in our age is endowed with providence. The rest of us have to rely on our brains. Consult yours for a change, Rutkowski. Take that Trpković, for example. His name is Adam Trpković, isn't it? Why shouldn't we start with him if we've already got him? And as for your hasty objection that he hasn't done anything that we could hold him in the basement for, and that he's not an enemy—I completely accept all that. But he's a member of an enemy nation, which is good enough in a time of emergency. You don't hate only the mosquito that bit you, Rutkowski, you hate all mosquitoes equally, right? You wrote in your report that the aforementioned Trpković is in some sense an official of the local authorities and that as such he's not a suspect. We had dealings with one such man in F. He was the mayor. During the day, that is. At night he presided over some kind of bandit liberation committee. I'll tell you how he ended up at the gallows. It was a penchant for logical analyses and inductive reasoning that killed him. He loved playing detective and formulating impeccable syllogisms. One night he blew up a fuel dump. The next day he was there to help out, as usual. And as usual he drew the logical conclusions from the situation. This time, however, his conclusions were a hair too logical. The only thing we could do was hang him. So where are we, Rutkowski? You have the bad habit of distracting me with stupid objections or your damned arrogant posture. Quit that, for god's sake!"

However, it was clear that I wasn't being heard at all. I wasn't there. He was talking to himself. There was no natural end to the soliloquy. THE INTEREST OF THE POLICE IS INFINITE AND ENCOMPASSES ALL ASPECTS OF LIFE. According to its internal structure, the diatribe would never end. It had to be interrupted by external circumstances. Or certain bodily requirements. The demands of the intestines, or sleep. I couldn't think of a third possibility.

This time it was Max. The Standartenführer receives a report. At the same time, Max plugs himself into the Standartenführer's logical system and becomes a source of an additional series of conclusions, which momentarily sever the connection to Adam. Before an analogy is finally found again, the Standartenführer recalls memories from his childhood and examines their use in putting pressure on prisoners, makes some critical remarks about my choice for the color of the walls, from which he elastically slips over to the pictures of the women, on to Rubens' *Saskia,* old painting techniques, the principles of guerrilla warfare employed by the Dutch against the Duke of Alba in 1568, and the principles applied by the resistance movement in the region of the Adriatic Coast. Today, Max was the occasion for a short breather. Tomorrow it will be an air raid— but the analysis can always continue happily in the shelter. The day after tomorrow he'll be interrupted by stomach cramps, but only in order to seize the chance to meditate on poisonous mushrooms, spiders, gases, and thus, via chemistry, he'll end up discussing the use of a truth serum in investigations. Hilmar, one day someone will put a bullet in him and blow out his brains—maybe, I thought, I'd be the one to do it—preventing him from realizing his innermost desire: to extract infinite generalizations from his own death.

"Your Adam,"—somehow he'd now become *my* Adam—"is, to be sure, no Egmont or Hoorn. He's an ordinary municipal scrivener. And of course I don't care a bit that he pissed all over the Italian flag. I'd piss all over it, too, with great satisfaction. But there's another problem here, Obersturmführer. Today the Italian flag, tomorrow ours. Today a flag, tomorrow a railway, and the day after that you and me. It was the wind, you say. Your report says that the wind made him do it. What kind of nonsense is that? Is a law less in effect in windy conditions than in humid conditions? Are we going to subordinate compliance with regulations to climactic conditions? Item 2, paragraph 5 of law such-and-such is applicable only up to 20°C. Item 1 of the same paragraph, however, is in effect only when it's raining. The trade winds invalidate all of paragraph 3. And under special circumstances, such as an earthquake or a hurricane, the law ceases to be valid in its entirety. General lawlessness comes into effect. That won't work, Rutkowski, it won't work. You yourself realize this. Your objection that it's stupid to mess around with some wretched file clerk is insulting, Obersturmführer. We don't do stupid work, Obersturmführer. And any stupid work that *we* do, automatically becomes intelligent. And we don't have any insignificant prisoners. Or insignificant cases. The fact that *we* are dealing with them gives them significance. And then there's that umbrella. The umbrella! Even you, an intellectual accustomed to perverse habits, couldn't accept it without raising your eyebrow. It puzzled you. That's evident in your report. Otherwise, why would you say anything about it? Why didn't you mention his shoes, for example? Why did you only write about the umbrella? You did it almost with enthusiasm! When you talk about it, you almost wax poetic. Finally, we've found a use even for you. Because if it weren't for your report and the bit about the umbrella, I'd have had the man released. Fortunately, for once, you caught a scent too. Because usually not even a skunk can get you moving. While we're on this, has the handle of the umbrella been examined? Yes? Nothing was found? Too bad. That demands a continuation of the investigation. The only question is who to have take it over. Haag's a blockhead. The umbrella would completely confuse him. Freissner is good, but I've got something else in mind for him. I won't suggest Rotkopf out of consideration for your Adam. So we're left with only one name."

Though I knew Steinbrecher and his satanic ability to discover people's innermost mental weaknesses and place them before carefully selected temptations, and even if certain technical circumstances (the fact, for instance, that I'd been the one to initially interrogate Adam) pointed to me independently of everything else, I was shaken like a cancer patient who, while aware that his disease is incurable, is unable to come to grips with the date of his impending death. There was a dark malice in the idea of having the file clerk be investigated by the man who only a few hours earlier had done everything in his power to get him released. At the same time, there was a certain vindictive equity in the choice. It struck the one who was really to blame for Adam's misfortune. Because if I hadn't tried so clumsily to get him removed from Münch's Register, if I'd let things unfold spontaneously, he'd have most probably been set free. Simply struck from the inventory as unserviceable. As it was, my unskilled intervention, combined with the careless fascination I'd shown for the umbrella, couldn't escape Standartenführer Steinbrecher's attention. My dear Hilmar, in all likelihood he must have reasoned as follows: *So our little Sonder-intellectual has tried to reach a settlement with his conscience again. It's time for the boy to choose sides. He can't serve both God and Mammon at the same time, and we've been looking the other way long enough. He's been left to stand on the shore and give instructions to those who are drowning long enough. Let's push him into the water, too, and see how well he can really swim.*

"Rutkowski!"

"Herr Standartenführer?"

"Did you choose the glass for the windows?"

"Yes."

"I can tell. I said for it to be milky, but not so much that you feel like you're sitting on the toilet."

"I'll take the appropriate steps, sir."

"Since we're already on steps, do you know how many steps a prisoner can walk in a three- by one-and-a-half-meter cell, assuming that he walks eight hours a day for one year?"

Hilmar, I didn't know. Do you know? Does anyone? Does anyone care? Does it matter to anyone? No. It doesn't matter to anyone. People are indifferent to a prisoner's steps. They don't want to hear them. They don't want to think about them. However, it did matter to Steinbrecher. He cared. He thought about it. Made calculations. Drew conclusions. And then turned them into deeds.

"I didn't expect you to know. That would mean you think about our prisoners. But you don't, Obersturmführer. When the office door closes behind them, they cease to exist for you. Then you read Goethe or play Chopin. What happens to them in the meantime, and outside of your interrogation, doesn't interest you. Don't you find that just a little heartless, Obersturmführer? Because it is precisely what happens to them between two interrogations that determines success or failure in advance. Men are broken *down below* and not *up above*, Rutkowski. Up here we put them back together in the desired form. Maybe you'll say that this is heartless, that it isn't heartless not to think about them but to think about them in this way. But there's where you're mistaken, Rutkowski. As usual, I might add. What's truly heartless in my view is dragging out the investigation, protracting their mental and bodily suffering. Especially when that's brought about by a lack of professionalism, negligence, clumsiness, and error. By a preference for Goethe and Chopin to their problems. By thinking about everything except how to break them as soon as possible and thus shorten their suffering. And this is where the steps come in, or more precisely the relationship between the possibility of inducing the appropriate contractions of a prisoner's striated muscles and his mental state, which is the real foundation of his resistance. In that regard, even the most strenuous gymnastic floor exercises can't replace the strengthening effects of taking a stroll. The moment a prisoner walks through the door of your office, you can tell the difference between a man who spent a day of incarceration in a cell of fifty square meters from one who has been cramped up in a little cavern of three- by one-and-a-half meters, or less. Everything else being equal, the latter will without doubt give you less trouble. And, vice versa, you'll be less trouble for him as well. Let's pursue this line of thought further. Let's limit our subject's ability to move at all. Eventually we'll reach a situation where none of his joints will be able to do anything except perform static, *useless* movements. The scapulo-humeral joint of the shoulder will, admittedly, move in at least two of its three degrees of expansion: flexion and extension in the sagittal plane, adduction and abduction in the frontal plane. Unfortunately, it won't move anything except *itself*—the arm will continue to remain motionless. The joint has lost it purpose. Its movements are senseless. In the end, it will be able to rotate, but that third degree of movement will nevertheless be ineffective. The arm will for all intents and purposes be dead. Do you know what I'm talking about, Rutkowski? About a privy, man, a privy! For you it's probably a mere instrument of harassment. And that only because you don't think about the prisoners, Rutkowski, but instead read Goethe and play Chopin. But there's nothing about privies in Goethe. The Herr Minister of Weimar was an intellectual and accordingly above privies. Above torture in general. The fact that his functionaries broke people's fingers, shins, and other bones suitable for that purpose didn't inspire him. He got excited about trading in souls. The soul as such and its possibilities in an alliance with the devil. I have the impression that this Faustian complex is what keeps you awake, that it's the only reason we're fortunate enough to enjoy your cooperation. But let's return to reducing movement and privies. In prisoners they yield, in addition to a constant fear of suffocation, the by-product of unbearable *fatigue*. And Rutkowski, as you know, fatigue is—apart from one's conscience—the most fertile basis for confessions. I'm not saying this on account of your Adam. How you deal with him is your business. I don't believe you'll employ a privy."

"We don't even have any, Herr Standartenführer."

"God, Rutkowski, you're really an idiot! Hopefully you don't think a privy has to be something antique, encrusted with jewels and artistic minutiae. Louis XVI, perhaps? Any solid box that you can fit a human body into in the most uncomfortable position is a privy. Any town is full of such privies. The world is chocked full of privies. All you need to do is cram people inside them."

"Herr Standartenführer," I said. "What is it that we actually want to find out from this man?"

"You mean you don't know, Rutkowski?"

"To tell the truth. . . ."

"So after two years of collaboration you come to me and ask what we want from a prisoner? Everything, Rutkowski, everything!

There's nothing we don't want! We'll pick out what we can use later. It's not for him to limit our interests. We're interested in everything, absolutely everything!"

"But I have to know in which direction to orient my questions, sir."

"In every direction, man! Not a single question may remain unasked, not a single aspect of life uncovered by the questionnaire. He must be questioned about everything, and everything must be recorded, verified, and compared. And several times at that, to avoid any mistakes. And once all theoretically possible questions have been asked, success is not far behind. An infinite system of interconnected questions always produces some result."

"I was asking where to begin. Which area, sir?"

"Any area, Rutkowski, any area! It's irrelevant, if your questions are logical and connected. No matter which area you start from, you'll always arrive at the same place. Sooner or later, of course. Our life forms a whole, Rutkowski. So the questions that concern it form a whole too. On all the roads of that sprawling traffic network, no matter where you begin, you always end up in Rome. Is that clear?"

"Completely, Herr Standartenführer."

"I doubt it. To make it really clear to you, I'll show you a copy of one of my old interrogations. You see, I keep all of them. Not out of vanity, Rutkowski, nor to endow them to a police museum. For my own private enjoyment. I peruse them in my rare moments of relaxation. Have a look at this interrogation transcript before you grapple with the clerk. You won't be sorry."

He went to a locked bookcase in which he kept his personal belongings. I always wondered: *What kind* of personal belongings such a man could have? What kind of memories? If the ancient custom whereby the heads of the vanquished belonged to the victor were still honored, and if investigators were allowed to keep the skulls of their suspects as trophies, I wouldn't have had any doubts. As it was, I had to await a moment when he was in a sentimental mood and let down his guard to find out what was in there. So it was transcripts of all the interrogations he'd carried out during his long police career. His mysterious treasure island in the sea of human misery. The infinite system of questions, which was always brought to its logical conclusion. But in the mist, beyond the ocean of words, lay the illogical ends of so many lives.

"I won't bother picking one out, Rutkowski. I'll close my eyes and pull out any one of the folders. Let's see what we've got. Ah! From 1938, the city of Mannheim, Rheinland. Industry. Workers. We've already talked about them. Hard nuts to crack. However, this case involved a traveling salesman named Fröhlich, one Gustav Fröhlich, who was reported for paying visits to a certain Lilly Schwartzkopf, a milliner, a designer of hats, who for her part maintained intimate relations with Herr D.R.D, the vice president of a Mannheim bank, whose nephew, formerly a student at Oxford, regularly corresponded with his English tutor, a professor in the German department, and also with the confident of someone else at the university who was the head of a team of analysts in the British intelligence service."

"Dear god!"

"It seems pretty involved, doesn't it? But in fact everything was quite clear. And logical. The tutor wasn't a friend of the other man from the university but a member of his intelligence team. The vice president's nephew was recruited as a young student, while still at college. There was blackmail involved, but the details are of no importance. What's important is that he, being without parents, lived in the house of his uncle, where he was in a position to find out confidential information concerning our economic policies."

"Now what did Fröhlich have to do with that?"

"We'll come to that immediately. The milliner Lilly Schwartz-kopf had a secret love affair with Herr D.R.D., the vice president. The milliner didn't really love him. Her motive for giving herself to him was intelligence."

"That was the cover for her meetings with the nephew, who gave her economic secrets."

"What economic secrets?"

"The ones she was learning from the vice president."

"Don't be an ass, Rutkowski. What kind of secrets can the vice president of a bank know? Everything he knows can be found in any annual industrial report or financial bulletin. The activity was proceeding in the opposite direction."

"So it was in the opposite direction?"

"Of course. Everything always moves in the direction opposite to the direction it appears to be moving in. The person supplying the information was in fact the milliner."

"And the vice president was the connection . . ."

". . . between the milliner and the nephew."

"But why didn't the milliner work directly with the nephew?"

"Because he was corresponding with the English tutor and because any contacts between a designer of women's hats and someone who corresponds with someone else in England would have been unfailingly suspicious."

"I understand. If this had been a matter of a designer of men's hats, everything would have appeared considerably more benign."

"In any case. . . ."

"But what if the nephew had corresponded with Italians? Then she could have remained a designer of women's hats, right?"

"In any case, I'm telling you, the nephew passed on the information that he received. How he did it, we never found out. Indeed, the letters were completely clean in this respect."

"So then how was it established that he was a spy?"

"By logic, Rutkowski. Everything was pointing in that direction. It stood out like a sore thumb. On the one hand, those studies in England under the direct tutelage of a British intelligence agent, and on the other that Fröhlich."

"What Fröhlich? What did Fröhlich have to do with it?"

"He was the heart of the conspiracy. He supplied Schwartzkopf with confidential information about the condition of our industry. He was the key. The milliner, the vice president, and the nephew were only a channel for the transfer of that information to London."

"So Fröhlich was indisputably shown to be a spy?"

"You bet. Likewise, primarily by logic. First of all, indicative of this was his indirect contact with the nephew—the notorious spy. And then everything else was against him, too. To begin with, his family."

"His own family accused him?"

"Unfortunately, no. Which was why we had to arrest all of them as well. Their interrogations are here, too, but we'll ignore them for the time being. His family led him to the commission of the crime; it was too big for his pocketbook. He had to find an additional source of income somewhere else. It goes without saying that criminal activity against the state suited him best, both technically and emotionally."

"Forgive me, Herr Standartenführer, but I don't believe that crimes against the state *go without saying*."

"No? Really? Your patriotism puts me to shame. You should write propaganda. Let's test the technical advantages in the meantime. Business trips in the industrial areas along the Rhine enabled him to gain access to economic and military secrets without drawing attention to himself. Correct?"

"Yes, but. . . ."

"It's completely within the realm of the probable that he didn't collect them for pleasure or to improve his professional standing."

"Completely, but. . . ."

"It follows logically that he collected them for purposes of espionage. Anyway, his contact with the milliner and the vice president, and through them with the notorious spying nephew, can be indisputably proven."

"Technically speaking, it really seems like the easiest method of earning money, Herr Standartenführer. But *emotionally?* Why would that have suited Fröhlich best emotionally?"

"Because he hated the state."

"Was that established?"

"Why should we lose time on that when it follows logically from the fact that he spied for its enemies? And finally, Fröhlich confessed. Without any physical force. Logic put the squeeze on him. Nothing else. Pure logic. I should add that all the others also confessed and were shot. Only the vice president got away."

"Because he was logically innocent?"

"No. Because he was the vice president."

Pay attention, Hilmar, to the iron logic of Steinbrecher's transcript. The nephew was a British spy. What proves that the nephew was a British spy? His contact with the notorious spy Fröhlich, obviously. But what proof is there of Fröhlich's espionage activities? The nephew's, naturally. Fröhlich is implicated by his contact with a person against whom he, Fröhlich, was instrumental in bringing charges. The nephew was a spy because Fröhlich was. Fröhlich was in turn a spy because the nephew was, with whom he corresponded—in matters of espionage, of course. Because two spies can have no contact outside of espionage contact. Relations between two spies must involve espionage. (Which is not at all contradicted by the fact that relations with prima donnas must not necessarily involve singing.) But, thank you very much, you'll say that we still haven't seen the real proof that the nephew was a British spy. Of course we have. Didn't we prove that he was in contact with the spy Fröhlich? But, you'll ask, how can Fröhlich's crime be proven in the meantime? What do we need evidence for when it is evident from Fröhlich's contact with the spying nephew?

Reflect a little on that, Hilmar. Look and see whether some of the proofs in your books aren't of this sort. Isn't the incompetence of some ruler deduced from the very fact that he ruled? Isn't some rebel justified because he was fighting for justice? Isn't the necessity of certain historical means proven by the importance of their intended goal? Weren't the conclusions about the value of those goals based on the worthlessness of some others? In brief, isn't Fröhlich condemned to death because he maintained contact with the nephew, who was a spy only because he maintained contact with Fröhlich, who according to the syllogism was also a spy?

Think about it, Hilmar. And we'll meet again tomorrow.

KONRAD

P.S. When a man dares to confide the story of such a life to another, who is in some sense an enemy (as you are, Hilmar), in order to obligate himself to the deepest possible humiliation and repentance, he's bound to show unlimited honesty. Otherwise, his confession has no meaning. Therefore, I'll return to my conversation with Standartenführer Steinbrecher to include an episode that I omitted out of the kind of vanity that makes a serial killer coldly confess all his crimes—and even describe them with a certain pride—while stubbornly refusing to acknowledge some tiny insult that he visited on his victims while committing the crime.

When the Standartenführer let it be known that he envisioned me as the future investigator of Adam's case, this is what I said:

"Herr Standartenführer, as the case is an unusual one, why don't you take it on yourself?"

With regard to the plan to save the clerk, this was definitely a betrayal, a withdrawal without a fight, desertion. Even more than that. As you've made Steinbrecher's acquaintance, you'll agree it was tantamount to murder.

Fortunately, the Standartenführer rejected my suggestion. But I had to pay for my shameful betrayal with a considerable worsening of the conditions in which I was to carry out the investigation. Namely, the Standartenführer decided to "meet me half-way," as he described his idea of determining the general direction of the investigation and all relevant questions himself, while I'd play the role of agent of his diabolic logic and submit reports to him every evening about the answers I'd obtained from Adam. Those answers would nourish new questions, which would produce new answers, and on and on until, of course, the file clerk and anything at all were shown to have the same connection that had made spies of the Oxford nephew and the traveling salesman Fröhlich.

"A suitable compromise," the Standartenführer said. "As someone with a penchant for compromises, I hope you'll know to value it."

■ □ ■ □ ■

LETTER 12

THE WORLDVIEW OF SS STANDARTENFÜHRER HEINRICH STEINBRECHER, OR *THE DECLINE OF THE WEST*

The Mediterranean Coast, 20 Sept. 1965

My dear Hilmar,

I have no intention of acquainting you with Steinbrecher's amazing Interrogation Transcript of 1938 in its entirety. If you're interested, you can find it in the drawer of my desk, which I've referred you to several times. I've studied it thoroughly. The first time was before I ordered Max to bring Adam to me, and then once more immediately after the end of the war, in the form of a copy which I compiled from memory. The original was returned to the Standartenführer and buried in the vault, and it was lost in the disorder during our withdrawal from the Balkans. The second time was brought about by the record of my case, which was kindly compiled by an American military investigator, Major Stein. Indeed, the relations between the questions and answers in both documents were guided by the same logic.

For the sake of illustration, let me discuss one formulation. On the eleventh day of interrogation, Gustav Fröhlich, once a traveling salesman and now a spy for the British intelligence service, was asked the following question: WHEN DID YOU FIRST SLEEP WITH MISS LILLY SCHWARTZKOPF? Let's not read the answer. Let's think, logically, in the fashion of the Standartenführer. The answer is, most certainly, negative. Fröhlich didn't sleep with the milliner at all. The question is repeated. The answer is still negative, but supported this time by certain explanations. Their purpose is to show that Fröhlich *could not* have slept with Lilly Schwartzkopf. (Of course he could have. He hadn't been castrated.) The question is repeated. The explanations become more confused, the denial less clear. Some contradictions even turn up. Mistakes in dates. Mistakes in whereabouts. Mistakes in general. They require more explanations, which in turn produce more contradictions. And the question is repeated all the same. Fröhlich is discreetly given to understand that sleeping with a milliner isn't a punishable act. Finally, after a few leading questions, the answer becomes affirmative. So, Fröhlich did in fact sleep with the milliner Schwartzkopf. (Soon he'll learn that this isn't at all as harmless as it seemed at first glance. That imaginary pleasure will turn out to cost him dearly.) When did this occur? On such-and-such a date. At which time of the day? At such-and-such time of the day. Fröhlich is left to add flesh to the skeleton of the false confession himself. A certain division of labor is the foundation of a good investigation. Compromise is its slogan—and all that despite the obvious fact that he didn't sleep with her. But it was logical that he should have. Quite natural, right? In the meantime, the fact that he didn't sleep with the milliner was only one of numerous possibilities for expanding their relationship, which wasn't exploited. It simply wasn't logical enough. It wasn't logical that a middle-aged, healthy, and potent traveling salesman (his bunch of children left no doubt at all about his sexual abilities) wouldn't sleep with a young and beautiful divorcée with whom, in addition to everything else, he was collaborating on a dirty business. Technically speaking, sentimental relationships are always a convenient screen for the transfer of spies' reports. These meetings had to be explained. Business contacts (Fröhlich indeed represented a textile factory) weren't a sufficient explanation. They could account for one meeting a month. They failed in particular to provide an explanation for the telephone conversations. Did any such telephone conversations take place, you ask? I couldn't tell you. The telephone exchanges keep no records. Logic, however, leads us. . . . And then, Hilmar, why would one vice consent to be alone? Experience tells us that vice loves company. Very often we come across murderers who drink themselves unconscious, frauds addicted to gambling, prostitutes who steal from their clients, dishonest politicians, drug addicts with an inclination for blackmail, and—of course—adulterers who spy for money to support their lovers. Vices usually give a hand to one another and mutually promote each other. A murderer kills while drunk, and then drinks even more to forget the murder. After another bout of drinking, he kills again and thus opens the door to more drinking. The gambler's hand reaches into the coffers, thereby committing fraud; it gambles away the stolen money, and then the gambler's hand returns again to the coffers and its embezzler's fate. The drug addict commits blackmail to secure funds for drugs that impel him to commit blackmail again. The socialite starts squandering money to become a still greater socialite and in the end a greater spendthrift. In order to keep the false promises he made to win the election, the politician continues politicking and telling more brazen lies. The adulterer becomes a spy to earn money to support his vice, which in turn forces him to produce more spy's reports. Such was the case with our Fröhlich. The fact that his adultery was deduced from his espionage relationship with the milliner doesn't invalidate the syllogism. In the same way, Fröhlich's espionage activity may be deduced from his adulterous affair with a female agent. Logic keeps a deathwatch on both sides of Fröhlich's fate. There's no possibility of escape. A man can dodge even bullets, but not logic. When something happens in the world of sterile, abstract concepts, there's not one damned fact of life in the world that's powerful enough to bend the logic of events to its will. Indeed, no fact of life should ever be so strong. But to ensure nevertheless that none of them will, Standartenführer Steinbrecher, that powerful mechanism for the production of positive answers, is hard at work. Responding with negative answers didn't help. In the end, denials were always transformed into affirmations. The person under examination thinks he'd have fared better if he'd immediately confessed to all the charges. Perhaps in that case he'd have remained on the level of torching the garage, and the Reichstag could have been avoided. But he's mistaken. He has no reason to reproach himself. If the program of the investigation included torching the Reichstag, the investigator wouldn't be satisfied with some insignificant garage. Either way you'd end up in front of the Reichstag with a gasoline can.

The Transcript of 1938 described that torturous path. One got the impression that both of its subjects, interrogator and interrogatee, were striving for the same goal—a confession. Everything in the Transcript strove for a confession, which is a unification with a logical reality, and no matter how they looked at the matter, that was the basic goal of every kind of Steinbrecherization: accepting logic in the place of reality, assuming responsibility for probable events that were never even actualized. The Transcript of 1938 was a magic carpet woven from logical questions and logical answers. If one knows that every logical question can have only one logical answer, further explanation of the procedure is unnecessary.

I imagined those questions to be a dense jungle of nooses hanging over Fröhlich's head. Which one would reach his neck first? Which of them would he be able to shake off? Which one would cinch around him only provisionally, to take his breath away and keep him from noticing just as the main, fatal noose slipped down around his neck to strangle him more logically than the others?

It seems, however, that in this regard Fröhlich was indifferent. Judging from his answers, at one point he stopped caring. (That's the magical moment every investigator dreams about, when his Transcript seemingly slips out of its languor and heads cheerfully for a universal and unlimited confession, the common goal of all police protocols.) Fröhlich's conclusion that any reasonable resistance was futile wasn't only practical. His actions testify to a deep philosophical consequence of this realization. Fröhlich had indeed become a philosopher along the way. He doubted not only the sense of any resistance but the point of being alive at all, the whole biological venture, the comical ascent of spermatozoa into the emptiness of eternity. If he could have formulated his despair in terms of some complex theory, that would have been philosophy. As things were, it remained the confusion of an otherwise rational mind, which was reflected even in a change of his name. At the end of the interrogation, after enduring a series of successive metamorphoses, his signature at the bottom of the record read: GUSTY FARTS. Indifferent to any future appellations, acts of posthumous rehabilitation, historical errata, and belated apologies, Gustav Fröhlich had taken refuge in a person with no face, no biography or address, into the chimerical Mr. Gusty Farts. He disappeared into a fairly vulgar, but wonderfully unintelligible, pseudonym, which suits perfectly the clandestine activities of a distinguished intelligence agent. In brief, he shrouded himself in the alogical cloak of farce.

When I think about that amazing work of logic from today's perspective, I can't escape the impression that it was in a way an empirical illustration or practical application of one of the cornerstones of contemporary philosophy: the TRACTATUS LOGICO-PHILOSOPHICUS of Ludwig Wittgenstein. (The prefix "stein" in *Steinbrecher* became a suffix in *Wittgenstein* and that withdrawal of their common denominator into the background almost seems to correspond to the shame that the intellectual felt at the consistent application of his own principles.) It's unlikely that Steinbrecher was a student of Wittgenstein, or that he ever even held the latter's *Tractatus Logico-Philosophicus*—published in the *Annale der Naturphilosophie* in 1921—in his hands. This serious shortcoming in the Standartenführer's education acquires a considerably more positive meaning in light of the fact that he arrived at Wittgenstein's conclusions independently, by way of deeds and not thoughts.

Let's just consider Wittgenstein's solipsism. It corresponded to Steinbrecher's Theory of Universal and Total Suspicion. The Standartenführer spoke to me about it on several occasions, most often because of my inclination to attach significance to the prisoners' answers. According to the Standartenführer, suspicion was a general frame of mind that followed from the impossibility to predict things on the basis of experience. This impossibility stood in direct relation to the nonexistence of a real causal link between events and phenomena of the real world. The claim that the sun will rise tomorrow is only a hypothesis. "When the sun rises tomorrow . . ." is a bad formulation. One should say "If the sun rises tomorrow. . . ." The rising of the sun is a possibility, perhaps even a probability, but in no way a certainty. All that's certain is the possibility of its rising. The possibility of such an event makes every sunrise a pure coincidence. And if we can't be certain even of such fundamentally existent phenomena, what about people and their behavior? A policeman who wanted to produce evidence about espionage activity from the assumption that Fröhlich was a spy would have miscalculated. Because that activity *must not* necessarily have had to exist. Fröhlich's guilt didn't in fact follow from his criminal activity, but from the contact with the spying nephew—just as the nephew's guilt follows from the assumption that Fröhlich, with whom he maintained a relation, was a notorious spy. This causation is exclusively the product of reason and logic. It needn't have any correlation in reality. Causation in reality is only a working assumption, like the rising of the sun tomorrow. If I say Fröhlich was a spy, that's likewise only a working hypothesis enabling me to arrest Fröhlich on logical grounds. During the interrogation, the validity of this hypothesis will be tested. If it proves to be correct—as usually happens with the application of other logical principles of the Steinbrecher-Wittgenstein system—the result is a self-fulfilling logical schema, which reality will subsequently adapt to. The logical precedes the real. The real follows from the logical. Or as Wittgenstein puts it: "Die Tatsachen im logischen Raum sind die Welt" (i.e., "The world is made up of facts in LOGICAL SPACE.")

For example, in Wittgenstein's view the world isn't described merely by naming all the objects in it; there must be knowledge of the facts that are component parts of the objects. Steinbrecher goes one step further. He isn't even satisfied with knowing the component facts. Because, according to him, all we might say about anything, even about Wittgenstein's idea of totality, are merely claims, assumptions, opinions. For them to become logical and thus effective, they must be supported by other assumptions. Saying that Fröhlich is a spy is offering an assumption. Without another corresponding assumption, it is dead, unproductive, nonfunctional—but, above all, stripped of logic.

Because why should Fröhlich have to be a spy? There are no reasons for assuming this in his personal life or his way of thinking. For this assumption to gain a logical basis, it must be supported by something. Fröhlich as spy is substantiated by the nephew as spy, with whom he maintained contact. And if we exclude the converse effect of this conclusion, which results in the nephew's espionage activity being substantiated by Fröhlich's, it's obvious that we could charge the nephew with spying only with the aid of some third assumption. This we could find in the milliner. The milliner provides evidence of the nephew's crime, and the nephew provides evidence of Fröhlich's crime. And vice-versa, naturally. But if this time we also wish to avoid the reversibility of the process, it's clear that we must resort to Vice President D.R.D. Thus, it's theoretically possible to fit all of humanity into a single net of informants. That this doesn't happen is the fault of various and antagonistic national interests. They don't allow police investigations to be carried to their ultimate, logical conclusions, which involve the arrest of the investigators themselves, thus closing the logical Steinbrecher-Wittgenstein circle.

Allow me a few more comparisons, this time in the form of quotations.

WITTGENSTEIN: *In der Logik ist nichts zufällig.* In logic nothing is accidental. If something can appear in a state of affairs, then the possibility of the state of affairs must be prejudiced in that thing. It would seem like a coincidence if some state of affairs subsequently fitted in with an object that could exist on its own. If objects can be in states of affairs, this possibility must exist in the objects themselves beforehand. Something logical cannot be merely possible. Logic is concerned with every possibility and all possibilities are its facts.

STEINBRECHER: If the traveling salesman Fröhlich can appear in his spying aspect or state, then that cannot be accidental, but prejudiced within him. Fröhlich is indeed *necessarily* a spy. Accordingly, it would seem arbitrary if Fröhlich, if he can be a spy, is not one.

WITTGENSTEIN: *Wenn ich den Gegenstand kenne, so kenne ich auch sämtliche Möglichkeiten seines Vorkommens in Sachverhalten.* If I know the object, then I likewise know all the possibilities of its appearance in states of affairs. Every such possibility must exist in the nature of the object. A new possibility cannot be discovered subsequently.

STEINBRECHER: If I know the spy Fröhlich, then I know all his possibilities, and thus all the manners and forms of his espionage activity. It cannot be subsequently established that he is not a spy.

WITTGENSTEIN: *Aus dem Bestehen oder Nichtbestehen eines Sachverhaltes kann nicht auf das Bestehen oder Nichtbestehen eines anderen geschlossen werden.* The existence or nonexistence of a state of affairs does not allow one to deduce the existence or nonexistence of another state of affairs.

STEINBRECHER: The fact that Fröhlich is a spy does not allow one to conclude that the nephew is not one. (As you can see, Hilmar, Steinbrecher had arrived at a somewhat simplified and more primitive form of Wittgenstein's conclusion. With him, one man's guilt for a crime did not exclude the guilt of all others. That provided a greater potential for intrigues, secret associations, and wide-scale conspiracies. Crimes committed by individuals didn't exist for him.)

WITTGENSTEIN: *Wir machen uns Bilder der Tatsachen.* We create images of the facts for ourselves. An image represents a state of affairs in logical space. An image is a model of reality. An image is a fact. The fact that the elements of the image are in a specific mutual relationship means that the objects themselves are in the same mutual relationship. The image is thus tied to reality. It extends to reality. It is the measure of reality.

STEINBRECHER: Facts are not directly accessible to us. We arrive at them by means of logic. Logic is the science of the formation of representations and images of facts and the relationships obtaining between them. A representation or image of Fröhlich's espionage activity is espionage in logical space. It is a model of reality. A model of Fröhlich's crime. An image or representation of Fröhlich as a spy—as long as it is logical—is the spy Fröhlich himself.

WITTGENSTEIN: *Das Bild bildet die Wirklichkeit ab, indem es eine Möglichkeit des Bestehens und Nichtbestehens von Sachverhalten darstellt.* The image reproduces reality by showing the possibility of the existence or nonexistence of states of affairs. The image shows one possible state of affairs in logical space. The image contains the possibility of the states of affairs that it shows. The image shows what it shows, independent of its truth or falsity, by the form of its reproduction. What an image shows is its meaning. Its truth or falsity lies in the conformity or nonconformity of its meaning with reality. In order to discover whether an image is truthful, we must compare it with reality. The truth or falsity of an image cannot be deduced from the image itself.

STEINBRECHER: (Here the Standartenführer's logical radicalism even surpasses that of Wittgenstein. This is understandable. Reality as the deciding factor between the truth or falsity of a police representation would destroy even the most perfect interrogation record. If one wishes to be truly logical, reality must be excluded from all our calculations.) It is theoretically correct that reality determines whether our representation of Fröhlich as a spy is truthful or not. But, because that reality is inaccessible to us except in the form of a representation, and we likewise gain information about reality only via a representation or image—which in turn requires the confirmation of reality, a confirmation which, as we have seen, is practically impossible—it follows that reality must be rejected as the measure of the truthfulness of an opinion, for practical as well as theoretical reasons. Consequently, we cannot find evidence either for Fröhlich's guilt or innocence *in reality.* Therefore, reality is irrelevant for the determination of Fröhlich's innocence.

WITTGENSTEIN: *Der Gedanke enthält die Möglichkeit der Sachlage, die er denkt. Was denkbar ist, ist auch möglich.* A thought contains the possibility of the conceived state of affairs. What is imaginable is possible. We cannot imagine something illogical; otherwise we would have to think illogically.

STEINBRECHER: As soon as I imagined Fröhlich as a spy, he can be one, because otherwise I would not even be able to imagine him as a spy. (This is not refuted by the fact that a cripple will not get up and run if I imagine him doing so.)

Hilmar, this much should be sufficient for you to grasp the logic that determined both the questions that were put to Fröhlich in 1938 as well as those that I had to ask Adam Trpković on behalf of the Standartenführer in 1943.

I'll write about that interrogation this evening. In the meantime, don't you think that logic is hell? And that the most hellish of all is to act according to logic?

Yours,

KONRAD

P.S. Sabina is getting impatient. She's complaining that I'm neglecting her. I hope I'll finish this report in a day or two, so I can make up for giving her so little attention. Deep in my heart, unfortunately, I'm aware that after this confession nothing will be as before. And that nothing in my life will be predictable anymore.

■ □ ■ □ ■

LETTER 13

PROFESSOR KONRAD RUTKOWSKI

DECLARES WAR

ON FASCISM, OR *PHAEDON;*

OR, OF THE SOUL

The Mediterranean Coast, 21 Sept. 1965

Dear Hilmar,

I assume yesterday's letter offended you. Although you've never read Wittgenstein, you worship him. Although you didn't understand Hegel, you worship him, too. The same goes for Kant, Schopenhauer, and Nietzsche. You owe this not only to your status as an academic, but also to your conviction that Ideas, especially philosophical ones, are a necessary corrective to the disgusting lives we're sometimes forced to lead. The idea that philosophy could inspire one such life, organize it, and defend it as ideal, seems blasphemous to you. I assure you, however, that something just like that is what's going on. If philosophy doesn't produce history, then it comes in afterward to explain and justify it. The fact that the majority of philosophical ideas aren't fallacious but nonsensical, if one considers the crippled logic and clumsy language of their formulation, doesn't sever the genetic link between Ideas and Reality.

Fortunately, it only limits the link occasionally. Regardless of whether they consider this world the best or worst of all possible worlds, whether they accept it in its ordinariness and mediocrity, whether they refuse to think about it in terms of human values, whether they deny or acknowledge its purposelessness, whether they explain it or merely describe it—Ideas *act,* Ideas *change* things, Ideas *create.* Your naive conviction (we'll see how naive it really is) that thinking philosophically means secluding oneself from reality and absolving oneself of all responsibility in connection with it—and that such seclusion is the *conditio sine qua non* of every unbiased philosophical view—stems from an insidious wish, camouflaged in a general independence of the intellect, to disavow any responsibility for this world, whereby your harmlessness acquires a completely different meaning. It represents Ideas' renunciation of their own deeds, the spirit in which the discoverers of atomic energy renounced the atomic bomb.

You refuse to believe in the existence and effectiveness of the Wittgenstein-Steinbrecher System. Fine. Maybe because its principles were demonstrated on a reality as bloody and filthy as that of the Gestapo. The thought that logical speculations could be connected in any way with beatings and the mutilation of people's souls seems to you to be a monstrous injustice—not against the people but against the speculations. An injustice against Wittgenstein, not against Fröhlich. (The explanation that the Intellect, even when it leads to crimes, can't be called to account for those crimes because they were unintentional cannot be accepted. Otherwise, all who kill out of negligence and recklessness would have to be excused from responsibility for their crimes.) But you see, Hilmar, as a historian you ought to know much more about the genetic relationship between Ideas and History. The Wittgenstein-Steinbrecher System isn't the only one to demonstrate this relationship successfully. I won't smother you with examples. I suggest you think about a single one, because it belongs in your area of expertise and many of its aspects are the historical dates you study.

Give Hegel a little more thought, Hilmar. Give yourself time to understand him. And then take a look at some of the states that have made the history of our century colorful. Think about Nietzsche, Hilmar (you can forget third-rate thinkers such as Giovanni

Gentile and Houston Stewart Chamberlain) and think about how much of Zarathustra there is in the Führer's thought. (Devoid of the poetry, of course, that makes it easier for us to accept Zarathustra's words as magical images of thought instead of calls to action.) In your work on the Third Reich, which was considered by some to be seminal, you very pedantically cite what Hitler read at various points in his political career, without once pointing out the logical correspondence between those writings and his policies. Between Ideas and History. Between the Spirit and Reality. Thoughts and Deeds.

The detonator of the hatred for the Jews, along with the instructions for its use, was implanted into Hitler by philosophers (you don't have to call them that if it makes it easier for you to swallow the painful truth): Otto Hauser in his *Geschichte des Judentums* (A History of the Jews); Werner Sombart in his *Die Juden und das Wirtschaftsleben* (The Jews and Economic Life); Gougenout des Mousseaux in his *Le Juif, le judaisme et la judaïsation des peuples chrétiens* (The Jews, Judaism, and the Judaization of the Christian Peoples); Theodor Fritsch in his *Handbuch der Judenfrage* (Handbook of the Jewish Question); and others. In addition to the aforementioned Chamberlain, his racial theories were based on such ghastly works as *L'Aryen, son rôle social* (The Aryans and Their Social Role). And in its context, a disdain for the weak, sick and unfortunate, disgraced and ignominious, was sparked by an academic monstrosity such as *Die Tüchtigkeit unserer Rasse und der Schutz der Schwachen* (The Fitness of Our Race and the Protection of the Weak) by Alfred Plötz, M.D. The theories of Lebensraum were taken from Ratzel, Haushofer, and Mackinder. Plato's *The State* inspired the thousand-year aristocratic SS Empire.[10] But the wise old Schopenhauer taught him the gloomy and hopeless pessimism that enabled the products of two other minds—Darwin's struggle for survival and Malthus' specter of overpopulation—to be happily joined into a brutal settling of accounts with the human race. His love of the Will was in the Nietzschean mold, and his hatred for Christianity was borrowed from Nietzsche and Gibbon's primitive idea that Christianity destroyed the Roman Empire. And let me put the icing on the cake. When you were in the Hitler-Jugend and you got carried away to the point of delirium during the Führer's speeches, sinking deeper and deeper into a nightmare of fanaticism, you didn't know he was simply applying Le Bon's and McDougall's philosophy of propaganda (*The Crowd* and *The Group Mind*).

But now, Hilmar, you're no longer a Hitler Youth wearing short pants. You're a professional historian. You ought to know this by now. That was the purpose of describing the Wittgenstein-Steinbrecher System in the previous letter.

Now let's leave Ideas to contest this accusation, and we'll go off to our first official meeting with the municipal clerk Adam Trpković. Let's not forget to bring along the Standartenführer's QUESTIONNAIRE (the monstrous offspring of the TRANSCRIPT OF 1938) and, just in case, the Transcript itself, that precious protocol of the interrogation of the traveling salesman Gustav Fröhlich.

We'll find Adam and his umbrella right where we sat him down when he came into our office, escorted by Hauptscharführer Max. We'll place the Protocol of 1938 to our left and to the right we'll unfold the Standartenführer's Questionnaire of 1943, and in the middle of the desk, right in front of my heart, we'll put a blank sheet of paper to be filled by Adam and myself with marks of our mutual misfortune. But so everything will be as it was then, we'll think once again: There's no way out of here, Konrad Rutkowski. The file clerk is your misfortune, just as you are his. The transcript is the pontoon that these two misfortunes will cross to commingle with one another. You can't leave here and go into the bathroom to shout THE EMPEROR HAS NO CLOTHES into the porcelain hole, and then vomit out a universal answer to the war, to Steinbrecher, to your own fate and the whole whorish tangled mess of life. You have to remain in your chair and attempt to *really* do something, for him and yourself. Primarily for yourself. Regardless of the fact that what you're doing for yourself will save his life and thus look as if you did it for him.

During this time he'll sit in his chair indifferently, as if none of this concerned him and he were leaving the whole trouble surrounding his fate to me. While I'm considering how to approach this matter, how to adjust Steinbrecher's questions to the noticeably neglected defensive system of the prisoner, he'll keep silent, dead in all aspects of his external appearance, except a gentle gleam under the lenses of his eyeglasses and a faint trembling of the umbrella between his thighs.

PROFESSOR KONRAD RUTKOWSKI DECLARES WAR ON FASCISM

What held him up? I think it was the umbrella, Hilmar, and not only from the perspective of what I learned about it later. That thought also occurred to me while I was interrogating him. Without doubt, the umbrella was the secret prop of the whole structure—without it the contraption would have fallen apart. One simply couldn't imagine him without the umbrella, and so it never occurred to anyone—not even to the unerring Münch—to take it from him. Perhaps he thought the umbrella was an organic part of the clerk's body. But when his Steinbrecherized brain realized that the man in front of him had been arrested with an umbrella, like some sort of accomplice, it was already too late. The umbrella had already been entered in the column for items left in the prisoner's possession. The mistake had occurred in a somnambulistic interval when Münch was convinced that he had before him some Balkan wonder and was afraid of inflicting some kind of injury on him by confiscating his silken protuberance, which would later have to be justified in the REMARKS column. As for me, I'd refused to see a prisoner in Adam from the start, and what someone at liberty carried on his person was none of my concern. Once it had been irrevocably inventoried by Münch's remark, I no longer had a choice. Though I hadn't yet arrived at the realization of its liberating significance *in extenso*, the umbrella's brazen contradiction of the regulations seemed to me to be a significant anti-Steinbrecherian act.

The greatest riddle of the attitude of the Geheime Staatspolizei toward the umbrella, however, was Standartenführer Steinbrecher's behavior. One would think he'd have immediately ordered its confiscation and then delighted us with a lecture on the harmful effects of all objects that distract the prisoners' attention from a confession as the *conditio sine qua non* of their existence. The umbrella wasn't confiscated, but the opportunity for a lecture wasn't passed up.

STEINBRECHER: A prisoner exists exclusively for the purpose of signing confessions. All his other functions are peripheral and may be disregarded as long as ignoring them doesn't hinder the realization of that primary function. As early as 1873, Herman demonstrated the functioning of muscle tissue in the complete absence of oxygen. Hill and Kupalov isolated the sartorius of a frog and placed it in Ringer's solution, completely depriving it of oxygen. And gentlemen, do you know what happened? In a period of twenty-four hours it contracted 1,500 times. The sole laboratory condition: the metabolic products had to be transported into the surrounding solution. As a result, the contractions were immeasurably more numerous than in natural conditions.

RUTKOWSKI'S COMMENTARY: Thus, theoretically speaking, a prisoner in strict isolation, subjected to a special regimen and placed in Steinbrecher's solution of logic and torture, can in the course of a one-week period of investigation contract his conscience x times, producing y confessions, on the sole condition that the waste products of the mental metabolism in a quantity z are promptly removed from the prisoner.

STEINBRECHER: One may deviate from the rule that a prisoner may not dispose of a single object that might distract his attention from the confession if and only if a purposeless item is placed at his disposal, which quickly loses its ability to distract his attention with some pointlessly repetitive activity. A ball of twine, a sharp nail, or a shard of colored glass from a beer bottle all have inestimable value for a prisoner. Not to mention social games like cards, dominoes, and chess. Animals and insects are especially dangerous to us. Gentlemen, the hunting pursuits of spiders can keep your interrogation transcript at a standstill for weeks. Industrious bands of black ants will discredit your investigative reputation more thoroughly than a prisoner's mental stability, strength in his convictions, or any possible hypalgesia. Nothing is more fatal for an investigation than some process that is not under its complete control. As we've seen, processes involving the exchange of matter—inspirations and expirations, temperature maintenance and digestion, and even thought—can to a certain extent be considered permissible only if we control them. By depriving a prisoner of oxygen (from the removal of windows and ventilation to the forcible prevention of his respiration—we'll leave the details to Hauptsturmführer Rotkopf), gentlemen, you'll make a powerful contribution to the disorganization of the suspect's defense. He simply won't be able to come up with intelligent answers. He won't have enough air. Or let's take digestion; the exchanges of matter involved are completely in our hands. However, gentlemen, a stray fly, a lost ladybug, anything that crawls and lives in the detention cells without our permission, any of those things undermine a well-planned investigation better than a well-planned defense. In this sense, any bug is more dangerous than the inductive abilities of some professor of classical philology.

And what's with the umbrella, you're asking? Leave it. Stand back and watch. What will a prisoner do with an umbrella? Open and close it. Over and over again. Hundreds and then thousands of times. Always in the same way, always with no purpose. At the start it absorbs his attention and works against us, but soon it disappoints him and begins to work for us. He'll comprehend the treacherous deceit. That umbrella won't protect him from anything. That umbrella is insultingly pointless. The prisoner will find more purpose in dealing with the questions he was asked than in opening and closing the umbrella. And gentlemen, I assure you that as soon as the prisoner starts thinking, he's on the wrong track. Logical thought in and of itself is incompatible with a clever defense. The umbrella will force him to do so sooner or later. But not an insect. I still haven't met a prisoner who would miss a duel between two insects to think out his strategy for an impending interrogation.

RUTKOWSKI'S COMMENTARY: Dear God!)

So, Hilmar, allow your correspondent to add his own little contribution to the Standartenführer's penchant for parenthetical remarks. Just enough for you to see to what extent I was Steinbrecherized at the time of the interrogation of Adam Trpković. My thoughts were, of course, theoretical in nature and the idea of applying them on the prisoners in the manner of the Standartenführer was the farthest thing from my mind. But the very fact that I thought about anything like that at all is incriminating enough.

Indeed, the Standartenführer had a habit of applying his theory of counterpoint treatment of prisoners with a regimen whereby, in wintertime, he let people keep their handkerchiefs but confiscated their sweaters. In my opinion, this was the single mistake I caught him making during the whole time we worked together. Because a handkerchief wasn't as harmless as the Standartenführer thought. A prisoner with a neatly folded handkerchief over his heart will contrive things that a man without one is simply incapable of. If he doesn't have a handkerchief in the pocket of his coat, the man without a sweater will shiver. The man with the handkerchief will never shiver under any circumstances. The handkerchief prevents this— it is the highest form of civil integrity that I know of from my experience. It's more dangerous than Steinbrecher's famed ladybugs, though I don't deny their importance. I don't know why handkerchiefs, if they're white (colored ones offer no kind of protection), harden a prisoner in his resistance. I suppose they remind the prisoner of the importance he had while at liberty, an importance he must defend at any price. When a gentleman on a deserted island changes his dress for supper, he does it out of self-respect. Similarly, the handkerchief obligates the prisoner. Interrogating someone who has a white handkerchief in his breast pocket is a task as devilishly difficult as questioning a general wearing a ribbon on his breast. And whereas Steinbrecher uncovered the danger of the ribbons with senior officers, the significance of a handkerchief slipped by him through some twist of fate. The higher the rank held by the accused officer, the greater the degree of *rank stripped.* Steinbrecher would tear off their ribbons, pull off their decorations, remove their rosettes, medals, insignia, the stripes on their trousers, braids and buttons, all the paraphernalia of their importance. He would strip them of their shoelaces and would even take their belts so that they had to preserve the last remnant of their human dignity with their hands and not their heads. He interrogated generals in their underwear, while letting them wear their hats as a matter of counterpoint. It was so much more odd that he missed the subversive significance of a white handkerchief. And I, to be sure, made every effort to keep from pointing it out to him.

Let's return to Adam. The resentment I felt toward him then, not knowing what to do with him and vexedly wondering how he got there, why he hadn't saluted that goddamned flag, why he hadn't given up the umbrella, and why that goddamned gust of wind had to have blown right when Adam was passing under the flag—Hilmar, that gall fills me even now. In the chair in front of me, a municipal file clerk is occupying the place of Prince Mieszko. With the Pole at least I wouldn't have any problems. From his history I wouldn't have to draw conclusions of decisive importance for my life. I'd transform him into beautiful footnotes: A. B. C. D. 7, ibid. 19, ibid. 138, ibid. Referring to this, relying on that, and disproving the old hypotheses along the way: Professor *X* is incorrect when he claims. . . . Professor *Y,* however. . . . The titles of the documents would be printed in italics as a laconic evaluation of their credibility. Different degrees of academic achievement would be set in different kinds of type. What others have discovered between the Oder and the Vistula would be set in diamond. As none of that is anything special, they'd have to be content with 0.376 mm. For significant discoveries, they'd get five or six points—pearl or nonpareil. I'm not jealous like you, Hilmar. Minion, with seven points (7 × 0.376 mm), would be quite suitable for conjuring a white margin between my discoveries and the pearl and nonpareil of my predecessors' findings. This is an unresearched historical area, terra incognita. I'd keep all typefaces of over seven points for myself—brevier for unproven assumptions, bourgeois for the half-proven, and long primer for the proven ones. Eight, nine, and ten points, respectively. Cicero, with its twelve points, would be reserved for the development of my general ideas, constructed on the basis of others' diamond, pearl, and nonpareil as well as my long primer, with cautious use of the half-proven hypotheses set in bourgeois. These ideas, in close contact with the philosophy of history, would suggest a method that my successors could use to boldly set off into the dark regions of minion. Numerous geographic maps would be appended. In black and white, of course—in history, colors produce a frivolous effect. I should also think about the lithographs. And then there are the acknowledgments. I'm indebted to Mr. so-and-so, who with generous scholarly solidarity (in spite of his attempts to hamstring me in the meantime) granted me access to his precious. . . . An exhaustive bibliography. An index. And on the jacket—me, with a pipe between my teeth. Price: 20 DEM.

There you go, dear Hilmar, all of that could have been squeezed out of a barbarian prince, if only he had been the one sitting in front of me. But what of significance could be learned from a bureaucrat of the lowest rank, with an umbrella like a giant, black silken member between his legs? Such mistaken notions are removed with a footnote. I'll correct this error with a trip to the municipal building. I'll inform the authorities that they've made a mistake with Adam Trpković and that the monument must be given another name. And the whole history of the municipal file clerk will end there. But what does this action refute and what does it strengthen? Where are the references? Without references there's no history, no scholarship.

What would Adam have mentioned in his defense, had he cared about it? (We've seen, however, that he didn't.) Münch's REMARK, which made his unimpeded ENTRY into our prison possible? The wind, which picked up just as he was passing under the Italian flag with his open umbrella? The "umbrasoll," that black, winged monstrosity? His children? His family? His homeland? His age? Innocence? Stupidity?

And what evidence could I present regarding his postmortem transformation, if I wanted to avoid any involvement in his fate? The fact that I'm a foreigner and that none of this is any concern of mine? (But nevertheless, I was born in this country and this language was at one time more familiar to me than my native German.) An identification process that in any case will erase Adam's name from the monument and blend him into a mixture of anonymous courage accessible to everyone? My preoccupation with the conversion of the Slavs in the Oder and Vistula river basins? The impossibility of supporting my claim with the long primer typeface of proof? (Both Steinbrecher and Rotkopf are dead. And the worker the monument should have been erected to is also dead.) What would be here under A., B., and C.? And where are the references? Without references there's no reality, no history, nothing at all. Even death has references. How would the footnote read? What would be positioned underneath the text? A photograph of Rotkopf's pizzle whip? Steinbrecher's questionnaire? Lists of suspicious persons, written in calligraphic script? A description of a men's umbrella of unusual size—a silk canopy that disrespected the Italian flag, mocked Steinbrecher's Gestapo world, and finally, like a black angel or a parachute drifting up in the wrong direction, carried Adam Trpković up into the heavens like the new Messiah of a tormented humanity—a weak, crazy, irresolute, unhappy Messiah—and carried him, I say, all the way to the hilltop above D., where he now gleams like some mysterious cosmic alloy? And what would the ibidems look like? One would suffice: See a basement of the Gestapo, September 1943. And further: Ibidem, Ibidem, Ibidem. Always the same thing: Ibidem.

Hilmar, you ask me where so much bitterness toward Adam is coming from? And isn't it a deceptive projection of dissatisfaction with oneself? It undoubtedly is. Both then, in 1943, and today, in 1965. However, that offers no relief at all. The partial awareness that I'm suffering less because of him than because of myself and the position I was put in doesn't excuse him in my eyes. Especially since he showed no sympathy at all for my predicament. To be sure, he didn't appear to care about his own, either. I can't find the right word to describe his bearing during those first hours of interrogation. Was he dominant, afraid, mocking, indifferent, suspicious, malicious, or adept? Perhaps the word "conscientious" would correspond more or less to the impression he made on me. Maybe "reservedly conscientious." It'll serve primarily to emphasize a certain assiduity for the situation, prepared to show itself if requested to do so, but capable of remaining in an unobtrusive, yet mobile state of expectation if its services weren't required.

He didn't ask why I didn't address him, what was expected of him, or why, after all, he was being held at all. Perhaps he himself also had Münch's professional respect for the REMARKS column in the protocol. Or was he simply mocking me? Or was he afraid of ruining the comfort of the silence with some careless intervention? As if, with the refined sense of the luckless, he felt a presentiment of a worsening of his situation in any change in the status quo. He didn't even get ruffled when this state of affairs continued into its third day. (In the meantime, I took the transcript of an imaginary interrogation to Steinbrecher for his examination every day, which will be discussed in the next letters.) As soon as Hauptscharführer Max led him in, he sat down on the chair and sank into a dull motionlessness, clutching that umbrella of his. At a set time in the morning and afternoon, Max would bring some "Turkith coffee." As he placed it on the table, I'd yell at the prisoner in an extreme, Rotkopfian way, or would icily Steinbrecherize over his head without any reaction on his part. Max would walk out nodding his head in agreement. He in particular "appwoved of energetic, tough meathureth." I'd pour some coffee for Adam, and he would drink it with no sign of gratitude, as an official part of the protocol, as something self-evident. Then I'd cautiously return to the minefield of the Questionnaire. Cautiously, I say, because the Standartenführer's mines were intended as much for me as for the file clerk. And he, that clerk, would continue to languish, wound gently around the handle of the umbrella-stalk like the tendrils of a grapevine.

For three days and nights, with pauses for lunch, trips to the toilet, and other needs, he sat in the chair for more than sixty-five hours, totally cut off from reality, except as in the form of black coffee and the intermittent curious glances he directed at me. Don't think that my intention was to torture him with that conveyor belt and force him to make some confession. The only thing I asked of him was that he sit in his chair and camouflage my battle with Steinbrecher. I undertook that intensive investigation out of necessity and for his own good. It shouldn't have been postponed. At any moment, something could have happened in the town, some kind of sabotage or terrorist attack, on account of which the clerk would be shot as a hostage.

I didn't feel compassion for him. I won't lie. I think I hated him at times. Perhaps that's not the right word. I don't know. He aroused my indignation, annoyed me. There was something going on between him and me. I found him annoying just as a scholar finds his day-to-day obligations annoying. This shows how much I had, in spite of everything, managed to protect myself from Steinbrecher's influence. If you've duly grasped it, Hilmar, Steinbrecherism necessarily included a high minimum of mental concern for one's victims. *Post festum,* of course, we might label it Jesuitical or inquisitorial, given its goal. But the concern remains a fact. I haven't encountered such a deep, intimate warmth for each individual prisoner with any other policeman except the *early* investigators in Stalin's purges, those amazing descendants of Porfiry Petrovich.

(STEINBRECHER: Love, Rutkowski, love for the prisoners is what many of you lack and what makes your investigations so dead and insipid, even when they're technically flawless. You can't stand your prisoners! If you don't hate them—you're too vain to give yourself over to such a feeling—you don't love them either. You barely tolerate them. Isn't that so, Rutkowski? As soon as you see them, you think: What the hell is this guy doing here? I have no use for him at all right now! But not only now—you'll never have any use for him. Prisoners only bother people like you, Rutkowski. They affect your refined intellectual digestion. Their predicaments annoy you. The struggle for their souls exhausts you. And do you know why? Because you don't value their souls. Because you only value *your own* soul. A prisoner's thoughts don't interest you. You're only concerned with your own thoughts, devoted to the creation of better worlds, a way in which a pig might be induced to experience a sty as if it were a palace, forgetting, of course, that for a pig a sty already is a palace, and that a palace would be a sty for it. This is the source of your professional failures, Rutkowski. Pulleys, inclined surfaces, and levers aren't required for a good investigation. What's required is a soul. One has to treat a prisoner as a doctor would, who, to be sure, isn't able to save him from dying but knows how to justify death impeccably. One has to act like a priest who can't give you forgiveness for your sins but can love you as he would love himself and by the power of that devotion reconcile you to your death. Rutkowski, you'll never have the satisfaction of having your prisoner request you to come after a death sentence has been issued, and weep for you. For you and no one else. Yes, Rutkowski, those people didn't request to see their mothers, wives, or sons, but wanted to see me, their investigator! Because I alone after all those months of interrogation could understand the language they were speaking!)

You're probably wondering why, if I had no love for Adam, I chose him for a battle with Steinbrecher. In those days I wasn't in any kind of paroxysm of atonement. I could have waited a few days. It would have even been logical for me to wait, logical considering my battle plan. The smallest mistake in Adam's case could have rendered me unable to act when our basements were filled with the real culprits, my secret allies, my brothers in arms. From that perspective, trying to save Adam was a tactical mistake, a completely unjustified fit of sentimentality, and so it's not surprising that it ended in total disaster.

I personally think that two factors were decisive for my choice: my intellectual vanity, which had been wounded by Steinbrecher's Questionnaire, and that umbrella. Above all the umbrella. I'll write to you about it this evening.

KONRAD

■ □ ■ □ ■

LETTER 14

THE WICKED BIOGRAPHY AND MALEFACTIONS OF A MEN'S UMBRELLA, OR *LOGICAL INVESTIGATIONS*

The Mediterranean Coast, 21 Sept. 1965

Dear Hilmar,

Regarding Kierkegaard's problem of *Entweder-Oder,* Leon Shestov writes in the *Revue philosophique* about the despair that seizes us upon the realization of the relativity of human knowledge and the fact that even a truth like "Socrates was poisoned" can be refuted. And that, consequently, even our basic truths will one day lie in ruins. Either "Socrates was poisoned" is an eternal truth that binds all sapient beings, or we're all insane. There's no middle ground. Kierkegaard's *Entweder-Oder* poses a threat: Either the eternal truths discovered by reason in the immediate facts of consciousness are only transitory and thus all the horrors of existence (the sufferings of Job bewailed by Jeremiah, which we can discern amid the storms of the Apocalypse) will vanish through the will of the Creator (just as our nightmares fade when we've woken up), OR WE'RE LIVING IN ONE CRAZY WORLD.

"The obvious cannot be saved by the principle of contradiction," Shestov writes. "When, tormented by a monster in a dream, a person feels that he is unable not only to defend himself but even to move a muscle, salvation appears with the contradictory awareness that A NIGHTMARE IS NOT REALITY, that it is only a passing illusion. That awareness is contradictory, because it presupposes that the sleeper believes it true that the state of awareness of the one dreaming is not truthful; thus, this is a matter of a truth that is self-destructive. In order to free himself from the nightmare, one must reject the principle of contradiction, on which in a state of waking all obvious things are based: He must make a great effort and wake himself." Shestov concludes: "Thus philosophy, as I told Husserl, is not a reflection (*Besinnung*) that prevents us from waking up, but a struggle (*Kampf*)." And then he advises: "We are not condemned to make gods from stones and to preach merciless cruelty toward others, as proclaimed by Nietzsche in one of those moments when reason was in control of him. In the overall economy of human spiritual activity, attempts TO SURMOUNT THE OBVIOUS have an enormous, albeit hidden meaning. BUT IN ORDER TO FIGHT AGAINST THE OBVIOUS, WE MUST CEASE 'EXAMINING' AND 'CALCULATING'."

Consistent with my conviction that in history as such, as well as in the stories of individual lives, some Idea always precedes Actions and Deeds, I began the following story, which could have been called THE BIOGRAPHY OF A MAGIC UMBRELLA, with Shestov's desperate call to arms against the obvious—the nightmare that oppresses all our hopes of salvation. You'll have to uncover the remaining correspondences between my philosophical positions and the events described on your own.

One of those treacherous elements of the obvious was Adam's umbrella and the absurdity of its presence in the cells of the Gestapo. I've already told what it meant to us, and especially to me. But what it did mean to him, Adam? Was it the eccentric signum of some Mediterranean oddball? A habit of unknown origin? A souvenir he never parted with? A bequest? A subconscious banner of the rebellion against Order, for which he himself had slaved away with calligraphic mastery, penning his intricate, flourished initials? The song of a refined soul held down by steel spreaders? Or simply protection from the rain and sun?

In order to test its obviousness to a certain degree at least, I decided to ask about it. Although the umbrella's owner could have surely told me the most about it, he wasn't the one I approached to find out more. I was afraid of receiving some answer that, when entered into the Transcript, might have done Adam some harm. Therefore, I paid a visit to his family, justifying this breach of procedure to Steinbrecher with my desire to get a firsthand impression of the conditions in which the file clerk's alleged criminal activity took place, and—if logic would serve me right—to find the necessary accomplices there. The Standartenführer praised my initiative, availing himself of the opportunity to develop a few general ideas about complicity as such.

(STEINBRECHER: Complicity is a logical element of crime. The existence of a network of accomplices is inherent to every criminal act. Only a lunatic works alone. An accomplice is, moreover, an irreplaceable syllogistic link that holds our premises together and makes it possible for a single logical formula to encompass the entire logical space of a crime. Without accomplices, crimes would be isolated geometric points incapable of forming any kind of functional network. Organized crime as a higher form of criminal activity would be impossible. Conspiracies would be precluded. Espionage would be impossible to carry out. Acts of sabotage and terrorism would be limited to isolated and illogical acts by the mentally ill. The consequences for investigative science would be immeasurable. The police would become a medical team, and prisons insane asylums.

RUTKOWSKI'S COMMENTARY: I wonder what the Standartenführer would say if he were alive and could see such a transformation taking place. Not only resistance against the deified order of things, but any ideological deviation therefrom is nowadays treated as a spiritual or mental illness and is accordingly treated with drugs, shock therapy, and procedures of psychological adaptation. I don't deny that there's some truth in such a conception, which has its foundation in certain philosophical and scientific hypotheses. An act that ignores the instinct for self-preservation can't be the mode of behavior of any intelligent human being. It's illogical to put oneself at risk. On the other hand, removing oneself from what is generally accepted, seeing things *differently* than everyone else sees them doesn't so much indicate a breakdown of one's social orientation as a disorder of the sense of sight, that is of those centers of the brain that control it. I've never dealt with this personally, nor do I know much about it. It seems to me, however, that Steinbrecher's theory of the necessity of complicity as a logical element of crime has been largely discarded. Perhaps it was determined that its consistent implementation would require the execution of everyone in the world. With the aid of the logical application of this theory, one country was at one time well on the way to exterminating all its inhabitants. The shortcomings of such a practice became evident when the heads of all the giant conspiracies against the state became the chiefs of police who in the meantime had mercilessly persecuted them, and when the presence of the crime was discovered in the anteroom of the head of state. Accusing him of a conspiracy against himself was a consistency in logic that a feeble human mind could not rise to. A compromise was found in the rejection of any form of complicity. Crime rings were disbanded overnight. Conspiracies sank into the bloody darkness of history. Crime again became humanly individual and self-sufficient, and as such it no longer demanded drastic punitive measures or collective revenge. It could now be treated as a simple dislocation of the brain from its social environment, like insanity.)

Thus, I visited Adam's wife. And here's what I learned from her:

Adam had never carried an umbrella. He didn't like to have to hold anything heavy in his hands. They had been created for the light handle of a pen, for old-fashioned goose quills. In rainy weather, he went around wearing a stiff hat and held an unfolded newspaper over that. Moreover, it wasn't more than about a hundred meters from his house to the Municipal Building. So the umbrella hadn't always been Adam's.

However, one night right around the eve of All Souls' Day, he came home late, long after midnight. He was drunk, which was rare for him. He was carrying a men's umbrella in his hands. It was large, as if it didn't belong to a man. It had a coarse, unfinished handle, which Adam tried to varnish. However, the varnish didn't take to the handle. The umbrella refused to submit to any kind of change. The way in which he came into possession of it was strange. He told his family about this when he came out of his stupor—because he wouldn't admit to being drunk. He hadn't had anything to drink at his friend's place, where he had spent the evening. But what had intoxicated him, he couldn't say. In any case, he didn't remember anything from the moment when the door of his friend's house closed behind him to the moment when his wife met him at their doorstep. It was hardly half a kilometer from one house to the other, but it had nevertheless taken Adam several hours to cover that distance. Where had he been during that time? How had he gotten lost, if that can happen to a local? He said it had been raining. However, it hadn't. The sky had been clear. He said he went through some sort of forest. That was also impossible. There wasn't any forest in the center of the town. And the surrounding countryside was nothing but karst, with an occasional olive tree or conifer here and there. He found the umbrella leaning against an oak tree (oak trees aren't found anywhere in the area either). Some traveler had obviously lost it. Adam asked around afterward, but the umbrella didn't belong to anyone he knew. It was concluded that some fairly tall foreigner had forgotten it in the city park, which the clerk, under the spell of drink, mistook for a forest. The case was forgotten, and Adam grew accustomed to the umbrella, so much that he didn't part with it. This continued right until the silk of the canopy was torn. Up until then there was nothing bad about the umbrella. The next day Adam wrapped up the umbrella and gave it to his son to take it to be repaired. When the repairman unwrapped the package, he found no hole in the silk, and that there had never been one. Adam stubbornly claimed that he had seen the hole with his own eyes, and even poked his index finger through it. No one believed him. Even the most painstaking examination failed to turn up any signs of patching. Thus, the umbrella regenerated lost tissue like a lizard and provoked misunderstandings for the first time in the family, which had until then lived quite harmoniously.

So far everything appeared to have an explanation. The story of wandering through a forest that didn't exist for anyone else, in rain that hadn't been falling for anyone else was a consequence of getting drunk, which the file clerk was ashamed to admit to. The hole in the silk, though unsettling, could also be explained as a hallucination, especially if it could be proved that Adam drank in secret.

From that evening onward, Adam's life took a fairly troublesome course. His health suddenly took a turn for the worse, though there was no reason for it. One of his sons drowned while fishing.

His chances for promotion, until then good, were unexpectedly ruined. In the words of his wife, domestic squabbles became more frequent—arguments about nothing. All the troubles involved the umbrella. Adam's health was adversely affected, because he tripped over the umbrella and broke two ribs. Their son had had the umbrella with him when he drowned. The waters washed the umbrella up on the shore, but not their son. And finally, the umbrella had indirectly caused his exclusion from the blanket promotions in the municipality. In an argument with the archivist, who was also the nephew of the mayor, regarding inappropriate remarks about Adam's transcripts, our clerk nudged him in the chest with the umbrella. Any other umbrella would hardly have soiled the man's shirt, but this umbrella left a bloody stain. And the wound got worse. Later the young man recovered, but the temporary suspension automatically resulted in Adam's exclusion from the promotion list.

I found the whole story to be exaggerated, and the link between the umbrella and Adam's troubles to be purely coincidental. His wife didn't share that opinion. She pointed out his arrest. If he hadn't been carrying the umbrella in his hands, he would have saluted the Italian flag. I reminded her that it had been raining. I know—she said—but he wouldn't have had to grip any other umbrella with both hands. Thus, in the eyes of his rather simpleminded wife, the umbrella was a scapegoat to be blamed for all the domestic problems that befell his house and family.

As for myself, Hilmar, I didn't find that all this in and of itself cast suspicion on the umbrella. The wind was much more responsible, but no one was accusing it of anything. The mayor's nephew hadn't been injured by the tip of an evil umbrella, but by the file clerk's overreaction, which had been provoked by an insult to his professional dignity. Blaming the umbrella for those two ribs while disregarding the clerk's poor eyesight and his secret alcoholism was truly unjust. Adam had tripped and fallen due to his own clumsiness. As for his son, he'd have drowned no matter what, with or without the umbrella. And Hilmar, isn't it natural that a current is more likely to wash up an object weighing a kilogram than one weighing sixty? And as for the family squabbles, need one even seek any reasons for them at all? Everything had a natural explanation, which, however, no one cared for.

The family's hostility toward the umbrella went so far that they claimed that there really had been a hole in the canopy, but that its real owner, the devil, had patched it overnight. Suddenly it was a hellish umbrella, a gatherer of woes, a lightning rod of evil. It was no wonder that Adam did everything to get rid of it. At first he wanted to sell it. There were no takers. No one needed an umbrella of that size. The family saw the devil's hand in that as well. He tried to give it away, without success. If someone won't buy something, they won't accept it as a gift either. In the meantime, the umbrella's criminal reputation grew in proportion to the family's failures to get rid of it. Adam finally tried "losing" it. Now, Hilmar, look how simple folk interpret even the most logical processes as the influence of evil forces. Namely, the umbrella always made its way back to him. Its reputation as a tool of the devil was thereby definitively confirmed.

I, however, thought that the umbrella had become identified with Adam in the minds of his neighbors and other locals. No one in the city had such an umbrella. Was it then really strange that it was always returned to him? Unfortunately, common sense did not sell well in the Trpković family. During those days, his wife said, they were beside themselves with fear. They expected some sort of new trouble to strike like lightning out of the bewitched umbrella, which the devil himself had evidently left behind. A devil resembling an ancient god—a foreigner passing through D. He'd obviously determined that this weapon of his inflicted more evil in human hands than in his own satanic hands. Therefore, he maliciously took care of it, patched it when it tore, recovered it when it sank, got it back when it was lost, and generally kept it in an evil state, inciting its wicked temperament.

There was no other solution. The umbrella had to be burned. They thought that in a carbonized state, deprived of its fateful trident form, it would not present any danger. On those days, however, it just wouldn't quit raining, as if out of spite. It rained for three days straight. Adam's family believed that the satanic umbrella had its hand in that as well. If it could kill, abuse, and wreck promotions that had already been approved, why couldn't it summon a cloudburst? Especially if its own neck was on the block. Causing rainfall was no problem for it and was difficult only because it also benefited the crops, which no matter how you look at it was more than an insignificant dilemma for a satanic umbrella. Its instinct for self-preservation prevailed, and thus it rained without interruption. Adam's terrified family decided not to wait any longer. Burning it inside was out of the question—the curse would be too great. Adam would take the umbrella into the municipal building, douse it with gasoline, and burn it in the bathroom. At the door of the municipal building, Maresciallo Dagllione arrested Adam, on an order from the caribinieri colonel who had seen him passing under the flag without saluting and clutching his satanic limb with both hands. In his defense, the file clerk pointed out the inclement weather. You know how his story was received. Diabolical causality inspired each step of this vicious circle. Satan's choreography finally had its masterpiece.

I didn't comment on the woman's story, especially the fabrication— as I then believed it to be—about the umbrella defending itself. Neither did I comment on her claim that Adam's arrest was the result of a mortal fear of fire on the part of the handle and the silken canopy (the steel wires needed not be concerned) and that it was a crime committed in self-defense. To an intelligent person—I thought—the coincidence was obvious, if perhaps somewhat exaggerated or even morbid. However, it was basically natural. It was impossible to convince his wife of this. She was sick of the umbrella and its devilish, malicious acts, sick of its gruesome orchestrations. She took a lively interest in my investigation. You might think she asked about her husband. Nonsense. She asked all about the umbrella. I told her Adam still had it, but that I didn't know how it was behaving. I had not looked at it in that diabolical light so far. But Adam hadn't complained either. His wife was astonished. So you didn't take it from him?—she asked. No, we didn't, Ma'am—I said. It was only entered into the REMARKS column. What could I say?

Sir, I didn't think carrying umbrellas was allowed in prisons, his wife said. That's right, I said. Well, why didn't you take it away from him, why didn't you rid us of our misfortune? Hilmar, I was struck by the realization that, if the woman was telling the truth, we in the Gestapo had also been charmed by the umbrella in some devilish manner. I wondered whether we hadn't, as Gestapo agents, given wholehearted support to that umbrella-demon under pressure from a deep, inner impulse. His wife couldn't get a grip on herself. She kept repeating that she couldn't understand how he had been permitted to keep the umbrella. I don't know—I repeated—that's how it happened, almost despite ourselves. There you go—she said— that's the umbrella's way. It was the will of the devil that it not be taken from him! She implored me to save them from this misfortune. I promised to do everything in my power, and that Adam would soon be released. Who's talking about Adam?—she asked. You are, Ma'am, I said. I'm talking about the umbrella, she said. Save us from that umbrella, sir, take it from him, for god's sake, take that fucking umbrella, and then everything else will get back to normal. If we don't get rid of it now during the war, we'll never be rid of it. It'll send us all straight to hell!

What could I do? I promised to free Adam of that harbinger of misfortune, which had parasitically attached itself to his thigh, and left.

I went off, Hilmar, to continue with Adam's interrogation and to test the philosophical dilemma I wrote about in the first paragraph on my own skin. That dilemma had been torturing me since I had read Steinbrecher's Transcript from 1938, and went as follows: Either the truth of "Fröhlich is a spy" is eternal and binding for all intelligent beings, or I'm a lunatic living in a crazy world, in a nightmare I'll never wake up from.

KONRAD

P.S. Something strange is happening. As this confession progresses deeper and deeper into the regions of my downfall, instead of becoming more and more open, it seems that I'm more and more prone to inappropriate mimicries. After reading the letter again before dropping it in the mailbox, I noticed that the reasons I gave for selecting Adam Trpković as the medium for my battle with Steinbrecher's perverted logic and the Nazism he embodied are at the very least unconvincing. They lacked a motive that could, *bona fide*, be called technical, but for which, from today's perspective, I have no intention of offering any kind of justification. Somehow, Hilmar, it turns out that I chose the file clerk only because with him I could have attained the maximum result of *liberation* with a minimal risk. Almost the same result that I would have attained, with an incomparably greater risk, by trying to save some obvious enemy. You might object that my salvation would have also been more complete then. You're correct. At the time I wasn't thinking of that. I was in a hurry. The war was nearing its end. I no longer had much time left. I hoped I'd later be able to focus on more complicated cases, on groups of the enemy already selected for extermination, and then even on to whole cities slated for decimation. That was another of my intellectual compromises—perhaps the only one that might meet with any understanding.

■ □ ■ □ ■

LETTER 15

HOW ADAM TRPKOVIĆ GOT INTO BED WITH MISS LILLY SCHWARTZKOPF, OR *PRAISE OF FOLLY*

The Mediterranean Coast, 22 Sept. 1965

Dear Hilmar,

When asked what he'd have wanted to be if he weren't a policeman, Steinbrecher answered: a police dog. (Rotkopf would have certainly preferred to be a baton.) They had it easy. The Standartenführer possessed the vital predaceous instinct of an antediluvian woolly mammoth hunter. Alas, this instinct was completely stunted in me—partly by natural degeneration, partly by an ideological rejection of hunting as a way of life.[11] This is why the interrogations, those intellectual hunts and pursuits of terrified human souls, were always so tedious and exhausting for me. Especially those in which I simultaneously played a voracious hunter and also passed by a thicket where an animal was hiding without shooting it. The interrogation of Adam Trpković was to be a well-organized hunt, which, however, wouldn't bag any game. I didn't dare count on any kind of conspiracy with him. A few questions at our first encounter failed to produce any answers that might promise a future for our tacit cooperation. Adam had, in fact, already stared down an attractive path, at the end of which death was waving its pruning knife. He'd decided to confess to disrespecting the Italian flag as a premeditated act. He was betting that our rage at the Italian betrayal would excuse him. The poor wretch didn't know that such a confession stood in a logical correlation with every other crime against the state just as much as deflating the tire of an army motorcycle was correlated to the burning of the Reich Chancellery—just as inevitably as sleeping with a British agent inevitably leads to espionage.

(STEINBRECHER: Gentlemen, the world is a whole in which all its components follow logically from one another. All crimes are interrelated. When our mothers warned us that someone who lies will also steal, that a thief will also commit murder, and that a murderer will end up on the gallows, they were giving expression to a philosophical experience that the police can only confirm.)

If I'd allowed Adam simply to fill out Steinbrecher's Questionnaire himself, the Standartenführer's questions would have led him straight into the abyss. I think he'd have been worse at answering them than Fröhlich himself. Adam would've Fröhlichified the matter thoroughly. If you've read the Transcript of 1938, you'll understand what I mean by that term.

Thus, I had to neutralize Adam somehow. That was the first step. But how can the interrogatee be removed from an interrogation? He's in fact an integral, essential component of the interrogation. Along with the confession, of course. Without him, the confession is impossible. Investigator, interrogatee, and confession were three pillars, three caryatids with their arms locked in sisterly fashion, holding up the state on their heads.

The difficulty thus lay in the fact that Adam belonged to the interrogation as sand does to a beach. But he had to be simultaneously removed from it. If I wanted to keep Steinbrecher from directing it all, I had to be the one to do it. Adam's answers were going to be directed in any case. I couldn't violate his liberty more than it had already been violated. The differences lay strictly in the aims of the stage direction.

(STEINBRECHER: The essence of the matter lies in the stage direction, gentlemen. We direct history, but it also directs us. We each direct each other. We direct events, just as they direct us. Gentlemen, everything in this world is one more or less successful stage production.)

But before getting down to that, my conscience compelled me to make one last attempt, to carry out a test on the basis of Adam's false confession that his failure to salute the Italian flag was a consequence of his hatred for the Italians. Perhaps he would understand my signal after all. I was hoping that as a file clerk he had witnessed an interrogation at one time or another. Clearly, he wasn't a police clerk but an administrative one. Still, perhaps he'd substituted for a police clerk on occasion. It was a small city, that D.—maybe there had been some urgent case and there hadn't been time to wait for a replacement. And thus our Adam took the pen in his hand. And if by some bit of luck the investigator was even slightly Steinbrecherized, Adam could have acquired some experience. If he'd had time between all those calligraphic flourishes of his, of course. I cast a fleeting glance at the paper in front of me, as if I were formulating a question based on some document:

"Tell us when it was that you slept with Miss Lilly Schwartzkopf of Mannheim for the first time."

The question was crazy. However, its spirit corresponded to that of the questions Steinbrecher was going to ask him via the Questionnaire. Monstrous in its conception, my question reproduced perfectly the numerous and unknown realities the file clerk would be thrust into.

(STEINBRECHER: From the perspective of an investigation, gentlemen, the value of a question is not measured by the degree to which it encapsulates reality, but by the degree to which the examinee, in rejecting that reality, accepts some other, likewise fabricated but less hazardous state of affairs. The crazier and more pointless the question is from the perspective of all known factors, the more chances it has of eliciting a confession to something less crazy and more moderate. The question asked at this point is never the question we want answered. The real questions appear on the agenda only when the prisoner has exhausted all his strength and all his powers of reason answering the phony questions.)

I wondered to what extent Adam comprehended the principles of the subterranean world he now inhabited, where nothing is impossible and where, as in *Alice in Wonderland,* there are no obstacles to the logical imagination. Would Adam, according to the principle of the acceptance of a lesser evil, consent to go to bed with the Mannheim informant? And if he did (the image of the clerk getting under the covers while keeping hold of his umbrella was comical enough in itself), how would he explain it afterward? It would fall to him to describe and explain all aspects of a reality once he accepted it as his own. According to Steinbrecher, the investigator shouldn't interfere with this under any circumstances. He could only warn of inconsistencies. Even in a perfectly fabricated world, facts must be mutually compatible and everything must function logically. With the Standartenführer, Trotsky wouldn't have been able to hold conspiratorial meetings in hotels that had been demolished long before or travel on flights that were never entered in an airport's log of arrivals. The prisoner's thought had to cope with that new reality all on its own. That was the only way the reality could become truly his, not only a part of his story, but a part of his experience, as had happened with that Fröhlich, for instance, whose case was fairly convoluted. In particular, he hadn't slept with Schwartzkopf in reality. But it was logical that he'd slept with her; accordingly, he had. Moreover, subjectively, he didn't even have to sleep with her, in order for it to be found that he'd slept with her objectively. A subjective determination didn't obligate anything to logicality. The logical was contained only in the objective. Thus, if Fröhlich had objectively been able to sleep with Ms. Schwartzkopf, he did sleep with her. Given the circumstances, the contrary was quite impossible. The fact that Fröhlich, despite all obvious facts, had nevertheless not slept with the milliner was his own fault, a sin against logic that had to be paid for. And Fröhlich had confessed not only to that affair, but had described the details in all their astonishing perversity.

But what would Adam do? I repeated the question. He leaned toward me slightly, gripped his umbrella more tightly, furrowed his brow as if he were expecting the return of a thought rummaging deep in his past, and answered slowly, with a certain derisive longing:

"On the fifteenth of July, 1935."

Hilmar, this was too much for my nerves. Was he mocking me? Wasn't his answer laughing at the same logic I was trying to find an antidote for? I don't deny it, I could hardly restrain myself from beating him black and blue with his own umbrella. It wasn't pity that stopped me. There was nothing to pity in his eyes—they sparkled with the strange greenish glow of a distant carbide flame. It was fear that stopped me, Hilmar, the icy breath of irreality issuing from him and his answer. No, this guy wasn't pretending, he wasn't mocking our logic, perhaps he really was . . . THE UMBRELLA, I thought! That was its way! I remembered what Adam's wife had said to me about it. I knew what Adam thought about it. Everything was clear to me. The umbrella confused him. His worry and fear of it temporarily removed him from reality. The umbrella was to blame for his insane answer. The objective fact that this was only his imagination had no significance. In Adam's eyes, the umbrella was continuing its dirty business, pushing him toward death.

"Trpković!" I shouted. "Get your hands off that umbrella!"

"Why?"

"Throw it away! I'm ordering you! Put it in the corner!" He obeyed. The iron tip scraped angrily across the floor.

"And now sit back down and answer the question again: When did you sleep for the first time with Miss Lilly Schwartzkopf, the milliner from Mannheim?"

"I told you, sir, on the 15th of July, 1935."

"Enough! Shut up!"

I didn't allow him to develop his story. Hilmar, I sat there on that chair as if spellbound and developed it myself. I could imagine every turn, every nuance, every pathway of that crazy Mannheim story:

Sir, it happened sometime around Nativity. (Details, especially irrelevant details, lend even the most outrageous lie the appearance of truthfulness. It's mistakenly thought that no one would go to the trouble of fabricating such unimportant things. Thus, they must be true—and with them the main theme of the concoction.)

Here in D. there weren't any jobs. (In such logical realities anything was possible, even a government announcing the dissolution of its administration.)

So, you see, I set off for Germany in search of a better life. (Such set phrases and colloquial clichés are always helpful. They sound so damned authentic.)

Why? To provide for my children, sir. (Spicing it with a dash of emotion gives the tale a lyric note—caring for one's children always meets with approval.)

And so I find myself in Mannheim. (Why in Mannheim of all places? Why not in Münster, Oldenburg, or Bayreuth? We can't believe it's because of the powerful industry that requires Balkan labor. It's more likely because Miss Lilly Schwartzkopf lives there. Bayreuth would come into consideration only in case it were some of Wagner's granddaughters that had to get in the sack.)

It was raining. (In Trpković's world it was constantly raining. That lends his crazy adventure its climactic coherence. It seems that everything happens naturally—naturally considering Adam, of course. If days of good and bad weather alternated in his life, the lie would be obvious. It would resemble our lives and reality too much. However, the tale took place in another reality, in which it was always raining.)

I wandered through the city. I was hungry, completely soaked, miserable. I knocked on many doors, but couldn't get any work. (And what did you think, Hilmar? One can't just hop into a German lady's bed straight from the railway station, even if it's required for a successful investigation.)

I knocked on her door too. Whose? Well, hers—Miss Lilly's. And so she let me in to spend the night, to sleep in the cellar. (I was already afraid that we'd head straight for the bed, which was already made, scented with violets, and warmed by a hot water bag under the covers. Because no investigator who was even slightly Stein-brecherized would have swallowed that. That would have simply eaten away his transcript, like vitriol. Indeed, it wouldn't have had sufficient psychological justification. After all, Adam wasn't Rudolph Valentino. His charm was hidden and only came to the surface gradually. German women aren't whores, they're just senti-mental. That would have been like a guards officer in some screen-play riding on a goose instead of on a ceremonial sorrel horse.)

She didn't give me a job until the next day. Working outside. (Something had to be risked as well. He couldn't say that he'd been hired as a gardener. Indeed, what if the milliner lived on the sixth floor? The neutral expression "outside" was quite good. There's al-ways some work to do outside. And in addition, something really did have to be risked.)

And so slowly, it happened, I'm not sure how myself. (He had to reach the bed as gradually, as naturally, and as leisurely as possible.

He had to avoid giving us any grounds to suspect that this was a case of rape.)

And if in addition to everything else the question of the identity of the woman were asked, the prisoner wouldn't have any reason to worry. He'd be asked what kind of hair that *blonde* Schwartzkopf had. Anyone could bet he'd answer that she was a blonde!

I asked him spitefully:

"What kind of hair did Miss Schwartzkopf have?"

"Blonde hair, sir," he answered. "Just like yours."

And then my dear astonished Hilmar, it turned out that all things are really possible in this world of ours, even when they spring from Steinbrecher's Transcript—it turned out that from 1933 to her arrest in 1938 the blonde British spy and Fröhlich's concubine had spent her vacations in D., and so, tipsy after a fishing party, *logically could have* lured some tipsy local into getting it on with her as well as circumstances would allow on a boat out on the open sea where, of course, it was raining again.

So now, Hilmar, use your head and try to think of some rational meaning in life, which in the meantime is developing like a series of senseless and gruesome images.

"Herr Obersturmführer?" Adam asked.

"Yes?"

"May I get my umbrella? I don't have anything to lean on while I'm sitting."

I gave him permission. There was no use in forbidding it. The umbrella could evidently exercise its negative effect even from a distance. It radiated illness like uranium. That was a risky concubinage, a sinful union with the black soul of Misfortune, which its partner can't break even as he realizes that it will be his undoing.

Someone else had to do that for him. I'd decided to be that person, even before I began to compile the Transcript. As if I'd acknowledged its demonic power and wished to neutralize it before I entered into the contest with Steinbrecher. Moreover, I'd promised Adam's wife that I'd sever the mysterious link between her husband and the umbrella, that I'd divorce the clerk from his evil companion, though the reverse would have been more correct: Adam was a blind follower, a companion and slave to the umbrella guide, which was pushing him down the path to death. Imagine, Hilmar, that the white cane in the hands of a blind man is alive, that it has an evil mind of its own, and you'll get an accurate picture of the nature of their association. I sent Adam away, and ordered Max to confiscate his umbrella on the way down to the basement and then to bring it to me. Soon I was alone with the umbrella. At first glance it revealed nothing. A heavy, awkward, fairly primitively manufactured object that appeared incapable of thought, especially intelligent thought, not to mention conceiving subtle and complex plots against someone's life. But where did Adam think its power lay? Where did its criminal mind reside? The handle looked more like some kind of medulla oblongata of evil. The metal tip was clearly intended for combat. Proof of this was the nephew's injury. The silken mushroom was obviously only a decoration, there to lend the device the appearance of an ordinary umbrella. The snap and the strap weren't even worth mentioning. All that was left was the steel mechanism and the handle. If its power were in the mechanism, that would be an imitation of human customs and habits. The handle was the most suspicious. A massive, crudely finished crook that couldn't stand for any human product to be applied to it.

I took from a drawer a nipple cutter and a few pairs of pliers of various sizes intended for pulling teeth and fingernails. My intention was to remove the handle from the stick and, unbeknownst to Adam, replace it with a copy that Max had commissioned from the local carpenter. In this way the device would be stripped of its evil power and the umbrella, rid of its hellish brain, would continue performing the regular civilian duties it was made for. (Have you noticed that I was unwittingly acting as if I believed the superstitions about its origin and nature?)

I didn't manage to turn my intentions into deeds. Just when I'd gripped its neck with the pliers, Standartenführer Steinbrecher entered the room and I was ordered to return the umbrella to its owner. I was punished with a one-hour Steinbrecheriad on the subject of the vital link between a prisoner's endangered possessive instinct on the brink of his confession and a men's umbrella, alias *Regenschirm, parapluie, ombrello, zontik,* a device which ordinarily serves as a portable rainproof "screen" and is therefore called an *umbrella,* unless it's used as protection against the sun, in which case it's called a *parasol* (about parasols some other time), an ancient symbol of power and honor among the Assyrians and Chinese, preserved in that honorific function only among some African tribes. (Our Führer, on the other hand, never carried one; he wore his impossible waterproof raincoat, which made him look like a motorcyclist.) It's made of a wooden or metal rod, a handle that's often carved, collapsible ribs (now made of metal but in the sixteenth and seventeenth centuries made of fishbones), and waterproof fabric, today thick silk but in earlier times waxed canvas; it served as the model for the parachute.

That is how the umbrella got a hold of Adam again. Worst of all, however, was that from then on I began to doubt its worldly origin. Steinbrecher's unexpected appearance right at the moment I was preparing to take its life, an appearance that he gave no explanation for, unprecedented in our professional relationship, convinced me that something really was wrong with that device. I wasn't yet one hundred percent certain. The healthy, rational core of my intellect rebelled against the idea that in 1943, amid the tumult of a bloody war, a crooked umbrella was strolling through the world and increasing the general misery on its own initiative. The events I'll describe to you in the following letters were what it took for me to realize—like some Hamlet of the police world—that, despite all our education and spiritual perfection, the most significant mysteries on heaven and earth remain unsolved and will never be revealed to us.

I'll leave you with that depressing remark. Tomorrow we'll compile Adam's Transcript. I think that tomorrow I'll try to keep the promise I gave to Adam's ghost. I'll go to the City Building to get his name removed from the pedestal that he so hates to stand on. I hope I'll be able to do it. Though I should be glad that he's suffering too, by having to bear the weight of someone else's history on his back, the thought that such a jerk is the object of someone's respect, even if by mistake, is more than I can endure.

Kind regards from your KONRAD.

■ □ ■ □ ■

LETTER 16

STEINBRECHER'S GAMBIT, OR *THE APOLOGY*

The Mediterranean Coast, 23 Sept. 1965

Dear Hilmar,

Don't expect me to give you a detailed description of the birth of a police Transcript like you might find in a slow-motion film, whose sequential images—all the phases of the development of a confession—would remain ingrained in your memory long after. There's no time for anything of the sort. That would require a study including research in all areas of anthropology, from certain sub-fields of biology (endocrinology, eugenics, reflexology, etc.) to medicine (psychosurgery, psychiatry, the psychology of utterances, etc.) and even including some of the philosophical disciplines (ethics, logic, etc.). The limitation of my intention, however, has not only been conditioned by a lack of time and knowledge (a letter from Steinbrecher on this topic would undoubtedly be much more competent), but is also a consequence of the special conditions under which the Transcript was born. The extraordinary circumstance wasn't in the fact that I myself gave answers to the questions that I asked in the Standartenführer's name, thus usurping Adam's legal right to choose his own manner of defense. Such an approach is natural and lies at the heart of all police transcripts—to varying degrees, of course. In the more extreme cases, which can at the same time be considered the most perfect, the investigator literally assumes the roles of all parties concerned: he asks the questions and gives the answers. In such cases, to which this one also belongs, the prisoner is practically superfluous up until the transcript is signed. In less ideal cases, the answers are ostensibly given by the person being interrogated, but in reality he's only articulating the investigator's suggestions. The extraordinary character of this interrogation consisted primarily in the redirection of its purpose. The method remained the same—what was different was the aim. The confession, paradoxically and contrary to its own nature, was to free the prisoner of culpability, instead of boxing him into it. And then, no matter how logical, rational and lacking in sentiment the construction of the Transcript looked *post festum,* the work on its completion, over the course of several days, seemed more like a nightmare than reality. Hilmar, it consisted of an exhausting mental effort, worthy of that which a chess champion under time pressure puts into his analyses during the period between the interruption and continuation of a lost game. Thus, the report has to be as confused as the reality it is based on. (I'm not repentant, Hilmar. I exclaim along with André Gide, whom you find so disgusting: "O Nathaniel, if our soul has been worthy of anything, it was only because it burned more brightly than others!")

What exactly is a confession?

Various definitions are in circulation, but I'm only thinking of those that might be deduced from police practice in totalitarian regimes. A CONFESSION COMES ABOUT AS AN UNCONDITIONAL ADOPTION OF SOMEONE ELSE'S (FABRICATED, ARTIFICIAL) REALITY AS ONE'S OWN. In a sense, it resembles insanity. We consider someone who claims to be Napoleon Buonaparte to be insane, though we *lack* any empirical evidence that he isn't the little Corsican. Our belief is based on the assumption that Napoleon is dead, which is in turn based on the assumption that all people are mortal. The truth here is only deduced logically—there's nothing self-evident in this judgment. However, if someone claims to have blown up a bridge that we're crossing in the meantime, we still consider him a criminal. There's an obvious fact involved here, but it doesn't influence our judgment. (Aren't we fighting against the obvious? The obvious is a banalization of the unimaginable complexity of life and must be rejected. I'd like to see what the great Leon Shestov would say if someone tried to illustrate his call for the struggle against the obvious with our police dossiers.) Let's ask ourselves why it doesn't, why certain obvious facts *inevitably* influence us to such a degree that they cannot be disregarded under any circumstances, whereas others demand to be neglected. No one with any sense will disregard a pothole in the street where he's walking. No one laughs at the obvious ability of fire to burn us to cinders. No one refuses to believe the obviousness of the elements when they threaten us. The only dubious catastrophes are those that befall others. Floods on other continents can be real or unreal, but if I find myself in a tub tossed about on a raging sea, there's no chance of my acting like I'm fishing in the Caribbean. Unless I'm crazy. So how is it that some obvious facts can—and sometimes even must—be neglected? Someone else's pain need not be taken into account, no matter how obvious it might be. Someone else's truth, though axiomatic, is not binding for us. Someone else's biography is always subject to negotiation. All the obvious is expunged from the domain of a technically correct interrogation, and everything is made from scratch, as on the first day of creation. Why is this so? I think it's because we, according to our very nature, have set up a certain hierarchy of realities as well, because we've declared some realities more valuable than others, and introduced a racist order among them. No matter what kind of standard we adopt—in our case it's a social one—we've divided reality into useful and useless obvious facts. The fact that Fröhlich wasn't a spy, for instance, is evident but not useful. However, the fact that he knew the milliner Lilly Schwartzkopf *is* useful. The former will be rejected, the latter accepted. Fröhlich's new reality will be born in compromises between a series of disavowed and acknowledged obvious facts. (It's been observed, however, that the obvious is capable of being transformed and is relative. An obvious fact that's been rejected can be accepted once again if circumstances change. Fröhlich can theoretically be pronounced not guilty, if the obvious fact that some Mr. X. Y. is not a spy is viewed to be more suitable for rejection. Rejected obvious facts are embraced passionately whenever the investigator finds himself in what he's previously called "the logical space of the crime" but now calls a goddamned madhouse. An investigator who is himself arrested and interrogated will defend the same obvious facts that he has until recently been destroying. In the beginning, of course—later, he'll abandon them and become Fröhlich's accomplice.)

If this definition can be called gnosiological, the one that follows is ethical: A CONFESSION IS THE REALIZATION OF ONE'S OWN GUILT IN THE LOGICAL (OBJECTIVE) SPACE OF A CRIME. No act is in and of itself criminal. What makes it criminal are the circumstances. War, for example, is a circumstance that makes mass murder a heroic act. Peace is a circumstance that makes the heroic act of mass murder a crime. Circumstances occasionally also have a retroactive effect. The Nuremberg verdicts were legally formulated on such a retroactive basis. Something that in its time was considered patriotism was declared, by virtue of the fact that the Allies won the war, to be genocide. With a change in external conditions, advocating a political view that was at one time considered mainstream can many years later result in one's being called to account. I should add that this definition found no application in our practice, not in its psychological sense. We didn't require our clients to realize their guilt or agree in their hearts with a verdict based on that guilt, but rather to confess their guilt and thus technically enable the verdict to be reached. Concern for their souls was unknown to us, and the deeply religious spirit of an investigation was foreign to us.

Let's call the third definition logistical: EVERY CONFESSION REPRESENTS A COMPROMISE BETWEEN THE REAL AND THE POSSIBLE. This definition excludes a priori theoretically impossible actions from a confession. That is why Fröhlich was never accused of having planned to cause a solar eclipse on the Führer's birthday. Likewise, Fröhlich didn't reveal German marine secrets, but the industrial secrets accessible to a traveling sales representative. He didn't code his reports—that was left to the educated Oxford student.

The fourth definition is physiological: A CONFESSION IS AN ACT OF THE WILL CONDITIONED BY A REFLEX. You'll understand it if we cite Professor Pavlov and Standartenführer Steinbrecher side by side:

PAVLOV: A dog is placed in a dark chamber and at a certain moment an electric light is turned on. The animal is allowed to eat for the following thirty seconds. This is repeated several times. The lighting, which until then remained unnoticed by the dog, and had no effect on its salivary glands, by being repeatedly switched on in combination with the food, becomes a specific stimulus for its salivary glands. The light becomes a conditioning stimulus for the secretion of saliva. The glands will secrete saliva even when the light isn't followed by an opportunity to eat.

STEINBRECHER: A prisoner who refuses to confess is asked a question, and then the light in the room is switched off. The prisoner is beaten for the next few minutes. This is repeated several times, until a confession is extracted. Later the prisoner will secrete confessions even when only the light is switched off.

And since we're already on the subject of Steinbrecher, here too is one of his personal definitions, which I'd call a technical-lyrical one: A CONFESSION IS A LOGICAL PEARL THAT IS GAINED BY CONSTANT IRRITATION OF THE SAME AREA OF A PERSON'S CONSCIOUSNESS. (Based on the principle according to which a pearl is produced by inserting a foreign object into the muscle of an oyster.)

The mention of chess a little while ago gives me an idea about how to make this story easier for me to tell and easier for you to read. Because the invisible struggle with Steinbrecher for Adam's head resembled a game of chess in which I had to make both the Standartenführer's and the clerk's *strongest* moves, I'll use this comparison to conjure up the birth of my transcript for you.

First of all I'm obligated to tell you what I was going to protect with the protocol. You'll see that Adam was an intermediary in a much greater gamble. As you know, I'd been given the task of obtaining a list of subversive elements from the mayor of the municipality of D., primarily of communists and Croatian separatists, which had been compiled before the war for the regional authorities. I was informed that the List had unfortunately been burned in accordance with the Rules of Procedure for State Archives in Case of a Hostile Invasion. The mayor's regret was so sincere that I had no doubt that he would have given me the List if he'd only had it. I reported this to Steinbrecher. I naturally didn't tell him that the adept Mayor knew a way to restore at least the greater portion of the List. The key was, as you might guess, in the man who had actually compiled the List—the file clerk Adam Trpković. The Mayor said that Trpković had unfortunately disappeared during the withdrawal of the carabinieri, so the List couldn't be restored. Although

I didn't inform him of the fact that the missing clerk was, helped along by Münch's REMARK, now sitting in our basement and that his regret was premature, I admit I was quite tempted to do so. I didn't risk it because I wasn't completely certain of his attitude toward the occupation, or whether he would inform Steinbrecher or the people on the List of my interest. (This indecision had severe consequences for D., but I bear no guilt for it whatsoever.)

All this meant that by saving Adam I'd be removing the lives of numerous people from danger, who would otherwise all be arrested and executed in one of Steinbrecher's exemplary stagings of the *Pax Germanicae*. (STEINBRECHER: I need bandits, Rutkowski. They get in other people's way, von Klattern can't even stand hearing about them, but I can't do without them. I have to give this town a quick lesson— a spectacular example of German retaliation, not pathetically beating someone to death in a ditch at night under cover of the drone of automobile motors. I need something like the ancient popular theater on the town square, some tragic *commedia dell'arte!*) My atonement would be greatly increased, based not only on some insignificant clerk, but on, most certainly, the significant people on the List.

Technically speaking, my task consisted of avoiding at all costs any mention of the fateful List when compiling Adam's answers. I hoped I wouldn't have to achieve that by making concessions to the file clerk's detriment. But at the very outset I was already prepared to buy up the safety of those people with some marginal sacrifices. If the immoral principle of the end justifying the means was ever applicable, it was in this case.

The White player was me, the investigator; the Black player was the suspect, Adam. In fact, Steinbrecher was White, with his moves sealed in the Questionnaire, and in Adam's absence I was Black. With this in mind let's call the variation of the sacrifice that opened the game STEINBRECHER'S GAMBIT.

The first question went as follows: WHY DIDN'T YOU SALUTE THE ITALIAN FLAG? The sacrifice was obvious. He wasn't interested in the answer. The Standartenführer didn't give a shit about the Italian flag. The pawn was sacrificed in order to open up a file for an attack against the opposing Black king, which symbolized the Great Secret. Black's mistake was anticipated: a move that would indicate a disrespect for the flag (calculated to elicit approval from Steinbrecher according to the principle of common hatred). The sacrifice was hastily accepted, and the offered pawn was taken. A lightning sequence of counter-questions would follow, which would quickly make of Adam a stock ripe for any kind of crime to be grafted onto it. (Disrespect for the Italian flag was logically transformed into scorn for Germany, the Germans and everything they stood for in 1943; the logical path from scorn to sabotage wouldn't be long now.)

The real question, which would lead to the main confession, was of course: WHAT KIND OF MEMORY DO YOU HAVE? If Adam had been answering the questions instead of me, he wouldn't have been able to resist bragging about his good memory. He would have exploited the seductive gap in the White pieces to dispatch the light figure of administrative vanity through them. The stray Knight would be surrounded by logical questions and taken out. The White Queen would finish it off with the following conclusion: IF YOU HAVE SUCH A GOOD MEMORY, THEN YOU CERTAINLY REMEMBER THE NAMES ON THE LIST OF SUBVERSIVE ELEMENTS THAT YOU COPIED WITH YOUR OWN HAND FOR USE BY THE REGIONAL ADMINISTRATION. The White Queen arrives at the crucial diagonal. Adam is seized with panic; he castles on the wrong side. To be fair, it should be said that he no longer has a better move. He has to admit that he remembers the list. Once he's bragged about his memory, a negative answer is now out of the question. In this game, the Black player was strictly bound by the TOUCH-MOVE RULE. The White player, however, wasn't bound by it. He could move his pieces back and forth an unlimited number of times. The White Queen would mate the Black King with an irresistable check, by saying: THEN WRITE THE LIST OUT AGAIN. The game would be lost in a wild, primitive series of rapid moves. The White troops would wipe out the Black clerk.

Fortunately for us, Steinbrecher didn't know of Adam's role in the compilation of the List of Subversive Elements of the Kingdom of Yugoslavia in the Municipality of D. The right opening wasn't chosen. The most formidable moves weren't made. A defense was possible. The sacrifice wasn't taken. Steinbrecher's gambit proved to be ineffective.

If we've called Steinbrecher's conduct of the investigation a gambit, my strategy would be most accurately termed RUTKOWSKI'S MOBILE DEFENSE. Black's only hope lay in a quick exchange of pieces in which the game would wade into the calm waters of a draw. In a tournament match with the Standartenführer, there was no possibility of bogging down the matter in trenchlike, positional complications. Because, as a prisoner, Black had no right to counterattack, and because White, by the nature of his color and investigative position, was completely focused on offense, the only defensive method left to Black was to maneuver freely around the board. The goal was to maneuver flexibly between the Standartenführer's forks while occasionally sacrificing a minor piece (that is, making some tangential confession from time to time) and thus to guard the main secret, personified in the Black King—the secret of the List of Suspicious Persons in D. The means were a maximal reduction of material and the removal of all pieces from the board, and, in turn, all questions from the Questionnaire. When the only pieces left on the bloody, black-and-red checkerboard were the two kings—the White King of the thirst for a confession of the Great Secret and the Black King of the Secret—the game would be won, regardless of the price that had been exacted for this draw, this compromise.

The main difficulty in my defense lay in the fact that I was forced to give answers based on a double foundation: they had to make sense both with regard to the Standartenführer's questions and to Adam's actual ability to formulate answers. They had to protect the Black King of the Secret, but couldn't exceed Adam's intelligence. Otherwise Steinbrecher would see immediately that this amateur player was being seconded by a master. There were areas of the board ideal for defense that I didn't dare occupy. A damned hard game, Hilmar, especially since it was followed by an analysis each morning. When the questions of one Questionnaire had been exhausted, and all the anticipated moves made, the game was stopped and I went off to a consultation with the Standartenführer. I had to anticipate his new moves beforehand and prepare the strongest responses. In addition to everything else, I had to choose which sacrifices to make, to choose what could be offered as a confession without putting Adam in a hopeless position. Too great a loss of material (making too many secondary confessions in order to postpone the central one) always led to the exposure of the Black King of the Secret and thus defeat. Worst were the fantasies of A WAY OUT OF THE SITUATION WITH NO LOSSES—seductive visions of something that's impossible once a person has already found himself in the interrogation chair. Everywhere on the board there reigned the frenzied trading of pawns, the Hunnic terror of bishops along the steppelike diagonals, the janissary devastation of the rooks along the ranks and files, the satanic mobility of the Queen, and predatory jumps of the knights resembling mobile gallows; everywhere the hellishly quick pace of the game was felt, under the icy shadow of a drooping flag; most acute of all was the terrible awareness that not a single move could be remade, not a single mistake corrected, and, once touched, no piece could be left where it was. The transcript was strictly governed by the principle *Pièce—touchée.*

The game is in full swing. My brain is working at a furious, exhausting pace. Steinbrecher asks a question. The White Knight moves—White Kd3–b4. What does he want to achieve with this move? Adam's bishop, which symbolizes Adam's intolerance of the occupier, is threatened. An admission of his hatred would lay the foundation for further admissions. (But answering that he loved the occupiers would be just as senseless.) Whoever hates will sooner or later back up his hatred with deeds. Does Adam have contact with the partisans? Was anyone in his immediate or extended family a member of the partisans? And what about his neighbors, friends, colleagues? It's enough to find just one man among the bandits whose contact with Adam is more than accidental, and then logic will swing into action. Adam worked in the municipal government. The municipal government assisted us in requisitioning property. Accordingly, the municipality was informed of the needs of the German army. Its strength could be calculated according to the level of those needs. Had Adam informed the partisans of that strength? Of course he had. If he could have gotten at any information, he had. If he could have passed it on to the woods, he'd done that, too.

Did Adam hate us? I don't think so. He feared us, scorned us perhaps, but he didn't hate us. He simply didn't have the courage for that. However, it was logical for him to hate us. Or do you think that a conqueror can be loved? Because we Germans in the Geheime Staatspolizei were in this respect the victims of a split, dichotomous (I might say even schizophrenic) logic, Hilmar. Proclaiming the New Europe to be Leibnitz' best of all possible orders, logically we'd have expected everyone to love us. That was what we thought as good Germans. However, as good policemen we knew that no one could love us, because that would have been illogical, given the premise that our enemies must have thought the New Europe to be the worst of all possible worlds. Thus, Adam could only hate us. And he had to actualize that hatred. He carried out that necessary actualization by spying for the partisans, by delivering to them reports with calligraphic flourishes at the beginning of every paragraph.

During the opening, it had to be kept in mind that Steinbrecher might find it profitable to exchange pieces, to trade one of his more severe charges for a lesser confession, to exchange a rook for a bishop, or a bishop for a pawn. What he needed were those initial confessions, even the most insignificant. Just a small step into a new reality, existing or imagined. The prisoner had to find his way around in it. Everything there was unfamiliar to him. One couldn't expect him to undertake some long and distant journey in that strange wonderland. Let him take a look around first—let him first get into bed with Miss Lilly Schwartzkopf. He has time to become a spy right up to the end. In the meantime, let's get warm between the legs of the divorcée. When we get used to the love of a woman whom we've never even seen, it'll be easier one night between two coituses to sign up with the British intelligence service, or any other, for that matter.

Thus, my dear Hilmar, I've been sitting for hours and making Adam's moves for him. He's sitting across from me and dozing, even snoring. Yes, Hilmar, he's SNORING! His head keeps knocking against the umbrella handle. The handle wakes him up; he opens his eyes. He gives me an innocent look. He smiles loyally. He earnestly requests permission to return to his cell. He hasn't slept since he doesn't know when. And he's not needed here anyway, no one's asking him any questions. Logic is taking care of everything quite nicely. Otherwise, couldn't someone put a "small box-spring mattress" on the floor for him?

I imagine Steinbrecher listening to this statement. I'm losing my composure. Blind with exhaustion, fear, and thought, I stagger up to him unaware of what I'm doing—on my honor, Hilmar—and slapped him across the face. A small box-spring mattress? What a jerk! The blow is weak, symbolic—it doesn't even knock off his pince-nez. And I'm trying combinations the whole time . . . White Ra3–b3; Black Kf4–d5. I want to remake my move. The rules don't allow it. The answer is recorded. But there were so many better ones! That jerk broke my concentration. As if I'm not tired as well! And how many great answers have I let slip by simply because that idiot isn't up to them?! I hate him, Hilmar! I feel an icy aversion for him, for that representative of a mediocrity that outlives all historical and biological catastrophes.

(Adam was tangible proof of the failure of Darwinism and Nietzscheanism. Because what's the meaning of Darwin's theories of the survival of the fittest and the strongest, or of Nietzsche's poetry about the same issue, in light of Adam's existence? In light of the fact that the most foul-smelling dung beetle will as a species outlive the fiercest wild animal, in light of the stunning truth that the more powerful, intelligent, strong, and better animals and people are, the fewer chances they have of surviving. What survives is a mediocrity that spawns. The extreme specimens disappear.)

The last question for today. I'm satisfied, as much as I can be. We haven't lost a lot of material. We bore up well. We made only the absolutely necessary confessions. Oh God, what a pace that was:

Did you keep records of the requisitions?—Records of the requisitions weren't kept. Did you memorize any of the requisition numbers?—I didn't memorize any of the requisition numbers. How is it possible that you didn't memorize any of the requisition numbers?—I'm too old to remember requisition numbers.

Behind all of this was Fröhlich, standing there like a dejected phantom with his black briefcase. Fabric samples in his briefcase, on his lips an incessant *No, I didn't!* Did you . . . ? —No, I didn't! Did you . . . ? —No, I didn't! Did you . . . ? —No, I didn't! But didn't you nevertheless . . . ? —Yes, I did! Yes, I did, as a matter of fact! And what use were all those hundred NO, I DIDN'TS, what use were the parenthetical remarks by Rotkopf's pizzle-whip, the blows and twisting shoulder joints to unprecedented angles, when that YES, I DID came out in the end? It was spoken because it was logical. "Yes, it was" and "Yes, I did" are always logical in the logical geography of police basements. "No, it wasn't" and "No, I didn't" are equally illogical. In principle, it's always more logical for something to have happened than for it not to have happened. If the reverse were true, this world would still be wrapped in animal skins and revolving around the Tree of Knowledge. We'd be in Eden, in the East. And hypotheticals always remain for remorse: If only Eve hadn't bitten into that damned apple! And once she had, if only she hadn't given it to Adam! And once she'd offered it to him, if only that blockhead hadn't taken it!

Hypotheticals, however, are of no use in reality. Reality occurs entirely in the positive and negative modes. Here at the Gestapo, of all modes of conclusion, the only one of any value is the positive one. The negative conclusions end up with Rotkopf.

At five in the morning, Max leads Adam out. Adam and his umbrella leave to excrete. As of late, the umbrella has been amazingly considerate of Adam. It doesn't trip him. As if it's dead, as if it had finished its work with Adam, and is waiting to be taken by a new owner. Adam is then led off to sleep. They inform me that he falls asleep as soon as his head hits the pillow. He even sleeps while walking, as if he doesn't care about anything. What's important is that we intellectuals are in action. While we balance out our relationships with eternity, he's got nothing to worry about. As long as we're atoning for ourselves with such endurance, the jerks of the world can lean on their umbrellas and snooze. The morning analysis of the transcript with Standartenführer Steinbrecher exceeds all expectations. He doesn't even give one of his famous lectures. He just nods. He's satisfied. I'm satisfied too, though I go to bed two hours after Adam. (In spite of all that, I get up two hours before he does.) And what kind of pathetic sleep is that, Hilmar? Adam's sleep is a mental lethargy that he sinks into. My sleep is a nightmare, in which questionnaires fly like glorious witches on broomsticks. Black umbrellas open everywhere and flap their wings like bats. The crazy music of pizzle whips echoes all around. Steinbrecher gives lectures. The ghosts of Gustav Fröhlich walk the gloomy streets of Mannheim. Lilly Schwartzkopf's legs open like a pair of clumsy, pale pliers. And in all that, from dream to dream, there's Adam Trpković and his evil fate, Adam Trpković waving the List of Subversive Elements. He'd like to offer it to the Standartenführer, but at the last moment I always prevent him from doing so.

And tomorrow, around noon, everything begins again. A pawn moves here, a pawn moves there. A pawn takes a pawn. A bishop takes a pawn. A knight takes the bishop. A rook takes the knight. The Queen takes the rook. There are now four pieces in the White Queen's belly: the pawn, bishop, knight, and rook. (Four confessions of medium importance.) Finally, the Black Queen captures the White Queen. (All mention of the list was avoided.) In the Queen's Black stomach there are a black pawn, a bishop, a knight, and a rook. And, of course, the White Queen. The White King finishes the feast. He takes the Black Queen and the black and white troops lie like brothers in his bloated belly. One night, at three o'clock in the morning, all that's left on the board are two weary kings. Adam's Great Secret, the List of Suspicious Persons, and Steinbrecher's desire to obtain some truly major confession. The flag falls. The clock is stopped. The game is over. It's declared a draw. I've beaten Steinbrecher. On his own turf. In the forbidden realm of his demonic logic.

And Adam? Has he stated anything? Yes. Adam deigned to make a statement. He complimented my handwriting. He said that, allowing for the bad lighting, it was quite good. Maybe in the future I could avoid making the loops of the letters "a" and "o" look identical. Otherwise—hats off. Then he signed the Transcript, page by page. Hilmar, that jerk signed MY Transcript, without even looking at it. The one thing he did do was to pen in, with his tongue between his teeth, one crummy loop on the initial letter of his crummy name everywhere it occurred.

Yours,

KONRAD

■ □ ■ □ ■

LETTER 17

A DEMONSTRATION THAT THERE ARE NO MINOR COMPROMISES, OR *A DEBATE ON HUMAN NATURE*

The Mediterranean Coast, 23 Sept. 1965

Dear Hilmar,

This morning I stopped by the Municipal Building and spoke with the mayor. I tried to debeatify and dethrone Adam Trpković. The mayor—the enterprising speaker with the affable Mediterranean manners from the unveiling of the Monument—was careful, who knows why, not to waste any of those nice qualities on our conversation. At first he was politely distrustful, if not rude. But then, when he had, apparently, finally understood me, he was a little kinder, but in the manner we use when we talk to—fools. Tomorrow, when I've regained my composure somewhat, I'll tell you how the mission ended (I call it a mission because I was summoned to action not only by my scorn for the clerk but also by his request) and how well it succeeded. For now, let's carry off the signed Transcript of Adam's interrogation to Standartenführer Steinbrecher, with pride in our hearts, to get it certified there at the empty desk, with salvos of logic flying back and forth across its polished surface like shells bursting over open terrain. In other words, to get the official seal pressed onto my hard won atonement.

You'll understand my pride. I've outplayed Steinbrecher. There are no more questions to be asked, they've all been used up. The depot of death is empty. No more moves. There are only the two Kings—the Black one and the White one—tired and dozing on the chessboard.

Of all the insidious charges brought against Adam, the only one we confessed to was having treated a wounded partisan relative in our house one night in 1942, so it's possible that, while attempting to dissuade him from his dangerous and senseless venture, we also told him something about the strength of the Italian garrison in D. It was a small but unavoidable confession, our ransom money.

Unfortunately, it turned out that there are no minor confessions.

My dear friend, I doubt you'll ever have to, and moreover I hope you'll never have occasion to come into official contact with the police except at traffic way intersections. Given your snailish life-style, your despicable indifference toward the realities of our world, and above all your mental cowardice, something like that hardly has a chance of happening to you. The most that can happen to you is being fined for walking across a lawn. But nevertheless, just in case, let someone who gained his first life experience in the offices of the police offer you some useful advice. The first piece of advice is the most important, in fact the ONLY advice: Do not, under any circumstances, admit to having walked on the lawn.

Don't let yourself be ruffled by the fact that you couldn't have reached a certain location without walking across the lawn. Tell them you flew, just don't admit that you walked across the grass. It's still better for them to declare you insane than to find you guilty. Don't worry at all about eyewitnesses, don't let the obvious bother you. Fight it. Why should the police be the only ones to resist the obvious?

Do what you want, just don't ever admit to anything. Remember: Nothing has such a thoroughly and irreparably disorganizing effect as the first *insignificant* confession.

Despite your promethean efforts to keep from sliding into the next one, it's clear you can't avoid it, after the first follow-up question. The admission that you were ever in Germany at all will lead inevitably to the admission that on the trip you visited Mannheim. The admission that you were in Mannheim will just as inevitably produce the admission that you knew Miss Lilly Schwartzkopf. (And do you know what that means?) The third admission will come by inertia. You'll eagerly get into her bed. You can bet you won't yet know that she's working for the British intelligence service—you'll find this out when you sign that you were very close. In the end, you won't even be able to know that in time, because you don't know her. And you never were in Mannheim. Perhaps you've been to Mansfield (England), Manhay (Belgium), Manama (Bahrain), Mankhera (India), and even to Manihika (a Pacific archipelago), why not? It's possible that you've even been to the Spanish town of Mansilla de las Mulas, in spite of the unreal name. But never to Mannheim. But are letters, those purely arbitrary signs, more powerful than absolute logic? Is the difference between Mannheim and Manama, although the former is in Germany and the latter on the Arabian peninsula, so unbridgeable—as if they were separated by an interstellar abyss? With today's advances in transportation? The exchange of people and goods? Postal communications? With the spirit of humanism that inspires us so much that it's manifested in the loss of the carnivorous instinct in animals? We're in the same dimensions, dammit! Aren't we then? Both places use the same letters. (Let's not forget that, according to the latest research, the essence of the world can be found exclusively in the formula THE ESSENCE OF THINGS AND PHENOMENA IS IN THEIR LANGUAGE—the essence of humans is in their speech, the essence of water is in its gurgling, the essence of a rifle is in its gunshot, etc.—so that we can reason seriously only within the field of linguistics, and we can express some final truth only in its terms.) Both cities have two *m*'s each. The three *a*'s in Manama to only one in Mannheim is approximately proportionate to the two *n*'s in Mannheim to one in Manama. So are we really going to split hairs on account of a crummy *i* and *h* with which, in terms of letters, the German town outnumbered the Arabian one? And here's what happens with a little help from linguistic philosophy: Following some internal logic (as no mutation is arbitrary), Manama acquires one more *n* and becomes Mannama, then Mannhama. The next thing you know it's Mannheima. The process could end here—Mannheima is sufficient for an intelligent investigation. As such a city does not exist, it's logical that it's actually Mannheim and that the prisoner is pronouncing the name incorrectly. (Please sign the Transcript here. Thank you.)

And so, there you are in Mannheim, although you're really in Manama, and we find you, your feet tired from such a long trip through the logical spaces of geography, going to bed with a designer of women's hats. In the meantime, you're getting somewhat used to this mode of unrestricted travel, this fascinating switch of words, this modification of concepts and change in meanings. To new interpretations of history. To the struggle against the merely obvious. You reach the comforting conviction that the small confessions you make are not only not harmful but also quite useful. To be sure, they distract the police from the main topic. (Never mind that you don't have one, or that you have nothing to hide. From the moment you make any kind of minor confession at all, you'll think you're protecting some great secret. This is fatal, because the moment will come when you'll really have to have one.) You'll be deceiving yourself, my friend: they won't be distracted by them. No one can ever distract the police from anything.

In the meantime, you're enjoying yourself. Of course, as much as you can looking straight into the glare of the electric reflector lamp and sitting on the hard chair they've been seating you in for a week already. You comfort yourself that you've thought out your little trick well. You've told them about some unimportant acquaintance who is innocent and who will surely get himself off the hook. These trivial acts of meanness were only a part of your tactics. After all, this higher goal requires one thing or another to be sacrificed. You can't make an omelet without breaking eggs. You can't make baklava without crushing nuts. Of course, it's always someone else's nuts you're crushing. That ought to be logical. It's always more tempting to reveal someone else's secrets than your own. Other people's secrets somehow always seem to be less important.

And so, my friend, you can accomplish all that. The one thing you can't do is to distract the police from their main goal. You can't count on them forgetting that you're a filthy spy on account of your patriotic negligence toward Manama, which you conquered in the name of the great German Reich before the Führer himself could

even manage to get there. You quickly realize that your "minor sacrificial confessions" aren't nearly as small as you'd hoped, that they're
anything but minor. That they are, dear friend, entire hecatombs—
a hundred bulls for the police feast. And that sleeping with a
German milliner, especially if the adultery takes place on our territory and not in Bahrain, costs you more than buying all the whores
in the local bordello. Because the police, my friend, aren't hungry
for your pawns, bishops, or rooks! They don't give a shit about your
Queen, which you're always trying to offer them! Chess is played for
the King. You've been protecting it with your psychological castlings
in vain, you've been avoiding any move that would expose it in vain,
your King will end up unprotected sooner or later. And in the
meantime, you've been playing your clever little tricks and combinations, mercilessly throwing away the minor pieces of your minor
confessions, which were the only thing that could protect your
King. Minor confessions can save you from major confessions only
if you don't make them—not even the least, most inconsequential
confession! None at all! Because now, you see, now you have no protection at all. The police agent correctly concludes that, since you
didn't try too hard to defend your Queen, you won't worry too
much about her royal spouse either. The deadly, checkmate questions will be repeated at regular intervals and will always demand
your surrender with the same persistence. There won't be any more
pawns to place out in front. You won't be able to say again that you
slept with Lilly Schwartzkopf. That pawn has already been taken,
my friend. Its loss has already been registered in the Protocol. And
you're suddenly aware of the significance of the pawn that you sacrificed so offhandedly. You realize you shouldn't have betrayed your
loyal spouse and slept with the milliner, not at any price. You especially shouldn't have changed the letters in Manama. Manama was
completely okay. On my honor, dear friend! You should have stuck
to that spelling. And if you cared so much for easy women, you
could have found them in Bahrain—those wouldn't have been spies,
at least. The minor confessions were therefore anything but minor.
BECAUSE, MY FRIEND, THERE ARE NO MINOR CONFESSIONS. Every
confession is a major one. Every pawn is important.

Does the realization of your fatal mistake stop you? Have you
decided not to give up even one more secret? Especially the ones you

don't have? Well, my dear, naive friend, once you've confessed to being a spy, do you really think you won't HAVE TO PROVE IT, TOO? You'll answer that that's the job of the police. Nonsense! It's the duty of the police to arrest you. Everything else in connection with the crime is entirely your affair. Thus, in the middle of the investigative process you'll be required to describe in full detail the military secrets you were gathering for the English, which, I believe, will be very difficult for you, because you're short-sighted and flat-footed and can't tell a mortar from a fire extinguisher. Don't worry. You'll get help. The sealed questions will contain all the necessary information. All you'll have to do is give them grammatical form. A great burden will be lifted from your shoulders—you were afraid that you'd seem uneducated and clueless in the eyes of the police, that you wouldn't be smart enough for them. Fortunately, as you see, the police will help you overnight to gain the kind of expertise that in peacetime it takes several years of training in a military academy to acquire. But it won't happen right away.

There is an optimistic period between the moment you resolve to protect each remaining pawn (and you don't have many left) like the apple of your eye and the moment you're again seized by a frenzied desire to sacrifice your pieces. Let's consider this for a minute. So you've decided that until the interrogation (it's only until "the interrogation" that people usually put up any struggle at all) you'll try to keep even the last, most insignificant pawn of your past—the one that was left on the very edge of the investigative board, on black square h4. You secretly hope to get a new Queen on that file. You imagine that your remaining pawn is some very great Secret of yours, equal to your phantom Queen. You sacrifice all your other pieces just to distract your opponent from that pawn and to get it to the opposite end of the board. You hope to win by surprise. In the end that will still be a victory, right?

Well, it won't. It won't be. As far as the police are concerned, your new Queen is still a wretched pawn, a trivial piece of information that doesn't interest them. In this bloody game, my friend, all values are fixed. There are no such "transformations," no secret promotions of pawns to rooks. A pawn is a pawn; a knight is a knight. Your trick didn't work. The police still want you to turn in your King. And he, of course, is no longer protecting your Secret. You gave away your Secret long ago. Your King is now only a bunch of names. Names and names only. Because the police don't need you. What the hell do they need you for? They've already got you. It's the others that they need, always the others. And some more of those others, all they need are some of those others. New players are needed. Someone has to be Black; White's existence depends on it. The Black sheep wouldn't be black if it weren't for the White ones, and there wouldn't even be any White ones without the Black one.

So your clever trick has failed, your twofold trick—to have saved face a little in your own eyes, and have told the police everything anyway. Everyone will cope with this dichotomy in his own way. You, for example, will see the futility of any further resistance and give up. You'll pull down the flag. (Sign the Transcript, please. Thank you.)

You want to return to your basement as soon as possible, to that shrunken world of the imagination. Nothing matters to you in your suicidal crisis. Since you're already dead, you vent your hatred on those who are still alive. You betray your wife, son, brother, mother, your friends. You throw unknown people on the altar of your self-torment—you are God in that virtual world of crime whose lightning strikes haphazardly, at random.

(Let's turn to science for assistance again. We'll call your condition *catharsis*. We have the right to do that. Freud made it possible for us. Breuer's patient was a cultured and talented young woman. But she fell ill while caring for her sick father, whom she loved dearly. She began to suffer from convulsions, inhibitions, and mental disorientation. Breuer—like any average policeman, by the way—realized that she could cure herself of her disorder only IF SHE WERE PUT IN A POSITION TO EXPRESS IN WORDS THE AFFECTIVE COMPLEX THAT WAS CONTROLLING HER. He put her in a state of deep hypnosis and let her tell about everything that was oppressing her soul. While under hypnosis she immediately revealed the links he was looking for. When we realize that this is the only way in which we can free ourselves from our dark complexes and subconscious disturbances, the fact that it leads us to the gallows becomes relatively unimportant.)

Now you hope it's all over and that you can go back to your underground world. You're wrong, my friend. The game has to be analyzed, the value of each and every move must be reviewed. Perhaps theory knows better moves. Maybe a better move was made somewhere else, in some other prison, in someone else's Protocol. The torture continues. You must repeat each move the way you played it. You can't change anything. That would open avenues to new variations of the investigation. But you didn't record your moves. The record book was with the White player. Finally, that is over, too. Everything comes to an end—everything except your torments. A kind of offer is made, which is usually accepted. And then you yourself become White, with all its duties but without a single right. The duty is to find more Black players for this round-robin tournament.

You're again overcome by a strict realism. The imaginary world in which everything was possible has disappeared. And the lost game doesn't hurt anymore anyway. A compromise has been found. Ordinary life may continue.

Pay attention to all of this, my friend, when they ask you whether you walked across that lawn. Tell them you can fly. Don't admit to having walked. Keep in mind that minor and unimportant confessions don't exist. Every confession is major. But in spite of nice theories, confessions must be made. Without confessions there are no interrogations. You'll say that a polite conversation is not an admission of guilt. But it is, my friend. Whoever speaks with a good police agent is already confessing to something. So don't say a thing. Be at least as smart as the prohibition-era gangsters were. Give only your name and address: Hilmar Wagner, Kutcherstrasse 17. Hilmar Wagner, Kutcherstrasse 17. Did you do it?—Hilmar Wagner, Kutcherstrasse 17. Did you?—Hilmar Wagner, Kutcherstrasse 17 . . . You can also request to see your attorney. (Though this isn't to be recommended; occasionally they arrest the attorney as well.) I want to see my attorney. Hilmar Wagner, Kutcherstrasse 17. Did you do it?—I want to see my attorney. Hilmar Wagner . . . It doesn't matter at all that you won't get to see him. (In the meantime, as I said, he's been arrested, too.) You don't request to see him so that you can actually see him. You don't want him—if you saw him, you'd have to talk to him. And talking is confessing. All you do is say the formula. Amen to that.

Hilmar, take that worker as an example—the one I've already told you about and will have more to say about, unfortunately. He didn't utter a single word from the moment he was arrested until his death. He didn't even give his name. Or address. He didn't demand to see his attorney either. The very salt of the earth. The eternal black stone in the Lord's tent. He didn't shout *Long live freedom!* And do you know why? You'd think that since he had overcome Steinbrecher and Rotkopf, he must have still had enough courage left for that. But he, that man, would have considered even that to be a confession. He knew: you either have freedom and no confessions, or confessions and no freedom. He knew that confessions kill freedom—even the confession that he loved freedom above everything.

As for me, Hilmar, if the police asked me if I wrote these lines I'd say that I DIDN'T. Konrad Adrian Rutkowski. Heidelberg, Scharlottenstrasse 123. I wish to speak to my attorney, please.

In the hope that you'll remember this, let's go enjoy the victory over Steinbrecher a little. At precisely eight o'clock we enter the foyer of the Standartenführer's office. We find Obersturmführer Meissner at Haag's desk. We're a little surprised—where's Haag, what's with little Haag?—we greet Meissner and ask what the hell is going on in the corridors. What's all this morning hubbub? Mornings the police are asleep. The night is their time. We won't wait for his answer because it doesn't concern us. We're hurrying to triumph over Steinbrecher. Nothing else has any importance for us. Everything else is an illusion.

The Standartenführer receives us at precisely 10:15, sitting at his empty desk. He's rubbing off an "illogical" spot on the glassy polished surface with his thumb. Then he stands up. That's his way. Words need space. A woman's face hangs discarded on the grassy green of the wall behind him.

We salute him and put the Transcript of the Interrogation of the Municipal File Clerk Adam Trpković on his desk in front of him. We give a brief, military-style report:

Seventy working hours of questioning. Brief interruptions for meals and psychological pressure, without the use of force. One blow. (A private matter, so to speak.) Covered the Herr Standartenführer's Questionnaire in its entirety. Established the rendering of assistance to a wounded bandit in the form of overnight shelter during the Italian occupation, but for reasons of consanguinity and not political conviction. A possible accidental passing of information about the garrison. On the whole, a matter of an insignificant municipal official who, as such, cooperates with us. Useless in any other sense. No grounds for proceedings, as the incident from 1942 was acknowledged as a sentimental error. Recommendation: release from custody.

The Standartenführer takes the Transcript, tosses it up slightly in his hand as if checking its weight, but he doesn't open it up.

Oh, we've foreseen this, too. It was clear that it wouldn't be simple. The questions were well formulated. How is it possible that they only produced such an insignificant confession?

Hilmar, the Standartenführer won't believe that all that's left on the board are the two Kings. He'll refuse the draw. He resembles a fanatical novice who continues to move his isolated King across the board even when all practical and theoretical chances for a decisive end have been exhausted, an enthusiast who, his eyes glowing and his jaws clenched in an epileptic cramp, holds on to the crown of his lonely King, his powerless White Majesty, and attempts with him and him alone to checkmate the equally helpless Black Ruler, the Keeper of the Great Secret.

Fine, we say to ourselves. We have to plod across the empty and senseless battlefield, on which no more battles can be won, for a little while yet. We'll have to hop from square to square for a while, as if from leg to leg, in place. Somewhere in the three-squared corner of logic. And then the end of it all will come.

And it did, Hilmar—but not the end I had foreseen.

"I can see from your transcript that your last interrogation ended at 3:15 in the morning, and that the prisoner was taken to his cell at 3:30. Thus, it was 3:35 when I visited him. At 3:45 I had in my hands the *List of Subversive Elements,* which Adam Trpković compiled from memory. Human memory is a deep well, Rutkowski.[12] You throw a stone into it, and you never hear it hit the bottom. But the stone isn't lost forever. There's a bucket and a pulley. Without the bucket and pulley of logic, we might as well close up shop. A meeting was held here at 4 o'clock. We didn't want to disturb you. You worked so much the last few nights, not without results. We'll talk about them a little more sometime. The meeting ended at 4:45. It was code-named OPERATION UMBRELLA: putting the enemy under Adam's umbrella. Meissner came up with that. I hope you appreciate the honor shown to your prisoner, Rutkowski. Preparations were made in the meantime, and at 5:45 the entire executive staff was in action. All our men left, one for each person on the list. The mayor led them—an agile gentleman who's known all those evil elements for a long time. And so I was left to think things over. And I thought about a lot of things. About you, among others. Remind me to discuss this after we execute your prisoner. You know, I actually wanted to release him. He did us a big favor with that List. We would have been powerless without him. But now there's no way I can do that. After your brilliant finding that back in 1942 he aided the bandits, my hands are officially tied, Rutkowski—do you understand that? Regardless of my personal sympathy for the man and regardless of the fact that he might burden your conscience. Because without your investigative genius, the episode with the bandits never would have come to the surface. All that would have been logically floating on the surface was that List. However, I can give you some solace. I'm not going to hang your Adam because he's guilty. I'm not yet such a puritan. I'm hanging him because of the numbers. The day after tomorrow we're going to hang three bandits who are impossible to work with. They won't even give their names. Rotkopf still has his hopes up. But Rotkopf's an incorrigible idealist. I know the type, Rutkowski, I've told you about them. They're all stone, with a little bit of political lichen and moss on the edge. However, I don't dare hang three people. That's a very unfortunate symbol—it reminds people of a historical injustice that people still complain about and that is also the reason why we're finishing off the Jews so easily. A single man would be a martyr, a legend, a murdered God, a future monument. Two men would be only two hung bodies. Three—I've just spoken about that. More than four would be a massacre. I don't care for mass murder. I prefer chamber music. And so that's why I'm taking your Adam. Four is the right number—logical, harmonious, closed on all sides. A quadrangle of reprisal. Am I boring you? No? Indeed, I can see you're having trouble standing up straight. Maybe you've got some internal problem? Don't take your health lightly, Rutkowski. You can see its importance from the fact that our boss Reichsführer Himmler is at the same time both Chief of the Police and the Reich Minister of Health. I'll be brief, don't worry. So, of thirty-nine people whose names are on the list, seventeen were located.[13] Twenty-two aren't in town. They're certainly in the woods. Let von Klattern take care of them; that makes more sense than reducing his front lines. Anyway, I'm not some goat that goes climbing around the mountains. My area is logic—logic in mental spaces. Of those apprehended, two resisted and were killed. In exchange, twenty-four others of varying ages and professions were brought into custody. And so the number matches the one on the List. Some kind of harmony between the idea and its execution must exist, right? Two of our troops were killed. One was accidentally shot by Haag. He himself received light injuries. He conducted himself bravely—he fired at one of our own men with no hesitation at all. The bandit escaped in the meantime. The formalities of their admission were taken care of quickly. Münch didn't enter anything into the REMARKS column. Everything was administratively impeccable. The interrogations began at once. This time, exceptionally, without an academic introduction. Our team is now working on this under the direction of Rotkopf and Freissner. I'm expecting the results any time now. Would you like to keep me company? If you feel like it, we could both reflect on an operation known as DONAR. Have you ever heard of Operation Donar, Obersturmführer?"[14]

As if at the signal of some demonic backstage director, Hauptsturmführer Rotkopf enters the office. His hand is bandaged. It seems that he's also been wounded in the raid, or maybe it's the consequence of a burst of investigative enthusiasm. Fortunately, it's his right hand, and Rotkopf is a lefty. He looks miserable; he's disheveled and sweaty, like the untidy carpet fringes that the Standartenführer hates. This time he has no comment. Rotkopf is the victim of his own idealism. The whole time he's been struggling with that damned worker. Steinbrecher shows discretion. He limits himself to raising his eyebrows.

"Well, Rotkopf?"

"Nothing, Herr Standartenführer."

"He didn't talk?"

"No."

"Not a word?"

"Not a word."

Steinbrecher turns to me:

"We'll have to turn to Obersturmführer Rutkowski for help. He got a good night's sleep last night. Though he has worked quite hard recently, and with brilliant results. Someday I'll show you his Transcript. It's a little masterpiece of logic. Do you think you're ready to take on that worker, Obersturmführer? To get at least his name and address out of him? Nothing more, just his name and address. Logic will do the rest. Are you *capable* of that, Rutkowski?"

"Yes, Herr Standartenführer."

"Then get to work. Remember: his name and address. Nothing more. Just his name and address."

I went to Rotkopf's office. A man was squatting inside, under guard, chained to the radiator. His face was bloody, like a Greek death mask. He seemed to be dozing. The floor glittered with the water that they'd doused him with. The room gleamed with a soft, Steinbrecherian green. It stank of sweat, vomit, and urine. I ordered the guard to leave the room. I went up to the desk. Next to a blank sheet of paper was Rotkopf's collection of instruments of torture. I picked one of them up at random. It was slender, surmounted at the tip with a lead cap, and its handle felt like coarse lizard skin. I didn't want to look at it. I didn't want to know what it was called. To myself I called it "the form." Holding it, I approached that other "form." I watched him, but could see nothing in him except a finite quantity of conscious matter formed into the three dimensions of space. Something that didn't differ *in any significant way* from the radiator it was attached to. I had to make lightning-speed intellectual preparations for what awaited me, though I knew that the outcome would be the same with or without them. It was necessary to reduce all definitions of man, which were so full of luxurious errors, to the one that would allow me to harm this one and go unpunished. Among other things, I had to reject my own definition, according to which man is A COMPROMISE BETWEEN ANIMAL AND GOD, between his two architendencies. Man had to become what he was and reject himself as a concept. Otherwise, I wouldn't have been able to do what I had to do. And if I didn't do it, my entire struggle up to then would have been futile. I'd never get another chance. I had to choose the lesser of two evils one more time.

Your name and address?!

Hilmar, I know that euphemisms won't help us get through this confession, which will give this heroic (in spite of everything!)

history of mine a monstrous turn. Marx said that history repeats itself: first it is tragedy; then it is farce. With me, even that was the other way around. It seems that its every date, its every event occurred once as a farce, and only later repeated as tragedy.

Your name and address?!

But maybe this wasn't a "turn" at all, in the real sense of the word. Maybe *this* is my true nature, which—in the form of a successful compromise between animal and God—roamed the world, knew Goethe by heart, read Schopenhauer and Nietzsche, played Chopin and reflected on the meaning of history?

Your name and address?!

In any case, I've lied to you, Hilmar. In my letter describing the unveiling of the monument on the height above D., I said that I knew the man whose likeness should be represented by that granite symbol. And that I knew *whose* face he spit into. I wrote that it was Rotkopf. It wasn't. It wasn't Rotkopf, Hilmar. IT WAS ME. MY FACE WAS SPIT INTO. The face of Konrad Adrian Rutkowski, Professor of Medieval History at the University of Heidelberg. The face of the author of A COMMENTARY ON THE RELATIONSHIPS OF THE ROMAN CATHOLIC SYMBOLS IN THE DECORATIVE EMBROIDERY OF THE CORONATION ROBE OF PRINCE MIESZKO PIASTOWICZ. The face of your sister's husband, your brother-in-law. The face of a liberal intellectual who thought he'd found a compromise between conscience and fear, between ideals and reason, between the will and the mind, the open sky and the underworld, heaven and hell, between each and every goddamned thing on this planet that might try to kick him out of his spectral bed of alibis.

There's not much to add to that. I regained consciousness on the leather ottoman in Steinbrecher's office. My uniform was torn from a struggle with my comrades who, as they said, attempted to pull me away from the worker. Bloody stains of vomit ran down my uniform, between the ribbons of two minor decorations. Rotkopf kept rubbing his bald head in amazement and repeating "My God, I've never seen anything like that in my life!" while Steinbrecher said in quiet meditation, "Nerves, gentlemen! Historically, nerves are our problem!" In my field of view, filled with the tranquil green of the Steinbrecherized walls, between all those animalistically godlike compromises standing around me, I could see, through the hazy opening of the doorway, the bloody legs of my man being dragged out by our soldiers to the police graveyard. And Hilmar, it occurred to me—were my attempts to save all those victims worth anything?

KONRAD

■ □ ■ □ ■

LETTER 18

SATAN'S EMISSARY,
OR *SIC ET NON*

The Mediterranean Coast, 24 Sept. 1965

Dear Hilmar,

The time has come for us to continue laying the current rail of this story, so we can reach our destination safely without fear of derailing and hurtling into the abyss of ambiguity and inconclusiveness.

Yesterday morning I paid a visit to the mayor of D., with the intention of informing him of the truth about Adam Trpković. I immediately recognized him to be the speaker at the unveiling of the monument. He received me with surprise, but stoically—more or less the way a healed leper reacts to recurring symptoms of his disease. After a few profound thoughts about the horrors of war and time as a universal healer—to which his contribution was conspicuously weak—I explained to him the reason for my visit, conscientiously but cautiously. I described in the most general terms how the file clerk was found in our basement, my efforts to save him during the interrogation and his betrayal. For the time being, I avoided complicating the story with the unfortunate worker. Don't think that I did this out of fear or shame. I simply didn't want to burden him with any unnecessary particulars. The fact that they had erected the Monument to the *wrong* man had to reach the mayor's brain unencumbered by any other details.

He rose from his chair, went to the window, and stared out at the summit of the height, where Adam Trpković's glowing, porphyrous eyes were staring back at him. A short while passed before he addressed me, without looking at me, somewhat absently, even bitterly, I'd say.

"So you say your name's Rutkowski?"

"Konrad Adrian Rutkowski."

"And you were here with the Gestapo Sonderkommando?"

"In September of 1943."

He went on talking as if he weren't speaking to me, but to someone outside, something that, though very distant, could hear him no matter how softly he spoke.

"Is that possible?"

"What, that you made a mistake with the monument?"

"No. That you're here and telling me about it. We're trying to forget the war and what you did to us then. We're receiving you all like welcome guests. And now one of you, and what's more one of those who were the reason why this war was harder than it had to be, comes to teach us *historical truths*. Is there any logic here, Mr. Rutkowski?"

"I don't know if there's any logic, but I know there's truth."

"Do you have any proof of this?"

"What proof?"

"The interrogation transcript, for example. Anything making it clear that Adam Trpković was the one who reconstructed the list of suspicious persons in the municipality of D.?"

I didn't have anything like that. In the withdrawal from the Balkans, one part of the Gestapo's archives had perished, another part was destroyed on orders from Berlin, and yet another part was lost to the enemy. The chances of locating the transcript after all those years would have been next to none.

"Do you have any witnesses?"

I didn't have any witnesses, either. Both Steinbrecher and Meissner are dead. Adam, too. Rotkopf never knew anything about the sources of our information. And Münch couldn't help out unless some administrative problem was uncovered. Only then would he remember something. But as long as everything went smoothly and according to protocol, he didn't care about anything. Of course, I didn't mention my hallucinations. You can't be mentioning phantoms when you yourself aren't even sure of their origins.

"So everything rests on your incoherent and contradictory, in short your unlikely story."

I was already prepared to admit this, when some inspiration—or the invisible Adam hidden in some corner of the office—came to my aid:

"Not at all," I said. "If you find your predecessor from during the war, he'll confirm it for you."

"We found him already," he said icily.

"Really? When?"

"In forty-four."

I understood. That was a fairly boggy area of the past I wasn't crazy about slogging around in. Confused, I said nothing, trying to figure out a safer path to my goal. In the meantime, the mayor explained to me how his collaborative predecessor was shot precisely because he gave us the List of Suspicious Persons and that this fact made my visit completely redundant.

"But how do you know it was him and not someone else who reconstructed that List?"

"We didn't know at first. At first we just assumed it."

"Just like that? You assumed it. And what was the basis for that?"

"Logic, sir. It was logical for him to have done it. It stuck out like a sore thumb. He'd been involved in the compilation of the List and had collaborated from the outset with the occupying army—it was pretty easy to figure out. The only people who came into consideration *logically* were the mayor, as the one who'd had the List compiled, and Adam, as the file clerk. Adam was hanged in front of the entire city after he was tortured—you saw yourself what he looked like. The mayor remained in his position right up to the liberation, obliging his people with several more such dastardly deeds. Would you really come to any other conclusion?"

"No," I said, "I guess I wouldn't."

"Of course you wouldn't. Otherwise you wouldn't have made it too far as a police agent. One has to think logically for that."

"I know," I said irritably, "I've already heard about that requirement. But still, as you see, even that omnipotent logic has proved to be in error."

"I'll have to disappoint you. That man wasn't done in by logic, but rather by the irrefutable evidence of his treason that logic merely led us to. Logic led to the evidence, and the evidence to the confession."

"I know something about confessions too," I said rudely. I couldn't help myself, though I knew that this way I was nourishing his indisposition toward me. I couldn't let myself be brushed off by that story that had been concocted for the occasion (I had to have some results to show Adam) or be demoralized by the man's open hostility. "You can believe what I say."

"I do. Our cemeteries are full of proof. And our municipality fared relatively well. Ours didn't lose more than two-fifths of our adult population."

"I'm sorry," I said.

"Get out of here," he said without anger, in an almost businesslike manner.

"So you don't believe me, and you're not going to do anything about the Monument?"

"Why don't you go down to the beach, Mr. Rutkowski? Leave our past to us, and you worry about yours. And while you're at it, think about the future, too. Because the more you think about the future, the less we'll have to think about the past. So long!"

"Listen, man, I'm telling you, that Adam wasn't any kind of hero!"

"And who said he was? He was just one of those who resisted the temptation to survive at all costs. Maybe other towns can boast of greater heroes, but we're loyal to the ones we have. No, Mr. Rutkowski, Adam wasn't a hero. Adam was more. He was human."

Ecce homo, I thought and left. And so last night I wrote you the letter dated the 23rd, in which I described my defeat in the "game of chess" with the Standartenführer, my failure to save Adam and my attempt to reach a compromise with death by unleashing it on others. I fell ill before the night was over. I suffered from a brief fever, the cause of which isn't clear to me. I assume my indisposition arose as a result of memories of something my conscience refused to accept, as a kind of reproduction of the swoon I awoke from on the ottoman in Steinbrecher's office in 1943. Apparently, the repetition of the constellation of people and objects in the letter of the 23rd resulted in similar mental consequences. Fortunately for me, the attack didn't last long, only from last night until this morning, and Sabina didn't notice my condition. Nor would I mention it had not Adam Trpković visited me during my delirium for the second time.

I was in the middle of a nightmare, when I was awoken by something cold and sharp pressing against my chest. It was the metal tip of Adam's umbrella. He was violently poking around at my ribs with it. He leaned over my bed and muttered:

"One more failure, huh, Obersturmführer?"

"I'm sorry," I said dryly. "I tried everything I could. Believe me, it's harder for me to watch you gleaming on that height than it is for you to gleam there. Unfortunately, the mayor had convincing arguments."

"The good-for-nothing," mumbled Adam. "I might have known."

"So you know him?"

"I knew him when he was still a complete nobody. I saw him for the last time at my execution. He was giving me some idiotic signals of reassurance, along the lines that he was with me. That all the people were with me! If he'd truly thought that way, he'd have climbed up on platform and let them hang him!—He wouldn't have just waved his hands. At the very least he'd have organized a rescue attempt."

"Faced with our security measures, that would have been impossible."

"Maybe. In any case, he shouldn't have been signaling to us and trying to assure us that everything was all right when it was obvious as hell that everything was all wrong. Do you know what that kind of thing looks like from our perspective? I mean, from the perspective of those who are about to die? Like complete bullshit, Rutkowski. That's what it looks like."

"Because something was wrong with that damned head of yours, Trpković, not because there was anything wrong with his sense of solidarity. In such situations, normal people are grateful for even the smallest sign of compassion."

"Well, sorry, I just didn't have time for it. People about to die are in principle fairly preoccupied. On top of everything else, you kept me busy holding up my underwear. Are you really enough of an ass to believe that in such a crappy situation anyone has time for such folkloric sentimentalities? But let's let bygones be bygones. Memories are for the weak. The weak live off memories and nothing else, they keep themselves artificially alive with the past, like with a perpetual transfusion. The strong know only the future. They know that if they don't kill their history, sooner or later it'll kill them."

"What's a man without his past?"

"A god!"

"You mean a demon?"

"Let's not get bogged down in terminological complications. A god in one world is a demon in another. But you don't have the guts to be one or the other. You prefer to remain a miserable terrestrial scorpion that will spend the rest of its life chewing on own tail. As soon as one loses sight of you, you immediately start focusing on yourself and that worthless history of yours. *Beatus ille, qui procul negotiis paterna rura bobis excercet suis,** where the land of your fathers is understood to be history and the bulls your tireless conscience."

"I didn't expect you'd know Latin."

"Knowledge is the prerequisite for all evil, Obersturmführer. Ignorance can be wicked when it gets the chance, but only the learned can be wicked in all circumstances. You know that much, don't you?"

"What exactly do you want from me?"

"Since you couldn't remove my plaque from the monument, remove the monument from the plaque."

"I'm not sure I understand what you mean."

"Demolish it, that's what."

"You've got to be insane to demand something like that of me!"

Adam laughed. An icy wind swept through the room.

"Beware of rash judgments, Obersturmführer. I'm aware you still consider me to be a hallucination, some kind of astral projection of your own guilty conscience. In that case, you're the one who's insane. I'm just an incarnation of your own insanity. And I'm not demanding anything from you that you yourself don't secretly

*"Happy is the man who, far away from business cares, works his ancestral acres with his steers" (Horace).

wish to do. You want to see that monument demolished, don't you, Rutkowski?"

I had to admit he was right.

"But since you're a coward and a man of compromise, you've chosen me to order you to do it. Because then, if someone called you to account for it, you could again say that you're not guilty and that you were merely carrying out orders."

"The monument must be demolished in a legal manner, with proper approval by the authorities and . . ."

"You Germans and your ideas of legality! A legality that on the whole consists of fulfilling certain administrative obligations when breaking the law—so that such violations are duly entered into the official registers. Don't be ridiculous, Obersturmführer. Hopefully you don't expect the chief of police to hold the fuse for you while you light it?"

"I'm an intellectual! Not a terrorist!"

"An intellectual with a pen in one hand and a file for grinding down prisoners' teeth in the other!"

"I never took a file to anyone's teeth!"

"No one asked you to, Rutkowski, no one asked you to. The question has to be formulated properly. We should ask you whether you'd have ground them down if that had been the only way to save your own teeth from being filed down. You don't have anything to say? You're not sure. Don't get desperate. No one can be sure of that. Not even those who've barely completed elementary school, let alone those with two or three doctorates! Finally, so we won't have to look any further, you yourself gave me a black eye. I had it when I went to the gallows and, as you can see, I still do."

"That doesn't count. That wasn't any kind of compromise. I hit you on an entirely personal level."

"*Factum infectum fieri nequit.** I suggest we forget it."

"Can you?"

"I'm not the one who's at issue. Sure I can. Can *you*?"

Yes, that was the real question, Hilmar.

"As things stand now," he continued, "you can't do it. So much is clear, Rutkowski. However, the situation can change. Under cer-

*"The deed cannot be undone."

tain conditions it's possible for someone to forget the past. One small agreement, one ordinary verbal convention between the two of us could put your life in order again."

"What would I have to do in return?"

"Demolish the monument. Nothing more."

"Are you suggesting to me that I in fact sell my soul?"

"Well, in the end there's not really much left of it, is there?"

"Enough not to lose all hope!"

"Hope for some kind of compromise, certainly? Then I don't see why you wouldn't give me a try. What I'm offering you is nothing other than your favorite out—a compromise. We're not traveling salesmen, Rutkowski. We don't deal. We conclude agreements. Arrangements which are beneficial for everyone involved. The only difference between ours and the ones you Germans made is that ours can't be broken."

I was already familiar with such alliances, Hilmar. As a historian, many human actions appeared to me to have been made to fulfill obligations imposed by these kinds of unnatural partnerships with the forces of Darkness, which, having been sealed with the renunciation of one's soul and its immortality, could not be invalidated by anything, requiring in the meantime blind obedience from the human party to the agreement. Such unions were as a rule established for mutual advantage. In exchange for the soul, the terrestrial partner in the deal would at first receive extraordinary benefits, paying for them only afterward with eternal suffering. At the moment when such an alliance was offered to me, I was already well on the way to viewing Adam Trpković not as a hallucinatory symptom of illness, but as an official representative of a secret subterranean world that we indeed know nothing about but whose presence we feel constantly underneath our personal and collective historical steps. Otherwise, I'd have had to consider myself a lunatic who has delusions of the fantastic. That isn't exactly a good alternative to good old superstition, is it? In any case, the interest that hell had for me was understandable. The rule of evil could be inaugurated only by some preliminary amnesia, the rejection of experience, the renunciation of history, and the total destruction of the past.

I thought about Adam. It seemed to me that he'd been in such an alliance before he died, an alliance in which the role of intermediary or controller was played by the umbrella. As there were no observable benefits in his case, as there had been with Dr. Faustus, for example—on the contrary, at variance with all rules, all that came into play was trouble—it was to be expected that the fulfillment of the essential preamble to the alliance, the payment of an earthly price for the soul, would come only at the end. However, Adam was executed, and the devil's reward, which will be discussed later, arrived in such a form that it didn't differ from an angel at all.

Before telling you how I responded to the offer, I'll present you with one more oddity of Adam's alliance with the umbrella. It'll help you to comprehend the extent of my dilemma. Similar cases that we know about from the Kabbala, black magic, and general demonology were in principle of a voluntary nature. Temptations could be employed, but the use of force was forbidden. (Something that hasn't yet occurred to those of us on earth.) The earthly partner would, for whatever reason, usually as the result of the irresistible pressure of some frustrated desire—a craving for happiness, knowledge, power, or adventure—seek out the aid of the devil. He didn't have to express this in words. It was enough for him to wish for Satan's help sincerely, with all his heart. In Adam's case, however, it's unclear whether there was any such invitation. The finding of the umbrella appeared to be accidental, if the matter is viewed from Adam's perspective. But if we view it from the devil's perspective, then it really appears to be a skillfully conceived trap. Thus, something outside of good demonic habits. Indeed, there's no way I can know what was really going on here and whether the formula hadn't been nevertheless spoken in some way. Because if it had, if his soul had been pawned for some sort of liberation, his downfall took place in the deepest areas of his being, still unpenetrated by any consciousness. In that case, the initiative, as was prescribed, fell to Adam's account. If the opposite was true, as I said . . .

To be brief, I'm telling you this only so you'll strike from your mind the devious idea that I was the one who arranged those godless meetings, and that Adam came at my beckoning. It'll be easier for you to understand the resoluteness with which I refused his offer.

"I'd give anything not to have the past that I have," I said, "but I can't sell the only thing that I might be able to redeem it with."

I was content with myself. My answer seemed to me to be almost

Roman. But the thing that was fundamentally new in it, as far as I was concerned, was the absence of any thoughts of compromise. I could feel, as much as my delirium allowed, that with this my spiritual life had turned a new, blank page.

Adam wasn't impressed.

"*Vederemo*," he said in Italian, the second language in his native region, and vanished in the ethereal skeins of new apparitions that overcame me.

Yours,

KONRAD

P.S. Hilmar, I don't think there are many of us who haven't at least once in our lives, in one way or another, called the devil to our aid. And if he didn't respond, it must be attributed primarily to the inborn insincerity and indecision of our hearts, which would like to keep us standing between two chairs, always ready to sit on both—the one in heaven and the one in hell. And to our insignificance as well. No one, not even the devil, likes to have to mess around with the so-called *homo statisticus.*

■ □ ■ □ ■

LETTER 19

GOLGOTHA IN D.,
OR *REASON AND EXISTENCE*

The Mediterranean Coast, 25 Sept. 1965

My dear Hilmar,

We're nearing the end of our correspondence. All we have left to do is attend a public execution in D., and then I'll reach a few conclusions regarding my life and scholarly work from everything that's been discussed over the last two weeks. In particular, I refuse to follow the old method by which both of us (along with our entire intellectual brotherhood) have been trying to recast history and reality—and even life itself—into food for thought but never into a cause for action. I wish that at least once actions would follow from these ruminations of mine, deeds from my thoughts, just as inevitably and naturally as a flame ignites from two sticks being rubbed together. I want to live the way I think, no matter where that leads me or whatever misfortunes it brings upon me.

In this letter I wish to describe in chronological order the events leading up to and including the execution of the municipal file clerk Adam Trpković, and to annotate this with Steinbrecher's learned commentaries, which most clearly manifest the Spirit of the Twentieth Century. Wherever possible, I'll limit my role to finding equivalents of the Standartenführer's commentaries in Western European philosophical thought, utilizing such examples to show where the responsibility for the history that you and I study really lies.

Standartenführer Steinbrecher and I were standing at an open window in his office on the second floor of the Geheime Staatspolizei in D., the room where the administration of the pensione is now located. The window looked out on the square, where that afternoon a few local bandits were to be executed.

Steinbrecher preluded absentmindedly:

"We say *to carry out an execution*. A firing squad *carries out* an execution. We *carry out* a hanging. Personally, I prefer the expression *to stage*. *To stage* a death sentence. A firing squad *stages* an execution. We *stage* a hanging. I think this term is more appropriate. How about you, Rutkowski? All that going on down there is a kind of performance, isn't it? Otherwise it wouldn't be public. It would take place in some dirty basement you enter through a narrow, slippery staircase, fearful of losing your footing and breaking your neck. And performances aren't carried out—performances are *staged*. Thus, we're staging an execution. The premier performance of an execution, actually. Something like this will never be repeated with the same cast, only with various alternates. The technical staff, of course, will remain the same: the directors, stage managers, set designers, ushers, the orchestra. But the actors always change. And if it is a performance, and it is, then—really!—behave in a manner appropriate for the occasion, Obersturmführer! You're in a loge, on the first balcony—not standing in the back row where you can munch mints and peanuts. Think a little. Think about language. We'd like to conquer the world, but we don't even have a proper language yet! Nor do we use the one we have correctly. We say *to carry out an execution* instead of *to stage an execution*. And that's just a trivial example. Our real linguistic tragedies occur during interrogations. As a rule, our understandings of certain terms differ from those of the prisoners. The language we use to interact with them is theirs as well, but it's as if any similarity ends in its external form. The meanings come from two different sources. When your prisoner claims that he's innocent, he imagines he's making a general statement about himself as such, regarding all possible charges, including the one he's currently facing. However, you accept his statement in its most limited sense, as a denial of the charge in question. If someone claims he's innocent of something, that doesn't mean he's not guilty of something else. Denying charges of sabotaging an automobile doesn't automatically exclude a future confession of sabotaging a train. Perhaps you think the semantic ambiguity of the language of investigation is a circumstance that works to our advantage, and that without such ambiguity the perfection and widening of the scope of the interrogation would be impossible or at least extremely difficult. Well, you're mistaken, Rutkowski—as usual, I might add! Linguistic confusion aids the prisoner, too. But something that serves both the jailer and the jailed well cannot be advantageous for the jailer. The ideal language of interrogation should be absolutely unambiguous, universal, and logically consistent. Truth would follow from *sentences,* and not from their *meanings.* In such a language, one thing would necessarily entail another—the latter would not follow only through our grammatical and logical interpretations or Rotkopf's pizzle whip! Antinomies would be precluded, and the thought process leading to a conclusion about someone's guilt—impeccable. A language in which you can say that 'Obersturmführer Konrad Rutkowski is the square root of stone tumbling downhill,' without such a statement contradicting any grammatical laws at all, is unsuitable for any purpose, let alone for police work. If effective measures are not undertaken soon, this language will make of us not the rulers of the world but the wardens of a nuthouse!"

(Can you recognize in Steinbrecher's linguistic jeremiad the semantic longings of Rudolf Carnap? The issue of our disputes is always the meaning of an utterance. If its meaning always followed from its form, misunderstandings and disputes would disappear, because all possible forms could be determined beforehand and even replaced with specific, fixed grammatical and logical codes. We'd be dealing exclusively with a prisoner's *sentences,* whereas at present we torment ourselves not only with their meanings but also with all the psychological, mental, and even physical origins conditioning them. Instead of dealing with their statements, without being concerned about anything else, we're still dealing primarily with the prisoners, and we take their statements as summary expressions of their existential conditions. In the Carnap-Steinbrecher system, it wouldn't be possible to have the first page of our freshly completed Transcript contain the sentence "The assertion on the last page of this Transcript is true," while the last page reads "The assertion on the first page of this Transcript is false." In such a system, we wouldn't have to carry out an additional investigation solely for the purpose of eliminating this one obvious antinomy. And those assertions are the very kind of antinomy which can be found everywhere in our Transcripts. There are so many of them that they're usually not even worth resolving. Transcripts—just take any police archive—are only chains of antinomies, assertions that logically contradict one another, though they do provide a harmonious basis for a verdict. Let's illustrate the example with a familiar name that's dear to our hearts. Let's say the first page of our Transcript reads as follows: "The assertion on the last page of this Transcript, that Gustav Fröhlich is a spy, is true." And then the last page reads something like this: "The assertion on the first page of this Transcript—that the assertion on the last page (that Gustav Fröhlich is a spy) is true—is false." The assumption that the assertion about Fröhlich being a spy is true then obviously entails its falsity, whereby it is falsely stated; but the assumption that it is false entails its truth, whereby that truth is proven. Everything would be so much simpler if Steinbrecher's dream, so similar to the dreams of the greatest living logicians, were to come true and if our Transcripts, instead of offering today's logical and grammatical confusion, provided an image of absolute harmony expressed in symbols. Then they would look more or less like this:

Steinbrecher: $(x - y) + (x + y) = ?$
Prisoner: $2x!$
Steinbrecher: $2x + (y - x) = ?$
Prisoner: $x + y!$
Steinbrecher: $(x + y) - (x + y) = ?$

How wonderful, dear Hilmar!)

Fine, Herr Standartenführer, the execution will be staged at precisely ten o'clock in the morning. It was a cool and rainy day. The grayish sky clung to the sea and shrouded the houses in a damp and dirty mist. There was no wind. The flags slack on the flagstaffs resembled the bloodstained rags used to mop up the floors of our offices after particularly difficult interrogations. Everything was in a kind of spellbound state, the winter hibernation of a provincial town that had been kept awake all night long by a methodical pounding of hammers.

Steinbrecher meditated:

"Rutkowski, have you noticed that executions are carried out as a rule either at night or at the break of dawn? Personally, I don't agree with this. Death is an integral part of our existence and not something that will come sooner or later to cut it short, not something external to us, unnatural and *contrary* to us, not something that we should be ashamed of, locking it in deep basements, the intensive care wards of hospitals, and dark bedrooms. It is death that, as Rilke put it, gives meaning to our life, without which life would be an interminable torment in inexpediencies such as despair, cancer, life prison sentences, or boredom. The constant threat of death, our fear of the indeterminacy of its onset and even its true meaning (unless you're religious, in which case the fear of nothingness is replaced by the still greater fear of being called to account), and the practical worry of avoiding or forgetting it, these things are the real source of all our existential pleasures. Because what can be done tomorrow, Rutkowski, what can always be repeated, can't be so important or irretrievable for us *today* that we would totally give ourselves over to it. Tomorrow kills all pleasure. If the act of sex were granted to us only once, and if on that single occasion we lost all our sexual urges and our ability to satisfy them again, that would be the *ultimate* sex. Thus, the man sentenced to death—if we want to be philosophers and not cutthroats—must be made to feel what he's losing. We have no right to deprive him of his FEAR, which according to Professor Heidegger is the essence of his earthly existence. Because if our existential worries and the accompanying fear are *our essence,* that which *makes us what we are,* in our higher manifestation and not only in our obvious and direct manifestations, and if that fear, as it stems not from anything that can be eliminated but from death, which is inevitable, is something innate in our existence, then it's natural for anything that aids the utmost possible expression and perfection of this fear and worry to be a rational and humane matter. In that sense death is humane—in and of itself and regardless of the social function in which it makes its appearance here. And the fear of the loss of one's life is a fruitful fear. At night that loss isn't so evident. Things are obscured, hidden in darkness as if under the black cloak of a magician. The crucial boundary between existence and nonexistence is erased. Darkness is a kind of harmless projection of death, an advance of death that we've grown accustomed to. What's more, you need artificial lighting: floodlights and stage equipment, occasionally even your own generators. You can't hang someone by flashlight or a millicandela candle. That's ridiculous. And you can't even see properly. In the dark you might even hang the judge. That would doubtless happen to our Haag—he'd hang the judge without fail. On the other hand, the monstrous union of the unreality of night and electrical lighting lends the whole confused scene the appearance of a theater rehearsal. You can't help thinking, for a moment at least, that it's all a simple stage performance, a trick, an equipment check, and even perhaps the dress rehearsal of an execution and that, if you make yourself useful and make a good showing, they'll take you back to your cell again. And you'll receive an amnesty in the meantime. Amnesties are, to be sure, always on the way. Or at least about to be approved. And there's no hero in the world who wouldn't rejoice at one. Night gives momentum to all probabilities. Day destroys even those that are possible. That's why I favor daytime. But by no means in the morning, Rutkowski. In the morning people are tired, drowsy, and not receptive to impressions. That goes for both those you're hanging and those on whose account you're hanging them. The latter are even more tired. Who knows how they spent the night before? It doesn't matter whether they were drinking or planting bombs under our vehicles, Rutkowski, in the morning all they want to do is sleep. They don't care about a thing. And since before lunch they're hungry, impatient, and incapable of reaching logical conclusions, and after lunch they're full and all they can think about is lying down for a nap, the only time left for our exemplary performance is ten o'clock in the morning. Do you agree, Obersturmführer? You do? Indeed, I'd like for you not to agree once in a while. That'd give me some inspiration. As things are, my best ideas drown in the disgusting muck of your loyal approval. Fine, let's give rainy weather a try. To see whether our opinions can diverge at least with regard to climactic conditions. What do you think about those rains during executions? I still haven't attended an execution when it wasn't raining. Nor have I ever heard of such a thing, though it must have happened somewhere. It probably can't rain in the Sahara just so one tradition—a repulsive one, I might add—can be upheld. But now it's too late. I've already said what I think. And you, most likely, agree. No, Rutkowski, I can't stand rain. I've been fooled by the erroneous forecasts of our radio service—not for the first time and not only about the weather. In my view, the condemned must to the fullest degree feel the definitiveness and finality, the totality and irrevocability of the act of dying. But what goddamned kind of definitiveness can anyone feel when water is running down his neck? He feels only water. The definitiveness of moisture. Not of the noose—of water!"

(I don't have much to add to this, Hilmar. The philosophical background was taken, in a somewhat simplified form and deprived of ethical correctives, from Husserl and Heidegger. He even cited the latter explicitly. Man in the world finds himself in enemy territory, surrounded by mysteries, limitations, and misunderstandings. Without any effective defenses, he's easy prey for death. His basic disposition is fear, his situation isolation, his answer despair, and his defense a withdrawal into his own existence. But since fear is also the essence of that existence—fear without limits or forms because it doesn't depend on limits or forms that death doesn't have—that withdrawal seems like someone jumping out of the frying pan and into the fire. But paradoxically, that jump is what saves us. It admits that death forms us, accepts its certainty, but turns it into existence. Existence is nothing other than *enduring* the indeterminate possibility of dying. Accordingly, fear is a constructive, and not a destructive factor in life. Whatever increases fear intensifies existence. Steinbrecher understood this within his narrow field of specialization and applied it well. The foundation of the constructive successes of totalitarianism and dictatorships on the coupling of death and fear, that is to say on the very essence of human existence, is the realization of this principle on the global scale of history. For an individual, a somewhat different logical conclusion would hold, and I don't doubt, not for a moment, that any living Standartenführer would agree with it: namely, it's occurred to me that, according to this principle, it would be best to live with a metastasis in your stomach, on a thin tightrope above a fiery abyss, with birds circling above and swooping down to attack you incessantly.)

The gallows had been erected on a wooden platform under the branch of a sycamore tree that obstructed our view. The gallows themselves looked like wild, unpruned sycamores, and the three nooses like three supple saplings bent back down toward the ground. The entire construction was adapted to the square to such a degree that it was almost indistinguishable from the meager flora there. On Steinbrecher's orders, the curtains of all the windows had been drawn and the blinds opened, but no one was there watching. Those rectangular glass eyes were black and blind.

Steinbrecher spoke on this topic:

"This is art, Rutkowski. Directing all the details of someone's death, so that it rises to an art form. But what is such an orchestration? An imitation of action, as Aristotle defined tragedy? But we don't want any tragedies. We prefer a farce. We can allow only ourselves a tragedy. Our enemies get a farce. When you see the condemned, you'll know what I mean. Our stage direction has turned what for them is a tragedy into a farce and thus eliminated any emotion that might be elicited by the act of killing. Shakespeare was similarly deluded in *Hamlet*. In Act III he says about the theater: 'The purpose of playing, whose end, both at first and now, was and is, to hold, as t'were the mirror up to nature; to show virtue her own feature, scorn her own image, and the very age and body of the time is his form and pressure.' (The fact that the Standartenführer knew English didn't, as you see, Hilmar, automatically make him a spy, as it did with Fröhlich's Oxford accomplice.) But we wouldn't want for a second to be mirrors of nature and to show the world its true form and imprint. That would lead *us* straight to the gallows! So then, what is such a staging as we understand it? It's obviously not an imitation of reality, but the creation of a new reality, the strings of which we hold in our hands. A kind of ritual puppet theater. Attending any of the party congresses would convince you of that. Thus, the first principle is: turn anything and everything into a theatrical performance. This is what our Führer is so successful at doing. The second principle: intelligently select the genre in which each piece is to be performed. Hindenburg's funeral should be enacted as a Greek tragedy, the burial of your Adam as a puppet farce. The third principle: carefully plan and supervise everything. And so we come to the stage on which our execution is to take place. I'll tell you more about the farce itself when they bring out the condemned and I can refer to examples. For now, let's stay with the decor and accessories. Every detail is important. The placing of the instruments, for example. You can't put them in basements or attics. Gallows require air and space. Perspective, too: they must be visible from all angles. In our theater, which is primarily intended for the people, we can't have any blind spots or seats from which you can't see the actors on the stage. And then there's the decor, the things surrounding the *échafaud*. It's tasteless and revolting to strangle people in front of nursery schools, churches, hospitals, or in cemeteries. What's the purpose of such primitive associations? How can something like this even occur to you? What was that? It didn't? So much the better. It would doubtless occur to Rotkopf. If he could, that man would kill people right in their coffins. The Middle Ages found the right place for all this—the agora, the square, the marketplace, where in ordinary circumstances the collective life of the city takes place. And when that life continues on this square tomorrow, there won't be a single one of the locals who won't feel that today's nooses are still swinging there in the treetops."

(As you can see, Hilmar, we haven't even neglected aesthetics. We've elevated life to art and thus fulfilled the philosopher's pledge. We've rejected the old division between comedy and tragedy and, according to today's teachings, blended them happily. Now we can laugh when they try to make us cry, and cry when they try to make us laugh. The ancient dream has been fulfilled. Art has lost its autonomy. We've subordinated it to man, turned it into an everyday, routine ritual, of both the individual and the whole nation. And can one really accomplish more in this imperfect world?)

The Schutzstaffel cordon formed a black tunnel that wound from the side steps of the wooden platform of the gallows around to the door of the former caribinieri barracks. Outside the cordon, which parted at the steps leading up to the gallows, skirted the platform, and closed again at the other end, as if gripping the platform like a pair of black pliers, the people of D. stood watching, packed into a crowd four deep—everyone Steinbrecher had been able to drag out of their houses in a surprise raid. Von Klattern's soldiers stood behind the townspeople in a thinner, green line, positioned to prevent the crowd from dispersing. But judging from their unenthusiastic expressions, they'd have been more inclined to join the crowd if it came to that.

While I describe the scene and while Standartenführer Steinbrecher prepares to give it a philosophical foundation, I can't resist the temptation to indulge in a little digression myself. After all, we too are capable of making a few of these damned generalizations. He didn't buy up the rights to all of them! Leaf through my previous letters so we can attend the unveiling of Adam's monument once more, but this time with some new information. Now, to be sure, we know that the monument is to the man whom we knew under the name of Adam Trpković, the municipal file clerk. We also know he didn't earn it. We know we're alone in this opinion and that the so-called facts are against us. We know, though this fact is of no use at all to us, that another man earned it, whom we likewise knew, and whom we *killed*. In an unconscious, unaccountable state, to be sure, but we killed him, no matter what our state. *Factum infectum fieri nequit.* We know also that his two compatriots earned it just as much as he did. They would, pursuant to the written propositions given to Hauptscharführer Münch, exit the door of the caribinieri barracks at the slow pace requested of them and pass through the motionless black formation, which according to Item 7, Subitem 12, was tasked with conjuring up the finality of the act, and to the accompaniment of a drum roll (also provided for in the said regulation), in a mental state that, despite the Standartenführer's frustration, had to be allowed a certain degree of freedom. But in return, they had to approach the gallows dressed only in their underwear (provided for in Item 11, Subitem 3)—and in the absence of their belts (as prescribed in Subitem 4 of the same Item), so that their hands were busy maintaining their dignity and not raised in defiant fists. And then, guided by the motherly hand of all of Steinbrecher's Items and Subitems, they would take three steps up to the platform. What tomorrow would be an indefinite human figure in granite was now only a human joint between a few wooden beams, from which three ropes were hanging, each smeared with soap—the device for the killing (provided for in Item 13, Subitem 4 of the Technical Section). It would never lose its basic purpose, though Steinbrecher would make sure it was adorned with deep psychological insights into his own crime as well as intellectual reflections on numerous topics. Hilmar, here the mystery of Genesis was being repeated once more in my spirit. However, while I kept the Standartenführer company during the execution, I had neither the time nor the inclination for such refined extrapolations. I waited for the Standartenführer to turn me into a generalization as well. I was to report to him after the execution. It seemed that the beating of Rotkopf's worker had not been accepted as a sufficient apology and that the episode of the false Transcript of Adam Trpković's interrogation had not been forgotten. I was tasked with participating in the preparations for the hanging. Meanwhile, in Steinbrecher's mind the Transcript was turned into harmonious, analytical propositions, smooth logical figures: $A = B$, $B = C$, $C = A$. My fate had already been logically defined. When they took me away at night, stripping me of my rank and spitting all over me, beating me to a pulp somewhere along the bottom of the garden wall in the light of a reflector lamp and to the roar of an automobile motor, I would finally be put in my real place. I would become one of Steinbrecher's famous mathematical propositions that were retold in the Gestapo corridors—a logical formula: $A = B$, $B = C$, $C = A$. $A = A$. No other result could be obtained without the logic itself being altered. He'd use these formulas to harass some other unfortunate Konrad Rutkowski. This Konrad Rutkowski, the one standing at the window, could see only this fact, the fact of his *own* possible death, and not at all the fact of Adam's death, nor any kind of correlation between the two. Intellectually speaking, I was thus entirely absorbed in myself and in testing the possibilities of extricating myself from the Standartenführer's formula. As for how I found a way to do that, and how my attempt was aborted, I'll tell that later. For now, let me merely underscore certain correlations between my position then and now. Indeed, I have a feeling that some logical conclusion must be drawn from this situation and that, after a confession, no one can act as if nothing has happened, as if nothing has changed.

I'm experiencing mystery of Genesis for the umpteenth time. This time, no one hails the deity. No one rushes to his feet. Men aren't molded out of gray clay. No kind of creative lightning bolt can overcome their horror and jolt them out of the warm security of nonexistence. The podium is empty and there's not a single human being who would give thanks to the Creator. There's no music to glorify the creation. Complete silence reigns. The music of the spheres. The music of death. Because this new deity, as I now realize, is the deity of death. And it isn't new. It's the same deity that created us, only now, in the form of a gallows, it has revealed its true intention. The purpose of creation. It created us only in order to have something to kill. The more of us it created, the more of us it had for killing. The blood lust summoned an ever-stronger lust for creation, and the latter an ever-stronger lust for death. It was a vicious circle—the geometric figure of our whole quarrel with history.

Let's hope that in the meantime Steinbrecher has thought up a suitable commentary that he'll use to explain the spectacle of the people in the dark green ring of our cynical orchestration. Of course he has. Let's listen to what he has to say:

"Rutkowski, I admit I'm fervent advocate of public executions. In this sense, I'm perhaps also somewhat old fashioned. Conventions, ceremonies, rituals, and the like. I wouldn't be able to kill someone on my own like that—in some basement, as you did. That's why I had to humble myself and ask General von Klattern for help with manpower. I don't need to tell you, that Pomeranian swine knew how to take advantage of the situation. Do you know what he said when we met? 'So, Steinbrecher, I'll give you my men, but I doubt they'll be any use to you. They're not, to be sure, trained cutthroats!' But *we* are! *We* are cutthroats! A man who comes to me and says 'They've burned my garage again. Do something about it'—he's not a cutthroat. I, who as a result does something about it, I *am*. I'm a criminal. If I do nothing, I'm still a criminal. I'm a criminal no matter what. But von Klattern is a gentleman in any case. Rutkowski, have you noticed how we're never mentioned in public? Our glorious army, which after four years of war is still approximately where it was at the beginning, and retreating at full speed, is the object of praise. We might eventually get a quick handshake in a dark corridor. No one talks about us, just as polite society doesn't talk about the deceased. We slip through the newspapers like a coffin carried through Australia, or a box of funeral decorations with the inscription *Empty Champagne Bottles* on the lid. The only people who aren't ashamed of us are in fact our enemies. They're the only ones we can rely on to make sure we're not forgotten. Our own people will say they didn't even know about us. The Gestapo—what the hell is that? Concentration camps—what concentration camps? Mass murder—what will you dream up next? We never heard about any 'final solution'! And even if all that *is* true, we didn't have anything to do with it. Go ask those dead ones! Go ask those—what do you call them?—Gestapo men! Put the squeeze on them! Hunt them down like wild animals! Hang them! Shoot them! Lock them up for life! They've earned it! They've degraded us in the eyes of humanity! They abused the respect we feel for polite traffic cops at intersections! They deceived us! Steinbrecher took us in! That dog! Rutkowski pulled the wool over our eyes, the swine! In the meantime, they dress von Klattern in a gown and set him in the chair of the honorary chancellor of some university. He's accepted into ten executive committees at the very least. He's also paid to write his memoirs, in which he'll explain at length the reasons why he didn't win the war, and among them Steinbrecher will figure in as the crown reason, because of his brutal methods that prevented otherwise willing nations from running into the outstretched arms of his soldiers. He'll die the center of attention and sympathy, which you could only do if you go to South America, change your name, and surround yourself with Amazonian savages! If you don't believe me, Rutkowski, then read up on the field a little yourself. Take a look through history. Remember how people write about Fouché, and how they write about his bosses Robespierre, Napoleon, Louis, and all the others. And in the whole business he fared well. He was a hybrid policeman, politician, and diplomat. His killings could pass as diplomatic games or political machinations. Ours?—Not a chance. Ours are murderous killings. But let's forget unpleasant things. Let's think about more pleasant probabilities. Let's daydream a little, Rutkowski, give ourselves over to imagination. Could our biological evolution help end our humiliation before von Klattern and other such swine? I mean the biological evolution of the police. Not technical evolution, Rutkowski—you're not listening to me again. I said *biological.* To illustrate this, let's compare ourselves to animals. In the majority of cases, the essential tools of a living being are integral parts of its organism. They harmonize with its nature and purpose. A beaver doesn't have pincers but strong teeth and a powerful tail. A tiger doesn't defend itself with ink like a cuttlefish. The ootheca of a praying mantis is constructed on the same principle as a thermos. The catapult systems that some animals use are miniature pieces of artillery, built into the organism by the evolutionary process, just as in an ideal world every soldier would be able to shoot directly from his mouth. You can see what I'm getting at. Snares, traps, nets, nooses, springs, adhesives, all the decoys nature uses to lure victims and then kill them, including hooks, spurs, barbs, pincers, proboscises, etc.—all of this, which we've taken from animals, we've been forced to mass produce in considerably less perfect form. Concerning the Service, I mean instruments of torture and liquidation, as well as dictaphones and other technical devices. The drawback of this practice is obvious. Despite the imperfections and the costs that we have to deal with, as well as the problems we have concealing them from the public, we often don't have them at hand. Imagine now that by heredity, through the course of a series of Rotkopfs, his hand, as a consequence of its constant use to beat people, evolved into a pizzle whip, an iron bar, or some other investigative device. We would have a subspecies of human called the *police,* and within it the Rotkopf variety, with an inborn club. A direct consequence would be a so-called 'hereditary police,' which is what all human functions are striving for by their very nature. They'd be technically perfect and would be much less of a burden on the state budget. But in my view, the most important consequence would be the fact that this would in some way biologically inaugurate the police into our lives. It would become just as natural as any other organ with its specialized function! What do you think of that, Rutkowski?"

(At the time I wasn't thinking anything. I was only thinking about how I could save my skin. However, now that my intellect has been freed from that immediate cause for worry, I don't see any difference between Steinbrecher's theory and the ideas of contemporary biology published by scientists such as Pierre Lecomte du Nouy, Lucien Cuenot, Julian Huxley and J. Rostand. The specter of the SUPERMAN appears in every new hypothesis, even those that hide scientific optimism behind the fear of the degeneration of the species. At the time of the writing of these lines, we've hardly reached the SUPERFROG. But the door has been opened, ever so slightly. "We must increase the number of brain cells," Rostand writes. "If the brain of a tadpole which has been given the pituitary hormone increased the number of its cells by 126%, there is no reason not to believe that, with special treatment, the human brain will not increase its cells as well." Rostand, to be sure, admits that he doesn't know what we'd do with a genius frog, but he does know what we'd gain with a Superman—a being, he says, that would understand what we don't, be capable of what we aren't, and would be to us what we are to a Neanderthal. Professor Vandel takes up the cause and carries it further, claiming that the past course of evolution is the best guarantor of the future. The prospects are great, and we have no reason to believe that intelligence, which has reached its pinnacle in man, will have to vanish with him as well. Man isn't the end of the story, but a transitional stage. *So the end of the story is certainly a Super-Rotkopf?* Such a development can be brought about. There's no need to sit with folded arms and wait for a possible correction of conditions on earth to destroy the chances for real progress, which can only be achieved with painstaking effort. Life for the esteemed Professor Vandel is constant toil. Woe to the lazy, happy, and content, for they are sinking in regression! Progress is on the other side: in making slow headway through hell. If humanity ever settled into the inert happiness of an earthly paradise—the professor insists—it would degenerate down to the level of an animal kingdom and renounce the lofty goals that can be attained only through suffering and battle. *But what good is morality, Herr Professor?* Vandel, in close proximity to vandalism, says nothing, dreaming of man without limits. And Paul Chauchard comes to the aid of the Steinbrecherian dream. He maintains that with the appearance of human consciousness evolution began a historical phase. *Does this mean, sir, that with the loss of human consciousness it will exit that phase?* "Biological discoveries have enabled us to overcome our blind nature and take the fate of evolution, the world and ourselves into our own hands. This duty follows from the fact that man, because he is Man, must also act like Man." This is a very interesting discovery, Hilmar. It was fairly novel for me, too. I'd never had the luck of meeting someone who would act like a man just because he was defined as such by his *biological* structure. "A BIOLOGICAL MORALITY is established. A protomorality, so to speak. An archimorality. According to it, evil is only what resists the rise of consciousness." In the meantime, it is not said what kind of consciousness, consciousness of what. "Whatever accelerates human progress is good." What this progress leads to, and how, is likewise shrouded in secrecy. All we know is that such a morality is determined just as its material correlates are. This is why voices of doubt are raised. A man is what responsibility makes of him. He is the first animal to think about itself and which is capable of choosing its own thoughts. *Doesn't determining him absolve him of all his responsibilities?* "So what?" asks Rostand, "What if that is the case? He who denies biological determinism," he who refuses to believe in the possible necessity of turning Rotkopf's hands into clubs, "doesn't he know that certain actions are forbidden as much as having a flat nose or brown eyes unless they've been genetically preconditioned as such? If you want to save the concept of individual responsibility, let's accept the principle that our chromosomes are ultimately responsible for everything." Hilmar, I don't think there's reason for worry. We can go ahead and yield to evolution, which, with the exception of man, hasn't produced a moral monster so far. With the help of our scientific consciousness, nature will at some point not only make sure that Rotkopf gets clubs instead of hands, but that they will also be organically equipped with an analgesic eye, a pain gauge, which will determine its ethically appropriate doses and reduce it to a minimum of necessity.)

Something's happened. A little while ago Sabina went to take a shower and now she's screaming frantically. Maybe she got burned by hot water. I'll end here.

KONRAD

P.S. I'll try to write the next letter this evening. Something strange has happened. I still don't know what to think of it. I'm hoping for the best. Namely, Sabina had a little unpleasant incident. Don't worry, it's already okay. We didn't even need to call the doctor. The plumber was sufficient. She went into the bathroom to take a shower and closed her eyes, expecting a refreshing stream of water. Instead, what she felt flowing over her was something warm and smelly. She opened her eyes and thought to her horror that she was showering in blood. Crimson blood was streaming from the shower-head. But it wasn't blood, of course. I could tell as soon as I ran into the bathroom. It was only a reddish liquid. Evidently some mineral soil had gotten into the water lines. The plumber came right away, and he had the same opinion. Especially since "the water had turned to blood" in the whole pensione. The incident was soon over. But the fact that the water became clear again all on its own and not as a re-sult of some technical repair (no break in the pipes was found) forced me to consider some other possibilities that you might consider silly, but which could not be excluded given the circumstances. First and foremost, this could have been a filthy attempt at blackmail by Adam Trpković, similar to Moses's attempt to deliver the chosen people from slavery by turning Egypt's waters to blood. I don't dare even to think about the second. It's too terrible for me to let out of this pen. But I'll soon know what this was all about. I took a sample of the red water without telling Sabina. Tomorrow I'll take it to be analyzed at the nearby Bone Tuberculosis Clinic. I'm hoping for the best.

■ □ ■ □ ■

LETTER 20

RIGHT AND LEFT,
OR *BEING AND TIME*

The Mediterranean Coast, 25 Sept. 1965

Dear Hilmar,

Sabina has recovered from the mysterious "blood-bath"—which can't be said of me—so I'll continue with my story where her scream interrupted me.

We're at the window again. From somewhere in the distance, it's impossible to tell where, I can hear the ghostly drone of kettle-drums. The church tower strikes nine hours and thirty minutes.

Steinbrecher notices my astonishment. He's satisfied, and begins explaining with heartfelt enthusiasm:

"This really is and isn't an innovation, Rutkowski. It's just a renewal of the good customs of old, of a romantic age when death still meant something, and people went to an execution as we go to the cinema today. In those circumstances, of course, no lapses due to sloppiness or haste could be permitted. A certain protocol was observed. Münch would find it satisfactory. There were also mistakes, of course. Once in a while the head couldn't be severed on the first blow. Torturous convulsions followed. But the audience was understanding. It wasn't spoiled, as it is today. It seemed even to pre-fer that things be dragged out a little. I wonder whether dragging things out like that wasn't provided for in the protocol. In any case, our great-grandfathers weren't hypocrites. When they killed people, they made an honest job of it. They didn't pretend they were just carrying out justice. They also knew how to freshen up executions with subtle details, for which, it seems, we no longer have the time or inclination today. We've industrialized everything, even death. In not too long, we'll be killing people on conveyor belts. So that's why I introduced music: Item 5, Subitem 9—musical accompaniment. I asked von Klattern for his regimental band. The swine refused me. He said his instructions from his superiors did obligate him to assist me with manpower, but nowhere was there any mention of piano accompaniment. So the sound is somewhat reduced. But the drums sound quite good, old fashioned and reliable. What do you think, Rutkowski? Nothing? Obersturmführer, it seems you never think anything. You're one of those who'll be saying tomorrow that you were only following orders. For heaven's sake, what's that big brain of yours good for? For *interrogation transcripts* alone? However, I do like drums, their monotony; their hopeless repetition of a musical phrase corresponds to the funereal music that, as you know, I couldn't provide, because of the general's refusal to cooperate. The perfect choice is a funeral march—logical, effective, direct. In the concentration camps they play *Rosamunde*. That's laughable. I don't see the point. I discussed this topic in Berlin with Sturmbannführer Klinger from subsection B4 IV of the office that under Eichmann specialized in the final solution of the Jewish question and partici-pated in the creation of a test ghetto in Vilnius. I told him I didn't understand what sense there was in playing *Rosamunde* when the Jews didn't know they were going to the crematorium and thus couldn't grasp the meaning of the counterpoint. He answered that this was precisely the point: to keep them from finding out. Otherwise they'd rebel and make trouble, disrupting the whole operation and bogging it down. He then told me about a working procedure they'd developed after prolonged experimentation. Al-though we don't work with mass groups, the idea might be of use to us as well. Klinger's main problem was how to prevent resistance, because hiding the truth was impossible in the long run. The only effective way was allowing them to retain a certain degree of hope for survival, and, as a consequence, occupying their minds with the task of finding out ways to save themselves. As soon as our troops entered Vilnius, the local population was incited to a few limited pogroms, with the goal of creating an atmosphere of fear and uncertainty. The idea of creating the Ghetto followed as an act by civilized authorities whose intention was to prevent disorder. And it was accepted by the Jews as a way out of a hopeless situation. However, any possibility of resistance was eliminated with a single subtle move, which later was continually repeated in different variations and which always produced excellent results. On its way to the Ghetto, the column of deportees found itself heading for an intersection that was visible from afar and where they were divided on their own choice into two groups: those who chose to go to the right headed off into the unknown, and those who chose to go to the left went to the Ghetto. Because the junction was on a rise and was visible from a great distance, the people who saw that the column was being split up had enough time to decide whether they wanted to go to the left or to the right. A decision like that required them to exert all their brainpower, even though the real decision is always made instinctively, and the people, completely absorbed in their fear of making a mistake, had no time for anything else. Their acquiescence to think about whether to go right or left, where it would have been normal to resist going in either direction, was an expression of their reconciliation to fate, evoked by a hope of survival. There was, of course, no survival in either direction. The path to the right led to a wood near the town of Ponar where they were instantly liquidated. The path to the left led to the Ghetto, where that liquidation was postponed for a certain time. The principle of choosing one's own fate, so comforting at first glance, was applied in the Ghetto as well. Sturmbannführer Klinger made a useful comparison. For him, the Jews of Vilnius were like a man who considers it an extraordinary victory to be able to choose whether he'll go ahead and be thrown from the window of the third floor or whether he can wait for the fifth floor. In the Ghetto, this principle was perfected by issuing various kinds of certificates. Those employed as workers in the German industry received them, but no one else did. At first the raids targeted only those without the certificates, which everyone then tried to obtain. Then they were totally preoccupied with that. There wasn't time for any kind of resistance. They had to get the worker's certificate before the next raid. However, it never took place. In the meantime, there was a change in the rules. Now there were two kinds of certificates being issued—those with identification photographs, and those without. It was up to you to decide which kind of document you were going to have in anticipation of the next human hunting party. The principle of "left or right" was in effect again. Now the raids targeted those whose pass had no photograph. Everyone tried to get theirs replaced. The administration took care that a third kind of document was introduced: a blank card with the stamp of the work office in Ponar. Rarely did anyone decide to get that one. That meager piece of paper promised no degree of security. The next night saw the arrest of many of those with the old documents, with and without photographs, in a proportion equal to those who had no documents at all. Everyone rushed to obtain the blank identity cards. In the meantime, the Administration found this division to be impractical. It was replaced by a division between the skilled and unskilled. No proof was required, only a statement. Right or left? The majority decided on some skill. Namely, it was thought that whoever was useful would be spared. In principle, that conclusion is valid. Soon it was discovered that the papers of skilled workers were being taken by those who had no right to them. As punishment, the next raid targeted everyone without discrimination—both those with the papers and those without. The Jews understood that they themselves were to blame for this. Sturmbannführer Klinger said he and his men were themselves astonished to find that the Jews almost approved of the punishment: *They believed us,* it was said, *and we deceived them.* When someone reaches this level of reasoning, you can do anything you want with him. Selections on the basis of identification papers were continued. Left or right was permanently in effect. By the time the last Jew had been liquidated, the identity cards had gone through the entire spectrum: from red to white. Their thoughts were always occupied. There was always a choice to be made. Left or right? Do you understand the ingenuity of the idea, Rutkowski? Only a speculative mind like that of the Germans could come up with this. Only the nation that gave birth to Kant and Hegel. Out of fairness, one must admit something about those Jews. Only their Talmudic intelligence could accept this game as an equal player. A primitive Anglo-Saxon, with no imagination or intellectual shrewdness, as soon as he saw that the rules of the game changed whenever he was on the way to winning, would have quit the game. The Jews kept on playing. Their passion for the game increased as the selections became more complicated and their numbers continually diminished. A strange people, Rutkowski, a truly strange people. In their place, any other people would have been erased from history ages ago. But you see, they're still filling our gas chambers and there's not much chance, at least at this stage in the game, of finally getting rid of them. How much time do we have left? Less than a half hour? Let's use it wisely. Let's reflect on this topic. I forgot to ask: Your Trpković—did he have any final wishes? He did? He must have wanted to see his children, right? He didn't ask to see his children? Then what did he ask for? A piece of string? What kind of string? What did he need string for? To tie his umbrella? Is that it? Clever. A peasant's possessive instinct. Let's respect that. A man's sense of order should always be supported. Note down that the umbrella should be returned to the family after the execution. We're not thieving Italians! However, that isn't what I wanted to talk about. I wanted to talk about executions. Do you know how many methods of execution have been employed to date? You don't? And you're supposed to be a competent historian! Well, three fourths of history consists of executions, and one fourth of the intrigues with which executions are prepared. Without worrying about chronological order, we have first of all decapitation by guillotine as an industrial spin-off. Then execution by free fall or the Roman method of throwing people off the Tarpeian cliff. And the Greek method of poisoning, which, like slitting the veins, relies on a certain degree of voluntarism. In this respect it's reminiscent of the way the Jews are dying today. If it can possibly be ensured, the cooperation of the victim is always welcome. Of the exotic methods I'd emphasize, among others, strangling someone with a cord or a Spanish garrote, impalement on a stake, crucifixion on a cross, stretching someone out on a wheel or tying someone to horses' tails, or drawing and quartering. Fill me in if I've left something out. Then we have execution by shooting in all its variations. I'm not thinking of rifles and pistols. In Toulon, Fouché dispatched his hostages with grapeshot. The machine gun is already a classic. Flame-throwers have been neglected thus far. It'd be hard to expect anything new in this area. The electric chair was the by-product of the industrial revolution and the American worship of electrical home appliances. Lastly, there's strangulation by mechanical means, gas and water. The goal—to prevent respiration. Let's examine the devices one at a time. The Anglo-Saxon sword was undoubtedly effective, but its lengthy tradition lent importance to the person it struck. And it also required skill. Can you imagine our clumsy Haag in the role of executioner? The French guillotine was somewhat more serviceable. It was downright ingenious, if one considers that it emerged from the most humane principles of the Revolution. It was the first expression of bourgeois practicality and respect for equal opportunities. Unlike the sword, it deprived its victim of any social importance. Unfortunately, in its familiar form it's fairly awkward and immobile, not to mention its miserable output—it's completely unsuited to any mass use. All that heavy iron, the blades, chains and bolts. And then, Rutkowski, it's always breaking down. Some handle loosens, a joint wears out, or the blade gets stuck halfway down—nothing but technical complications. The main drawback of the Romans' method of throwing someone from a cliff was that it couldn't be employed in the flatlands, and a method, if it will claim to be perfect, must be applicable in all geographic regions. This also applies to drowning in water. It was limited to coastal peoples. Drowning someone in a barrel seems silly to me. The Greek method was hypocritical in the Balkan fashion. The victim was required to cooperate and assume part of the responsibility; besides, it wasn't a very reliable method. You never knew whether the one to whom you sent the tablet with the death sentence would kill himself or slip over to the East, from where he would send one such tablet back to you. The Italian Renaissance introduced poison. You go to sleep alive and wake up dead. Typical of the Italians, who make everything indefinite, everything semilegal. Everything is some kind of contraband! In addition, there's something subversive, conspiratorial, Carbonarian, in a word *seditious* about it. You can get by with shooting, but on a large scale, as Sturmbannführer Klinger reported to me, it causes psychological complications in the executioner. A personalization of death occurs, its transformation from an abstract formula into a human face. I reject the electric chair. I accept American home appliances, I don't have anything against electricity, but I don't want a whole bunch of scientists to get between me and my convict. That's soulless, Rutkowski! All those people in white lab coats with stethoscopes, then men in blue coats waving wrenches around and holding isolation tape in their teeth, men wearing black with crucifixes falling out of their pockets, and those in gray nervously chewing on mechanical pencils—it's really loathsome, if you consider that the hullabaloo takes place in front of a person who is sitting half-naked and waiting to have his head jolted by one more proof of our technical genius. If you ask me, I'd do it by burning. Chemically, it's the cleanest method. The Inquisition knew this. And in general—that Inquisition! I didn't even ask about this method; it wouldn't have been approved. Everyone would think it morbid. The cremation of entire cities, in the meantime, isn't morbid. When you burn a man you've just anaesthetized, that's morbid. When thousands of conscious beings burn in a phosphorescent flame, it's natural. Fine! Ideal solutions are always impossible anyway. What's left is hanging or breaking the neck, however you want to put it. The best combination of our will and natural conditions. Hanging best approximates natural death. It's only a slightly accelerated anoxia. There are no technical complications. The material is natural—everything is more or less vegetable matter. Vegetarian. Ah, there's your Adam!"

(Dear Hilmar, I won't waste time grounding these thoughts in the progress of our technology. The connection is obvious. Each individual tool, from axes to rifles to the electric chair, was only a temporary peak in the ongoing ascent of our scientific consciousness. Even ordinary strangulation requires the twining of a rope. The use of poison requires medical and chemical skill. Only the connection between pushing someone off the Tarpeian cliff and the state of scientific thought is somewhat tenuous. It surfaces only when we remember that it's there, only hidden in experience. Shoving someone off a cliff would be pointless were we not aware of the physical laws that will kill him.)

The door of the barracks opens out with a deep creaking sound. The convicts step into the black cordon. Because of the position of the window, we can't see them at the start; we then follow them from behind. There are three of them—in spite of the traditional interpretation of such an arrangement. Steinbrecher found that in this case Adam's betrayal lends the symbolism a sense of irony, even of the grotesque. As seen from behind, the trio indeed appeared incredibly silly. Like three provincial clowns entering a circus arena. Yes, Hilmar, just like that. Those two made a circusy effect in their underwear, which resembled white shalwars, and which slipped down at every step. Adam also cut a circusy figure with his oversized, satanic umbrella, which he spread over himself and his friends like a black wing. I'm aware that the expressions "clownish" and "circusy" are apt descriptions not only of the scene (though they were so accurate that not even the terrified townspeople could avoid such an impression) but also of my inverted, nihilistic spirit, as it was then, in the face of death. A spirit that mocked the secrets of existence in the spirit of Caliban. Because what kind of people of understanding, imagination and feeling can laugh at a man merely because he is dying in his underwear under an umbrella? Would a parade really help here? A top hat, perhaps, with glacé gloves and a magician's cloak lined with white silk? Or would that elicit laughter as well? Maybe men should be hanged in beaver coats, gymnasts' suits, folk costumes, firemen's uniforms, major-domos' liveries, historical costumes rented from museums for the occasion? In diving suits with underwater fishing equipment? In chefs' aprons, in miners' overalls, hospital gowns? Perhaps the requisite solemnity is to be found in the feathered headbands of Seminole chiefs? In the leather dolman of a 1917 revolutionary or Jacques' open shirt from 1358? A nobleman's collar from 1600 or a brown shirt from 1934?

There are at least a few things in this world that a man ought be able to sense instinctively. He'd should, say, instinctively see something *unprecedented* in violent death, no matter how much death itself was otherwise the most well known thing in our accursed lives. Such an irregular, unnatural death would always have to surprise him. Astonish him. Disappoint him. Revolt him. But never make him laugh. So even if someone did decide on killing a man who was in his underwear and holding up an umbrella, it would be just so he could have that urge stifled in the repulsive reflex of laughter.

But Hilmar, I still laughed.

Steinbrecher said dryly:

"Don't you see yourself how things are, Rutkowski? Do you sense the advantage of farce over all other forms of human humiliation? Farce kills truth, destroys faith, ridicules every feat of heroism. Can someone be a hero in his underwear while holding an umbrella? No, he can't, Obersturmführer. Not even Achilles could have managed that. One can be a hero only in a suit of armor. Perhaps wearing Danton's open shirt. Only a clown can be dressed in peasant's underwear with a long belt beneath an umbrella. A circus performer! No kind of standard-bearer, legend, myth. Now you understand why I had them undressed. Even though I don't care to look at their bare asses! And even if one of them were bold enough to shout out, to call out, to yell out a slogan, do you really think there's a single sensible person who'd respond to an alarm sounded by such buffoons? So you see, Rutkowski, what all can be done with people. And even worse things—if the Service requires, and with a higher goal. But one *doesn't dare* laugh at that. An intelligent and conscientious man doesn't laugh at that. Especially if there's a possibility that he too will tomorrow walk some umbrella to his grave!"

Steinbrecher sensed how funny all this was, like every unnatural counterpoint. An ordinary man who doesn't want to look silly doesn't sleep with a whore and a prayer book at the same time; he doesn't go to the beach dressed in a tuxedo, except when he's going to drown himself; he doesn't go to the theater naked, unless there's a costume party; he doesn't carry an umbrella when he's being led to the gallows, unless he's crazy. But in that case it is all really very funny. He sensed it—the Standartenführer sensed that everything he was directing appeared nearly unreal in its inhumanity, as if it weren't even going to happen. Instead, the whole marionettish mechanism would stop all on its own, when the spring-loaded invertedness of the scene wound down. He knew it was all a satanic, heathen comedy that he was playing with all of us for reasons of the state, a practical joke that perhaps some higher law was playing on us and him. He knew all this, but he still didn't laugh.

I, Konrad Rutkowski, an intellectual in the Christian tradition, of bourgeois upbringing and subtle nature, I did.

And that was the last time I laughed, in the many years of darkness that followed.

Your—again unsettled—KONRAD

RIGHT AND LEFT

■ □ ■ □ ■

LETTER 21

DEATH AND TRANSFIGURATION, OR *BEING AND NOTHINGNESS*

The Mediterranean Coast, 26 Sept. 1965

My dear Hilmar,

We've reached the end, rock bottom. This is the last letter. I don't believe I'd have the strength for another. I'm not well. It's not that I'm suffering from something definite, that could be treated with therapy. I'm not experiencing any kind of health problems, though my unstable inner state surfaces in my physical condition, which has even started to worry Sabina. The problem is primarily my state of apathy, an unusual and debilitating collapse of my will. It's as if nothing matters to me at all. Indeed, this lasts until I fall into a stupor, which soon turns into a hysterical delirium. Suddenly everything seems attainable and possible. And then this mood fades as well, carrying away with it each time more and more of the dark past that surrounds me. If you can imagine a man who jumps into the water to cool off, enjoying that splash, only to realize later that he's crawling on hot sand, then my situation will be clear to you. It's very likely my nerves, strained by this painful confession—as well as some circumstances connected with it, which have left me deeply troubled.

In particular, I went to the Institute this morning to have the red fluid examined, which, as I told you, had come out of the shower head when Sabina turned it on. In the meantime, the emulsion coagulated and my fear, no matter how I tried to suppress it as inappropriate, grew with every minute of waiting for the result.

Hilmar, the result was positive. It was human blood.[15] The laboratory's findings in this regard leave no room for doubt. The report puts its age at about twenty years. And its composition and characteristics apparently indicate the blood of a single individual.

What that means or whose blood it might be—I don't even dare to think, Hilmar. I'm sure I'd go insane if busied myself with that. I know I'm talking nonsense, that my assumptions are incredible and scientifically unfounded, but I'm unable to reject them. I can only stop tormenting myself with them.

Hilmar, I must be careful in the description of what followed after the moment when the three condemned were halfway to the gallows, up until the time when the noose was placed around Adam's neck, and his satanic umbrella began its satanic action. Because with this execution we part ways with my past (both rails of the story are already proceeding parallel to one another) and begin to draw logical conclusions from it. To *C* from *A* via *B*. Here the history of Konrad Rutkowski reaches its culmination, and the sum effect is such that it resembles those unique situations in life which, if they are by some magic ever repeated, have immeasurable consequences. Somewhere in all this there must be a "revelation," the one reason why such a story occurred in the first place. So let's proceed cautiously and conscientiously. First of all, let me state a couple of assumptions that until now I've kept to myself. In this way, the events can be better comprehended and their turns, no matter how unnatural and inexplicable, more easily accepted as possible.

Down below, everything was proceeding exactly as anticipated. Although I couldn't see them from the window, Rotkopf, Meissner, Freissner, Hauptscharführer Max, and even the freshly recovered Untersturmführer Haag were down at the gallows. Each member of the Sonderkommando had become an oiled, Steinbrecherized cog in a demonic ceremonial machine, the flywheel of which was the

Standartenführer, and its transfer belt Hauptscharführer Münch. No one was left in the headquarters, except the guard in the basement and the prisoners in the cells.

The Standartenführer was standing to the side of the window, watching the scene and Steinbrecherizing animatedly. It seemed that the whole spectacle felt much more comfortable in his logical generalizations than in its own reality.

I stood behind him and prepared to kill him.

No, Hilmar, you're wrong. I wasn't going to do it to escape retribution for the Interrogation Transcript. Though I admit the Standartenführer's death would have saved me. No one knew of my betrayal. He'd jealously taken that case back to his lair so he could gnaw on it with his conclusions undisturbed. Nor was I acting like one of the damned in hell, who, despite all torment, are sustained by the hope that they'll someday be able to return to the world and warn people of the danger awaiting them. I wasn't acting the part of any kind of awakened conscience that metes out justice and punishes in the name of higher principles. I'd had enough of all the higher principles of this world. I longed for a principle, be it even the lowest, which would allow me a life beyond Steinbrecher's syllogistic Ringer's solution, without the fear or humiliation that the iron steps of the logic of compromise and ruin lead us to. Then, of course, I thought differently. I saw myself as a weapon of collective revenge, just as any ancient champion of tribal justice must have felt in the fight against dragons or other forces of darkness. Now I know, Hilmar: That wasn't true. And it wouldn't have been even if I had in some apparent desire to survive and testify the next day—in some compromise with shame—concealed my desire to survive and never said a word about anything. (Which, by the way, was what happened.) But not even that's the whole truth. My instinct for survival, already gnawed away by alibis, wouldn't have borne the weight of such an act, even if I had been absolutely certain that I wouldn't get caught. It had to be cured and drugged with an insane hatred, which had almost nothing to do with Steinbrecher's victims or the divine laws of humanity that he violated in thought and deed—a hatred whose sole motivation was a fatal insult to my person. Thus, I was going to kill him for the simple reason that he had brutally pulled me down into a quagmire of individual responsibility and forced me to feel the "real fates of real people"—which had flowed into me through a lead-tipped rubber truncheon as if through a transfusion tube—and then left me to act as if that didn't concern me. I was going to kill him because he'd forced me into a voluntary agreement to participate with all my treacherous compromises in his capitulation ratio of one to three instead of three to one.

Standartenführer Steinbrecher was the mirror that the enraged Caliban had decided to smash.

The plan was a good one. There was little danger of anything going wrong. We were alone in the building. I had secretly locked the office door. Not until the execution was over would anyone come, nor would the Standartenführer wish to leave. He had his back to me. He was not wearing his hat, the back of his head was exposed. He was in the modern position for execution by shooting, recommended by the young school of butchers from the B4 Department of the IV Section of the Reichssicherheitshauptamt. At the Standartenführer's order, the opaque glass of the windows had been temporarily replaced with transparent glass. The window was closed, and the angle of the sun, which had just begun to gleam softly through the nimbus clouds, did not cause my shadow to give me away. At the moment the convicts stepped up onto the platform, the drums would start up. The drum roll would grow "dramatically, Rutkowski, hellishly Wagnerian," and when my bullet was fired in that Wagnerian orchestration of death, no one would hear it. The attention of those present would be directed to the gallows, which would creak from the weight of the three convulsing bodies. I doubted that any of the convicts, even in a moment of insight immediately before death, would be able to see in through the darkened glass of the window and see Steinbrecher's head explode like a giant, putrid boil. I'd return my pistol to its holster after quickly cleaning it, and leave the room. I'd blend into the crowd just as the tension let up and I might again draw people's attention.

Because I—as I'd tell the investigator—was down there from the beginning. At the explicit order of the deceased Herr Standartenführer. The deceased Herr Standartenführer commanded me to supervise the organization of the execution personally. *But wasn't that the duty of Sturmbannführer Freissner?* Correct, sir. I was a kind of personal informant. Without the right to intervene, of course. I was, after all, his adjutant. *In that case, do you know why the deceased Standartenführer wished to be alone in the office?* I don't know, sir, I couldn't tell you that no matter how much I might wish to. But I can assure you that he had some logical reason for it. Indeed, the Herr Standartenführer never did anything without solid premises. *So you were all outside down there, the whole Sonderkommando?* That's correct, sir, we even had to borrow men from General von Klattern. (Clear, concise, logical, Steinbrecheresque.) *But in that case, why wasn't Standartenführer Steinbrecher with all of you down on the square?* He must have wanted to have an overall view of the scene. (No, my dear little Lilly, we're not going to bed!) And that's how the bandits got him, I can't see any other alternative. *Okay, Obersturmführer, you're probably right: But how did they get in?* (Lilly wasn't giving up. She was obviously a nymphomaniac.) Unfortunately, that was our mistake, sir. (One must assume some of the guilt. The pawn won't help the investigation anyway. Indeed, it originated in the deceased's concept of the game.) We couldn't exercise control over everything! There were so damned few of us! (An affectation lends conviction to these words.) We left the rear of the barracks unguarded. One of the windows to the basements had not been barred over, and the bandits broke it. (I was actually the one who broke it. A few minutes before I would join Steinbrecher.) *Okay, Obersturmführer, that's clear and logical.* Of course, sir, Steinbrecheresquely logical, as we liked to say. *However, how could they have known that the Standartenführer would be in his office? Wasn't it more likely that he'd be on the square?* They saw him at the window, sir. *How could they have seen him?* Just as the others saw him. I also saw him. If that partisan could see him, so could I, correct? (That was the classic Steinbrecher equation. What proof is there that the partisan could see him at the window?—The fact that Obersturmführer Rutkowski could see him. But what proof is there that Obersturmführer Rutkowski could even see him? Well, didn't the partisan see him? And does one brachycephalic bandit have better eyes than a dolichocephalic officer?) But if we nevertheless run into complications, and the question is raised as to whether anyone could have seen him at the window, the answer would be that everyone can testify to that. Let's ask, for example, Hauptscharführer Max. Naturally, I'd get a hold of Max beforehand, who has the requisite amount of stupidity for my purposes. I'd find him as soon as I stepped out of the building and tell him that the Standartenführer was quite satisfied with all that he saw *from the window.* Especially with his precision. Didn't Max see him up there? Of course he did. What kind of Hauptscharführer wouldn't spot a Standartenführer who was admiring his professionalism from the window? And when questioned like this, Max would state that during the execution he saw the Standartenführer smoking at the window. (Care must be taken that the deceased Herr Standartenführer didn't happen to be a nonsmoker, because one such act of restraint on his part would, as a final consequence, only fill little Lilly's bed.) The fact that at the time the Standartenführer couldn't have been at the window, because his splintered skull was lying under the windowsill—put to death by a bandit who must have killed him *before* the execution, and therefore before the Standartenführer could have arrived at his evaluation of Max—this logic wouldn't spoil the beauty of the news itself. Max was glad to receive any praise, even from an officer who was already dead. In any case, the execution was over, and I went up to Max and informed him of the Standartenführer's opinion; Max looked up with devotion at the window where the Standartenführer, who had praised him, was supposed to be standing. But the Standartenführer wasn't there. Would that mean catastrophe for me? Not at all. The execution was over and there was nothing else to watch. It was natural for the Standartenführer to leave the window, where the two of us had spotted him during the execution. Because he *must* have been standing there. Otherwise he wouldn't have seen Max in action. The Hauptscharführer wouldn't have received his praise. But the Hauptscharführer needed praise, and he wasn't too much of an idiot to see the only person who had praised him for anything in the last few months. For Max, it was a closed case. After the Standartenführer praised him, he could drop dead with a bandit's bullet in the back of his head.

That was my plan. And here's how it was carried out.

I looked down at the square. Three men trudged slowly through the black cordon under the demonic umbrella.

Steinbrecher was explaining the physiological and anatomical aspects of a hanging:

DEATH AND TRANSFIGURATION

"The medulla oblongata is separated from the spinal cord. Like a thread when it breaks. Respiratory movements are rendered impossible. The process of respiration stops. Flourence's "knot of life" is broken. Do you know where that knot is, Rutkowski? Where your life is? Where the *formatio reticularis* is located?"

He turns around abruptly. A shudder passes through me. Fortunately, I haven't yet opened the holster of my revolver. My hand is still resting on it.

"Stretch out your neck, Obersturmführer! The middle third of the medulla oblongata. That's it, right here!"

He gently touches my skin over the knot of life. With his black-gloved finger. With a black finger like a black kiss.

The convicts walk up to the steps. In which order will they climb them? In the order of logic—the order of death? Or in the order of chance—the order of life? As they stand there, there's a moment of hesitation.

Steinbrecher meditates:

"In a state of complete rest, a human being completes on an average sixteen to twenty inspirations and expirations a minute, with an exchange of 0.4 to 0.6 cubic liters of air in each inhalation and exhalation. Frequencies of under ten and over twenty breaths are observed only rarely. The ventilation of the lungs, however, can increase to up to 100 cubic liters a minute, with a respiratory frequency of forty breaths. Accordingly, Rutkowski, dying means nothing more than reducing a single frequency to zero, and cutting off a single transportation route from the spot where it's regulated. Death is an ordinary mathematical equation: E (expirations) $- I$ (inspirations) $= 0$. And this is what people make so much fuss is about!! Of course, death can be defined in other ways. With biologists, you'll say death is the permanent cessation of all bodily functions. With physicians, you'll say it's an absolute dysfunction with a transitory probability equal to zero. With, chemists you'll define death as the absence of the body's ability to synthesize its molecules into an integrated and organized system. With theologians, you'll say it's the definitive separation of the eternal soul from the temporal body. Philosophers will define it in thousands of ways, each of which will starkly contradict the others. But it'll always remain what it is: $E - I = 0$."

Then they climb the steps. Adam first. They assist him. His place, however, doesn't get him any privileges. The order of their ascent was determined by Item 12, Subitem 2; the order of death by Subitem 3 of the same item. Who would be hung first was still unknown. It might surprise you that the Standartenführer didn't determine it with the roll of a die. Left or right! A red or a white certificate! That would bring chance into the program. And the Standartenführer hated chance. There's nothing the Standartenführer hated more than chance. Chance means exceptions. Chance is a violation of law. Chance is illogical. Therefore, it can't be. And therefore, it doesn't exist. There's no chance. Everything is intentional, willful, premeditated. No one can meet with anyone by accident. It always happens intentionally. No one can learn of anything by accident, he must have always been working at it. There's no such thing as negligence, carelessness, coincidence. Everything is always planned and organized. There are no mitigating circumstances. All circumstances are, by their very nature, aggravating.

Steinbrecher meditates:

"Indeed, everything lies in the combination of numbers, in which death has the role of zero. With the cessation of breathing in a hanging, the body's tissues continue for a certain time to take the residual oxygen from the lungs, slipping them carbon dioxide in return like a cuckoo's egg. A considerable amount of oxygen, around 750 cm^3 of every five liters of air, and around 320 cm^3 of every two liters of alveolar air, is used up at a rapid pace. The level of O_2 in the blood drops. Body tissues die without oxygen. A human, however, no longer feels it. He's already brain dead. And is that moral, Rutkowski? Is it logical for the principal culprit in someone's death to die first and not to see the fruit of its crime? For consciousness of death to die before the body, which is completely innocent in all this bullshit? But that's just like consciousness—it always bugs out first. Especially with you intellectuals."

On the square, Rotkopf is reading the sentence. The blood of treacherously murdered German soldiers demands it. The blood of the dead, however, never demands anything. It doesn't have time for that. It coagulates. It isn't troubled by an absence of justice, but by a lack of hemoglobin.

In the meantime, Steinbrecher concludes that everything has been arranged for the benefit of intelligence and to the detriment of other aspects of life:

"Intelligence never succeeds in drawing the logical consequences from its guilt in the destruction of the body. It departs first, in bliss ignorance of the crime. Whereas other cells endure their agony for quite some time still, consciousness has already been dazed by some convenient abstraction. In our case, by the abstraction of death. Because death, about which consciousness can't draw conclusions based on its own experience—based on its own death—is only an abstraction. In the meantime, the cells of the higher nerve centers, the entire army of the CNS, stop functioning due to the insufficient supply of oxygen. Like our Wehrmacht in Russia. In a cat, for example, the cessation of cardiovascular circulation for a mere twenty seconds results in the suspension of rhythmic changes in the potential of the cortex, and after five minutes the nerve cells are destroyed beyond repair. And why, Obersturmführer? Why? Because they didn't receive their 0.6% of air. And depending on 0.6% of something isn't exactly glorious, is it? Especially if you're Socrates."

The reading of the verdict draws to a close. Adam, apparently, will be the last. That's clear now. They tie the hands of the other two. No one should have to fumble with his underwear when being hanged. I'm eagerly Steinbrecherizing in that vein only so I won't watch myself unsnap the holster of my pistol.

The Standartenführer continues Steinbrecherizing too:

"It's assumed that consciousness, before disappearing, nevertheless has at its disposal a minimal interval of superconsciousness, in which it can reach some reasonable conclusion. Its futility is of no significance. I firmly hope that this is the case. That would confirm my theories of intelligence. As a result of a lack of oxygen, as when we climb to high elevations, there must be a brief condition of rapture, ecstatic intoxication, in which consciousness, its time and space having been disrupted, already completely beyond our logical dimensions, can reject every earthly sense of mortal danger and soar to the next world without any comprehension of its own responsibility. Memory has been erased, history blown away, innocence established. One breathes one's last breath with no pangs of conscience. That's the way of you intellectuals!"

The two workers have been hanged. Quietly. Logically. Without even a parenthetical remark by the Standartenführer. The proletariat doesn't deserve parentheses, but a bullet. Nothing remains behind them, not even one of the Standartenführer's incidental generalizations, like a modest gravestone.

In the condensation on the inside of the windowpane, Steinbrecher's black finger traces the silhouette of the medulla oblongata, which resembles a gray flower's calyx with tender, dewy edges:

"The brachium posterior, corpus restiforme, tuberculum acusticum, nucleus cuneatus, tuberculum cinereum. Neural flowers . . . dianthus chinensis, helianthus annuus . . . As if they were tender plants, and not nerve junctions, and indeed the last two aren't. The last two, in fact, are carnations and sunflowers. But there's no difference! There's no difference between the *formatio reticularis* and the *helianthus annuus,* although the first is your knot of life, and the other only a miserable sunflower!"

I raise the pistol. My hand is pointing it at the dark skin of the Standartenführer's neck. At his *formatio reticularis,* with which he secures his 0.6 liters of air with every inhalation. That hairy lawn covers the paths of logic, with which one is first sent to Lilly Schwartzkopf's bed and then to the gallows. But if I shift my gaze only a few centimeters to the side, then I have a gray, rainy view of Adam's hands being tied in front of him, his open umbrella being thrust back into his hands, and the noose being tightened around his invisible *formatio reticularis.*

I notice something else that astonishes me—his face is black, broken, ruined, as if some sloppy creator had begun to alter his form but suddenly left it unfinished. I'm seized by the fear that that monstrosity is an infernal consequence of the half-hearted blow I'd given him, a last reminder of his desecrated humanity. But then I disregard all that, it's probably an illusion arising from a conspiracy of distance, shadows and my shame. And I see him open his mouth and shout something.

I couldn't hear him. But I didn't care. His *formatio reticularis* was no concern of mine. Steinbrecher's was. Any second now I'm going to put a bullet in it. The essential brachium posterior will be destroyed! The tender petals of the tuberculum cinereum will fly apart! The nucleus cuneatus will burst like a seed pod! The corpus restiforme will splatter!

As I fire a bullet into all that, I'll at the same time be killing all his magic dianthus chinesis, golden sunflowers, the poisonous flowers of his brain, of his ideas and aims! The potential for endless analyses and unexpected conclusions will disappear! Together with his severed neural and floral cells and his ingenious generalizations, Standartenführer Steinbrecher will become my personal generalization, one of my better themes.

Something strange is happening on the platform. It's as if a dark film were dropping down over the scene, in which nothing was visibly changing, only there was a sense that—with that darkening—events were no longer subject to the Standartenführer's program or our earthly laws; rather, they were given over to the fiefdom of something stronger and not of this world. Even Steinbrecher had fallen silent and was watching the scene in disbelief, a scene from which all logic was withdrawing step by step.

I draw satisfaction from the fact that by killing I nevertheless don't become a murderer. Because I, in fact, am not killing the Standartenführer. I'm merely reducing a simple frequency to zero. I'm not destroying his medulla oblongata but disrupting the combination of certain of his characteristic quantities. That his personal equation is destroyed, that the disrupted transport of 0.4–0.6 liters of air per inhalation and exhalation will be his share of the universe, air from God intended for him alone, and that his last reserve will be those rapidly evaporating 320 cm^3 of O_2 for every two liters of alveolar air, the index of the length of his life, insufficient for any of the Standartenführer's generalizations—these facts cast no doubt on my generalization, according to which everything, life and death, is only a game of numbers, a purely stereometric venture.

But then the umbrella in Adam's hand spread out like a black cherub's wing and, after raising him slowly up off the platform— from which his executioners were watching his miraculous ascension and where the limp bodies of the bandits were still swaying— it lifted him with a fatherly motion, devoid of all pomp, into the sunlit nimbus clouds as if into some phosphorescent tunnel, and this motion, to the noisy applause of the people and a military salute from the German troops, carried him upward into the heavens.[16]

Thus was the ascension of our clerk, Adam Trpković. And I testify these things—I, Konrad Rutkowski, who holds the pen in his hand, and who saw all these things and wrote them down according to what he saw. And who is ready to speak of this in more detail with you when we meet in Heidelberg.

KONRAD

■ □ ■ □ ■

LETTER 22

THE UNUSUAL ILLNESS

OF PROFESSOR RUTKOWSKI,

OR *CREATIVE EVOLUTION*

The Mediterranean Coast, 28 Sept. 1965

Hilmar,

Something *really is* wrong with me.[17] I've been feeling out of sorts for two days already. To be precise, since the evening of the 26th, when I completed the last letter. If I'd been going down to the beach I'd say I've come down with sunstroke. However, I don't have a headache or a fever. I took my temperature. And Sabina's too, just in case. Maybe we ate some bad food. True, things don't seem unclean here, but again, it's summertime, you never know . . . After Sabina's bloody shower, it seems I've become suspicious. Not of the people, of course. I know the people couldn't have anything to do with any kind of supernatural treachery. That would only occur to Standartenführer Steinbrecher, were he still alive . . . I don't feel like eating, either. My head is heavy, as if it weren't my own, as if it had been attached to my body by mistake. But it doesn't ache, I couldn't say that. It just doesn't fit, it doesn't perform its function. You know my memory, the letters are proof of it, but now I don't even know what I should be writing about or why. The story is over. What else is there left to do? . . . I really think I'm terrified—of what, I couldn't say. Last night, for instance, I felt like I was choking, as if someone were sitting on my chest and crushing me, crushing me, reducing my life functions to zero. I woke up halfway suffocated. As if I'd been hanged and the rope had suddenly broken, and I was starting to breathe again. What do you make of it, Hilmar? Can it be because I described Adam's hanging in such painstaking detail? I don't believe so. We're smart people, intellectuals, historians. We're not Steinbrechers. Steinbrecher was crazy, I've realized that for certain. But that was obscured by his extraordinary intelligence. The municipal file clerk's impossible ascension by umbrella, Steinbrecher faked it all—Item X, Subitem Y of the Secret Protocol appended to the Execution Program. He set it up so that Adam would be pulled into the crowns of the trees by a cord, and bore him all strangled up to the heavens. But maybe he didn't even completely finish him off, and left him to wander the town with a brain whose cells had been permanently damaged due to a temporary loss of 0.6% of their oxygen. And that's what led to our nightly conversations . . . Because the Standartenführer pulled all the strings. Everything was tied together and he held the end of the rope. We were only marionettes, subhuman creatures with no will or independent purpose. Sort of like the Jews were. And for us the world was as the Standartenführer's friend and correspondent, SS Untersturmführer Kurt Franz of Treblinka, imagined it in his struggle for perfection: "We must reach a point where we don't have to do anything any more, not even push a button when we get up in the morning. We'll create a perfect system and then watch it do its work. Because we're the masters, and our role is not to act but *to be*." (That world of Kurt's was a concentration camp. In spite of it all, Hilmar, it's impossible for us not to be overcome with admiration in the face of an intellect that turns a provincial waiter into a Heideggerian thinker!) . . . I told Sabina, she was reading a book, Sabina, I'm choking again![18] Why *again,* she asked, were you choking earlier? Yes, once, a while ago. Just like this. But it passed. Well, this'll probably pass too. In your family, there's certainly no room for crybabies, you can whine only about great patriotic or racial themes. Otherwise you endure. Maybe she'd have been more considerate if

I'd told her everything. But how? I'd have had to tell her about Adam and perhaps even that worker. You know *her*. It would have ended up with something having to be done—at the very least we'd have to visit Adam's family. And if I dared to tell her the truth about the umbrella and the file clerk's ascension, she'd take me to the doctor. That's the real reason, and not some fear of the consequences. I'm a foreign national—I know what international law is . . . But still, one can never be sure. Have you heard about what that Wiesenthal is doing? Now I'm not one to think that war criminals shouldn't be . . . If Steinbrecher were alive and they kidnapped him, I wouldn't be making an issue out of the formalities. I'm not Münch. Entry, Exit, Remark. With me it's another case. I resisted. I was revolted. I didn't agree. I comprehended the utter indecency of a pizzle whip in the hands of an intellectual! It can't be said that I didn't. I even fell ill after they forced me to beat a man. And I only assented to doing that in the name of higher goals—to survive so I could take revenge on the Standartenführer. I'd already even raised the pistol to do it, when Adam rose up away from the gallows and thus disrupted all logic in the world. Everything was so confused. One thing, however, was certain: I'd risked being killed and falsified Adam's Interrogation Transcript in order to save the people on his List. Unfortunately, there are no witnesses. The archives were destroyed before we withdrew from Belgrade. Steinbrecher's dead. Rotkopf is certainly still alive. But he doesn't know anything about the Transcript. He knows only that I gave the man a beating. And worst of all, he believed I was the one who got Adam to confess. He even congratulated me. Bravo, Rutkowski! So there's no use in going in that direction. And I always yelled at the file clerk in front of Max. Any testimony from him would be the end of me. The only one left is Münch. He'd be able to confirm that I'd wanted to get Adam out of there that first night. Only he'd never say something like that. He couldn't. He didn't take my intervention to be an effort to save the prisoner—otherwise he'd have reported me—he believed I was objecting to administrative inconsistencies in the ENTRY column. I'd end up looking like a jackass. And if my other witness Rotkopf heard what I was alluding to, his Steinbrecherian logic would automatically kick in: I hadn't tried to save Adam, because if I'd done so I'd have been shot after it came out that Adam knew about the List, which my Interrogation Transcript failed to mention. Since Adam was hanged, I'd performed my Gestapo duty. If Rutkowski were innocent, he'd have been shot. Since he's alive, he's guilty and should be shot. And even if everything had been different, I wouldn't have gotten away. I had, to be precise, the BLACK EYE.[19] . . . Sabina said my fits of choking came from unhealthy living. I spent whole nights scribbling things down, I didn't go out in the sun, I didn't get any exercise. My muscles had stiffened, fallen asleep. If I were more active and didn't think so much, things would get better. I assume you think the same thing too. You'll also use the opportunity to correct some historical delusions. Not *everything* in the Third Reich was bad. No one can deny that physical education was encouraged, which in democracies and especially plutocracies is completely neglected. In Berlin in 1936, we took 36 gold medals. And then there was the Autobahn, social welfare, the development of industrial technology, the sense of community through organizations, the collective conscience of the nation, public toilets, advances in martial music, the increased birth rate and the unification of all Germans under one umbrella—none of that can be denied merely on account of some megalomaniac delusions . . . You might have the right to reproach me for spiritual apathy. When I'm not writing, I lie or sit and stare into space. I think. Often I don't even think, though it seems I've become absorbed in some profound thoughts. It was as if writing these letters were the only thing keeping me going, and now that there's no longer any need for them, I've ground to a halt . . . Really, Hilmar, somehow I don't give a damn about anything. I don't care about anything. I don't even think I'll send you this letter. But I still continue to write it. You yourself can see how things are. I'm no longer certain of anything. Not even of the old letters. At times they depress me, at others I think I'm tackling significant problems with them . . . And my own case, does it matter to anyone? People are interested in Heinrich Himmler, and maybe even Heinrich Steinbrecher, but what do they care about SS Obersturmführer Konrad Rutkowski? There are millions of him. History consists of him alone. All the others—the Führer, Stalin, Mussolini, Napoleon, Nero, Caesar, Alexander—they're only the *titles* of history's chapters. History is Rutkowski. But who knows this? Who's interested in whether the ascension of Adam Trpković took place or not? People would be taken with that only if some religion arose from it. Some system. Such as Muhammadanism. But like this, what? . . . And in general, I don't know, I can't say . . . Maybe you don't even understand me, Hilmar. I admit I'm not being clear. As a result of my illness, my thoughts are dissipating, but I fear you wouldn't understand even if I were being biblically clear. No wonder. Don't take offense, but you're a lot like your sister. With her everything's cut and dry. Everything is in stark logical contrasts. Either Fröhlich slept with Lilly or he didn't. It can't be both. In reality, however, we've seen . . . Sabina doesn't understand me, she never has. You certainly haven't. Your attitude toward me was a rather poor compromise between scorn and the unpleasant fact that I was your brother-in-law . . . Anyway, why complain when no one understands you? Nothing but misunderstandings from childhood on. In 1941, for example, I didn't feel liberated in any way at all. But my parents immediately joined the NSDAP. To be sure, they weren't fanatics. They were peasants. As Steinbrecher said, those people don't lose their heads easily, unless there's some benefit for the livestock and harvest involved. I remember all those festivals, May Day parades, Kulturbunde, Horst-Wessel Lieder, and short pants. I've always hated short pants, especially on guys as big as me. And above all, that constant stamping of feet, as if you hated the very ground you were walking on . . . Then came the army and new misunderstandings. The SS and the Gestapo. I'd just finished my studies and begun teaching at the Pančevo Grammar School when I was conscripted into the police. Stupid, Hilmar! I know you hang that on me as another compromise—a compromise that substituted for a trip to the Eastern Front. But that's not true. I was simply selected and sent to work for the Gestapo. If you think I could have refused, ask yourself why you didn't refuse all your appointments, why you didn't resist your promotion through the ranks of the service.[20] . . . You really never could stand me. And you turned Sabina against me. You told people I was crazy. Once you even went to the Chancellor and accused me of ruining old books by correcting them. Where's the logic in that? How can something be ruined by corrections? By the time something needs correcting, there must be something wrong with it. Especially if the act of correction is acknowledged by the accusation itself . . . It's always been clear to me that you envied me for abilities you didn't have. All you ever had was good documentation, but nothing else. And we all know who collects documentation. Write this about Prince Mieszko and about the embroidery. A few robes and gowns do exist, but there are no references. References are what's important, not excavations and clay jugs. History doesn't consist of tin necklaces, broken vases, and femoral bones preserved in lava, Hilmar, but in *relationships,* which don't get preserved. In life that's been burned up in the meantime . . . I don't deny it, though—something can also be gleaned from femoral bones. From the condition of the teeth, for instance, one can glimpse the state of a people's health, the attitude of a race toward the body, and then that carries with it an index of the general relationship between the material and the spiritual. And here you're already on the fairly solid ground of the typology of civilizations, at O. Spengler's Table of "Contemporary" Culture Epochs. But how can you arrive at the most profound knowledge of the modes of thought and behavior of extinct peoples? Hilmar, you can't even manage that when it's a matter of what you've personally witnessed and served. The difficulty is in the fact that you don't have the conscience for what you have talent for, and you're not talented at what you're conscientious in doing. That's why you don't have any ideas worthy of cicero. You took your best ideas from others— they're nothing but diamond, pearl, and nonpareil. It's hard to find two bourgeois-sized thoughts in the whole book. Everything else is nothing but minion, marred by the blots of unproved assumptions. Is that really the history you squander tome after tome on? . . . Martin Bormann did not hold the *N.* Conference on the 7th of May 1944, but on the 8th. Professor *X. Y.*'s error stems from the fact that the Protocol of the Meeting does not say that the meeting began in the wee hours of the 8th. But Professor *X. Y.* makes an even more catastrophic mistake when he writes that the Führer never saw the town of Kitzingen. Because from the fact that on the Day of the Party in September 1941, the Leader of the Reich was traveling by train from Frankfurt to Nuremberg (a parenthetical note follows about the party conferences in Nuremberg), and since he was traveling by day and the train was supposed to stop in Kitzingen according to the railway schedule (documentation compiled from statements by the railway personnel of the Kitzingen station follows), and the time of the train's stop coincided with the usual time of the Leader's walks (a digression about his habits with a fair number of parallels with other historical figures), it inevitably follows that he must have at least walked out on the platform and thus saw Kitzingen, if not preferring to make a few rounds around the platform itself accompanied by his German shepherd Wolf (here there follows a final digression about the role of that dog in the life of the Chancellery staffs, and a little more about dogs in general). If Professor X. Y. now dared to try to prove in a large study that the Führer always traveled in a special train (here there follows a digression about Hitler's travels, with a few details about diesel locomotives *sub specie* . . .), and thus nevertheless didn't see Kitzingen, because such a train never made any stops en route (facsimiles of the statements of the staff of the Führer's official train follow), you would get your glorious bourgeois-sized passage, your contribution to historical scholarship would be made. You'd respond in an offprint: On the critical day, the Führer's private train was for once *nevertheless* out of service, Nuremberg unavoidable as always, and Kitzingen was *nevertheless* seen from the passenger train he took on this occasion. So you see, Hilmar, that's what you study, what history is for you . . . But history is really our adaptation, the adaptation of the human race, to the inevitability of an individual death. History is—according to Hegel—the realization of freedom by means of a series of successive enslavements to different kinds of necessity. Hilmar, history is everything except our uncertainty about the Führer's knowledge of Kitzingen . . . I'm tired. Lately I've been tired all the time. I don't think there's anything physical about it. I think in fact I'm tired of misunderstandings. Let's just consider the one with the army. If they recruit you even when they know you're not a trained killer, the misunderstanding is evident. What do you call it when your knowledge of Serbian, which until then you had used so you and the Serbs could understand each other, is used to create misunderstandings with them? A misunderstanding, obviously. And I've already written about the misunderstandings in the police. Move your knight here. Move your bishop there. Left or right? Just think—squandering so much effort and intellectual energy on the wrong man! I should have tried to save the worker, not Adam. But I beat the worker to death, and didn't manage to save Adam anyway . . . I'm afraid all my compromises were misunderstandings as well, all my compromises with reality or my conscience, each at different times. They were always lame. Did you know that I never succeeded in convincing a single prisoner that I was maltreating him exclusively for *his own good?* That every time I was compelled to slap him, it was only a compromise with the prescribed beatings he had coming to him according to the most lenient practices of the Service? That every beating was a substitute for electroshocks and dislocating his limbs and thus again a compromise? . . . And there's no end in sight to those misunderstandings. I was always having some misunderstanding with your sister, too. She was constantly demanding that I drop my Poles and study something intelligent like her dear old big brother. Who's interested in the Poles any more? One should work on something shocking and exciting. Genocide. Massacres. Pogroms. Catastrophes. National tragedies. Besides money, there are consequences to be drawn from such things. No consequences can be drawn from the embroidery on Mieszko's royal robes, other than in the field of fashion . . . Hilmar, your histories are, for instance, chiefly the biographies of criminals and the chronologies of crimes, which you dress in euphemistic names, such as: the Polish Question, the Czech Question, the Austrian Question, the Question of Danzig and the Corridor, the Question of Rearmament. And then: the Solution to the Jewish Question, the Munich Agreement, Crystal Night, the Night of the Long Knives, etc., etc. Here history is just a crime drama, equipped, in order to be disguised as scholarship, with numerous footnotes and ibidems. Sadism and exhibitionism printed in pure diamond. Paranoia with references to epilepsy. Megalomania and hypochondria with psychoneurotic footnotes. Psychopaths of a powerful, abnormal self-consciousness with references to politics . . . I don't deny it, maybe I'd be qualified to study the police aspects of contemporary history. That would even have some philosophical justification. Man would have his faith in progress and the ascent of history renewed, which was destroyed by Spengler's closed circles of civilization. The police are something that an optimist could relate to. If progress in history is dubious, if it's the result of illusion, the advance of police skill is beyond doubt. And that returns a certain amount of hope for the meaning of history, right? *Eppur, si muove!* . . . Standartenführer

Steinbrecher spoke about that once too. I don't know whether I'll manage to recall everything he said on that topic, but the idea about constant progress was clear. He said that all the constituent ingredients of political criminal proceedings are already to be found in the first biblical episode of human history: Forbiddance, Threats, Crime, Investigation, Interrogation, Judgment, and Punishment. First of all, forbidding that fruit be taken from *one* tree, fruit completely indistinguishable from the fruit of any other tree, could have as its goal only the enthronement of prohibition as such and to test its effect on people. Plucking fruit from that tree in particular, amid all the others, proves that this was not a matter of ordinary theft, but a premeditated act aimed at violating divine order—and thus rebellion. That was the first known political crime. The whole legal action encompassed elements in effect for any political police at any time, and so for the Gestapo as well, of course: the logical craving to violate the prohibition and to disturb the established order, a conspiracy of man and woman with that as its goal (abetment and solicitation); the participation of the serpent as an agent provocateur and a probable informant; and finally one person, God, who appeared in every legal guise—as legislator, investigator, prosecutor, and judge. Even the warden of the execution chamber. And above all, the similarity is confirmed by the punishment—death. That's what Steinbrecher said about it. And then he rushed through the history of police service in easy bounds. The first portrayal of police life was excavated from a grave of the XII Dynasty (around 2,000 years before Christ) near Beni Hassan in Egypt. The image showed a man being held by three policemen while a fourth beat him with a bamboo stick and a fifth (obviously the commander) supervised the procedure. A disappointing scene. It seems that nothing has changed in 4,000 years. Policemen and prisoners still provide more or less the same picture. Impressions, however, are deceptive. Historical changes are not sudden. They more closely resemble biological processes, the physical consequences of which—like aging, for example—are noticeable only after a series of successive declines in vitality. The first forced confession—leaving the Bible aside—is again recorded in Egyptian Thebes. The Commander in Chief of the City of the Dead had a man suspected of sacrilegious grave robbing beaten until he, in order to escape torture, confessed his guilt.

Then he was buried alive in the grave he had desecrated. We find a similar link between Crime and Punishment among the Assyrians, who punished incompetent surgeons by performing the exact same operation on them that they made on the patient, with the same mistake. While here the correspondence between the kind of crime and the punishment is obvious, it's not entirely clear why prostitutes were covered with asphalt. The first legal privileges were observed in Rome and have been retained to this day. The *quaestores parricidii* of the Roman Republic were allowed to force confessions via torture only from slaves. Citizens were *intacti tormentis*. Steinbrecher was a bitter opponent of such policy. He claimed that, in addition to the obvious technical drawbacks, it undermined the confidence of the citizens in the concept of equality before the law. How is it possible to foil conspiracies if those who usually conceive and lead them are protected by law? He viewed the Roman episode as some kind of historical regression. He didn't make any explicit comment regarding the Persian experience. The news that Persian judges sat on chairs upholstered with the flayed skin of their corrupt predecessors didn't excite him. Namely, he never made mistakes. He considered the trial of Christ to be an example of a failed third degree. No change occurred in the attitude of the condemned toward his guilt. No names other than that of God could be gotten out of him. The ends of the conspiracy were left untied and the participants were allowed to slip away. The result is known. Rome fell owing to the incompetence of the Sanhedrin political police and the aristocratic ignorance of Pontius Pilate. (In the end, this is what the Jews wanted, so it's not inconceivable that they intentionally conducted the trial in a sloppy manner!) Emperor Trajan was the first to combine, on a scientific basis, intellectual persuasion of the Russian kind with the psychological pressure exerted by the Anglo-Saxons and the German physical system. As early as his long dispute with Galien, the Christian convert, Rotkopf's pizzle whip filled any occasional gaps in the argumentation. The dawn of barbarism brings nothing new and it seems the possibilities for the development of the police were exhausted and finally reduced to a club. All that happened was a change in the legal perspective: the life of a Frankish nobleman was worth 600 gold pieces, whereas that of a Roman citizen was now hardly worth fifty. However, in the eastern half of Europe there were advances in the technology of interrogation. The interrogatee is seated on a narrow, oiled stake and is left to slide down on it from his own weight until he starts talking. Sometimes salt was put on the tip of the stake. The Turks later bastardized the Byzantine techniques. Impalement on a stake was a prolonged punishment, appropriate in sparsely populated parts of Europe and particularly in the Middle East, where time wasn't at a premium. SS Untersturmführer Kurt Franz wouldn't have gotten anywhere with such techniques. The equipment would have overwhelmed him. The raw materials would have killed him before he could have undertaken anything with them. Steinbrecher thought that collective revenge was one of the oldest forms of effective punishment—practiced very often in the Bible—but that it acquired its modern sense only in its Saxon-Norman version. The customary tribal law of Alfred the Great, according to which every free man was a member of a group of ten co-tribesmen, for whom he was *responsible* in every respect, was exploited by William the Conqueror to neutralize any possible Saxon resistance. The remaining Norman innovations were castration, blinding, and drawing and quartering. In the psychological domain no progress was made up until the Holy Inquisition, which truly represented the first revolutionary step in elevating police service to the level of a scientific discipline.[21] (By the way, you must be aware that the torture handbook of the honorable fathers Jacobus Sprenger and Heinrich Krämer, entitled MALLEUS MALEFICARIUM and published in 1486, was the favorite book of the Geheime Staatspolizei.) The goal was no longer purely technical—to establish as much guilt as possible and learn as many correspondences as possible—though these technical aspects were not forgotten. Nor was the police service of the *Sanctum officium* indifferent to the arrestees, as were all earlier institutions of persecution. The goal was now immaterial and elevated, so to speak: To save the lost criminal soul, to force it to comprehend its sin and repent publicly. But that demanded a complete change of the principles that until then had formed the basis of the relationship between investigator and suspect. Instead of a device for forcible extraction, the investigator became a confessor, an assistant, a comforter, and even a rescuer, although in the majority of cases all that could be saved was the soul. The shell of the sin, the body, had to be burned. No longer could just anyone with a powerful voice and a heavy fist be an investigator. Only very educated people, prone to speculations and unsurpassable in dialectics, could count on becoming inquisitors, which had inestimable consequences for the development of the police cadre of the future. An investigator, in addition to knowledge, had to have faith as well, something that was completely unessential to an Egyptian, Roman, or Byzantine policeman; he had to be absolutely convinced that he was doing God's will. Otherwise, he'd have had difficulty bearing the new techniques of torture, described so perfectly in Fox's BOOK OF MARTYRS. (Piercing sensitive parts of the body with thin rods in search of bloodless demonic zones; tearing off flesh with red-hot tongs; submersion under water to the point of suffocation; "strappado," or pushing the suspect from a certain height onto a hard surface; forcibly dislocating limbs from joints, which, after they had been reset by doctors, were wrenched again; "*peine forte et dure,*" or crushing to death, which consisted of subjecting the prostrate suspect to the weight of greater and greater quantities of rock and iron—these were only a few forms of torture, which have been retained in somewhat modernized forms to this day.) Steinbrecher didn't consider anything in that period significant other than perhaps the laws of Edward I of England, which made of every citizen a policeman, a primitive and early form of the modern dream, and, of course, the proclamation of Charles V of France, which founded the French police for the purpose of "increasing the people's happiness." He considered the *Lettre de cachet* to be a mere technical advance, although he didn't dispute that it had a certain ideational value. The century of the industrial revolution, by its nature, practically and pragmatically speaking, couldn't profoundly change police methods. It simply raised them from the workshop level to the level of mass production. The American innovation could be seen mainly in the application of machines during interrogation: powerful reflector lamps, electric shocks, and tear gas, although working someone's kidneys over while his back was covered with a wet towel was kept everywhere as a time-honored tradition. (In Europe, where traditions were stronger, the transition was made more slowly and with less clear-cut distinctions. Thus, for example, a fire for burning the vagina was replaced with an electric bulb over which a stream of water flowed. The cult of the past is obvious here.) As I've emphasized to you so many times, Hilmar, Steinbrecher was above all a conscientious policeman. And no matter how much it humiliated him and embittered him personally, he had to admit that, from the time of Charlemagne's mounted police up to the Gestapo, we Germans had contributed precious little to the perfection of the police and its methods. In his view, we were always the best students of more inventive nations. That honor, in our century, belonged to the East. Preventing biological processes (sleep deprivation, which enhanced the traditional starvation and dehydration), intellectually inducing dementia, brainwashing with the aid of "magic rooms," mescaline, scopolamine, or LSD (with artificial schizophrenia of a more recent date) and depersonalization—these are the milestones of contemporary police doctrine. The "sweet box" (an American invention in which the suspect was placed in a hot room filled with the stench of skunks) seems in comparison to be like a bow and arrow versus a rifle—primitive and laughable. I personally think that Steinbrecher was wrong and that he was being unfair, both to us Germans and to the West as a whole. The West has no real reason to be ashamed in the face of the achievements of the East in this area. Not one of them, particularly those in the area of psychology, would have been possible without the scientific foundations which came from the West. With the exception of Pavlov, all of them, Jean Charcot, Janet, Freud, Jung, Adler, etc. were westerners. As for us Germans, even if we didn't at all prove ourselves in individual cases, our findings in the area of mass operations are beyond dispute. We were the first to industrially exploit our victims. Stalin only exploited them as slave labor, a historically totally antiquated process of extracting extra profit. No one had attempted turn their bodies into goods before. A disdain of corpses has marked our dynamic civilization. We've returned respect to death. We've prolonged the life of the human body. We've made it socially useful in its worthless state. Gold teeth, hair, fat, and even skin—everything has served some purpose . . . What in the name of God am I talking about? How did I get here—to soap? You see how things are, Hilmar. I can't even deal with my own thoughts any more. I need to turn the page to see what I've just been writing about . . . Yes, about the failure to understand. When everything is taken together, I think the

Standartenführer was the one man who *really* understood me. And that turned out to be a misunderstanding. Isn't that unfair, Hilmar? Once in your life you come across someone who understands you, and then he starts tormenting you because of a lack of understanding . . . It's no wonder I'm in such shape, that I have insomnia and attacks of depression. And that I avoid people. And all of that befell me after Adam's ascension, too. To be sure, I didn't pass out then and there. I only went temporarily blind. My eyes grew dim while the file clerk was still passing through the clouds. And I don't remember how I got to the toilet. How long I was there, or what I did. They found me on the stool with a pistol in my hand. I was very ill, though I don't remember what that illness consisted of. Everyone claimed I'd wanted to kill myself and had locked myself in the toilet to do so. The Standartenführer was livid. He shared Untersturmführer Kurt Franz' opinion of suicide. For him it was a sign that a person had not been Steinbrecherized to a sufficient degree, that they, in spite of the most refined treatment which had as its goal the complete destruction of independent will, had still retained their last, yet vital right: To be or not to be. That right, however, did belong to Standartenführer Steinbrecher and Untersturmführer Franz. The suicide of prisoners, and even of subordinate officials, was a flagrant violation of their competency . . . I don't know, though. I don't remember wanting to kill myself, although it would certainly be better if I had. I wouldn't be upset like this, or afraid that there will be a repeat of my crisis. But all indications have been that there will be. As soon as I described Adam's ascension, I felt nauseous and ran to the toilet to puke my guts out. That's what I have left from the Gestapo. Whenever things got difficult for me—I headed straight for the toilet. There I was at least alone. I know I shouldn't do so (and I'm not much for superstition anyway), but I swear some kind of spells must be involved here. It happens that certain states repeat if everything is arranged in the same positions, if the same constellation of objects is achieved. That's the principle of all witchcraft. It's possible that I induced this process with the magic description of the events that induced it in 1943 . . . I likewise think the Standartenführer should be cleared once and for all from any suspicion regarding Adam's ascension. He was undoubtedly a gifted and capable policeman, but he couldn't cast spells or arrange miracles . . . (Untersturmführer Franz was better in that area. He erected the facade of a cute railroad station in Treblinka and thereby cast a spell on all the Jewish transports unloaded there to be cremated. Not even the fact that the wooden clock on the platform always showed the same time—three o'clock in the afternoon—could fool anyone into thinking that Treblinka wasn't a well-organized labor camp.) . . . Only that satanic umbrella of Adam's could pull off something like that. That was its *way!* When I recovered a little, I asked around. I couldn't get at anything. Sure, everyone claimed there'd been something unusual and odd about that hanging, but no one knew exactly what it was. No one had seen Adam rising up into the sky. That was apparently only granted to me . . . But since accidents don't happen in such cases (rather, everything is a calculated act on someone's part, usually that of a supernatural being), it's clear that the fact that I was chosen as the medium had some meaning . . . Inasmuch as something really did happen, and everything wasn't a hallucination. Because in Freissner's photograph, taken right before Adam was actually hanged, nothing out of the ordinary can be seen. Unfortunately, that doesn't prove anything. The shot could have been taken immediately before his ascension. (Freissner was a passionate amateur photographer. He specialized in photographing horrible scenes. Otherwise, he was a professor of ethics at Berlin University.) . . . I didn't manage to complete the investigation because I was taken to the hospital. I spent two months there and recovered completely. Steinbrecher didn't give me any problems when it was medically established that I wasn't faking. He visited me fairly often and Steinbrecherized. But that was already in Belgrade, after we returned . . . But by then he had problems of his own, too. General von Klattern had reported him to Berlin, accusing him of holding popular fiestas with hangings, convicts in their underwear, and umbrellas. Nothing happened to him, of course . . . The administration and Müller himself were behind him. Kaltenbrunner intervened on Steinbrecher's behalf in his capacity as Oberstgruppenführer of the SS and chief of the RSHA, and there were no consequences, except that General von Klattern was transferred to the Eastern Front . . . I'll have to quit, Hilmar . . . Sabina's right . . . I'm not getting enough air and exercise. That's where the choking, the sweating, and dizziness are coming from . . .

But how can I get out? It's raining outside, and Sabina left her umbrella and parasol in front of the door to dry . . . The umbrellas, unfortunately, slipped down and ended up lying across each other, blocking the doorway. Like a magic sign of forbiddance . . . Now it's not Adam's wicked umbrella, so there's nothing to fear . . . But again, you never know, do you? . . . Take their ability to change their form. An umbrella is only an umbrella. Mostly tame and obliging—even when it's wild and disobedient, there's always some way for it to be put in order . . . But when they're in company, together, alongside each other, they suddenly look like SS lightning bolts . . . A store with umbrellas becomes a Waffen SS barracks . . . If you cross two umbrellas at the middle, do you know what you get? . . . A swastika, Hilmar! The Hakenkreuz! . . . Don't you see now what the problem is, and why you can never be careful enough? . . . Hitler started out with one man, himself, and look how far he got . . . If Sabina's umbrellas are benign, why didn't they fall in some other way instead of crossing into a swastika right away? . . . Maybe they too are capable of committing maleficences? . . . Maybe after all they are part of a satanic plot that . . .

KONRAD

■ □ ■ □ ■

LETTER 23

A MAGICAL RECOVERY,
OR *CIVITATES DEI*

The Mediterranean Coast, 29 Sept. 1965

My dear, dearest Hilmar,[22]

If, out of your well-known magnanimity, you've continued to read my letters, even the one I scribbled out at the peak of a mental crisis, it won't escape you that they imitate our earthly cycle with a mocking consistency. Like us, they're born under the unfathomable star of chance. To be sure, there was a desire to come to D., no one is denying that, but no kind of confession was envisioned, and so it all reminds us of a child we didn't want to have and weren't thinking about when we gave ourselves over to the pleasures of the first night of our marriage to our wartime and police memories. Born into a family rich in wretched episodes but that, in the meantime, has still found a modus vivendi (in public but not in private), the letters spend their early youth continuously rehashing loathsome memories of home. Despite this, they've retained the enthusiasm and freshness of that original inspiration; the perspectives are still unobscured, and all their paragraphs live in the conviction that the mistakes of their parents' house will be corrected or explained and even redeemed by some exceptional *stylistic turn of phrase.*

How broadly, clearly, and fluidly my thoughts came forth when I, pushing Piastowicz aside, took the pen in my hand! True, a dark pre-life was waiting to be portrayed, but alongside its shameful burden there was also a goal: the possibility of its finally being cast off. The mental blow suffered by a child learning that his father is a murderer can't be harder and more cruel than that which I had to endure while portraying an event I had until then remembered as a tragedy but now recognized to be a crime. (Over the years, I'd developed an unusual, basically compromising attitude toward the past. I admitted it to be mine in the same way a son admits to a blood link with his parents and a partial responsibility for their actions. This Konrad Rutkowski, though older than the one who committed the misdeed, was younger than him, because he had been conceived and born while the original Rutkowski was ingloriously dying in fear and shame amid the last echoes of the guns in May 1945.) The mature period of my correspondence coincided with that painful realization. So even in those circumstances, in which other letters would have deteriorated into raving, these maintained a clarity of comprehension. Owing to my extraordinary memory, life could be dismantled like a faulty clock mechanism in order to find the part in it that was broken and affecting its accuracy. The occasional nervousness in the correspondence can be explained more as an overabundance of memories than a fear of facing their reality. In any case, it appeared that nothing could keep these letters from advancing toward their goal: the fateful conclusion that would turn my whole life upside down. Unfortunately, if these letters repeat our life cycle, and if we were satisfied with them while they were feeding on its youth, we must remain loyal to them when they age with us as well.

To put it simply, there are two possible ways for life to end. On the one hand, we can burn out imperceptibly, gradually sinking into ever-lower levels of thought and ever-simpler forms of rhetoric, and reducing our relationships with the world to a minimum—until one day in this respect we become so far removed from reality that it no longer acknowledges us, no longer recognizes us or notices our disappearance. Or, on the other hand, at the height of our expansion, something hits us and with a single blow our axle snaps, our brakes go out, and the car of our life goes careening off into an abyss at lightning speed, wiping out everything in its path. Obviously, the letters, like my life, chose the first way. They're dying off with me and my powers.

The fact of the matter is that everything here happened under the sign of compromise as well. My axle *had* been broken, it just hadn't flown apart yet, and the drive continued for twenty more years after it came to its natural end. I maintain that Adam's ascension, my failure to kill Standartenführer Steinbrecher, and my pitiful attempt at suicide were the events that broke the axle of my life. Everything that happened between those events and my return to D. was an optical illusion, the afterglow of a life that had ended. I consider these last twenty years to be the most successful in my life, but look—I haven't even dedicated a few sentences to them in these letters. A life with nothing to say for itself—what the hell is that?

This needs to be said. A space needs to be cleared out around the decision that awaits me. But before I go on to that—it's still unclear even to me, so let it straighten itself out while we talk about other things—allow me to clarify things between us with regard to the last letter. I have the impression that I insulted you rather badly in it. I denied that you have any talent and tried to make you look foolish. I hope you understand that this deficit of logic was just another symptom of my state of illness. Because it goes without saying that you're talented. And it's well known that you're the hope of our historiography. From the fact that you're our hope, it follows inevitably that you're talented, because if you weren't you wouldn't be our great hope. You'd be something like me—the worst intellectual and moral failure in my whole class. And from the fact that you're talented it follows naturally that you're our hope. Let's leave it to logic to excuse me, and let's turn to umbrellas.

I solved the problem of Sabina's umbrellas, which were blocking the way out of my room, yesterday evening. After a protracted mental battle, I mustered the courage to grab them by their necks with a pair of tongs and carry them to the pier, and then threw them into the water. I convinced Sabina that someone had stolen them, and she turned that into a very long excursion into the realm of ethics. Today I'm already sorry I did it. Because, as you see, I felt better soon after anyway, and so if I hadn't been in such a hurry the umbrellas would still be alive. Considering it calmly, there was no chance of their being related to Adam's.

But to be sure of this, I visited Adam's family this morning. There was no need to introduce myself. Mrs. Trpković, who was at home by herself, recognized me immediately. For a while we revived our memories (mainly of her husband) over some brandy, and finally I took advantage of the opportunity and delicately brought up the subject of the umbrella. She said that it was still in the family's possession, but that no one used it any more. They kept it more as a keepsake of Adam's. When asked how they came into possession of it, she said that it was handed over to them together with the file clerk's belongings after his execution. Answering the cautious question of how it now behaved, the woman said they couldn't complain, although at first things had been fairly difficult. But not, in fact, immediately after it came back. After Adam's death the family was in turmoil and didn't pay any attention to it. It was kept with the file clerk's remaining personal effects in an unlocked cabinet. Only after some time was it determined that the umbrella would disappear at night and return again in the morning, sometimes bloody and torn. For those who knew about its nature, these strolls were no surprise. But since they didn't result in any kind of trouble *for the family*—it seemed that the umbrella had had enough of the Trpković's—nothing was done to hinder it. What it did out on the street after the curfew was none of their concern, as long as they weren't involved. Anyway, it was wartime and the umbrella's dirty deeds, if indeed there were any, were camouflaged by the misfortunes that came with the war. No one could distinguish the former from the natural misfortunes of the occupation, and thus the umbrella was left to its clandestine work. (They must have secretly hoped it was killing Germans.) A few attempts to get rid of it in the meantime failed. It retained its independence. The real trouble began only after the liberation. The umbrella continued to disappear from the cabinet, but it was no longer possible to close one's eyes to its actions. There was no war to cover them up. Whenever it disappeared, something would happen in the town. Either a fire would break out, or someone would die, or there would be a traffic accident on a nearby road. It even happened that the roofs on some houses began to collapse. The situation became intolerable when the umbrella began to interfere with the reconstruction of the country after the war. A few acts of sabotage in the factory buildings of the local industry were, at least in the eyes of the family, its doing. There was a danger that the connection would be discovered at some point and that the Trpkovićes, though they weren't accomplices, would be charged with negligence if nothing else. Only then was it decided that something had to be done. One night they called an Orthodox priest to the house, who said prayers over the umbrella all night long, poured holy water on its silk canopy and rubbed its handle while reciting incantations of exorcism. For a time the umbrella calmed down and didn't go out. And then it started all over again. It seemed that the prayers had only lulled it to sleep temporarily and had not had any lasting effect on the devil in it. After that they guarded it. In turns, every night. Unfortunately, that arrangement didn't prove to be practical. If someone was left to guard it, he would generally fall asleep, apparently charmed. Something more effective had to be found. The woman could no longer remember, that was quite a long time ago, who it was that hit upon the good idea of treating the umbrella as if it were a vampire. If it couldn't be destroyed, then at least its movement could be inhibited. The umbrella was placed in an old safe that had been bought at the junkyard of a neighboring city, the safe locked, and a crucifix hung on its door. Since then they hadn't had any difficulties with it. I wondered whether they hadn't been mistaken about the umbrella's nightly outings. There was a possibility that those tragedies were not its doing and that the outings had a completely different purpose. *What would that have been?*—asked the woman. To find someone who would use it and thus enable it to begin its demonic life again. Maybe it spent most of the night leaning peaceably against some tree in the hope that someone would take it as Adam had done once. *If that were the case,* the woman asked, *why would it return to the cabinet again?* I didn't know what to say. With otherwise logical supernatural phenomena there's always something that defies comprehension. I was already about to take my leave when a troubling thought occurred to me: If the umbrella in the safe was Adam's, whose umbrella was it that his astral figure was carrying when it spoke with me? Cautiously, so as not to upset the woman, I asked if it wouldn't be possible to see the umbrella before I left. She was reluctant, but as the umbrella had never disappeared while it was surrounded by watchful and rational people, she was prepared, for a small amount of monetary compensation, to take the risk. The safe was tucked in the cellar, where no one had gone for a long time. We had a hard time getting at it, clearing away heaps of old junk. Hilmar, you can imagine the woman's surprise—I, however, remained calm, I had already suspected something of that kind—when she saw that the crucifix had been removed from the lock, the safe open and the umbrella gone. In search of an explanation, she accused the neighbor children, who had the habit of jumping into the cellar through an unprotected window and rummaging through the old things. But despite all that, she didn't hide her feeling of deep relief that the umbrella had left the Trpković family once and for all, it seemed. I didn't want to deprive her of that satisfaction. In a sense, it was justified. But, naturally, I had a simpler and more sensible explanation of the whole event. The one who had opened the safe and taken the umbrella was Adam. The traditional protection of the crucifix had once again proved to be inadequate.

There was only one more thing to clear up before I left. I asked Mrs. Trpković whether she had attended the execution of her husband. She said that on the day when the soldiers had gathered people from the streets and their homes, she had fortunately not been in D. Had she heard anything in particular being told around concerning the execution? She hadn't, other than that he had conducted himself bravely, of course. I bade her farewell and left.

As I've already touched on that important question—namely, the question of whether there were any other witnesses to Adam's ascension besides myself—let me finish my report about the investigation I undertook in that regard as soon as I recovered from my shock. (Later the crisis resumed in a considerably stronger form, and I had to go to the hospital in Belgrade.)

I told you that the men of the Sonderkommando hadn't noticed anything and that Freissner's photograph—which you'll find in the drawer of my desk—doesn't reveal anything unnatural in the scene of the hanging. However, I also made inquiries among the townspeople and von Klattern's soldiers. The problem was that I didn't dare ask anyone the question openly. I was afraid of being turned in and subjected to a medical examination. I asked everyone whether they had noticed anything unusual during the execution. The more primitive among them considered the men's underwear to be the most conspicuous thing. The more educated among them gave precedence to the umbrella. The fact that this detail had not escaped the latter was a consequence of their refined perception and intellect. I decided to narrow my search and concentrate on them. It turned out that they didn't wish to say much about it. I realized they were ashamed that they had witnessed such a flagrant violation of human dignity. Naturally, they didn't reproach the Standartenführer for killing bandits. That was natural and justified. What they did reproach him for was taking such a serious matter and turning it into a circus, degrading not only the condemned but also themselves, the spectators. In all, only a few noncommissioned officers showed any willingness to go into more detailed recollections. I could tell that they had all sensed how preposterous the event was and how horrified they'd been, even if they couldn't keep from laughing about it. As for details, they had noticed a wind that made the umbrella start swinging at the moment of the hanging and a darkening of the scene when a cloud moved in. The locals responded somewhat differently. Although nothing in the statements of the townspeople directly indicated an ascension, a certain respect for Adam seemed to imply the possibility. Several women who mentioned Adam's name while at prayer in the church were brought into Gestapo custody. A kind of cult began to spread. As if this were a matter of the new Messiah, who was gaining his first followers among the women. The women were executed. Their defense, that mentioning Adam was part of the Orthodox funeral liturgy, didn't hold up logically. Not even factually. Questioned about this, an Orthodox priest stated that Adam isn't mentioned anywhere in the liturgy. Concerning one Jewish lady among the women who claimed that she was not praying to Adam, but to the god Adonai, she was acquitted and simply killed as a Jew.

Although I have my doubts about the Intellect in a moral sense, which will be the topic of discussion below, what I can't dispute without damaging its foundation and disavowing its purpose is that it tackles every problem life presents us with. In that sense, strictly philosophically, there are no topics forbidden to the Intellect, nor speculations that are in and of themselves immoral. Only their *use* can be immoral. We cannot accuse scientists of discovering the principles that we used to make the atomic bomb. We should not claim that discoveries in the fields of eugenics, genetics, neuropsychiatry, and theoretical biology are immoral *up to the point* that they start readjusting our brains, and even then only if they are developed in the wrong way. I'll cite two examples from police practice so you can see the difference between Idea and Deed, Reflection and Action, Speculation and Realization.

Imagine you're a scientist approached by a respected crematorium in need of technical assistance. The problem to be solved is how to burn the most human bodies in the shortest time with the lowest expenditures. There's no doubt that you'd take on the job, certain that you were furthering general progress. You'd begin by making an on-site inspection and then begin experimentation. There's no other way to determine the most effective method of cremation. You'd begin with the logical assumption that not all bodies burn with equal intensity, that some are relatively flammable while others are fire-resistant and that there are innumerable varieties between these extreme cases. (If one is seeking some industrial application, the process has to be simple.) Through research and experimentation you'll reach the conclusion that bodies of the elderly burn better than bodies of young people. (This was the result of a parallel with dry and green wood.) That fat people burn more quickly than thin people, and women faster than men, and that in this respect children are somewhere in between on the scale: namely, children burn more quickly than adult males, but a little slower than adult females. ACCORDINGLY, THE IDEALLY FLAMMABLE BODY IS THE CORPSE OF AN OLD FAT WOMAN. These categories will predetermine the techniques of the procedure, the type and quantity of kindling, as well as all technical aspects of the cremation. *Pure speculative logic + laboratory experimentation = maximum result.*

Thinking and experimenting in this manner, faced with the task of burning, in the shortest possible time and with a shortage of oil and wood, around 700,000 Jews suffocated in the gas chambers of Treblinka, one Herbert Floss, an expert in cremation, had to devise a way of getting the job done without it taking a hundred years and depleting all of Poland's forests or the entire German military oil reserves. Through pure abstract reasoning, followed by experiments, he arrived at the ingenious conclusion that the process would be cheapest if the flammable bodies were left to ignite the fire-resistant ones. The result was pyramids of corpses, which had thin males at the top and women near the bottom (children were in the middle), while layers of old fat ladies were positioned at the base. The daily rate was almost 10,000 corpses burned.

Mr. Floss's work was intellectual in the highest degree. The fact that it was conducted in unfavorable historical circumstances does not *in principle* diminish its ingenuity.

Allow me another example, this time from the realm of intellectual controversy. You're aware that great intellectual disputes and conflicts have always defined the real problems of a civilization. The dialogue between the Christians and the polytheists, occasionally interrupted by a lion's roar from the arena, was undoubtedly the greatest intellectual controversy of ancient times, and centered on God. The other great controversy of thought—the precise number of victims has never been determined—was that between the iconophiles and the iconoclasts in eighth-century Byzantium; it opened the door to a new era and also centered on God. The third philosophical conflict of global proportions centered on God, too. This time the argument was between the adherents of the Reformation and the Counterreformation, who, on horseback and foot, were led by their brightest minds, from Luther to More and Loyola. Only the fourth controversy put Man and his fate at the center of the argument. It alone could be labeled humanistic in the full sense of the word. The fact that it occurred between us Germans must not be a cause for arrogance on our part. We were the only ones to have the opportunity to draw certain consequences to their logical conclusion, and the fact that this controversy was learned about only at the postwar trials in Nuremberg doesn't diminish the significance it had for our history and future. The issue was which was more humane: the "towel policy" or the "hammer policy." In other words, was it more humane (the problem of productivity arose only later) to give the Jews who were going off to the gas chambers towels for the alleged showers and thus keep them in the dark about the fate awaiting them on the other side of the door to the shower room, or was it more opportune, since everything they possessed (from their real estate to their hair) had been confiscated from them, to expedite the process with panic and pizzle whips, a truth whose effect would have had the power of a hammer, and thus end the torment of their uncertainty. The commander of Auschwitz, Rudolf Hess, was a fervent advocate of the first method and a sharp critic of the method applied in Treblinka by our acquaintance Untersturmführer Kurt Franz. Franz maintained that Hess's theory had neither a human nor an economic justification. Speed, which was of primary importance if one desired the greatest possible daily rate of suffocation, was impossible to attain with the towel method. Not only because the victims went into the chambers slowly, but also because they died more slowly than those of his in Treblinka, as they were fairly calm and mentally disengaged and thus with a reduced respiratory rate. In front of the Treblinka crematorium, it became clear to everyone where they were going and why. Beatings by our Ukrainian collaborators and the SS men caused agitation, panic, and a dramatic rush to the shower room. Their powerfully exerted lungs were forced to work quickly. Death came in two thirds of the time that it did in Auschwitz.

That gives me the right, for purely speculative purposes, to compare Adam's execution to that of Christ. There was no mockery by the crowd, of course, but that didn't even happen in the Messiah's case. It was the soldiers who tortured him, and they did so only mildly and primarily in the form of humiliation. Steinbrecher took into account how much the barbaric conduct of Christ's escort negatively affected future generations. Moreover, that was a Hebrew, Semitic, Mediterranean kind of execution. This one was to be Germanic, Aryan, Northern. Naturally, there did have to be some differences. That meant a gallows instead of a cross. The difference here was only in the fact that at the origin of *our* faith we had a just man between two thieves, but in this *new* one, a thief between two just men. As a consequence of the natural acceleration of historical processes, death occurred simultaneously to resurrection.

Christianity needed a few hundred years to organize itself as the leading spiritual and physical force of Europe. And though phenomena develop more quickly in our day, and disappear more quickly, twenty years are not enough to . . .²³

■ □ ■ □ ■

LETTER 24

THE FIRST CRUSADE AGAINST THE
UMBRELLA, OR *THE REBELLIOUS MAN*

The Mediterranean Coast, 1 Oct. 1965

Dear Hilmar,

It's already been two days since I've written a word. I had a lot to take care of . . . You're guessing that I tore myself out of my languor and decided to do something . . . Writing is no use . . . I also had an argument with Sabina . . . I don't have time to go into that now . . . For an awakened intellectual there are things more important than personal matters and motives . . . My decision was preceded by the realization that the parody of the crucifixion wasn't devoid of purpose . . . It was some kind of sign. But what kind? . . . This is something I've been thinking about a lot these days. There was some key to be found there . . . Then I remembered how Christ described the end of the world . . . Beware, he said, because there will be many who will come in my name and say: I am Christ! Many will be deceived and nation will rise up against nation and kingdom against kingdom . . . And there will be hunger and pestilence, and the ground will quake all over the earth . . . And many will be corrupted. And friend will come to hate friend, and friend will betray friend . . . And many false prophets will go out and deceive many, and lawlessness will multiply

. . . I don't know, I shouldn't judge from the Transcript . . . but everything indicates that Adam was also one of those false prophets. And
maybe even the Antichrist, though I'm not convinced he had the
intellectual powers and courage for anything like that . . . Somehow
it turned out to be logical that Adam was one of the devil's compan-
ions, or the devil himself, with that satanic Umbrella of his . . . Or trident of his that, assuming the form of the Umbrella, adapted to our
civilization . . . Adam, to be sure, couldn't have walked around with a
trident in his hands. No one would have taken him seriously, not even
those who had already gone over to Satan. They'd have taken him for
an agent provocateur . . . And the authorities would have packed him
off to the mental ward, and degraded the trident to a pitchfork for
stacking hay . . . I wouldn't be able to tolerate such a state of affairs,
Hilmar, so I've decided to take certain steps . . . To renounce my meditations and get down to work, first and foremost to deal with the
Umbrella, which was the only thing in that whole hellish mechanism
that was accessible to me . . . It was obvious that there was something
wrong with the idea of the Umbrella as a symbol of human civilization . . . That was logical. It followed from the satanic behavior of
Adam's Umbrella . . . If I say that one bomb is bad because it kills, will
I say of another that it's good, though it kills, too? In a purely theoretical sense, one bomb may be better than another for two reasons:
because it's technically superior and because it's dropped for more just
causes . . . But such distinctions have no place here. One Umbrella
can't be better than another if they're of the *same* construction.
Differences in size, the form of the handle (Beliar's head), the color of
the silk vestment, and sometimes in the material and mechanism (the
method of putting the evil powers to work), can't influence the degree
of their godlessness. It's conceivable in theory that Adam's was actually the *protoumbrella,* from which all the others spawned in hellish
debauchery. And that all the Umbrellas in the world are different generations of the descendants from that one of Adam's . . . In a word,
that they're the devil's brood . . . As you know, Hilmar, the war
between them and the forces of good is eternal . . . In a certain sense,
it's a war with one's very self. The necessity of the existence of the devil
is logical. Evil is the intellectual requirement of a mind that meditates
on good . . . Naturally, I don't want to claim that we intellectuals also
invented evil—though we perfected some of its worst forms—but it's

certain that we made it logically necessary in the establishment of the idea of any kind of better world . . . The idea of evil, according to even the most primitive logician, is *necessary* for one to have a representation of the concept of good . . . Thus, things sank lower and lower. The Umbrellas multiplied. The number of Umbrellas is striking. No matter which way you turn—Umbrellas everywhere . . . Good doesn't multiply so quickly, nor does it latch onto people so well. Accordingly . . . It follows logically that Umbrellas are evil. From the fact that they're evil it follows that they multiply quickly, and from the fact that they multiply quickly if follows that they're evil . . . I wouldn't want to claim, I don't know, maybe not all owners of Umbrellas are directly in the service of the devil . . . But it's clear that they enjoy his favor. It turns out that God created rain to annoy us, but Satan sent the Umbrella to protect us from rain. The conclusion is unambiguous . . . In our subconscious, Satan appears as the Savior . . . But he's really just a false Messiah, the herald of the End . . . I don't want to get involved in theological disputes, I don't have time for that, but the indifference of church dogmas to the Umbrella problem is most troubling and testifies to the fact that the demonic conspiracy has penetrated to the very heart of the official faith . . . that the devil has already carried off many a prelate. Especially those who quite openly march in processions under the open Sky, a rare form of Umbrella . . . He even carried off your sister, Hilmar. She's got three of them. You, too, if I'm not mistaken. (This number is not especially high, if it is taken into account that the *Legion,* or 6,666, is the maximum number of demons that can possess us.) But none of that's important now. What's important is that I've finally decided on a course of action . . . I know people will laugh at me. They laugh at everything at first. They even laughed at Hitler and his first speeches. The extermination of all the Jews seemed to them to be a silly exaggeration . . . (They considered sporadic and limited pogroms sufficient for the purpose.) They'll think my call for the extermination of all Umbrellas in the world to be a delusional exaggeration. So let them laugh. The duty of an intellectual is to persevere, even in his delusions. I'll be the happiest man in the world if it turns out that I wasn't right and that there was no need for so much destruction . . . So as to avoid complications, I began with my immediate vicinity. In a roundabout way and nicely. That was the day before yesterday. I went out for a walk and met Mr. Klopstock from the company *Klopstock & Klop-stock*, whose suite is opposite ours, in the former office of Sturmbann-führer Freissner. Mr. Klopstock was just then taking his elegant Umbrella out for some air. The sky was clear and there was no need for an Umbrella, for me that was one more proof that Mr. Klopstock was also infected. I had to be very circumspect. I knew Mr. Klopstock had served under Karl Ernst in the Berlin SA. Thus, he was a man of considerable strength and savagery. I asked whether he was maybe expecting rain and if the radio hadn't announced something like that. He answered that it hadn't and that he was taking his Umbrella along to use as a cane. The expression "use as a cane" was symptomatic. The Umbrella was evidently giving him support. This revealed the part-nership between them and confirmed my blackest expectations. At the same time, I realized that any attempt to convince him of the harmfulness of Umbrellas would be a hard sell; so I withdrew, noting down Mr. Klopstock's name on a list that I had started for this pur-pose . . . Then I gave it a try with a certain Mrs. Anagreta Friedmann, a widow from Hamburg. She was carrying a Parasol. I tried in a roundabout way to convince her that it was illogical for someone to go to the Mediterranean to vacation in the sun, and then to protect themselves the entire time with a Parasol. It seemed I managed that with a fair amount of success. She soon folded up her accursed device and rushed off to the hotel . . . I had a little problem with Mr. Procházka, a doctor from Prague. While we were sitting on a bench and talking, I was playing with his Umbrella and, I must admit, dam-aged it on purpose. "You Germans destroy everything you touch!" he said and walked off. Fine. But he couldn't use the Umbrella any more . . . However, none of this was enough, and I calculated that at that rate it would take me several years to make people give up Umbrellas in D. alone. More radical steps had to be taken. "The final solution of the Umbrella question" could not be reached merely by persuasion, like many other tasks which thought places before us . . . Action had to be taken. I began with Sabina's Umbrellas and Parasols . . . However, she herself was the real cause . . . This is what hap-pened . . . I had assembled the cooks and cleaning ladies in the kitchen. I was just laying out to them the urgent need to get rid of their Umbrellas when your sister appeared and made an unbelievable scene. She simply dragged me off to our room . . . That was not only an unprecedented assault on my person but also a challenge to my mission, and that was what gave the attack its weight . . . An offense against my umbrella-war. . . We had words. I won't repeat what was said . . . It was all really very unpleasant for me, but I couldn't give in to human ignorance at the very outset of my crusade . . . For her own good, just to prove to her how we would all benefit if there were no Umbrellas, I also broke her other one . . . Then she slapped me and called me a damned lunatic! . . . So then I roughed her up a bit . . . I don't know, I can't say for sure . . . Maybe my foot got her, too . . . It wasn't easy to see what was going on in that uproar . . . Guests, the pensione staff . . . A real scandal. To make a long story short, your sister locked herself in the room and she's still there . . . But that night I scored a victory on another front . . . I can't remember whether I told you that my suspicions had even extended to the large Parasols that we ate under on the terrace. It was a matter of their construction. I grew accustomed to drawing certain parallels way back in my police days . . . What's logical, what's illogical . . . What's possible, what's not . . . Left or right? Steinbrecher taught me all about that, and so I applied the method now too . . . In particular, what proves that the hotel Parasols are satanic devices? Their resemblance to Adam's Umbrella. But what proves the satanic nature of that Umbrella? The fact that it resembles the hotel Parasols that we've just determined to be evil . . . That night I sneaked out of the pensione—I was sleeping in the salon because Sabina had locked herself in the bedroom—with the intention of liquidating them . . . Unfortunately, I didn't succeed, at least as far as the stands and poles are concerned. They were mounted in concrete blocks, but I didn't have any tools or explosives . . . I only ripped up their canopies as much as I could . . . Despite the initial setback, I found a good amount of prey that night; on the grounds of the pensione alone I definitely destroyed the following:

7 men's Umbrellas
3 women's Umbrellas
1 children's Umbrella
4 Parasols (including Mrs. Friedmann's).
I can say with certainty that I inflicted considerable damage on:
3 men's Umbrasolls
2 women's Umbrasolls

1 Parasol
5 hotel Parasols.[24]

The crowning achievement of that successful night—a crusade if I may call it that—was the destruction of a tent that some hippies had set up not far from the pensione . . . Certainly, that was over-doing it. A tent, after all, isn't an Umbrella . . . But what can you do, you can't make an omelet without breaking eggs. In a just struggle there have to be innocent victims sometimes . . . My mistakes, if there were any, were made only in my fervor, the sole transgression, which already contains its justification in itself . . . If there were more time, I wouldn't have made them . . . Maybe your sister would have fared better, too . . . Maybe a sedative reformatory process could have been resorted to, and the massacre avoided . . . There was a possibility, which I had already hit upon in 1943, that the whole devilish power of the Umbrella is to be found in its handle . . . That didn't contradict the observations of individuals who were possessed. In the case of a fifteen-year-old girl from Lyons, in the seventeenth century, the demonic presence was observed exclusively in her right hand, which to her horror and despite her desperate resistance scrawled obscene words on the walls of the chapel . . . If it were scientifically determined that the encephalon and the medulla oblongata of evil were located in the handle, great material damage could be avoided . . . It would be enough to replace the handles on all Umbrellas . . . Of course, that wouldn't eliminate the danger of demons settling into the new handles sometime later . . . No, that wouldn't be a solution. We know what compromises lead to . . . We've felt that on our own backs and won't make any more compromises under any conditions . . . I know that nitpickers in love with historical parallels would accuse me of trying to solve the Umbrella question in the same way we tried to solve the Jewish question . . . The need to cleanse the world of certain categories of people who are considered to be the sources of mental corruption and evil is a constant feature of history. The Christians were the first victims of this urge. They were accused of having secret societies in which incest, sacrilege, and cannibalism were practiced. Later, the Jews were accused of the same crimes. Then came the waves of persecution against satanic societies in the fourteenth century . . .

But I'm concerned that my operation not be compared with these errors, though the fact that at its head—just as in all other mass purges to date—there stands an intellectual . . . could speak against it . . . Appearances are deceptive . . . I didn't use torture to obtain false statements about the satanic alliance between Adam and the Umbrella. I have no personal motives for this massacre, as the pagans of Lyons did when under Marcus Aurelius in 177 A.D. they settled the score with their more affluent Christian compatriots . . . In this war, pure idealism is my inspiration and guide . . . The good of the people . . . Progress . . . Universal interests . . . A higher goal! The same thing that inspired my secret struggle against Steinbrecher during the war, my resistance to Nazism . . . The only difference is I've learned that in such matters you have to avoid making any kind of compromise . . . A small compromise, and then a larger one. Later an even larger one . . . In the end all that remains are compromises and no struggle at all . . . Compromises and bitterness in the heart . . . If I forgive even a single solitary Umbrella, if I have compassion for a single solitary Parasol, if I let myself be corrupted by an innocent look from any one of them—and how they can play the fool!—I'll be putting the entire operation in jeopardy. Whoever proves weak on one occasion will give in on another . . . A small Umbrella and then a larger one. Then an even larger one . . . In the end the only things left in the world will be Umbrellas . . . I don't think I'm making sense any more, Hilmar . . . I'm tired . . . Fortunately, it's not the weariness of a resigned man, but of a soldier after a successful battle . . . I must rest. Tomorrow a more difficult task awaits me . . . The attack on the Umbrellas of two neighboring hotels . . . No matter how ashamed I am of it, my experience of working for the Gestapo helps me out a fair amount in cleverly organizing my raids . . . Until soon, your

KONRAD

P.S. Lest I forget—I visited the spa's doctor. An extraordinarily sloppy and slovenly general practitioner. All during the consultation he was picking his ears with a scalpel and extracting cerumen. Then he would look at it and smear it on a patient's case file . . . There was no use going there . . . He couldn't tell me anything concrete. But he was interested. Touchingly curious and earnest. Like Steinbrecher. Generalizations and dialectics. (Apparently the world is full of Steinbrechers. Steinbrecherization is very fashionable) . . . He asked me what my parents died from. I said they were killed in the Second World War. In answer to the question of what their parents died from, I said they were killed in the First. However, all four of their parents were killed either in the Austro-German War of 1866 or the Franco-Prussian War of 1871. As for others from the more distant past, I couldn't tell him anything. It's logical—the doctor said—they must have kicked the bucket during the Napoleonic Wars . . . You see, Hilmar, how logic helps to clear the mists of time . . . He also questioned me about certain personal matters. They mainly concerned Sabina. This he did with a considerable amount of lust and cerumen from his ears . . . Via sexual intercourse we arrived by a parallel to Umbrellas. I said what I think of them and what I had done in that regard . . . That was a mistake. But a mistake the examination wouldn't have made any sense without. In that damned desire for compromise again, I wanted to get official confirmation that my acts were a consequence of moral and intellectual indignation, and not of a mental disorder as your sister claimed . . . No, sir—I repeated—I feel absolutely no need to tear up Umbrellas. On the contrary, the whole affair is repulsive to me. In a certain sense, I pity them. As one would pity individuals who are possessed, whose bestial actions are the fault of a demon. But in a war of ideas, there's no room for sentimentality . . . No, sir, I didn't see my mother in an unseemly pose, at some moment when an Umbrella had assumed a completely different form . . . No sir, I chose Umbrellas exclusively because of the fact that they're possessed. If there had been a demonization of kitchen bowls, clothes' hangers, or mustaches, I'd have exorcised them . . . No sir, I never hated my father, who, by the way, didn't carry an Umbrella either . . . I never found any particular pleasure in caressing umbrella handles, and to respond to your vulgar question, I never attempted anything which, because of rejection, would have led me to take revenge on them . . . No sir, I couldn't tell you how much truth there is in the claim of the Holy Inquisition that, when mating, a satanic Umbrella is as cold as ice and studded with iron points . . . Do I like Umbrellas? What kind of question is that? Of course I don't. I like rain. He who likes rain cannot like Umbrellas . . . In the meantime, the doctor was generously secreting cerumen and Stein-brecherizing: . . . The matter is, of course, serious. One shouldn't surrender to illusions. The roots are deep. One never knows where the serpent sleeps . . . In the Freudian sense it might be . . . However, considering Jung's modification, it's probably the other way around . . . The truth is most likely in some compromise . . . The Umbrella as a surrogate, a compromise between the ideal and the sinful EGO . . . With you a certain confusion is also evident. I don't want to go into the forensic significance. Do you know about that one famous case? A patient is asked: Why were you brought here? He answers: Because of a parquet floor that has putty in it. However, that's not right. There's no putty in parquet floors. The patient only seemed to be a floorer . . . You, for example, don't notice bloody tears drip-ping from the eyes of stone Madonnas? Do you maybe feel like the Dalai Lama? Do you have someone else in mind? . . . You don't? Then the matter is opened radially. An electrical engineer, otherwise an educated man, during a banquet luncheon, in the company of members of the Red Cross, fired shots at those present, then mas-turbated and urinated, and only then ate his dessert . . . A com-pletely unexplored territory, sir . . . Especially for us out here in the middle of nowhere. Here we don't have any lunatics to show off like they do in big cities. The nest of insanity is built in the big com-munities. Everything is better organized there. Funding for medical care. Ideas. Everything . . . Here all we have is a small group of senile retirees . . . Not even one case of *Morbus Addisoni,* not one *Hydrocephalus,* not one *Sclerosis multiplex.* We do have a little men-strual psychosis, which according to Heller is found in 35 percent of suicidal women, and one person with an unusual EGO. . . . He's some former sea captain, a paranoid grumbler with a strong libido and a hyperrhythmic temperament who collects fish excrement . . . And what can be done with that? What kind of generalization when all we get are cases of *delirium tremens* and *commotio cerebri,* that is brain concussions and once in a while, when it's hot, one or two sea-sonal pyromaniacs . . . You're the first one with any real dimensions to his insanity . . . And then it turns out you're only passing through. However, my honest recommendation to you is a return home and adaptation to Umbrellas by psychodrama. In the mean-time: sedatives, restraint, and rest. Only an empty brain is a healthy brain . . . That's how it was, my dear Hilmar. The only benefit I got out of my visit was that I tore up his Umbrella in the waiting room and that, comparing myself with him, I came to the definitive conviction that I'm normal and rational. *Ergo,* that everything I'm doing is rational. Because from the fact that I'm rational it follows logically that everything I do is rational, and from the fact that everything I do is rational . . .

■ □ ■ □ ■

LETTER 25

THE ROPE AND THE STOOL,
OR *THE POVERTY OF PHILOSOPHY*

The Mediterranean Coast, 3 Oct. 1965

My dear Sabina and Hilmar,

(I'm writing to her, too, because I assume she's with you—where else would she be after leaving her worthless husband except at her dear big brother's?) I remember developing a comparison not long ago between my letters and the cyclic development of human life. The length of my confession, it appears, is inversely proportional to the length of the period of my life that inspired it. Decades go unexplained, leaving the entire space to the year that concerns us, mostly without rhyme or reason, because we're indeed incapable of determining exactly what's of major and minor importance for us. If we had the ability to make that choice in even the smallest degree, our lives would be better. We wouldn't waste them on minutiae. We'd dedicate ourselves only to their main currents. (For a man to get to the bottom of life, a certain degree of fanatic attachment to life is required; but that precludes a common-sense approach to values. Thus, a full life and a wise life are mutually exclusive.) To this we can add one more paradox: the more quickly the events described take place, the slower they are to be recorded. Thus, I found myself at the doctor's office only after Sabina's demonstrative departure, without writing any on this letter in the meantime.

Sabina will no doubt speak about me with your family's characteristic objectivity, which I believe also compelled you to spend your life correcting an insignificant historical calendar. I only wish for it to be known that I'm completely aware of my unseemly conduct toward Sabina, though I think her departure to Heidelberg was a bit of an overreaction. If I were in a bad mood, I might interpret Sabina's conduct as desertion, and under particularly grave *wartime* circumstances to boot. (The war on Umbrellas is in full swing, though somewhat slowed due to the interest of the local police in the pestilence among the umbrasolls.) And everyone knows what the punishment for desertion is. Fortunately, I'm in a buoyant mood and am prepared to take complete responsibility for the incident and, moreover, to extract from it the basic hypothesis on which I intend to base my future life. Whether it will be a life together will be decided by Sabina when she hears what it will look like.

In the meantime, there's no reason for concern at all. I feel great. I'm taking sedatives and taking it easy. I hope my condition is evident from this manuscript. My sentences are no longer fragmented and choppy, nor are my thoughts confused. And although my conclusion hasn't yet assumed its final form, its outlines are already visible. Under such conditions, I could come back to you in Heidelberg and finish settling accounts with the past. However, I fear you'll take advantage of my still vulnerable state and thwart this impending liberation. I know you'd thrust me back into the tenth century, Hilmar. You'd tell me not to waste time puttering around in the present day, which I don't understand and observe through the mistakes of my own personal past. Fortunately, I no longer have anything to seek between the Oder and the Vistula. I have absolutely no interest in how Prince Mieszko was baptized. I'm not interested in anything older than my future and the future of the world I live in.

To all appearances, the question has been formulated incorrectly. The problem wasn't finding the key to my past—which was what I was passionately trying to do in my letters—but to find the one to my future. Tomorrow is what makes me human; yesterday is what makes me a corpse. The mistake was reviving something I should have taken long ago and buried forever. Our problem is not how to revive, but how to quiet our vampires. THE PAST IS A VAMPIRE AND THE REAL QUESTION IS HOW TO QUIET IT FOREVER.[25] We don't have a third option. Either we drive a stake though the vampire's heart or our blood is soon completely sucked dry. In order to achieve the former, we must for once begin with the excretion of the poisonous spirit of intellectual analysis from our lives. Otherwise, we'll be turned into pure syllogisms, and thereby be returned to the nothingness of the word from which we were created—but what would we have from such divine logic?

I was just in the process of making this realization and searching for the most effective ways to apply it as a liberating force when Sabina came in. My disgusting behavior was only the destructive and nihilistic act of an intellect in withdrawal. I was about to drive it into a corner. Sabina ran into it as it was on its way there. She was knocked to the ground and trampled as anything is trampled which was ever in the path of an intellect in pursuit of deeper realizations about man and being. In a certain way, however, she should be proud. Despite her injuries, she became proof. She stopped being Sabina and became an intellectual act, or in any case, its essential premise. It's the dream of every intellectual to cease being human and become an intellectual act—a part of a perfect logical system. She succeeded in this. Now she's a logical symbol, with two or three references and several Ibidems.

This realization, partially achieved with the help of Sabina's bodily remains crumpled on the parquet floor, which I hope have been put back together in some hospital, would remain speculation if it were all I focused on. Were I the old Konrad Rutkowski, I'd continue gathering evidence pro and contra, and the scales of my opinion would become a silent seesaw perpetually in motion: first its left pan (the pan of faith) sinks, then its right pan (the pan of doubt) does, but the needle never shows an exact balance. My intellectual conscience wouldn't allow that. Whenever it would threaten to stop on some deed with a heavier share of faith, I'd throw a new suspicion on the other pan, and the balance would start happily moving again, swinging in dark uncertainty. But when the accumulated doubt reached the very edge of death, I'd smother myself with faith over on the other pan and that seesaw swinging of my soul would begin all over again. In actuality, I feared action as much as death, which is the complete absence of action. I knew that a conclusion, if it doesn't dispose of a counter-conclusion, demands deeds and leads to action. But action is the death of thought. He who acts has no time for balances and scales. Everything has already been weighed out for him. Since I'm an intellectual, and it's my nature to think about things, because that thought is what makes me an intellectual—not my academic rank, social position, and education, but my speculative abilities, even if they led to answering the question of whether a child's body burns faster than the body of an adult male—I'm terrified of definitive conclusions. I want to have my "although," "maybe," "nevertheless," and "on the other hand." Without "although," I'm as helpless as a hedgehog lying on its back. Defeating this delusion was a real feat of heroism, because it stood blocking all the paths to freedom, like a sentry.

I'm sending you a copy of certain notes on that theme as a separate letter. The essay is of a strictly private character and is intended to serve as a kind of philosophical clarification of what happened with Sabina. There's no longer any doubt in my mind that your sister was thrown on the floor and trampled while I was formulating the conclusions presented in it. Because NOW I DARE. NOW I'M A CHAMPION OF THE WILL, A MAN OF ACTION. The pan of faith has finally prevailed. All doubts have been cast away. The balance of thought has stopped. The rivers have thawed and the ice has started flowing downstream. But if you're hoping this turn of events will produce another one of those beautifully bound books, which nowadays take the place of real history for us, you're sorely mistaken. I'm familiar with the hypocritical role of books and public speeches. They exist to fool us with their apparent similarity to *deeds,* to reconcile us to inaction with a compromise. Because we say: I speak, therefore I act. And we say: I write, therefore I act. And at the beginning of the deceit it is written: I think, therefore I am. And I exist, therefore I act. But I say unto you: TO ACT IS TO MOVE OBJECTS, NOT TO COMPREHEND THEIR POSITIONS. THERE IS NO ACTION BEYOND ACTION! ALL ELSE IS DECEIT.

KONRAD

P.S. Hilmar, what's wrong with me? Weakness and resignation have struck me again. Since this took hold of me yesterday, I haven't left my room. I haven't eaten, either . . . The gentlemen from the reception desk have indeed come to inquire whether I'm not perhaps ill . . . I'm not ill, it's just that I'm completely apathetic. Everything seems senseless to me . . . Especially any kind of Action . . . What can Action do? Who needs Action? Hasn't there been enough of it already? Haven't we gotten our fill of it? . . . I'm surprised at my fervor. I must not have had my wits about me. I must have seemed silly in my messianic ecstasy . . . I promise, it won't happen again. I know where it comes from. Hopefully I'll know how to defend myself next time . . . I've learned where those unbearable attacks of initiative come from. Whenever Adam Trpković visited me, afterward I felt strong and ready for action. I always undertook something, even when I tried to resist . . . It was as if every time we met some of his demonic power flowed into me and later turned into imprudence . . . The last time he was here was before I sat down to write this letter. He tried once again to get me to demolish the Monument. He made promises and threatened me . . . The typical Steinbrecherian counterpoint technique. Sandwiches and cigarettes mixed with pizzle whips . . . I didn't give in, but he nevertheless accomplished something . . . He got me to rave about Action, and to make a compromise in thought at least . . . And we all know how it is with compromises. At first a little one, and then a bigger one. At first a deedlet, and then a deed. In the end one finds himself in a sea of mindless activities that he no longer has any control over . . . Everything has its consequences. Every step leads somewhere. Untersturmführer Kurt Franz was an extraordinary waiter. And then he made just one wrong move: he went to a meeting of the NSDAP. That inevitably led to the SA. The SA inevitably led to the SS. Membership in the SS took him to Treblinka. And once he found himself there, he had to exterminate Jews. That was a logical consequence of serving in a concentration camp. But in a broader sense, it was the natural consequence of a gloomy, provincial Sunday afternoon in 1933, when the waiter Kurt Franz had been unbearably bored and when, instead of going to the cinema, he went to a meeting with Adolf Hitler . . . Adam underhandedly calculated that thoughts of action, as the sole authentic way of life, would through a series of compromises finally lead to a misdeed: the demolition of the monument . . . And since we're on the subject of Adam, some other suspicions gain credence . . . I don't know, but the very course of events . . . Why, for example, did your sister agree so readily to come to D.? That wasn't in her stubborn nature . . . It wouldn't surprise me if she knew what had happened in this town during the war and the role I'd played in it . . . Or, even if she didn't know everything, she'd been goaded into such behavior . . . Demonic powers know no geographic boundaries. Persian spirits used to travel down as far as the holy Jordan River. Their mobility was practically unlimited . . . Thus, Adam could have kept Sabina from resisting my choice. If it was my choice at all, if it hadn't been suggested to me, too. Yugoslavia was in any case Sabina's idea . . . Everything hints at intrigue, a dark conspiracy with the goal of bringing me to D., confronting me with the past and blackmailing me with it, but then saving me with the offer of an alliance with Satan . . . If to that I add Sabina's insistence that we attend the unveiling of the monument, the plot against me becomes obvious. In the context of such damning logical evidence, what good is your telegram? . . . Yes, I received it. They pushed it in under the door . . . DEAR KONRAD STOP DON'T DRIVE HERE BY YOURSELF STOP DEAR HILMAR IS COMING TO GET YOU ON SATURDAY STOP EVERYTHING'S FORGOTTEN STOP LOVE SABINA . . . However, the point is that it hasn't been forgotten, and that nothing can be forgotten . . . One would have to lose one's sanity first. Indeed, that's the only real way. Insanity is the hawthorn stake for the memory. Anything else is just a half-measure . . . But there's no sense in blaming Adam. He was just doing what the Umbrella ordered, he was only carrying out orders. He was a complete prisoner of the Umbrella, just as we were prisoners of our oaths . . . Paradoxically, however, it was only in that alliance that he became free. Only as an absolute slave did he acquire absolute freedom of action. Hegel sensed that when he saw the freedom as the embodiment of successive necessities. Satanic necessities, of course. Human freedom is a hell of alternatives, dilemmas, and choices. True freedom is having no choices. Hell is nothing other than absolute freedom, and the devil has been its champion since his rebellion against God . . . Just look at what kind of image we have of heaven. Whenever some painter attempts to reveal the Power and Glory of God, we feel like we're attending an SS parade at the Luipold Arena in Nuremberg . . . Phalanxes of identical, expressionless, and blond angels and archangels, cherubim and seraphim surround the Throne as specified in Reinhardt's mathematical staging, conjuring the most brutal vision of an authoritarian state I've ever seen . . . And what does Hieronymus Bosch show us? In his portrayals of hell, especially in the Rotterdam *Demons,* I don't see any order or system . . . In the triptych *Garden of Delight,* there's certainly order, everything is there in proportions that are always under the control of heavenly laws, and everything has identical, monolithic, spherical shapes . . . But that's Heaven, that's Paradise! . . . But go to the Vienna Academy and look at his three-panel altarpiece with the *Last Judgment.* Successive necessities, realizing paradisiacal freedom, are transformed along the vertical axes of the composition into chaos and the true freedom of hell. High up, in the golden nimbus, symmetry reigns as in a Wehrmacht barracks; there's still a humble order and a system in the falling of the angels, but farther down . . . my god! Farther down an absolute oriental chaos reigns! Each abusing each as he pleases! Each does as he likes! Everything is in total confusion! An insane chaos attains the freedom and beauty of the ideal democratic state . . . It's all so convoluted. Who can figure it out? Where's the truth? . . . Is truth necessary at all? Can't logic replace it? Steinbrecher always maintained that it could, that logic is something permanent, whereas truth changes . . . I saw that in 1945 . . . The major who investigated my case was named Stein (certainly a Jew) and was the attorney general in Columbus, Ohio . . . *Can't you see, Rutkowski, that your criminal activity follows not only from the premise that you worked for the Gestapo, but also from the premise that you're German? Are you German, Rutkowski? . . .* Yes, sir, Major Stein! . . . *So there you go. Accordingly, you're also a criminal! . . .* I'm not a criminal, sir. I did commit some improprieties, that's correct, but those were compromises intended to alleviate the situation brought on by the war . . . *How is that possible? It's illogical for you not to be a criminal, Rutkowski, completely illogical. Let's make inductions from what we know. If all Germans were Nazis, then you must have been one, too. Otherwise you wouldn't have been a German. And you admitted that you're German for the transcript. I hope we're not going to have to go*

back to the start, for God's sake, Rutkowski! Don't be such a bloody fool!
You're supposed to be an intellectual. We're both fuckin' intellectuals,
aren't we? Come now, let's use some fuckin' logic for a change! If you're
German, then you're a Nazi, too, and if you're a Nazi, then you're also
a criminal, and so let's go ahead and sign the fuckin' transcripts so we
can all get the fuck home! . . . To my claim that not all Germans were
in fact Nazis, the major said that was pretty damned illogical,
because if they hadn't, they probably wouldn't have committed such
damned awful crimes! To my insistence that he acknowledge at
least the theoretical possibility of the existence of some innocent
goddamned Germans, Stein said he didn't deny the possibility. In
principle, namely, it's likely that there are some among Americans of
German ancestry . . . *But they're not under investigation, Rutkowski,*
old boy! You are! Do you get the message? . . . In 1945 I got off with
one year of "intensive de-Nazification." . . . It never was clear to me
why this also consisted of hard physical labor and lectures, when in
its time the process of Nazification consisted of the very same thing
. . . Today I don't have many chances of getting off. I don't have an
answer to a single question. And the ones I do have aren't worth
anything. There's no answer that doesn't lead into the abyss . . . I feel
like I'm in Steinbrecher's office to be examined. With him, being
innocent didn't help. All my answers led to a lost game . . . The fact
that someone was innocent technically didn't prevent them from
being sent to the gallows. Hanging was prevented only if the noose
broke . . . But mine doesn't have much chance of breaking. I made
it from a sailing rope, strengthened it with Steinbrecher's logic and
smeared it with soap. I spent all day at this, locked here in my room
. . . The noose is hanging from the chandelier hook. There's a stool
under it . . . Someone's knocking at the door, but I won't open it.
It's too late for anything . . . There's nothing left to be done, and
barely anything to be said. There are no more forks in the road.
There's no longer any left or right . . . Don't hold this last compromise against me. It was unavoidable and logical. Otherwise a
harder fall would be waiting for me . . . And maybe also a dementia that would make roughing up Sabina look like a small down payment . . . The knocking's getting more persistent, I have to hurry
. . . Burn all my manuscripts . . . Don't allow my books to be
reprinted. Don't ever talk about me. Act as if I never existed. Try

with your souls to attain what was impossible for me: to forget and to acquire innocence . . . And beware of compromises . . . (I'm not superstitious, but it wouldn't hurt if you drove a hawthorn stake into my heart before you lowered me into the grave. That would give Hilmar particular satisfaction.) . . .

Yours,

KONRAD

■ □ ■ □ ■

LETTER 26

HOW PROFESSOR RUTKOWSKI SOLD
HIS SOUL TO THE DEVIL,
OR *BEYOND GOOD AND EVIL*

The Mediterranean Coast, 5 Oct. 1965

My dear Sabina and Hilmar,

I received the second telegram, too. It was handed to me during a charming renewal of energy, after a brief period of exhaustion that came over me. I can't thank you enough for your concern. Especially Hilmar—dear, good Hilmar—for his sacrificial decision to spend a precious few days away from writing his book and waste them on me. Fortunately, along with my repeated gratitude I'm able to decline the favor. There's no reason at all for you to come down here. I'm in full control of myself; this letter should provide you with proof of that. Unless, of course, you intend to join me in my operation, but since you don't know anything about it yet, that's hardly likely. And there wouldn't be time anyway. (I settled my account with the pensione, took the car to a garage to have it checked—don't worry about that—and I've packed my things. I'm leaving for Germany at around seven o'clock this evening. I'll drive at night because of the heat, and for some other reasons as well, which I'll explain to you in due time.)

I feel extraordinarily well, almost like the first man on the first day of creation, as if all my blood had been changed overnight and my veins were flowing not with that sluggish, infected, and poisonous sludge, but with the very current of life. I can't remember ever feeling so vigorous, venturesome, and confident. I don't know anything I could compare this state to. But if Hilmar can recall how he once interpreted for us the indescribable sensation of total immersion in a community of the soul that seized and intoxicated him whenever he was in a parade of the Hitler-Jugend or listened to one of the Führer's speeches, then you'll get an approximate idea of my state. The crucial difference, of course, is that my euphoria is the result of a total and absolute union with an idea, and not with people as its intermediaries.

You know how much I've always suffered from chronic perplexity, dilemmas, hesitation, wavering, and procrastination, how much I've been ready to compromise. All that's over now. My goals are clear; their self-evidence is complete, and my readiness to attain them unshakable.[26] Apparently some crucial element in me changed, at a moment when all others were already braided into a noose hung over the chandelier hook. I don't believe you would even recognize me. As I write these lines, I'm looking at myself in the mirror, and I confirm with wonder and joyful excitement rather than fear that I've changed. I wouldn't be able to say what the nature of the change is. Nothing in my physical appearance is any different. Maybe my sudden loss of weight has given me a sharper appearance—bladelike, with the steel blue tint characteristic of prophets and others convinced of their calling such as John the Baptist, Savonarola, or the head of the RSHA Reinhard Heydrich. Perhaps that impression can be ascribed to a greenish acetylene feverishness in my eyes, which is barely softened by the high diopter of my eyeglasses. In any case, the nature of the change can't be expressed in familiar terms, or I don't know what those terms are. What I'm certain of, however, and what I can express in words, fills me with confidence and assurance. All hardships have disappeared, as if they've been removed by magic. I have to suppress my appetite, though I think that reflects more a thirst for life than a hunger for earthly food. My thoughts have become miraculously clear, and my power of reasoning has undergone an incredible acceleration. It's as if I've gained the ability to reach valid conclusions without a single logical premise, without any mediation by the empirical or experience. I reach them, I almost dare to say, through REVELATION. I use this exaggerated comparison to stress the extraordinary speed in making decisions and their spontaneous harmony with the whole of my being. My memory has been completely restored, fortunately by no means in its old, repentant, demonic aspect, which was well on the way to wrecking me mentally and destroying me physically, but rather the other way around: as the realization of the complete irrelevance of the past for our authentic lives. (A feeling of freedom equal to that experienced by a drowning man when he reaches the surface again!) Without the past, I've become free again! In the meantime, there's one process that has been strengthening this attitude. The events of the war are mixing together and fusing into a morass in which it is getting harder and harder to distinguish anything—to isolate a date, pick out a face, replay a scene. Personages such as Steinbrecher even begin to lose their individuality and turn into floods of unconnected thoughts, ideas and words. The past is evaporating, as if it were boiling slowly on a low flame; I'm being liberated. My dilemmas have vanished. Was that even me at all, that man with listless eyes and a pen in his hand who was preparing to kill himself? Was that monster devouring Umbrellas even Konrad Rutkowski at all? That monster of petit bourgeois conscience who attempted with false accusations to turn the most wonderful device in the world into a devilish trident? Was it Konrad Rutkowski who was killing himself with his ostensible share of guilt in the war twenty-two years after it ended? Where did he even get the idea that he was guilty of anything? Why would he be guilty? He was but an unoiled—what am I saying?—a *stripped* screw in the German war machine. He neither held anything together nor kept anything moving. Wherever he was screwed in, everything came loose, everything came flying apart . . .

Let's forget the past. Let's get rid of it like a smelly rag that's making the air in our room stifling. Let's accept the innocence that renouncing it offers us. Let no shadow taint the ground we'll walk from now on, bathing in the distant light of our goal. Let us know: Forgetting, rejecting, and destroying the past are essential features of the new state of being from where I'm now speaking to you and to which I now invite you as brothers!

You ask me how this came to pass, so you may join in it? It struck like lightning, like thunder. As it will come to you, when your hour strikes. Development is omitted, history suspended. I awoke like a new person, as you, too, will one day awake!

I had already pulled the noose down around my neck when I heard someone knock. At first I didn't pay any attention, but the knocking persisted. I hesitated. If I didn't open up, the visitor might think it suspicious. There would be an alarm, the door would be smashed in, and I would be pulled down from the rope. Reason demanded that I politely rid myself of the intruder, whoever it might be. In the end, that would mean only a slight delay. I opened the door slightly: there was no one in the hallway. It seemed I'd been mistaken; the knocking had been on someone else's door. I locked the door and put the noose around my neck again. The knocking interrupted me again. A coarse, commanding, wooden knock, it was stronger this time, more persistent. It was undoubtedly coming from my door. I opened it again, and again there was no one there. But now I noticed a large men's umbrella next to the door. It was leaning against the left jamb; it must have been put there awhile before, I just hadn't noticed it in my excitement. I recognized it immediately: it was Adam's demonic ally. I was shocked and horrified. I couldn't understand the reason for this disturbance. I assumed it was some kind of pressure from Adam. I calmed down and even laughed, realizing the futility of such Steinbrecherian pressures in the context of my noose. The Umbrella could no longer do me any harm or drag me into any more crimes. It was powerless in the face of death. At first I considered leaving it where it was, but then I realized it would continue beating on the door, which would upset the guests or the hotel staff. They might come to intervene and hinder me. Besides, I didn't wish to die to the demonic music of its knocking. I picked it up, took it into the room, and locked the door. I leaned the Umbrella against the wall and returned to my gallows. I remember nothing of what happened from that moment to the following morning. And the next morning I awoke in a new state, in which my desire to die was replaced by an abundance of life-energy and gratitude to the Umbrella that had saved me, evidently leading me to reexamine my suicidal decision from all angles.

Let's leave the Umbrella in its black, monklike rigidity, and return to our mission.

Its primary goal is THE DESTRUCTION OF THE PAST AND THE ELIMINATION OF ITS OFFSPRING, HISTORY. O my brothers in spirit, history is a millstone hung around the neck of life. It's Aladdin's magic lamp releasing the punitive spirit of regret and penitence to render any future odious to us, a flying carpet that we ride, battered by memories, speeding toward hell through a phony sky of false historical ideas. Let's reject all of it! Let's carry all its sources to the trash heap—all its written annals, letters, official documents, newspapers, charters, records, literary works, diaries, memoirs, historical readers, epitaphs, everything written about anything! Let's topple all the monuments of the past, anything that might ever teach us new failures! Let's raze even ancient ruins to the ground, where we'll tread freely and gloriously as on a clear plain! Let's restore things to their divine innocence and obscurity! For I am teaching you innocence, my brothers! The virtue of carelessness! Does a boulder look back when it rolls downhill, crushing everything in its path, to take its happy place at the bottom as soon as it can? So don't you look back either! There's nothing behind you that's worthy of you! All that's behind you are the rutted paths of your downfall! Be the Orpheus who didn't turn around! Have eyes and hearts only for what's out ahead of you! Be supermen!

For what is the history that we so marvel at and which we strive to learn so much from? What do we read about in the *Holy Scriptures* (if they are the false history of the Jewish people), in the writings of Herodotus, Polybios, Sallustius, Livius, Tacitus, Svetonius, Flavius, Plutarch? Is history the fairy tales told to us by Carlyle, Thierry, Gibbon, Mommsen, Ranke, Spengler, or Toynbee? Are all those tales facts? Are they true? Not at all, o brothers in spirit! They're merely hypotheses created by our reason, orthopedic analogies, the limelike, phantasmagorical shadows of onetime facts. The presentation of the evidence is good, but it's supporting a false charge. The logic is impeccable beginning with the first premise, but that first premise is false. The documentation is exhaustive, but serves a mistaken assumption. Mankind's drawing conclusions from its past is no different from your trying to figure out what I'm writing about from the mere fact of my sitting at this desk, relying solely on the fact that I am a historian and on my mood. You'd be deluded if you tried that. You'd believe that I'm restoring history, while in fact I'm destroying it. And even when you've read these letters, do you think you'll understand me? Do you think you'll be able to say with a clear conscience *Now we know who Konrad Rutkowski was?* How very terribly mistaken you are! What you see is only a mirror's reflection of a shadow. What I haven't said about myself takes precedence over what I have said. And there's considerably less of what I know about myself than there is of what I don't know and will never find out. So what then is History? The lifeless ghost of existence in the place of existence. A stew of assumptions, lies, deceits, interpolations, falsifications, mistakes, and even typographical errors, on the basis of which we create our picture of history. The tradition that we intellectuals have used to construct our idea of the future is a permanent misunderstanding with the past. The whispers of the deaf, dumb, and blind calling through the centuries. We're constructing the future on the quicksand of our delusions. Is it then odd that we're not inspired with confidence and that we await every change with fear?

But, don't be impatient, o brothers in spirit! I'm not a tired whiner about false idols! I'm the builder of true ones! In locating your wound I've also found the cure for it! And just as Christ delivered you from original sin (in vain, because anything is refuted more easily than shame), I shall save you from the newfangled sin of the West: the sin of rationality, logic, restraint, mediocrity, calculations, and compromises!

If you obey me, and grow stronger than your pasts and equal to your futures, if by rejecting humanity you can rise beyond good and evil, you'll be guaranteed a seat in the last car to drive through Berlin.[27] And he who assures you of this is one who preaches that everything is founded on life and that without it nothing is worth anything at all. Reject the past! Let's destroy it wherever it enslaves us in our innocence and creative ignorance! Let's raze the libraries to the ground! Let's burn the state archives! Let's renounce our memories, that lair of small men, and the recollections that have overgrown us like a bramble, making us look like ghostly scarecrows in an arid field! Let's rip up those nonsensical old letters, which will one day bring the roof crashing down on our heads! Let's forget when and where we were born and who bore us! Let's toss the documents with that information on the trash heap! Let the photographs, newsreels, and Dictaphone recordings follow them into ruin! Let's grind the false stars of Gutenberg's slave galaxy into dust! Let's forbid any human tracks to be left in the sand and obliterate all those whose vanity or cowardice puts them in the face of death! Let's bring all the printing presses to a halt; let's forbid printing entirely! And if we think this consistency too bold for a beginning, let's print the papers on self-destructive material! Let a newspaper read in the morning spontaneously combust at evening! Let the correspondence exchanged during the day crumble into dust by evening! Let film cassettes explode immediately after their showings!

And if you ask me how we're going to succeed in this, how we'll cast the stone of the past from our backs, I'll say unto you that you've formulated the question wrongly and that you won't succeed as long as you keep formulating it like that. If the past were only a stone on our backs, we'd have felt its burden, and would have cast it off long ago as something that is *outside* us. Were it within us, we'd have vomited it out or died long ago, because you either expunge poison or it kills you. O brothers in spirit, there isn't any past inside us, rather *we're in the past,* as in a hot and stifling swampland. We can only extricate ourselves from it if we pull ourselves out by our own bootstraps, like Baron von Münchhausen when he got stuck in the mud.

The past will not be destroyed until our sense of transience becomes as profound as transience itself. In order to defeat it, people must grow accustomed to death. Because we don't die nowadays. We only pretend we do. We flow off secretly into the swamp that stifles posterity. Let's extricate ourselves! Let's be as great in renunciation as we are merciless in conquest! Until we've killed the past, we won't give birth to the future! We'll be giving birth to posthumous children instead!

Only when the past has ceased to exist will every man become a creator and a builder. Every being will create a world from scratch. I offer you the lesson of the ultimate bravery: I teach you death! Human mortality and superhuman eternity! All else is smoke and the shadows of shadows!

You ask what's special, unusual, or new about this? There have been great and glorious destroyers before. There have been destroyers, my brothers in spirit, but not a one who destroyed as a creator. For it is said that the doors everywhere are low and that even the great ones shall enter, but they must stoop down to do so. But I say unto you that we're not going to stoop down. We wish to remain great. We'll tear down all the doors and build others according to our own size. It has also been said that anything that can be smashed against our truths should be smashed. But I say unto you: Smash everything. Stars are only born out of chaos!

What benefit did Alexander get from burning Persepolis, since he didn't destroy Athens? What did Antioch and Vespasian get from the destruction of the Great Temple of Jerusalem, since the Holy Teachings survived? What was changed by burying Carthage under a layer of salt, if Rome continued to flourish? What significance for the future was there in torching the Library of Alexandria if all the others survived?

It is said that you follow the path of greatness and that no path remains behind you because your foot has destroyed it. But I say unto you: There never was any path at all; the path was the land scarred by your iron foot!

And then it is said that of all that has ever been written only that penned in blood is worthy, and that it will take only one more century of writers and readers for the spirit to smell foul. But I say unto you: Its smell has been foul for ages! It's had a foul smell since the first time a chisel was hammered into a stone tablet, since the first reindeer was painted, as if spellbound, on the rock walls of Altamira!

So let's glorify the martyrs of destruction and the saints of demolition, because they had no fear of the future as they raised their hand to smite the past. Glory to the silent loners in the world of words, who were the first to understand that words are a treacherous compromise with inaction, which is in turn an even more treacherous compromise with nothingness. They dared to light the first flame of freedom and to keep it burning to this day, despite the humiliations and injustices they've been subjected to down through the centuries. And especially to the first among them to set fire to the books of Prothagoras. Let us pay tribute to Pope Innocent II, St. Bernhard, the city councils of Soissons and Sens, which torched all of Abelard's books, and also to the city councilors of Constance, who took care of Jan Hus and his works. Let's also not forget the Council of Worms, which first kindled a stake under Luther's writings, those who fed Pascal's *Léttres à un Provincial* into another fire, and especially the illustrious Parliament of Paris, which overcame the pressures of ignorance and destroyed copies of J. J. Rousseau's *Emile*. On 18 August 1770, the same parliament had the honor of burning (among other things) three Baron Holbachs, one Boulanger, and one Voltaire. We'll forgive them a moment of weakness toward the latter. It was corrected later, so that nothing written by that old hypocrite escaped the cleansing flames. Owing to the same constructive spirit, we rid ourselves—at least temporarily—of D'Aubigne, Beaumarchais, Helvetius, Marivaux, Milton (*Defensio*), Marlowe, Raleigh (*History of the World,* volume 1), Locke, Hobbes (*Leviathan*), Swift, Defoe, and so many other wordsmiths and windbags. It is, though, regrettable to some extent that in the more serious cases the authors were burned along with their books (their place in the fire could be replaced by their desks in the minor cases). It is and will be our view that such measures are justified only if the burning of certain works can't afford us sufficient guarantees that the writers won't restore them from memory or compose new ones to replace them. And at the same time, let's not out of modesty (which is the defense of the weak) neglect to mention the unforgettable 10th of August 1933, when the ritual of book burning began at universities in our Fatherland. (Here both Manns, Zweig, Gide, Proust, Heine, Remarque, Zola, Shaw, London, Freud, etc. were justly burned.) Especially because it was the first time that intellectuals were the main ones taking part in the solemn task—students and their professors. In earlier times, intellectuals had been limited to filing charges and issuing verdicts. The actual burning was left to the servants. And I say unto you: It took them long enough to realize that simply not reading, the method employed by ordinary people, couldn't kill books.

Let's not content ourselves with admiration. For it is said that we are striving toward fortresses of stone pillars and that, the higher we rise and ascend the heights, the more beautiful and tender we become, but the harder and more resistant within. And that we mix our balm from our own poisons. For no evil will issue from us then, except the evil coming from the struggle of our virtues. Let's perfect our devils if we have them. Thus, we'll become light, we'll fly, we'll have only ourselves before our eyes, and God will be dancing in us. Let's not worry whether something is good or evil, because we don't know what good and evil are. That's known only to the creators who have glimpsed the goal (because only in relation to that can something be good or evil) and who give the country its meaning and future (because only in relation to that can good and evil exist). Thus it is said. But I say unto you: There's neither good nor evil until we reach the goal.

And so you won't take this once again for the ramblings of a fearful sage in his bourgeois mousehole, I say unto you that the great cleansing of delusions, the great cleaning of the world, has already begun and that I've been the one to begin it.

First I sent a message to the Holy Father regarding his Biblioteca Apostolica Vaticana (800,000 volumes). I called upon him to feed that garbage into the fire without delay. And though the Church is never quick to act, and though it's bound by its dogmas and canons, I trust that it will, inspired by its experience with the Index Librorum Prohibitorum (Copernicus, Dante, Gibbon, Hume, Mill, Stern, Kant, Lawrence, Stendhal, and innumerable others), set an example which will be taken to heart.

Then I contacted HM The Queen Elizabeth II. (70,000,000 volumes in public libraries alone; 6,000,000 in the British Museum; 5,000,000 in Cambridge and Oxford.) I counted on the fact that the English, who didn't hesitate to burn Tyndall's translation of the *New Testament* in front of Old St. Paul's Cathedral, wouldn't show any more respect for profane books.

I also wrote the Russians. (Over 25,000,000,000 books in 400,000 libraries!) I'm aware of the unfortunate fact that they won't undertake anything without an agreement with the Americans (around 100,000,000 volumes in the three dozen largest libraries alone), so I simultaneously appealed to the President of the United States with the same words. I shudder at the thought of some ass in the UN proposing the formation of some subcommittee, where the matter will get bogged down interminably—in the meantime the world's shelves will keep filling up—and instead of discussing the technical problems of torches (as Herr Herbert Floss once did in Treblinka), they will go on and on about defensive and offensive books, books of this or that intellectual caliber and range.

So they won't feel left out, I also contacted the French, citing the glorious traditions of the Paris Parliament. To my own country I sent a brief telegram that read: GET STARTED! I consider that sufficient, because when something's supposed to be done there, they know what it is.

It'll be the first revolution without human victims. (Some stubborn night watchman might die, say, in Reykjavik—only 180,000 volumes.) But I'm not afraid of blood. Don't be afraid of blood, o brothers in spirit, if it turns out to be necessary. It is said that the goals in the name of which the blood is spilled consecrate the blood. But I say: Blood is that which consecrates, it consecrates all things.

Thus, this is how I want man and woman to be: Man must be able to fight wars, and woman able to bear children. And both of them must be able to use their heads as well as their hands. Thus it is said and thus let it remain!

Know that chaos alone has the power to create. From it alone worlds are born. Earthquakes cover up old sources and break open new ones. So it is said, but I say unto you: Don't wait for an earthquake! Be earthquakes yourselves! Only rotten fruit falls to the ground if you don't shake the tree. And the harder and more savagely you shake it, the more fruit will fall to the ground.

Look straight ahead. Because if you were supposed to look behind you, you'd have eyes in the back of your head. Love the land of *your children,* and not that of *your forefathers.* Because honor doesn't depend on where you've *been* but where you're *going.*

Don't be terrified of the bottom. Love the bottom. All the most profound realizations assume some bottom. And don't ask how big it is. One can stand on the bottom even if it's only a few inches wide. And there's no bottom so far down you can't see the light of the stars from it.

Reject everything, as I reject it:

I reject Laws, because they are the chains used to bind me by those who think themselves to be good but are merely powerless; I choose the lawlessness of the Will, which structures the world according to itself! For I am a creator, for it is granted to me, and because I can do it! I reject their Tablets and break them over my Will, as Moses broke the Sinai Tablets!

I reject Justice, because it renders every path wide enough to be taken by both the worthy and unworthy, by both the useful and those who are not, those who know where the path leads and those who don't!

I reject Equality, because it makes every path crowded, and makes of each step a war; wars must be saved for the fight with oneself and one's humanity!

I reject Kindness, because whenever I took a path, no matter which path, it held me back and weakened me; I bent down in sympathy for the fallen, who instead of thanking me put their hands around my neck and pulled me down to the ground to suffer and die with them!

I reject Remorse and Shame, because they force me to lower my head and eyes to the ground, depriving me of the pleasure of looking up at the goal! Had conscience always won out, the world would be ruled by monkeys today!

I reject Wisdom, because one's own insanity is more elevated than the wisdom of others!

I reject Love, because it doesn't know how to choose; I choose Hatred, because it does and never errs. I reject love, because I know that God too has his hell, which is his love for mankind!

I reject Suffering and give no reasons; whoever doesn't see them himself is born to die and doesn't deserve to live!

I reject Freedom, because it has intoxicated me and made me fall from the path on which the only ones who remained were those who held each other humbly by the hand; those who knew that a man can't scale the summit of the world on his own—one man holds the compass, another hammers in the pitons, and the third carries the pack, but they also must know at the base of the mountain who will plant the flag on the summit and who the mountain will be named after!

I reject the Past, because it created me as I am, and I accept the future which I am creating as I wish it to be; because one can be pregnant only with one's own child; and because I wish to have a clock at the very outset of my time and not for it to be handed to me at the end when I no longer have any time to keep track of!

I reject Mankind and Humanity, because I am for the Superman and Supermankind!

I have wandered, sought, and found. My spirit helps me to write boldly:

IN THE BEGINNING WAS THE DEED.

For once, at last, *mine* and not *yours,* KONRAD RUTKOWSKI.[28]

Part II

Professor Konrad Rutkowski's Postscripts

■ □ ■ □ ■

POSTSCRIPT 1

THE TRANSCRIPT OF THE INTERROGATION OF GUSTAV FRÖHLICH

STEINBRECHER: So you admit to knowing Miss Lilly Schwartzkopf?

FRÖHLICH: Yes.

STEINBRECHER: Sign the statement. . . . But why then did you claim that you don't know her?

FRÖHLICH: I didn't claim I don't know her. I said I don't know her *well.*

STEINBRECHER: How well *do* you know her?

FRÖHLICH: I know her professionally.

STEINBRECHER: The question was *how well* you know her, not *how* you know her. So how well do you know her?

FRÖHLICH: I know her only casually.

STEINBRECHER: The question was how *well* you know her, not how *casually* you know her.

FRÖHLICH: I don't know her well.

STEINBRECHER: Do you consider yourself a good salesman?

FRÖHLICH: They're satisfied with me.

STEINBRECHER: Who's satisfied with you?

FRÖHLICH: My employers.

STEINBRECHER: Who are your employers?

FRÖHLICH: I've told you ten times already!

STEINBRECHER: In the meantime, have there arisen any new circumstances due to which you should refuse to name them?

FRÖHLICH: Of course not. Why would I do that?

STEINBRECHER: That's what I'm wondering. Nevertheless, you're refusing to name them for some reason.

FRÖHLICH: I'm not refusing.

STEINBRECHER: Yes you are, Fröhlich. Just a moment ago you refused to name them. Do you still refuse to do so?

FRÖHLICH: No.

STEINBRECHER: Well?

FRÖHLICH: The company is called Urban, Urban, & Urban.

STEINBRECHER: A troika?

FRÖHLICH: It's a family-owned business.

STEINBRECHER: What's the address?

FRÖHLICH: (Gives the address of Urban, Urban, & Urban.)

STEINBRECHER: Tell us everything you know about the business dealings of Urban, Urban, & Urban.

(The following forty-eight pages of the Transcript cover the firm Urban, Urban, & Urban; the transcript includes the addresses of its employees as well as descriptions of their family backgrounds. It also includes an account of their opinions and attitudes, insofar as the suspect Gustav Fröhlich was able to say anything about them, or insofar as it was possible to make logical inferences about them.)

STEINBRECHER: You said your employers are satisfied with you. Does that mean you're a successful salesman?

FRÖHLICH: Yes.

STEINBRECHER: And does that mean you've engaged in ethical business practices?

FRÖHLICH: Yes.

STEINBRECHER: Yes, it does, Fröhlich. There's absolutely no doubt that it does. Or rather, it does in every case but yours. As in other areas, which we'll also address, you're somewhat of an exception in this respect. You did just the opposite: you were successful precisely because you disregarded ethical business practices.

FRÖHLICH: I've never engaged in unethical business practices!

STEINBRECHER: How so, if you've done business with people you don't even know?

FRÖHLICH: I've never done business with people I don't know.

STEINBRECHER: What about Miss Lilly Schwartzkopf?

FRÖHLICH: But I did know her.

STEINBRECHER: Did you know her well?

FRÖHLICH: Well enough.

STEINBRECHER: Enough for what?

FRÖHLICH: For the purpose at hand.

STEINBRECHER: What purpose would that be?

FRÖHLICH: The purpose of doing business with her.

STEINBRECHER: Oh, I see. You consider something good if it's only passable. You consider any deal good if it's not completely worthless. So your superficial acquaintance with Miss Lilly Schwartzkopf was good enough for entering into a serious relationship with her?

FRÖHLICH: The acquaintance wasn't superficial.

STEINBRECHER: Were you friends then?

FRÖHLICH: I knew her well enough. I wouldn't say we were friends.

STEINBRECHER: So you knew her well enough? What's enough?

FRÖHLICH: I knew her well enough to avoid risk in doing business with her.

STEINBRECHER: What risk—for the company or for you?

FRÖHLICH: In fact, for both the company and me.

STEINBRECHER: What risk would the company be taking in doing business with her?

FRÖHLICH: Miss Schwartzkopf could have been insolvent.

STEINBRECHER: So the company could have suffered financial losses?

FRÖHLICH: Yes.

STEINBRECHER: And you?

FRÖHLICH: I could have suffered financial losses, too.

STEINBRECHER: How could you have suffered financial losses?

FRÖHLICH: According to my contract, I have to reimburse the company for any financial losses resulting from the business deals I negotiate.

STEINBRECHER: Does that in fact mean you were the only party taking a risk in the deal?

FRÖHLICH: That's how the contract works.

STEINBRECHER: Consequently, in order to avoid a personal financial risk in doing business with Miss Schwartzkopf, you had to obtain a certain amount of reliable information about her?

FRÖHLICH: Yes.

STEINBRECHER: All right. That fits logically. Criminal activities always involve a certain amount of risk.

FRÖHLICH: What criminal activities?

STEINBRECHER: Your criminal activities.

FRÖHLICH: I didn't do anything wrong!

STEINBRECHER: Then why are you here?

FRÖHLICH: I don't know!

STEINBRECHER: Do you wish to say you're here for no reason at all?

FRÖHLICH: I have no idea why I'm here.

STEINBRECHER: And that the German police arrest innocent people?

FRÖHLICH: I didn't say the German police arrest innocent people! I just said *I'm* innocent!

STEINBRECHER: But you're nevertheless under arrest, aren't you? Thus, it follows that we just arrest innocent people out on the street. That is, either you're guilty and we only arrest those guilty of some wrongdoing, or you're innocent and we arrest the innocent, too. There's not a third possibility, logically speaking!

FRÖHLICH: What about a mistake?

STEINBRECHER: Only idiots make mistakes. Do you consider us idiots, Fröhlich?

FRÖHLICH: Of course not.

STEINBRECHER: Then don't act as if you do. That won't help you in the least. Especially considering the statement you just gave.

FRÖHLICH: I didn't give any statement.

STEINBRECHER: You said we arrest innocent people; that claim is considered hostile propaganda and is punishable by law.

FRÖHLICH: I didn't say that.

STEINBRECHER: Well, I'm glad you didn't. I'm glad for both of us. You see, broadening the interrogation to include new charges is always a hell of a job. So you don't think that we arrest innocent people?

FRÖHLICH: No, I don't.

STEINBRECHER: Whom do we arrest?

FRÖHLICH: Those guilty of some wrongdoing.

STEINBRECHER: Accordingly, you can't be innocent, can you? Otherwise, your own generalization wouldn't hold, would it?

FRÖHLICH: Well, it wouldn't, but . . .

STEINBRECHER: In logic, Fröhlich, there aren't any "buts." Logic is a science. Logic isn't a business deal—you can't negotiate the conclusions. If the first premise is that we arrest only those guilty of some wrongdoing, and the second is that we've arrested you, what's the inevitable logical conclusion?

FRÖHLICH: That I'm guilty as well.

STEINBRECHER: Correct. Sign the statement. . . . There you go. Thank you. Let's continue. Where did you inquire about Miss Schwartzkopf?

FRÖHLICH: In the firms she had business dealings with.

STEINBRECHER: Which firms? Give me their names and addresses.

(There follows a list of the firms where Gustav Fröhlich inquired about the solvency of the milliner Lilly Schwartzkopf. The list also contains the names and addresses of the employees whom the suspect knew or whom he had any kind of contact with. Some of the names reappear later, in the final stages of this transcript, as the accomplices of the Fröhlich-Schwartzkopf intelligence network. These individuals seemed to function as "pump-out agents" who gathered industrial secrets at their workplaces and forwarded them to the espionage headquarters.)

STEINBRECHER: For the sake of concision, can we label your activities regarding Miss Schwartzkopf as spying?

FRÖHLICH: I didn't spy on her!

STEINBRECHER: Was she aware of your activities?

FRÖHLICH: No, but she could've expected that I'd inquire about her. That's a common practice when you enter into a new business relationship.

STEINBRECHER: Inquiring means gathering information regarding someone or something, right?

FRÖHLICH: Right.

STEINBRECHER: Would we distort the meaning of your words if we put down that you "gathered information about Miss Schwartzkopf"?

FRÖHLICH: I don't think so, though it's not any more concise than if you simply wrote that I inquired about her.

STEINBRECHER: In case you're concerned, Fröhlich, let me assure you that we have enough paper to finish your interrogation. No need to worry about a shortage of either paper or time. . . . Was the information you gathered any good?

FRÖHLICH: Yes.

STEINBRECHER: Could we say that the information gave you a clear idea of who your business partner was?

FRÖHLICH: Yes, we could.

STEINBRECHER: Consequently, you got to know her well, which directly contradicts your previous statement that you were only casual acquaintances.

FRÖHLICH: I said that the information was good, but that doesn't mean I was able to get to know her well on the basis of that information.

STEINBRECHER: So your information was insufficient?

FRÖHLICH: No.

STEINBRECHER: False?

FRÖHLICH: Not at all.

STEINBRECHER: Then the only explanation we're left with is that you simply didn't read your own information.

FRÖHLICH: But I did, of course I did!

STEINBRECHER: So it was detailed, reliable information that you conscientiously took into consideration?

FRÖHLICH: Yes.

STEINBRECHER: Then one of us is either a lunatic or a liar. What do you think, Fröhlich, am I a liar?

FRÖHLICH: No, Sir, you're not. Why would you lie?

STEINBRECHER: You've finally said something sensible. Exactly— why would I lie? I'm not under interrogation. Consequently, I'm a lunatic. Am I a lunatic, Fröhlich?

FRÖHLICH: Of course not, Sir.

STEINBRECHER: What about you?

FRÖHLICH: I don't think I'm a lunatic, Sir.

STEINBRECHER: But you aren't positive, are you?

FRÖHLICH: I'm positive, Sir.

STEINBRECHER: If that's the case, then you're blatantly lying when you insist you didn't know Miss Schwartzkopf well. Why are you lying, Fröhlich? What are you hiding from us? Why is it that you're *afraid to admit* that you knew Miss Schwartzkopf well?

FRÖHLICH: I'm not hiding anything, Sir. I swear to God I'm not hiding anything.

STEINBRECHER: Do you think a close friendship with someone who happens to be a milliner is dangerous in and of itself?

FRÖHLICH: No.

STEINBRECHER: Do you think that we at the Gestapo have gone mad with suspicion, and that we consider it a crime if a person knows someone or something well?

FRÖHLICH: Not at all!

STEINBRECHER: Then why are you reluctant to admit that you knew her well?

FRÖHLICH: I'm not reluctant, Sir. I only thought that it's too strong a word to describe my knowledge of her.

STEINBRECHER: It may be too strong, but it's close enough.

FRÖHLICH: That's right.

STEINBRECHER: Sign the statement.

FRÖHLICH: But here it says that I knew Miss Schwartzkopf *intimately!*

STEINBRECHER: Didn't you?

FRÖHLICH: Well, of course not! I knew her professionally, as a business partner, but certainly not intimately!

STEINBRECHER: Calm down, Fröhlich. This statement isn't carved in stone. If we've made a mistake, we'll correct it. We'll erase "intimately" and put down "well" instead. Satisfied?

FRÖHLICH: Yes.

STEINBRECHER: I hope you can see now that we're not enemies who are planning to get you into trouble; therefore, your emphatically defensive stance is out of place. Does that make sense?

FRÖHLICH: Yes.

STEINBRECHER: Will you sign the statement now? There you go. Thanks. . . .

(Even in the early stages of the interrogation, Steinbrecher didn't accept Fröhlich's denial of his acquaintanceship with the milliner Lilly Schwartzkopf—the denial that resulted from the suspect's instinctive

realization that it was safer to admit to knowing fewer people. From that moment on, Fröhlich used all his inner strength and intelligence to avoid at least admitting to getting to know Lilly any better. His partial success can't be denied. "Knowing Miss Schwartzkopf to some extent" was as far as he allowed himself to go in his relationship with the milliner. Naturally, the phrase implied only a business relationship. Accused of having an intimate relationship with her, Fröhlich could only negotiate. Thus, the "intimate relationship" was exchanged for "a close relationship." Consequently, according to the Transcript, Fröhlich now knew the milliner well, and this was precisely the point he'd wanted to avoid ending up at. But he succeeded in one thing at least—he eliminated any possibility of defining their relationship as "intimate." Fröhlich must have felt satisfied, even proud. Little did he know that, as the interrogation progressed, the "intimate relationship" would re-emerge like an apparition and be accepted as the only way of avoiding the third possibility, espionage. Nor did he suspect that in the end this last term would also be accepted because, after all, one is better off as an industrial spy than as a saboteur or a terrorist.)

STEINBRECHER: On whose orders did you contact the aforementioned Lilly Schwartzkopf?

FRÖHLICH: On the order of my employers.

STEINBRECHER: Who are your employers?

FRÖHLICH: I told you—Urban, Urban, & Urban.

STEINBRECHER: The address, please.

(There follows a monotonous repetition of all the details that Fröhlich had already given. There were no discrepancies and the interrogation continues.)

STEINBRECHER: Who's the owner of the firm?

FRÖHLICH: Mr. Urban.

STEINBRECHER: Do you know him well?

FRÖHLICH: I do business with him.

STEINBRECHER: The question was . . .

FRÖHLICH: I don't know him well.

(Fröhlich knew all the moves in advance. He knew they would lead to his inevitable defeat, but he repeated them with a mechanical persistence. This could point at some sort of plan on his part. But I don't think he had any plan. Fröhlich was only instinctively following the basic rule that one never admits anything when under interrogation.)

STEINBRECHER: How come you don't know him well if you work for him?

FRÖHLICH: Mr. Urban doesn't have a habit of establishing close relationships with his subordinates.

STEINBRECHER: I see. He's withdrawn, reserved, mysterious. Which one of these?

FRÖHLICH: He's businesslike.

STEINBRECHER: And you know him only as being businesslike?

FRÖHLICH: Yes.

STEINBRECHER: Formulate the statement for the File in your own words, please.

FRÖHLICH: Answering the question how well he knows Mr. Urban, Mr. Fröhlich . . .

STEINBRECHER: Which Mr. Fröhlich? Who's Mr. Fröhlich?

FRÖHLICH: That's me.

STEINBRECHER: He can't be you. You're not a mister. You're a suspected criminal. So who's the second Fröhlich and where does he live?

(There follows an intricate exchange with constantly shifting logical assumptions, in which Fröhlich finally succeeds in convincing Steinbrecher that he did not have anyone else in mind; calling himself "mister" was simply a mistake, and not a slip of tongue that revealed the existence of some other Fröhlich. Having thus saved the life of an innocent relative, the first Fröhlich continues to define his relationship with Mr. Urban with a sense of victorious pride.)

FRÖHLICH: Fröhlich says that he knows Mr. Urban only as his employer.

STEINBRECHER: Does that sound right?

FRÖHLICH: It does.

STEINBRECHER: Don't you consider an employer to be a human being as well?

FRÖHLICH: Of course I do.

STEINBRECHER: If you do, you must know him both as an employer and as a human being.

FRÖHLICH: Certainly, insofar as he acts like a human being in doing business.

STEINBRECHER: He probably doesn't act like an animal. Or does he?

THE TRANSCRIPT OF THE INTERROGATION OF GUSTAV FRÖHLICH

FRÖHLICH: Of course not.

STEINBRECHER: So there's no need for him to be reported to the Reich Bureau of Labor?

FRÖHLICH: No, there isn't. He's a good man.

STEINBRECHER: How do you know that?

FRÖHLICH: I just do.

STEINBRECHER: But then you know him well, don't you?

FRÖHLICH: Yes. I know him well.

STEINBRECHER: Sign the statement. . . . Thank you. How well do you know him?

FRÖHLICH: Like my own brother.

(Fröhlich has obviously lost his temper. He allowed himself to make an exaggerated, sarcastic comment. He shouldn't have done that. An interrogation doesn't understand exaggerations. In an interrogation, everything is possible and everything is allowed. Steinbrecher provides instant proof of this.)

STEINBRECHER: What's your brother's name, what does he do for living, and where does he live?

FRÖHLICH: I don't have a brother. I'm an only child.

STEINBRECHER: Then why did you say you know Mr. Urban like your own brother?

FRÖHLICH: That's what you say when you want to emphasize how well you know someone.

STEINBRECHER: Listen, Fröhlich, save such remarks for later when you're writing a dictionary of German idioms. But in the meantime, don't obstruct the interrogation process. Got it?

FRÖHLICH: Yes, Sir.

STEINBRECHER: Did you often talk with Mr. Urban?

FRÖHLICH: No, I didn't talk with him often.

STEINBRECHER: Why didn't you talk often?

FRÖHLICH: Because I travel a lot.

STEINBRECHER: Why do you travel a lot?

FRÖHLICH: Because I'm a traveling salesman.

STEINBRECHER: Did you often talk with him when you weren't away on business?

FRÖHLICH: Occasionally. Not too often.

STEINBRECHER: What did you talk about most of the time?

FRÖHLICH: Most of the time about business, the situation on the market, the way merchandise sells . . .

STEINBRECHER: You lied again, Fröhlich. You did talk with Mr. Urban frequently, because it's impossible to talk with someone about something *most of the time* and yet to talk with that person *rarely.*

FRÖHLICH: I don't know. It seemed to me that we talked very rarely.

STEINBRECHER: That's only because you wished that your conversations had been more frequent. That's a psychological condition all subordinate employees suffer from. They can never get enough of their superiors. Let's negotiate the formulation of your statement: Although Fröhlich talked with Mr. Urban frequently, he insists that, in the view of their common cause, it was not often enough . . . Why are you mumbling? Articulate your objection!

FRÖHLICH: I don't agree with the part that says that we talked about some common cause.

STEINBRECHER: Okay. We'll leave that out. Let's have only the part in which you admit that you talked with Mr. Urban very frequently. How does it look like now?

FRÖHLICH: Excellent.

STEINBRECHER: We'll naturally leave out the part in which you deny that you talked with your employer frequently. Otherwise you'd look like a liar. Was Mr. Urban kind to you?

FRÖHLICH: Yes, Sir.

STEINBRECHER: Then I don't understand what you had against him.

FRÖHLICH: I didn't have anything against him.

STEINBRECHER: In that case, I can't really understand why you avoided him.

FRÖHLICH: Who said I avoided him?

STEINBRECHER: You've never said you would have met with him even more often than you did if you'd had the opportunity. Are you a freak, a misanthrope, an asocial person, or just a disloyal employee?

FRÖHLICH: I'm not asocial, I like people. I would've met with Mr. Urban even more frequently than I did if I'd had the opportunity, but we move in different social circles.

STEINBRECHER: Let's write that down: Fröhlich states that he and Mr. Urban would have met with one another more often had the situation in Germany so allowed.

FRÖHLICH: I don't understand—what situation in Germany?

STEINBRECHER: The circles you mentioned.

FRÖHLICH: Oh, yes, the circles.

STEINBRECHER: Sign the statement. . . . Thank you. Your desire to meet with Mr. Urban more frequently logically implies that you trusted him. Did you trust him?

FRÖHLICH: I did, although trusting him didn't have anything to do with our conversations.

STEINBRECHER: Did you see eye to eye with him in those conversations?

FRÖHLICH: Mostly.

STEINBRECHER: Did you or didn't you?

(Fröhlich tries to think fast. If he says he didn't always agree with Mr. Urban, he'll have to explain what they disagreed about and so one of them—this time Mr. Urban—will certainly be in trouble. Besides, it's only natural to expect that a well-to-do and educated man such as Mr. Urban knows more than a salesman, and that he's much more intelligent. In principle, it's less risky to agree with such an interlocutor. Therefore Fröhlich decides to appear less reserved.)

FRÖHLICH: Yes, I did.

STEINBRECHER: What do we call people who agree in their opinions?

FRÖHLICH: Like-minded people.

STEINBRECHER: When did you last confer with your like-minded Mr. Urban?

FRÖHLICH: Mr. Urban and I never conferred together. Only important people confer. I only talked with . . .

STEINBRECHER: Is Mr. Urban an important man?

FRÖHLICH: I think he is.

STEINBRECHER: So, in principle, he can confer with someone?

FRÖHLICH: Yes, he can.

STEINBRECHER: While you, being unimportant, can't confer? You can only talk?

FRÖHLICH: That's right.

STEINBRECHER: Would you be satisfied if we omit you entirely from the next paragraph and reduce everything to the point of your not conferring with Mr. Urban but Mr. Urban's conferring with you? Would that description match what went on between the two of you?

FRÖHLICH: It would.

STEINBRECHER: Put your signature here. . . . Thank you. Where did the aforementioned conference take place?

FRÖHLICH: I don't remember.

STEINBRECHER: Try to remember.

(This exchange is repeated a few times. Then Fröhlich remembers.)

FRÖHLICH: In a church portal.

STEINBRECHER: Consequently, you're religious?

FRÖHLICH: God forbid, I'm not!

STEINBRECHER: Then you must have gone to the church only in order to have a clandestine meeting with Mr. Urban.

FRÖHLICH: That's not true!

STEINBRECHER: Then what were you looking for in the church?

FRÖHLICH: For God!

STEINBRECHER: Whom you nevertheless don't believe in. Or do you? Do you believe in God, Fröhlich?

FRÖHLICH: I don't.

STEINBRECHER: Why do you pray to him?

FRÖHLICH: So that he helps me. Why else do people pray to God?

STEINBRECHER: That's logical. Only, how can he help you if you don't believe in him?

FRÖHLICH: Who said I don't?

STEINBRECHER: You said you don't!

FRÖHLICH: I didn't say that.

STEINBRECHER: You did. Why did you say that? Why did you lie?

FRÖHLICH: I don't know. I thought . . .

STEINBRECHER: That it would be better that way?

FRÖHLICH: Yes.

STEINBRECHER: Why would it be better that way? Maybe because in Germany religious people are frowned upon?

FRÖHLICH: Yes.

STEINBRECHER: How are religious people looked upon in your opinion, Fröhlich?

FRÖHLICH: With a certain amount of distrust.

STEINBRECHER: What makes you think that?

FRÖHLICH: Because they aren't allowed in certain positions.

STEINBRECHER: Which positions?

FRÖHLICH: Government positions. Diplomatic, military, police, and so on.

STEINBRECHER: You mean all government positions?

FRÖHLICH: I didn't say that.

STEINBRECHER: And what does a state consist of, if not the military and the police?

FRÖHLICH: I think there are other government positions as well.

STEINBRECHER: Say, garbage collectors.

FRÖHLICH: Yes, but there are others . . .

STEINBRECHER: So religious people should be allowed to collect garbage. Do you consider that just?

FRÖHLICH: Yes.

STEINBRECHER: What do we call it when some people are forbidden what others are allowed?

FRÖHLICH: Injustice.

STEINBRECHER: So in your opinion, it is injustice when a carpenter is not allowed to operate on cancer patients?

FRÖHLICH: I don't know . . .

STEINBRECHER: In other words, when a carpenter is forbidden what a doctor is allowed to do?

FRÖHLICH: I don't understand what you're talking about. I'm a bit tired. Would you mind if I get up from the chair and stretch my legs for a moment?

STEINBRECHER: You'll get up when we're finished.

FRÖHLICH: When will that be?

STEINBRECHER: That all depends on you. Stop being uncooperative and we'll be finished in a minute. But more than that, stop broadening the interrogation by making one incriminating statement after another!

FRÖHLICH: I haven't made any incriminating statements!

STEINBRECHER: You insisted that we discriminate against certain parts of the population. Read the Transcript!

FRÖHLICH: I refuse to sign that.

STEINBRECHER: No one's making you sign it. We still haven't reached the bottom of the page!

FRÖHLICH: I'm not going to sign anything like that even when we do.

STEINBRECHER: You have the right to refuse to do so.

(Standartenführer Steinbrecher changes the subject. Fröhlich accepts

the change with relief. Delighted at having escaped the quicksand of religious issues, he becomes somewhat reckless and makes a few unnecessary admissions regarding other, less dangerous matters that he'd have certainly avoided under different circumstances. But all in all, he's satisfied. The interrogation is going better than he expected. It hasn't been like in the horrible stories he's heard about the Gestapo. He hasn't been hit once. It's true that he doesn't know how long the interrogation has been going on—thick drapes cover the windows and the reflector lamp shining in his eyes somewhat dulls his sense of time—but in all other aspects the interrogation resembles a polite exchange between two systems of logical thought, which occasionally clash with one another but eventually reach a compromise that results in mutual satisfaction. Fröhlich certainly thinks it's essential to avoid a confrontation with the great truths of the Doctrine, not the least of which is an animosity for the Church. And he's succeeded in that. Unfortunately, Steinbrecher doesn't share his opinion. After some ten pages, the Transcript addresses this issue again.)

STEINBRECHER: Tell me, Fröhlich—this is in fact a personal question and won't go into the Transcript—do you think there are a lot of religious people in Germany?

FRÖHLICH: I don't know, Sir. I think so.

STEINBRECHER: More than those who aren't religious? I mean, do you think the religious people represent the majority of the German population?

FRÖHLICH: I think . . .

STEINBRECHER: So you think they do. Considering your statement regarding the discrimination against certain parts of the population in Germany, recorded on page 127 in this Transcript, it can be concluded that you're of the opinion that the large majority of the German people is discriminated against . . .

FRÖHLICH: That's not what I think!

STEINBRECHER: Then at least the majority? Not a large majority, but still majority?

FRÖHLICH: No, not even that!

STEINBRECHER: Then only certain parts of the population?

FRÖHLICH: Yes.

STEINBRECHER: Will you sign that statement? That is, we're at the bottom of the page.

FRÖHLICH: I will.

STEINBRECHER: Thank you. . . . I asked you because I thought that earlier—was it yesterday?—you were of a different opinion regarding the issue. No matter. It's important that we've finally found out what you really think.

FRÖHLICH: It's not just my opinion. Even Party members say that religion should be taken care of sooner or later.

FRÖHLICH: Members of which party?

FRÖHLICH: Well, there's just one party.

STEINBRECHER: Consequently, we have a one-party dictatorship here?

FRÖHLICH: I didn't say that.

STEINBRECHER: But that's what you meant, since you said we have only one party. If you claim there's no dictatorship in Germany, you must have the existence of some other parties in mind. Well?

FRÖHLICH: We have a number of parties.

STEINBRECHER: What are those parties? What are their names?

FRÖHLICH: The NSDAP—the National Socialist German Workers' Party.

STEINBRECHER: What about the other parties?

FRÖHLICH: I don't know. But if I don't know about them, that doesn't mean we don't have them. That only means I'm ill informed.

STEINBRECHER: Why would other parties *have* to exist, Fröhlich?

FRÖHLICH: Because it's only logical, Sir. Because we don't have a dictatorship!

(Fröhlich has also finally learned something about logic. This knowledge should have been of some use to him. However, the strength of logic doesn't depend on its application per se, but on the person applying it.)

STEINBRECHER: Don't be a damned idiot, Fröhlich! It's only too natural that we have a one-party dictatorship! You're the first and only one to deny that. Are you ashamed of this?

FRÖHLICH: Actually, I'm proud of it!

STEINBRECHER: Or is it that you know of some other party that we don't? Do you know of some other party, Fröhlich?

FRÖHLICH: No, Sir, I don't. I only know about our National Socialist Party.

STEINBRECHER: Then don't rave like some lunatic, for God's sake, and stop giving answers that look like they were obtained from you with thumbscrews! . . . Sign here. Not there! . . . Here! It follows from the Transcript that you claim that some parts of the population in Germany are discriminated against.

FRÖHLICH: That's what follows from it.

STEINBRECHER: Have you talked about this with anyone?

FRÖHLICH: Only with my wife.

STEINBRECHER: What's her name and address?

(The name of Fröhlich's wife, her address, and her family connections including all the accompanying information, fill the next twenty pages.)

STEINBRECHER: You and your wife discussed discrimination in Germany. Thus, you were involved in spreading hostile propaganda.

FRÖHLICH: No, I wasn't!

STEINBRECHER: Fröhlich, when someone tries to convince someone else that there's injustice in their country, isn't that spreading hostile propaganda?

FRÖHLICH: Yes.

STEINBRECHER: Then you did so by trying to convince your wife . . .

FRÖHLICH: I didn't try to convince her of anything!

STEINBRECHER: Then she tried to convince you!

FRÖHLICH: I swear to God it's not true!

STEINBRECHER: Listen, Fröhlich, this isn't working. One of you *had* to be trying to convince the other; otherwise, I can't make any sense of your statements regarding your conversations with your wife. Well? Who was trying to convince whom?

FRÖHLICH: I don't remember.

STEINBRECHER: Then we'll put down that you tried to convince her. In any case, it's more logical.

FRÖHLICH: But that's not true! Now I remember! She tried to convince me!

STEINBRECHER: Sign it. There you go. Will you write down her name and address on a piece of paper? There you go. . . . I suppose now you'll insist that you tried to dissuade her?

(There follows Steinbrecher's own note from which we learn that the interrogatee Fröhlich fainted at precisely 15:15 and regained consciousness at 16:05, when the interrogation was resumed with a repetition of the last question.)

FRÖHLICH: Yes, I did.

STEINBRECHER: Did she attack us ever more fiercely as you persisted in defending us?

FRÖHLICH: Well, sort of.

STEINBRECHER: And in this way you cunningly induced her to go even further?

FRÖHLICH: I stopped when I realized that.

STEINBRECHER: So you let her spit all over everything that we hold sacred? You know, Fröhlich, that's a model example of criminal collaboration. And if it were only that! Your wife obviously convinced you. If she hadn't, you wouldn't tell me such crap and try to recruit me as a like-minded accomplice for your criminal activities right in the middle of a government office! But we'll discuss that issue later on. In the meantime, do you think we persecute segments of the population besides the religious?

FRÖHLICH: No.

STEINBRECHER: But what are we going to do with the Jews?

FRÖHLICH: What Jews?! Jews are swine!

STEINBRECHER: Consequently, they're not human?

FRÖHLICH: They are, but they're evil.

STEINBRECHER: Judging from your statement, you seem to approve of the measures taken against them.

FRÖHLICH: Not only do I approve . . .

STEINBRECHER: Restrain your blood lust, Fröhlich. Answer my questions and don't deliver any political speeches! Tell me, how does the commandment about our fellow man go?

FRÖHLICH: Love thy neighbor like thyself.

STEINBRECHER: Do you love the Jews like that?

FRÖHLICH: They're not our neighbors.

STEINBRECHER: But they *are* human?

FRÖHLICH: Yes.

STEINBRECHER: I don't understand you, Fröhlich. On the one hand, you believe in God . . .

FRÖHLICH: I signed that statement!

STEINBRECHER: Calm down, Fröhlich! You've said and signed all sorts of things so far. Both that you do believe and that you don't believe! One can never tell what you mean. We'll need a month to purge this Transcript of all the contradictory statements you've filled it with!

(Fröhlich faints for the second time, but now only for some ten minutes.)

STEINBRECHER: Such an impressionable person should be forbidden to meddle in politics. . . . Does your religion oblige you to love thy neighbor?

FRÖHLICH: It does.

STEINBRECHER: Then how can you call Jews swine?

FRÖHLICH: I don't know!

STEINBRECHER: Are Jews swine?

FRÖHLICH: No! I'm a swine!

STEINBRECHER: Finally, the two of us agree about something! Sign the statement. There you go. Let's continue. From what you've said we can conclude that you actually don't support the measures that are being taken against them and that you lied to us when you said you do. Did your love for the Jews make you accept the job with Mr. Urban?

FRÖHLICH: Mr. Urban isn't Jewish!

STEINBRECHER: But his wife has some Jewish blood in her veins. Why didn't you notify the authorities of that?

FRÖHLICH: I didn't know I was required to do so.

STEINBRECHER: What do we call a person who fails to report a crime?

FRÖHLICH: A witness.

STEINBRECHER: That's not true. A witness is someone who reports a crime. If not, he's an accomplice. Accordingly, Fröhlich, you're an accomplice to a crime!

FRÖHLICH: Being Jewish isn't a crime.

STEINBRECHER: Then why did you claim that you support the measures taken against them? Whom are such measures taken against, Fröhlich?

FRÖHLICH: Against criminals.

STEINBRECHER: Consequently, the Jews are criminals. What are the Jews?

FRÖHLICH: Criminals.

STEINBRECHER: And what is a person who helps criminals?

FRÖHLICH: A criminal.

STEINBRECHER: Accordingly, Fröhlich, you're a criminal.

FRÖHLICH: But I retracted the statement in which I said that I supported those measures. In fact, I never supported them.

THE TRANSCRIPT OF THE INTERROGATION OF GUSTAV FRÖHLICH

STEINBRECHER: What is a person who doesn't respect the laws of his own country?

FRÖHLICH: A criminal.

STEINBRECHER: So even in that case you're a criminal. You're a criminal no matter what. What are you, Fröhlich?

FRÖHLICH: A criminal no matter what.

STEINBRECHER: Let's sign the statement. Write legibly, please. Thank you. And now describe your meetings with Mr. Urban.

FRÖHLICH: Those weren't meetings. Just occasional encounters. They always happened by chance.

STEINBRECHER: Does your employer go to church on regular basis?

FRÖHLICH: He sings in a church choir.

STEINBRECHER: So you know you'll find him in church on Sundays?

FRÖHLICH: Yes, I do.

STEINBRECHER: Those aren't chance encounters, Fröhlich. A pre-arranged meeting isn't an accident. What do we call a meeting that's arranged beforehand?

FRÖHLICH: Planned in advance.

STEINBRECHER: That's right. Planned in advance. Premeditated. Organized. Why did you hold clandestine meetings with Mr. Urban?

FRÖHLICH: For God's sake, there wasn't anything clandestine about those meetings!

STEINBRECHER: Don't swear! What kind of inappropriate behavior is that? Do you really want me to lose all trust in you? . . . Be sensible! Did you ever tell anyone about your intention to hold meetings with Mr. Urban? No. Did you announce those meetings on the bulletin board in the church lobby? No. Did you make the news available for the press or radio? No. No one but you knew about those meetings.

FRÖHLICH: Even Mr. Urban didn't know about them.

STEINBRECHER: There you go. What kind of meeting is the meeting that no one knows about? What kind of meeting is that, Fröhlich?

FRÖHLICH: Clandestine.

STEINBRECHER: So why are you arguing then? Sign the page. What was the purpose of the clandestine meeting between you and Mr. Urban?

FRÖHLICH: I asked for a raise.

STEINBRECHER: Do you really think I'm going to swallow that, Fröhlich? That I'll believe you when you say that you held secret meetings in the church because of your raise, which you could have easily asked for in his office? Besides, you don't have fixed salary—you work on commission!

(I've noticed that the Standartenführer often supported his accusations with evidence that had no logical foundation whatsoever. This confused the examinee Fröhlich, wasting his intellectual energy on trifles.)

FRÖHLICH: I wanted to ask him to raise the commission I received as a salesman.

STEINBRECHER: Why didn't you do that in his office?

FRÖHLICH: I didn't dare. We were never alone there.

STEINBRECHER: Let's describe the situation concisely: Fröhlich claims that—considering its confidential and dangerous nature—the conversation couldn't be held in the presence of witnesses . . .

FRÖHLICH: That's an exaggeration, Sir. There was nothing confidential about it. The issue was simply embarrassing.

STEINBRECHER: But you said, "I didn't dare." Logically, this phrase accords with the word "confidential." The word "embarrassing" requires the phrase "I couldn't," which you didn't use.

FRÖHLICH: I didn't mean that.

STEINBRECHER: So you don't mean what you say!? You're obstructing the interrogation! Do you want to lead us in the wrong direction? Sit up! Raise your head! Look me in my eyes! Admit that you lied in order to conceal the subversive nature of your conversation with that man Urban!

FRÖHLICH: It's true that I lied, but our conversation wasn't subversive. It was just confidential.

STEINBRECHER: A moment ago you denied even that.

(As has been often the case during this slow and tedious journey through Fröhlich's confused, subversive past, Steinbrecher's questioning suddenly changes course. Such a turn always causes a powerful shock, and many of Fröhlich's unfortified lines of defense simply collapse. Now Steinbrecher asks which Party members Fröhlich knows. What follows is a list of names, occupations, and characteristics of all the NSDAP members and functionaries known to Fröhlich. Since such lists have already been compiled a few times, they are compared with one another. It's dis-

THE TRANSCRIPT OF THE INTERROGATION OF GUSTAV FRÖHLICH

covered that one name that was included in the first list is missing from the last one. Fröhlich is further interrogated because of this omission. There must be a serious reason for such a lapse of memory. The only reason that can be considered really serious is some subversive activity on the part of that particular Party member. The logical conclusion is that such activity is underway and that it was the cause of Fröhlich's lapse. It's also only natural that Fröhlich wasn't forgetful at the time the first list was compiled. Namely, at that time Fröhlich wasn't yet fully aware of the real nature of the interrogation, and his instinctive system of defense had not yet been fully activated. The clarification of this issue continues for another twenty-nine pages. It's interesting to follow the change in Fröhlich's signature in the course of the minor threads of the interrogation. His signature has again acquired its original firmness and legibility, and there's no danger that Fröhlich's name will end up as some kind of farts. And then suddenly the Standartenführer returns to Mr. Urban, the general manager of the textile company where the examinee was employed. Lilly Schwartzkopf, the mysterious milliner and the British spy, is still out of sight. She flashed by at the very beginning of the interrogation, and then disappeared like the winter sun in the clouds of Steinbrecher's logical maze. But let's not fool ourselves. Her bed has been made and, leaning against the window, she waits for her knight, Fröhlich, who will come to her, somewhere near the very end of the Transcript, riding on one of Steinbrecher's questions as if on a steed that knows its way all on its own.)

STEINBRECHER: Tell me, why did you hold these highly confidential talks with Urban in such fear of someone finding out about them?

FRÖHLICH: I was ashamed.

STEINBRECHER: Ashamed of your betrayal?

FRÖHLICH: Ashamed of the circumstances in which I lived.

STEINBRECHER: For God's sake, Fröhlich, are you also going to bother me with stories about your unhappy childhood? I simply wouldn't be able to endure them. I'm sick of that. After all, you don't have a right to something like that. You're not an intellectual. You're only a wretched salesman. No one but the Gestapo is interested in your life. And since this is the case, you could show a little bit of gratitude and stop bothering me with personal confessions.

FRÖHLICH: What I meant are my *present* circumstances, Sir.

STEINBRECHER: What about them? What are your circumstances?

FRÖHLICH: I live in miserable circumstances, Herr Hauptsturm-führer. No one wears hats any more. Just helmets. And I have eleven kids. The twelfth will be with us soon. We've also been awarded the honor cross for motherhood.

STEINBRECHER: I'm only interested in the one who will be with you soon. Where did you send your child and for what purpose?

FRÖHLICH: What I meant is that it's on its way, it hasn't been born as yet.

STEINBRECHER: Then speak it up clearly! You're in a police office, not in the academy of fine arts! Did you get that? And what do you mean by your miserable circumstances? Do you want to say that poverty reigns in our country?

FRÖHLICH: Not at all, sir. I'm the only one who's miserable.

STEINBRECHER: And with the exception of you, Germany is a land of milk and honey?

FRÖHLICH: Yes, sir.

STEINBRECHER: Don't speak nonsense, Fröhlich. A country that's preparing for a defensive war can't be a land of milk and honey. While we're tightening our belts, you're turning our efforts into hostile propaganda.

FRÖHLICH: I haven't told anyone that I live in poverty.

STEINBRECHER: What about Mr. Urban?

FRÖHLICH: Not a living soul!

STEINBRECHER: At the interrogation of 4 February 1938, the witness Urban from the company Urban, Urban, & Urban claimed that during their clandestine meetings the aforementioned Fröhlich portrayed his situation in the worst possible terms. . . . What do you have to say to that?

FRÖHLICH: I had to tell him. Because of my raise.

STEINBRECHER: And your wife?

FRÖHLICH: She was the one who told me!

STEINBRECHER: From her statement we can conclude something else, Fröhlich. We can conclude that the two of you actually lived like kings! Naturally, she didn't know where the money came from.

FRÖHLICH: I didn't know about that! I swear to God! Maybe she lived like a king! I was always away on business! How could I know how she lived when I wasn't at home?!

STEINBRECHER: There's something else, Fröhlich. She claims it was you who insisted that this country is afflicted by poverty and injustice, while she tried to persuade you otherwise. . . . Why are you constantly trying to fool me, Fröhlich? Are you a damned pathological liar?

(Fröhlich parted with his consciousness for the third time. Something was done to him at this point, though Steinbrecher doesn't give any details. He only notes the time when the interrogation resumed.)

STEINBRECHER: Tell me, Fröhlich, what is it that makes you think life is miserable here?

FRÖHLICH: I didn't say that everyone lives in poverty. I said that I live in poverty.

STEINBRECHER: I say! In the whole of Germany—only you! Gustav Fröhlich, a salesman!

FRÖHLICH: Well, there are probably others who live in poverty.

STEINBRECHER: So you say that, besides you, there are many other people who live in poverty?

FRÖHLICH: Not many, but there are some. That's logical. There's no country without poverty.

STEINBRECHER: Have you traveled abroad a lot?

FRÖHLICH: No, Sir. Never.

STEINBRECHER: Then how do you know about life abroad? Whether there is or isn't poverty abroad?

FRÖHLICH: I made a logical conclusion.

STEINBRECHER: What logical conclusion? What kind of logic leads you to think that poverty exists everywhere? According to that logic, it's reasonable to conclude that we live in poverty, too.

FRÖHLICH: I don't know . . .

STEINBRECHER: Is it or isn't it?

FRÖHLICH: It is.

STEINBRECHER: Fröhlich claims that Germany is afflicted by poverty and that the National Socialist Party hasn't succeed even in providing bread for the Germans. Sign it!

FRÖHLICH: I didn't say that.

STEINBRECHER: What didn't you say?

FRÖHLICH: I didn't say the Party is to be blamed for everything.

STEINBRECHER: All right. We'll leave that out. But there's still the part that refers to poverty. Fröhlich claims that Germany is afflicted by poverty. Sign it!

FRÖHLICH: Can we add that the reason is the fact that we have to prepare for war?

STEINBRECHER: We're not going to go into details. It's enough to say reasons exist. Therefore—Fröhlich claims that because of the well-known reasons Germany is afflicted by poverty. Are you finally satisfied?

FRÖHLICH: Yes, I am now.

STEINBRECHER: Sign it, then. You're really difficult to satisfy, Fröhlich. You're a perfectionist in fact. I'm also a kind of a perfectionist. That makes all this easier. Speaking of that, let's polish up the part of the Transcript that refers to your so-called poverty. What's your salary, Fröhlich? How much do you earn a month?

FRÖHLICH: It depends, sir.

STEINBRECHER: Is your salary really that low?

FRÖHLICH: To tell you the truth, my salary isn't so low; however, my expenses are high.

STEINBRECHER: Prices are, consequently, prohibitive for the majority of the population?

FRÖHLICH: I didn't say that prices are prohibitive, I said they're high.

STEINBRECHER: What do we call prices that are too high for an average salary?

FRÖHLICH: Prohibitive.

STEINBRECHER: Why are you complaining, then? One always gets mixed up in some semantic crap with you! When you talked about this with Mr. Urban, did he sympathize with you?

FRÖHLICH: Yes, he did.

STEINBRECHER: Did he give you a raise?

FRÖHLICH: No.

STEINBRECHER: Why didn't he, if he accepted your reasons?

FRÖHLICH: He wasn't able to give me a raise due to the high cost of his expenses.

STEINBRECHER: His living expenses?

FRÖHLICH: His production costs. What I want to say is that his high expenses didn't prevent him from living well; they just prevented him from giving me a raise.

STEINBRECHER: Could something else be going on here? Maybe Mr. Urban knew that you had sources of considerable additional income?

FRÖHLICH: But I didn't have any.

STEINBRECHER: That remains to be seen, Fröhlich. In the meantime, let's confirm and sign that Urban complained about the situation, which he saw as an impediment to giving you a raise. Is that so?

FRÖHLICH: Yes. Where shall I sign?

STEINBRECHER: Sign here. Thank you. . . . However, Urban claims he didn't complain. He says you complained about the situation to him, and that in his opinion our situation is excellent. But that in your opinion Germany is going to hell in a handbag!

FRÖHLICH: That's a lie. He's the one who thinks that Germany is going to hell in a handbag!

STEINBRECHER: Then we'll put that you both share the opinion that Germany is going to hell in a handbag. It's obvious that Urban was very dissatisfied with the situation. Now, what do we call a person who's dissatisfied?

FRÖHLICH: I think . . . a malcontent.

STEINBRECHER: That's right. And if someone is dissatisfied with his country, can he be a patriot?

FRÖHLICH: I don't think so.

STEINBRECHER: That's right, Fröhlich. Consequently, Urban is an enemy of Germany.

FRÖHLICH: The swine! If I'd known that, I'd have informed on him myself!

STEINBRECHER: But you did know that, Fröhlich. You even shared his opinions!

FRÖHLICH: I never shared his opinions!

(Steinbrecher quotes the part of the Transcript in which Fröhlich claimed that he shared Mr. Urban's opinions, which proves once more that sharing your superior's views isn't necessarily smart if you're not sure what they are.)

STEINBRECHER: And what do we call it when a group of like-minded people meet?

FRÖHLICH: There were only two of us!

STEINBRECHER: Do you think it takes a thousand people to make a group? You learned at school what groups and sets are.

FRÖHLICH: In any case, a group consists of more than two people.

STEINBRECHER: No need to teach me the techniques of organizing subversive groups, Fröhlich! I very well know what *troikas* are!

FRÖHLICH: But there were only *two* of us.

STEINBRECHER: This is what we'll put down: Fröhlich claims that in the beginning they organized their meetings "in groups of two," and it was only later that they switched to a system of "troikas." Were you alone in the church?

FRÖHLICH: No. It was Sunday. The church was full.

STEINBRECHER: Then how can you prove that there were only the two of you and not more in the group? In principle, is there anything to keep two conspirators from being joined by someone else and then another . . .

FRÖHLICH: But we weren't conspirators!

STEINBRECHER: I'm asking in principle. You don't have to take everything so damned personally!

FRÖHLICH: No, nothing would keep that from happening in principle.

STEINBRECHER: Leave the principles alone, Fröhlich! It's the principles that got you in here! Did anyone ever join you during your conversations?

FRÖHLICH: You know, sir, it's a church. People know each other.

STEINBRECHER: And so they come up to each other?

FRÖHLICH: Yes.

STEINBRECHER: And thus they form groups of various sizes.

FRÖHLICH: Yes.

STEINBRECHER: Fröhlich claims that the church was the place where the groups were formed. Sign the statement. . . . Let's add "subversive" for the sake of clarity.

FRÖHLICH: Why subversive? People get together on lots of occasions, at the annual celebration of a fire department, for instance.

STEINBRECHER: Did you and Urban get together in order to go to the annual celebration of a fire department?

FRÖHLICH: No, we didn't.

STEINBRECHER: No, you didn't, Fröhlich, no, you didn't. Instead, you were involved in subversive conversations!

FRÖHLICH: For heaven's sake, Herr Hauptsturmführer, can't people talk about the weather sometimes?

STEINBRECHER: What kind of weather? The dark storm clouds gathering over Germany right now?

FRÖHLICH: No, the rain and sun!

STEINBRECHER: So did you and Urban always discuss the rain and the sun?

FRÖHLICH: Of course we didn't. . . .

STEINBRECHER: So you see? For God's sake, stop torturing me, Fröhlich! Don't you have a heart? Didn't you confess that Urban is the enemy of the state?

FRÖHLICH: Yes, but . . .

STEINBRECHER: And that you shared his opinions?

FRÖHLICH: Yes, but . . .

STEINBRECHER: Didn't you confess that you and Urban not only shared the same opinions, but met in a subversive group?

FRÖHLICH: Yes, but . . .

STEINBRECHER: And that you were involved in antagonistic conversations?

FRÖHLICH: That I didn't confess!

STEINBRECHER: But you will! Sit up! Raise your head! Look me in the eyes! Did you confess that you and Urban were enemies?

FRÖHLICH: Yes, I did.

STEINBRECHER: And you're not going to retract that? Let's hope not at least. Because in that case we'd have to start all over again.

FRÖHLICH: I'm not going to retract it!

STEINBRECHER: Can enemies have a friendly conversation? No, they can't. They can have only a hostile conversation. And what do we call a group that's engaged in holding hostile conversations?

FRÖHLICH: An enemy group.

STEINBRECHER: We'll say that Fröhlich confessed that for a long time he's been a member of an illegal enemy organization, whose objectives and connections with foreign intelligence circles will be discussed in detail during the next round of interrogation . . .

(Fröhlich signed the statement and went back down into his cell. The word "next" destroyed the last remnants of his pride, dignity, and sensibility. The next round of interrogation was only a hazy dream, hidden by the seven veils of the morrow. This round of interrogation was what counted, and that was what he'd had to save himself from. He'd be able to think up something by the time of the next round. In the end, the

organization could be reduced to only a few members. Mr. Urban—such a bastard anyway—his wife—also a bitch—Fröhlich himself, and perhaps someone else. Maybe that Schwartzkopf lady. His prospects didn't seem so bad after all, did they?)

THE TRANSCRIPT OF THE INTERROGATION OF GUSTAV FRÖHLICH

■ □ ■ □ ■

POSTSCRIPT 2

PROFESSOR KONRAD RUTKOWSKI'S SECRET TESTAMENT, OR *TRACTATUS LOGICO-PHILOSOPHICUS*

I. The Dichotomy of the Spiritual Man and Its Historical Origin in the Reality He Created by His Inability to Resolve the Dichotomy

I. 1. An intellectual's spiritual principles are the fruit of a tradition that he *himself* created in his conflict with reality—the reality that he *himself* likewise created in his aspiration to surpass it with some more faithful projection of his spiritual principles.

(I. 1. a. The spiritual principles of the Fabianites are the fruit of the rationalist tradition, which they followed *as intellectuals* in their conflict with the brutal reality of English industrial society, which, in the meantime, they built *as citizens*.)

I. 2. Since principles are idealistic in nature and are formed without any preconditions except in the spirit, which—as their creator—is sympathetic to them and thus unsuited to resisting them in earnest, they develop freely and without compromise, perfecting themselves independently of any kind of reality.

(I. 2. a. The majority of philosophical definitions confirm this state of affairs. The central ideas of systems of thought are mostly logical radicalizations with very little or no connection to real experience.

An unknown thinker says that man was created in the image of god; it is still too early to foresee whether Darwinism will claim that man was created from beasts, and in their image.

Thales considers water to be most perfect thing in the world.

Anaximander, however, claims that our souls, which are air, surround us just as air surrounds the world.

Pythagoras proclaims that all things are numbers.[29]

Heraclitus, for his part, suggests that good and evil are one and that souls in Hades have a pleasant odor. He also thinks that everything changes.

Parmenides opposes this with the assertion that nothing changes. Because if something is coming into being, then it doesn't exist, nor does it exist if it's just about to come into being. Something either exists forever or forever does not exist.

As the soul is preexistent and eternal, for Plato all knowledge is *memory.* And the basic elements of the material world are two kinds of right triangles, one which is half of a square and another which is half of an equilateral triangle.[30]

Aristotle allows that birth and death occur only from the Moon *downward;* from the Moon *upward,* everything is unborn and indestructible.

ZENO: Virtue is a solid material.

CHRYSIPPUS: A good man is always happy, a bad man always unhappy.

M. AURELIUS: The wickedness of one man does not cause harm to others.

ST. AUGUSTINE: The reason why the world was created in six days is that six is a perfect number.

T. À KEMPIS: God cannot make himself nonexistent.[31]

HOBBES: Life is the motion of the limbs, and freedom the absence of external impediments to that motion.[32]

DESCARTES: Cogito, ergo sum.

LEIBNITZ: This world is the best of all possible worlds.[33]

LOCKE: Things are good or evil only with respect to pleasure or pain, so that we call those good which cause or increase pleasure, or diminish pain. The greatest and most important goal of men who join together in a social community and subordinate themselves to the state is the preservation of their property.[34]

HUME: The SELF is a collection of diverse perceptions succeeding each other with incredible rapidity.

KANT: Infinite progress is possible under the presupposition of an infinitely enduring existence and an infinitely enduring personality of the same rational being, which is called *immortality* of the soul. Thus, the highest good is possible only on the assumption of the immortality of the soul.

HERBART: As they arrest or obscure one another, concepts lose as much intensity as the weakest of them possesses, and the arrested portion of the concepts affects the individual concepts in inverse ratio to their original strengths, so that, if in the simplest case $a > b$, a has after arrest a remainder of

$$\frac{a + ab - b^2}{a + b}$$

and b has a remainder of

$$\frac{b^2}{a + b}$$

FICHTE: The EGO can be conceived only insofar as it contrasts from some NONEGO, but since the NONEGO is nevertheless posited only in the EGO—a historically expressed object is posited only in the consciousness—the EGO and the NONEGO (i.e., the subject and object) can be defined only in the consciousness.

SPINOZA: Not a single virtue can be understood as existing prior to the instinct for self-preservation. The struggle for self-preservation is the first and only basis of virtue. Not one thing can be bad by what it has in common with our nature. The more a thing conforms to our nature, the more it is necessarily good.

HEGEL: The state is moral life in its concrete existence and real-ization, and thus the embodiment of rational freedom that realizes and sees itself in one objective form, and the German Spirit is the spirit of a new world, the aim of which is the realization of absolute truth as the infinite self-determination of freedom, that freedom which has as its content its absolute form.[35]

SCHOPENHAUER: Everything is nothing. And only in nothingness can we hope to find something.

NIETZSCHE: If we believe in morality, we condemn life. Morality must be replaced with the will to attain our goals and the means to do so. The courage of natural instincts must be returned to man. Self-depreciation must be eradicated. The contradictions must be removed from things, since it is evident that we were the ones who put them there in the first place. Social idiosyncrasies—crime, punishment, justice, humiliation, freedom, love, etc.—must be eliminated. Our holiest convictions, which reside in us constantly in the form of the highest values, are the outcome of our physical strength. The best preventatives and medicines against nihilism are universal compulsory military service including wars, where everything is dead serious; a national conscience that simplifies things and puts them into perspective; better nutrition, mostly meat; more cleanliness and hygienic living; the domination of physiology over theology; and military discipline in the execution of one's duties.[36]

BERGSON: We are free when our actions emerge from the whole of our personality, when they express it and bear a semblance to it that cannot be defined, but which is occasionally found between an artist and his work.

W. JAMES: An idea is truthful as long as believing it is beneficial to our life.

HEIDEGGER: Since direct existence, as "potentiality-for-Being," also includes "the not-yet" in the mode of existence of the possibility of "coming into being," and since as yet unrealized human possibilities belong to man's existential being, then *man always exists ahead of himself.* In the being of the existent, nothing is nullified.

CARNAP: Heidegger's thought, "In the being of the existent nothing is nullified," is meaningless because "nothing," which is the absence of everything, cannot be used as the name of an object and thus for the presence of something, and because, even if "nothing" existed, by definition no activity could be extracted from it, not even "being nullified."

WITTGENSTEIN: The majority of positions and questions that

have been presented concerning philosophical matters are not false but meaningless. Thus, to questions of this kind we cannot give any answer but only establish their meaninglessness. And thus it is not strange that the most profound problems are not even problems at all. If an answer cannot be given, then no question can be asked either. There is no mystery. If a question can be asked at all, it can also be answered. But if something cannot be discussed, one should keep silent about it.)

I. 3. On the other hand, since reality is nothing other than the collision of opposites that must be reconciled in order for reality to exist at all, the world is only a form of compromise; reality is only a collection and series of compromises, of which the first is inherent in the very origin of reality: its transience is only a compromise between complete nonexistence and eternal existence.

(I. 3. a. The number of examples of this is practically unlimited and the principle can be successfully applied to all forms of life, thought and existence. Our solutions are compromises between necessities and our limitations. Philosophy was at first a compromise between theology and life, and then between theology and science. The traditional ethic of the liberal society of the nineteenth century was, with the aid of rationalistic ideas, based on a compromise between Christian values and the principles of a capitalist economy, between love for one's neighbor and the exploitation of that neighbor. In the area of history, compromise is in the final account the single a priori condition of events. Thus, the Polish state was a historical compromise between the imperialistic aspirations of Germany and Russia. Our defeat in 1945 was a compromise between the defeat of Great Britain in 1940 and the defeat of the Soviet Union in 1941. Deportation to a concentration camp was a compromise between the murder and release of innocent people, etc., etc.)

I. 4. The Spirit and Reality are developing in two opposite directions—the Spirit toward heaven and Reality underground, the Spirit in unceasing progress toward ever more perfect ideals and uncompromising demands, and Reality sinking ever deeper into reconciliations that make of it a monstrous product. And the abyss between them grows ever wider, according to the spiritual principles of irresolvable contradictions. Thoughts and Words, and then Words and Deeds—which should be one and the same, since otherwise Thought has no meaning, Deeds are erroneous and Words useless—become irreconcilably antagonistic. Reality tries to tame thought, and thought tries to defeat and alter reality. In a spiritual person, as a creator of both the one and the other, this dichotomy must be resolved. Otherwise it leads to the self-destruction of the spirit, or the spirit rebels and attacks some aspect of reality accessible to it.

(I. 4. a. On the grand scale of humanity, this is how revolutions occur, and on the smaller scale—how personal scores get settled. Like my kicking Sabina, for example, for which this Treatise, I hope, offers a final explanation and satisfaction. Everything else is the physician's task. As an intellectual, namely, I also nurtured very elevated spiritual principles, based on a tradition that was formed by people like me, but on the pretext of a reality that we also created. The war into which I, allegedly without consent, was sent, was declared by me. I and my spiritual forefathers made it possible and even necessary. But it nevertheless took me by surprise, as if it were an accident and lacked any connection to myself. In denying responsibility for it, I also denied my own reality, as if one were capable of disowning his own hand whenever it commits a deed that his thought is ashamed of. However, I felt that the dichotomy was not resolved by this. I knew that if I didn't succeed, I was headed either for insanity as the self-destruction of my spirit or for some senseless act of vengeance against an insignificant aspect of that reality—say, Standartenführer Steinbrecher.)

I. 5. Progress in history doesn't exist. Progress in history is logically impossible, despite the appearance that it's made necessary by a dialectic expressed through the synthetic predominance of the contradiction between thesis and antithesis. Because what we gain by synthesis as compromise is always a form lower than the forms we already had in the thesis and antithesis. Assuming that any progress exists in history—except perhaps constant progress in the realization that no kind of progress is possible—is the same as hoping to mix red and white and get a third color that will be better than the two original colors. What we in fact get is a compromise: diluted red and diluted white. If progressive theories of the world view history as a slow yet continual ascent toward ever more complex and higher states of being, an ascent that over 500 billion years (which the astronomer Sir James Jeans guarantees the human race) will create and destroy 1,743,000,000 more civilizations (in addition to around twenty civilizations so far) and if cyclic theories reduce history to a tale told by an idiot, signifying nothing, then a compromise between these two theories leads us to the realization that history itself is only a compromise between progress and regress. Civilizations truly behave like living organisms that obey the laws of birth, aging, and death, and in the life cycle of each of them one can detect advances at least in the phases of their youth and maturity. But advances are relative and illusory if the process is viewed in its entirety. The historical process as a whole is controlled by an inexorable regression. But that retrogress is also revealed to be relative and illusory, if we put it in the context of the unlimitedness of time. In that context, we are neither advancing nor regressing, but standing still.

(I. 5. a. There was a time when the total destruction of the human race figured only as a theoretical possibility, completely in the hands of the gods. A few practical attempts at this, in the floods of the Jewish Noah and the Greek Deucalion, didn't have as a goal the destruction of the human race but rather its punishment and a slightly exaggerated warning for the future. Today, such destruction is completely within the bounds of the real and is in our own hands. Can that be called progress, even on the condition that this ability of ours is at the same time a victory over fate? There was a time when slavery existed for the benefit, immediate advantage, and good of the masters; today all enslavement is implemented in the name of ideals, very distant goals and for the good of the enslaved. And although the motives for contemporary enslavements are undoubtedly more ethical than they were at the time of Tutankhamen or Nero, can we really consider them progressive? In the circumstances of the depletion of the resources vital for the continuation of life of the planet, can the numerical increase of humanity be taken as progress? Especially if one considers that, along with the number of people, the problems connected with their survival and happiness multiply as well? If we claim our knowledge is continually progressing, we'll be in trouble if someone asks us: With respect to what? One can't know *more* in a world where one can never know *everything*. If we accept that we exist in infinity, we also accept the impossibility of progress, because no progress can be made in relation to something that goes on forever. In relation to that, we'll always be in the same place—the spot where we squatted down to start our first fire by rubbing two sticks together.)

II. A Typology of Solutions to the Dichotomy of the Spiritual
Man and the Betrayal of His Principles as a Consequence
of the Impossibility of the Spirit's Successfully Resisting
Its Creation in Reality

II. 1. Those rare loners, enthusiasts and creators of life resolve the inner conflict in that they, aware of their guilt, assume responsibility for it both before themselves and history, and thus struggle against their own works with the same relentlessness they had when they created them, and in so doing risk destroying themselves along with their creations. They are the Will, whereas reality is the Mind.

(II. 1. a. The graveyard of history is full of such heroes. We need mention only Fouché and Trotsky. And although my struggle against Nazism was only a shadow of the battle that those two waged against their very own revolutionary handiwork, they've earned my respect. For if I scorn those who say "Everything under the sun is vanity," I'm disgusted still more by those who say "I know, and that's enough"; however, I don't scorn those who say from on high, "I can, but why should I?"—I detest them. I love those who are willing to act. Even if they don't know, even if they're not able to express what it is that they want to do. Because "I'm willing to act" is already a deed, and deeds are the highest form of knowledge. The Will is the sole creator. Man must carry the primeval chaos in his bosom if he's to give birth to a star! And chaos reigns within such men! Such men are charged with the lightning that will strike us! They're filled with an insanity that they'll inject into us like a vaccine! For their spirit is free from guilt and they are free of heart. Their minds are only the insides of their hearts, and their hearts are filled with the chaos that gives birth to the light of stars! Stars are only born in explosions!)

II. 2. But such men, strong as they are, perish. By their nature, Deeds are stronger than the Creator, reality is stronger than the spirit.

(II. 2. a. The Idea wanted to be like Kronos and eat its own child, reality. What happened was the reverse. Reality appeared in the role of Zeus, who killed his father Kronos. Revolutions don't eat their children, but their fathers. The projection of the ideal, in fact, aims to devour the projection of the real, but ends up in its belly. But I love those who are unable to live except in downfall. Because where is there beauty but in the will?—Where I'm willing to perish only so one vision will not remain merely an image, and ideas merely words?!)

II. 3. And who survives? All the others do. The survivors are the weak and the frugal, those who can't live according to the ambitious principles of their own tradition and are unable or unwilling to restructure the world according their own ideas; consequently, they offer and accept every compromise with reality usually on the pretense that they're thus gaining time. They would say that this compromise is small and illusory, just a necessary and wise tactical concession, and that it will protect them until the first opportunity they get to bring about a reign of pure, spiritual principles, rejecting any agreement with the imperfections of reality.

(II. 3. a. But that never happens. The compromises multiply. It's in the nature of compromise to engulf everything, once it's become the sole form of existence. One compromise entails another. The second yields its place to a third. The third leads to a fourth. And they become deeper and greater. But only in their appearance. Because, just as there are no minor confessions, there are no minor compromises either. Every compromise is major and decisive. No more than a single germ is necessary to catch the smallpox. Whoever is ready to commit a small betrayal is capable of a great one. It's not the height that's terrifying, but the fall. If the height isn't important, every fall is equally hard. Let's illustrate the claim with my case. I entered the war over the pontoon of a compromise between the obvious impossibility of avoiding it and the hope of making it more bearable in my sphere of activity. The compromise that tasked me with humanizing the war led to other compromises, and they seemed to me to be very agreeable, especially since they unavoidably followed from the premise of the first compromise—my participation in the war. Therefore, when I slapped the clerk Adam it wasn't actually any kind of real blow but an ordinary compromise—a compromise between the need to beat him black and blue and the principle that said I shouldn't even have laid a finger on him. Reality demanded that I beat the hell out of him, but my Spirit resisted this: the God in Adam was protected by the principle of inviolability. That blow didn't originate in my shoulder but rather in the pure antinomy that in the end I succeeded in resolving. The second, higher degree of the same compromise on the path of humanizing the war was my beating of Rotkopf's worker. At first glance, it might seem paradoxical that the beating of people is accepted as a contribution to the humanization of reality. Nevertheless, in those harsh circumstances, it was a humanization, logically and unconditionally. Just as Rotkopf's beating of the same worker logically and unconditionally remained merely senseless torture. Because, in the Hauptsturmführer's case, the beating wasn't an expression of an effort to humanize the war. Thus, what in my case was only a small compromise on the way to good became in Rotkopf's case a crime, logically and unconditionally. The fact that I slapped Adam became my reality, in which I no longer felt any kind of contradiction between the slap and the elevated principles I was trying to serve. That was a concession I'd already agreed to, and if everything hadn't gone wrong, I'd have slapped people right up to the end of the war without remorse, seeing each one of them only as a single episode of my humanitarian mission. As slapping people had now become my working spiritual principle, whereas reality demanded that I murder the worker, I again resorted to a compromise: I beat him up and in that way saved him from death. The fact that he nevertheless died from my blows lacks any theoretical significance. That was an error in dosage, not in the motive. I did what I could. You can't expect the impossible, not even from an intellectual. In that sense, I could be satisfied. I had repaired reality within my sphere of activity: I substituted single blows for beatings, beatings for killings, individual killings for massacres. Even my failed attempt to murder Standartenführer Steinbrecher was a compromise between the already adopted principle of beating people and the reality that demanded that the Standartenführer be tied to horses' tails and torn limb from limb on the spot. Only from the standpoint of my intellectual obligations, I decided to kill him, to euthanize him so to speak, by shooting him in the medulla oblongata. The *formatio reticularis* was a quite suitable, minor compromise. The fact that those trivial compromises would undoubtedly turn me into a monster likewise has no significance, if the monster and his monstrous conduct were only one more compromise between a spiritual principle—that had now gone as far as an ordinary murder, a justifiable homicide—and a reality that would as always place exaggerated demands on one to destroy, for no reason, for no purpose or aim, in brief—to become a complete madman.)

III. The Regression of Reality as a Logical Consequence of the Sum of the Individual Dichotomies That the Spiritual Man Has Resolved through Compromise

III. 1. The reality into which those who betray their own principles are integrated cannot be perfected by such integration. It doesn't improve and come closer to those principles, but rather drifts away from them and thus deteriorates. The fact that in this initial phase (the phase of lower compromises between inner demands and external possibilities) men of spirit are aware of the lack of dignity of their conformism only appears to make things easier. It doesn't make things easier for the reality in which intellectuals act true to the obligations they've taken on and true to the renunciation of their principles; it makes it easier for *those very intellectuals* to mitigate their betrayal with the view that it's only provisional, a temporary protective measure chosen under the pressure of circumstances and under the constant control of their free will and thus is always ready to be renounced in more favorable conditions in the name of some uncompromising solution. That, of course, is never achieved, simply because under more propitious circumstances the spirit has more immediate worries.

(III. 1. a. An ordinary man will be satisfied with a murder, if it liberates him from the pressures of reality. And the case ends with that. He'll strangle his ill wife, not in order to end her suffering, but so the insurance policy can be collected. An intelligent person, however, won't be satisfied with such a vulgar justification. An intelligent man must rationalize his murder logically, with higher motives, he must spiritualize it with ideology, complicate it with precedents, in brief— he must give it a theoretical foundation. In history, the thirst for power and even clinical insanity often assume the elevated forms of historical necessity. The same thing happens in life. A murder committed by an intellectual can't be regarded as the product of alcoholic depression. That would be too shallow an interpretation. Such an explanation is perhaps suitable when compiling depositions for court cases in rural areas, but completely inadequate when one must explain why the educated professor of electrical engineering of the University of X. Y., whom we last saw nibbling on fruit and almonds after he'd so successfully masturbated and urinated, took an automatic pistol out of his briefcase and, instead of delivering his scheduled speech, started shooting randomly at the ladies from the Red Cross. That act must be connected with some horrifying image from a shattered childhood, which, through nihilistic conceptions of the world and according to the principles of electric circuits—in which charges of the same sign are repelled when they come into contact with a reality charged with the horrible ladies from the Red Cross—had to find a logical compromise in eliminating several of them. A negative charge was repelled by a charge of the same sign. The pistol ended up in the professor's hands accidentally. The fact that the ladies from the Red Cross wouldn't have killed the professor even if they had been armed proves nothing. They, no doubt, lacked the appropriate images from childhood. Let's transpose the example to the subject of my letters. Let's ask ourselves—what could the reality of the D. Sonderkommando of the Gestapo have been? What could it have been when it was commanded by a Steinbrecher who had already advanced so far in the field of compromises that he could express them in equations with several unknowns, equations in which the letters x, y, z stood for people? What could that reality have been when the only known quantity was a torrent of logical generalizations that brought those people into mutual relationships and into contact with death as the final conclusion, not unbearable in the least, by the way, because it was hidden in the innocent formula: $A + B + 3CH = 0$? What kind of reality was it that included the monstrous photo album of a professor of ethics, Sturmbannführer Freissner? That album, containing so many photographs of murders, was really a threefold compromise between a reality that offered abundant opportunities for murder, Freissner's spiritual principles that in principle refused those opportunities, and his natural criminal urges that craved them. And finally, how did Konrad

Rutkowski further the reality of the Gestapo according to his spiritual principles? With his improvements of that reality. What did those improvements consist of? It all depended on the level of a given compromise. Once it was a matter of a simple slap to someone's face, another time it was a beating, and occasionally, God knows, even aiming a pistol at someone's *formatio reticularis*.)

IV. Nihilism as the Rationalization of a Guilty Conscience

IV. 1. As said before, the conscience hasn't completely vanished. Paradoxically, this is indeed what's worst about it. In particular, it appears that this last remnant of common sense ensures that there will be future attempts to break the shameful alliance with reality. According to the inner logic of the dichotomous composition of the spirit, what happens is the opposite. The greatest danger for an intellectual in fact lies in the retention of that minimum of common sense. If it no longer existed, he'd fall downward like everyone else, in a *free fall*. His acceleration as he nears the bottom would be normal, determined by the universal laws of falling objects. However, now that his fall has begun, that tiny engine of common sense starts up, drawing fuel from the reserves of the conscience, and causes the whole damned process of ruination to reach a tremendous speed. The fall accelerates in proportion to the quantity of conscience retained. Under pressure from the conscience, the intellectual endeavors to extricate himself from the compromise with reality that he has accepted. He struggles with it. Reality never gives up anything once it has borne its brand. It never withdraws. It attacks. It places conditions even more difficult for survival on our revolted, combative intellectual. The compromise into which he's forced in order to save himself is always more difficult than the previous one, which is now being betrayed. The new compromise must be accepted, not only because otherwise the party violating the agreement would be destroyed, but above all because he would thereby lose any possibility of continuing the struggle. Usually we think there's no point in abandoning all our prior efforts because of some insignificant worsening of conditions, especially when it was brought on by some stupidity on our part. By this time, reason is indeed called stupidity, and the conscience designated as insane. Of course, the rule only holds for weak intellectuals, those who have no will of their own. It doesn't hold for the strong ones, but they don't exist. By their very nature, the strong can't be intellectuals.

(IV. 1. a. If I hadn't tried to intervene on Adam's behalf and thereby attempted to improve the reality of the Gestapo, he wouldn't have been detained, let alone questioned. If I hadn't tried to save him by falsifying the transcript, which was a compromise between imbecility and intellectual vanity, Adam would have certainly been hanged [he wasn't killed because he was guilty, but because he was *there*], although I wouldn't have had to choose between my own death and the killing of someone else, between being beaten or beating someone I didn't know.)

IV. 2. Plummeting from compromise to compromise, reason itself begins to sense how untenable the dichotomy is. It detects the dangers of continually rejecting the compromises it has adopted. The conclusion is reached that inertia is the only state in which a fall decelerates. But no one can survive defenseless and with a guilty conscience (which will gradually become vaguer and vaguer until it dissipates into the collective guilt of whole nations and races). That guilty conscience will once more incite a revolt and accelerate the fall. And our intelligence will come running to our aid again. It, by the way, was to blame for the loss of our freedom, because it pushed us into trials that we weren't up to. It's only fair for it to find a way out.

IV. 3. The mind is put to work. It hurriedly collects evidence of the misery and nothingness of the world that is its own creation. An entire nihilistic defense system is prepared, in which all forms of spiritual fortification participate equally: the impenetrable ramparts of rationalistic philosophy, surmounted with the powerful turrets of science and dotted with ideological loopholes through which history snipes at men; the smokescreens of spiritualism, the sawtoothed barricades of the philosophy of relativism, whose sharp barbs point in all directions and block the approach of any definitiveness, because any definitiveness is a conclusion, and every conclusion is the gateway to a deed; the bottomless trenches of religion and mysticism . . . All instruments of the mind are assembled here to fortify a betrayal. And the logic thus born is the universal logic of a denial of life—the logic of death.

IV. 4. Nihilism proceeds in two directions that converge only at the conclusion. On the one hand, everything is declared to be an *illusion.* Naturally, in a world of illusion, not even betrayal can be real. It too is illusory. If the world does not exist, there can be no betrayal of that world either. On the other hand, everything is *worthless,* primarily because it is illusory, but beyond that it's worthless in and of itself. Everything is empty, repetitive, past. All our fruit is rotten. Everything we've done has been futile. All is vanity and vanity alone. Nothing is of any use for anything except ruin. And in a world of no value, betrayal can even be good. Because if this world is evil and condemned to ruin, everything that hastens that ruination is good.

(IV. 4. a. The denial of reality in all its manifestations, even in all its possibilities, has become the predominant idea of intellectual history. Even the strong among us, those who haven't broken down themselves, have gradually been seized by the hysteria of the destruction of values, which was induced by the weak and which suits them alone. They placed their strongest mental powers and even their noble creative will at the disposal of the need of the weak for systems that justify their weakness, whereby it is proved once again that an alliance of the powerful and the helpless, the strong and the weak, benefits only the latter. The *proactive* denial of reality combines happily with a *retroactive* denial, which is the product of an "analysis" of reality. To make a long story short, analyses of the brain and excrement led to the conviction that both are equally worthless if they have the same origin and the same fate, whereby in the analysis one proceeded from excrement as the initial postulate. Maybe the difference wouldn't have been discovered even if the brain had been taken as the premise, but it was symptomatic that excrement was nevertheless selected as the model. Soon we won't even have a heart any more! But who cares?! In exchange we'll dispose of its mechanical, acoustic, and electrical characteristics and be able to replace any of its movements with the electrocardiograph signs $P, Q, R, S, T.$ We'll reach the point where instead of eyes we'll have only an accommodation index. We'll see by means of $B = D + A$ or $A = B - D.$ Ordinary people will differ solely by virtue of their diopters. Maybe we'll persecute the colorblind and burn them at the stake as heretics. The nobility will be recruited from those who, suffering from optical agnosia, can't see the point in the objects of reality. Their small numbers will be the guaranty for their nobility and their right to power. The aristocratic principle will finally receive fundamental scientific support. The ruling class won't be based on heredity, inasmuch as their illness isn't either. The democratic principle will be preserved in such a way that the leader will be chosen according to the degree of complexity of the equation expressing his deviation from the norm. You might think that such a method of selection is a step in the wrong direction, but that's only because you're viewing it from the wrong angle. A very advanced specimen of this kind was Standartenführer Steinbrecher. For him the world was a fairly primitive illusion, which he accepted only as a convenient occasion for reflection. The world, translated at first into concepts and then into formations of concepts in the guise of equations, became merely a logical simulation in which various concepts entered into various mutual relationships. The massacres that resulted from them were the consequence of the fact that people, as the contents of those concepts, adhered to their own logical forms and simply acted on their inevitable conclusions. A lower reality submitted to a higher, spiritual one. There was something Hegelian in all this. Killing a man without touching him, only by reducing certain frequencies to zero, was already in and of itself wondrous. But isn't my humble attempt to express the struggle for one human life in terms of the various combinations of pieces on sixty-four black and white squares also wondrous?)

IV. 5. Therefore, words take the prerogatives of living beings, and their intersection begins to replace the real world. Soon even words will become superfluous. They'll be replaced by the initial letters of concepts and then by numbers. People, of course, will keep suffering and dying, but they'll endure it more easily, because misfortunes will lose their critical significance for life and become logical categories. In the long run, concepts will perhaps entirely free themselves of real content, and so the end goal of the intellectual—the idealization of reality—will be attained. But there's still some time before that happens. In the meantime, the poison of nihilism is succeeding in infecting everything of any value, power, or influence, in subjecting everything to ridicule and finding a negative side to everything.

(IV. 5.a. In the world of the Gestapo, the process of idealization was in full swing. Intellectual euphemisms such as "the solution to the Jewish question" blossomed abundantly. There were "cleansing operations," "scientific experiments," and "emergency pacification operations." On a larger scale there were various "equalizations," the "acquisition of living space," and the "New Order," etc. Behind logistical formulas like AO, NSDAP, BDM, DNB, FS, GFP, HJ, KdF, KZ, NSKK, RSHA, SD, SS, VoMI, WVHA, WNV, FU III, etc., etc., elite National Socialist realities existed and operated comfortably. Our Gestapo was only one of them. Enormous scientific plans for the transformation of the world rested in dossiers with labels that read *Case Green*—one would think it had to do with forestation—*Case White, Sea Lion,* or *Barbarossa.*)

IV. 6. Need it be stressed that an intellectual can only scorn such a life? The fact that he himself is to blame for it, doesn't take away his right to scorn it. On the contrary. That right thus becomes even more justified. Because who can know the shortcomings of his work better than the creator himself? But, at the same time, he fears life as well. He hates the life he's betrayed, a life that now, of course, doesn't offer him anything but new betrayals and deeper falls.

V. Nihilism as the Co-Creator of the World

V. 1. Because nihilism—both its overt version and its covert version that hides beneath optimistic doctrines—is the prevalent philosophy, it has sovereign power over the formation of new levels of reality. And it's natural for nihilism to shape them according to the monstrous features of its own sense of guilt. The chasm between spiritual principles and reality deepens. It seems that the guilty conscience ought to deepen with that chasm. Surprisingly, the opposite happens. The greater the fall, the milder the pangs of conscience. The deeper we sink, the farther the bottom becomes. This, of course, is a psychological illusion. As our downfall continues, our sense of guilt slips into ever-deeper layers of our subconscious, from which to the conscience everything appears totally unclear, isolated, and insignificant. And while our lives are slogging through muck, our spirits still bathe in the clear waters of knowledge.

(V.1. a. When I hit Adam, it was a greater shock for me than when I beat up the worker—up until I learned that he'd died—because the latter act was safeguarded by my fear for my own life. Long before I neared the bottom, while there was still hope, I thought that I was finished. When I got close enough to see it, it seemed that I needed only a little more effort to save myself.)

V.2. Constructing an alibi for itself, nihilism has undermined the foundations of the struggle to alter reality. By refusing to acknowledge the world and denying it, the need for the world to be altered is delicately removed. If something doesn't exist, save as an illusion, then why replace it with anything else? If evil is everlasting, then why the wish to change the unchangeable? If we deny in principle that anything has any value, then changes aren't worth anything either. An intellectual arrives at the conviction that it's impossible to fight evil and that for the Spirit the only possible position is to be detached and neutral. And because neutrality is more often than not impossible—collaboration is the only option.

(V. 2. a. When Standartenführer Steinbrecher ordered me to take part in organizing the execution, I carried out my task with extreme care, as I had been taught a lesson by my bad experience with falsifying the Transcript.)

V. 3. Alienated even from our sense of guilt and, because that's our sole unmistakable mark, alienated from the essence of the world, we begin to hate that world, as if it had been created not by our own hand but had always been here. We flee from it in disgust into a molehill of personal security. We finally feel relieved. We think that a way out has finally been found and that the dichotomy has been resolved to everyone's satisfaction: reality is happy, and our all principles are present and accounted for. Or as the Greeks put it:

και το ψωμί σωστόν, και ο σκύοζ χορτασμέυοζ*

(V. 3. a. For we don't love the world as creators, as those who give birth and who are joyous when things come into being; we hate it as destroyers do, because it's a creation of ours that we're ashamed of. It's pointless to believe a divine soul is woven into our knowledge, because deep down we know that even if we waited pregnant on the horizon for centuries, we'd never give birth to anything but excrement. We prefer to be merely spectators and not to be out in the blazing sun. We languish in the icy shadows of concepts like the ghosts of great, betrayed ideas. Our mouths are full of limy words, so that the naive might believe our hearts are full of them, too. But

*"Just as the bread is good, the dog is sated."

they're not. They're empty. They're as empty as the jugs that will be smashed on Judgment Day. Because whoever doesn't believe himself and his own gut instincts is lying to himself and everyone else! And he's only good for creating—and then destroying—one last little world where the last little man will skip from rock to rock, searching blindly for the causes of his ruin.)

VI. Nihilism as the Destroyer of the World

VI. 1. Everything strives for equilibrium; everything demands to be counterbalanced. A suppressed feeling of guilt seeks expression, and if it can't get that through legitimate and conscious paths of engagement, it will surface in the form of prevalent ideas that obsessively lead one down the path to ruin. In the majority of cases, the prognosis is as follows: depressive psychopathy accompanied by delusions of rebirth and the salvation of mankind.

VI. 2. If such insanity is given the opportunity to gain a foothold in history and become one of its driving forces, the results are worldwide movements, religions, fanaticisms, or collective missions. But if, on the other hand, these individuals fail to grab hold of history, they write delusional books or rush through the streets bearing crosses on their backs, foaming at the mouth and brandishing knives. In the first case, the escalation of insanity sometimes even assumes the guise of civilization. Entire state machineries are placed at insanity's disposal so it can create a new world with their help and according to its own warped image of itself. In the second case, the story ends in an insane asylum. When all is said and done, I have to say I don't see any particular justice in that.[37, 38, 39]

Part III

Editor's Notes

■ □ ■ □ ■

Note 1, page 22

Although it is still too early to speak of any abnormality in Professor Rutkowski's thoughts and behavior, it is time to acquaint the reader with the consultation team charged with forming an opinion about the origin and type of Rutkowski's abnormality on the basis of his correspondence. Let me introduce Dr. Schick first. In his opinion, Rutkowski was suffering from a mental illness, most likely hereditary, long before the breakdown became so painfully obvious in his altering of reality according to the models of the ideas preoccupying him. In fact, he viewed Rutowski's pathological hatred of grammatical and orthographic mistakes as the first sign of this. His striving for perfection, his desire for impeccability and intolerance of mistakes are clear evidence of a mental imbalance. A person who is obsessed with thoughts of perfection is undoubtedly a psychopath, and in our case a psychopath of the cycloid type, whose symptoms resemble manically melancholic psychosis combined with paranoid delusions. At that stage, however, there was not yet anything indicating that this was a matter of psychopathy in the form of a mental illness; rather, his war on orthographic mistakes appeared to be one of the many exaggerated and imbalanced activities characteristic of otherwise normal people. However, Dr. Schick's opponent, Prof. Dr. Birnbaum, held the view that even later

Rutkowski could not be said to have a mental disorder; nor was he insane in the clinical sense of the word. Rather, all his abnormal actions, even the most unexpected of them, were within the possible parameters of a healthy, albeit idiosyncratic, human brain. According to the third member of the consultation team, Prof. Dr. Holtmannhäuser, Konrad Rutkowski had up to September 1943 been a healthy and normal human being of above-average intelligence, with a powerful imagination, an extensive education, and a healthy moral instinct; he went insane only when he was faced with a set of circumstances that his mind could not comprehend and his conscience could not condone. The editor does not have a view of his own, but leans toward the most dangerous version, according to which Konrad Rutkowski's insane behavior was the consequence of the retrograde orientation of an otherwise shining example of a human mind.

Note 2, page 28

The editor does not know where Rutkowski got the idea that Steinbrecher committed suicide; there is no evidence of this at all in the official documents and statements. A possibility is that he hallucinated it (Dr. Holtmannhäuser maintains that Steinbrecher's "suicide" was a surrogate for the execution that Rutkowski failed to carry out. This is supported by the fact that he credited himself, at least indirectly, with the Standartenführer's death. Thus, he killed him nevertheless!)

Note 3, page 34

For those who prefer dry facts, here are some from the biography of Konrad Rutkowski. He was born in 1916 in the territory of the K.u.K. Austro-Hungarian Empire, in Bavanište—Pančevo district, southern Banat—the son of Johann Georg Rutkowski, a farmer of moderate wealth, and Magdalene née Schlegell. He was the third child of this family whose origin was undoubtedly Slavic. The time of its settlement in Pannonia, according to tradition at least, is connected to the expulsion of the Husites in the fifteenth century. He was baptized Konrad Adrian in the Evangelical faith. He completed the grammar school in Pančevo with very good grades, except in history and Latin, where he was outstanding. With assistance from a fund of dubious origin and purpose, he studied medieval history at the University of Heidelberg from 1934 to 1938 and received his doctorate there in 1940 with a thesis on German-Polish relations before the Reformation. That same year he was awarded the post of assistant instructor at the Pančevo Grammar School. In 1941, he failed to respond to the mobilization call of the Yugoslav High Command and was pronounced a deserter; immediately after the arrival of German troops that year, he became a member of the SS and an agent of the RSHA (i.e., its Section IV, the Gestapo) as a second lieutenant (*Untersturmführer*) and then a first lieutenant (*Obersturmführer*). He performed his police activities in the Belgrade sector, except during two brief periods, both in connection with special operations: first in D. on the Adriatic coast, and later at the end of the year in Turjak in Slovenia. Between those two operations, he was treated in the Belgrade Military Hospital for something that was recorded in the hospital protocol as "extreme nervous exhaustion." In 1944, he again experienced problems with his health, but he recovered fully by the end of the year, and an examination by the Allied military authorities declared him completely healthy and fit to stand trial (he was subject to criminal proceedings as an SS officer and a member of the *Geheime Staatspolizei*). He was sentenced to a year of so-called work rehabilitation, after which he spent two years without permanent employment or place of residence, right until his former professor brought him to Heidelberg as a lecturer in his department. From that point on, his academic career flourished, and his name gained recognition in Polonistic circles both in Germany and abroad.

Note 4, page 52

According to Goering's directive of 10 February 1934, "the police exists to (1) execute the will of a single head, and (2) to protect the German people from all attempts at destruction by internal and external enemies. In order to achieve that goal, the police must be *omnipotent.*" It seems, however, that Steinbrecher, while imagining the ideal police force to be omnipotent, did not envision it as subordinated to any power higher than itself. In the Standartenführer's view, all police power should stem from the very nature of the police and develop independently of all other circumstances, like the self-development of the idea of absolute power, in the sense in which the Hegelian world is only the development of an idea. When he spoke of the "police state" (as did St. Augustine about the divine state in *De civitate Dei*) he was not thinking of a state that would employ universal control as one of its instruments, but of an idea of universal control that would employ the state as a form of itself. At that point the problems of the police ceased being historical, legal, and sociological—they became ontological.

Note 5, page 59

Of all religious conceptions of heaven, only the Viking version can be compared to Steinbrecher's. In contrast to all others, it is characterized by uninterrupted fighting and unrest, conditions which are quite alien to our visions of heaven. Not even in Valhalla does battle end for the dead warriors. Every day the god Odin holds a feast for the most worthy of them, and every day the dead fight to the death again for their places at the table. It is comforting, however, that those killed are resurrected the next day for a new battle and that their chances for a feast with God never vanish completely. Chosen by the Valkyrie during the earthly battles for Heaven, you are not retired when you finally end up in Heaven. On the contrary, whereas on earth you had a little peace between wars, in Valhalla you must hack away at each other day after day, eternally, without rest.

Note 6, page 63

All county administrations and township authorities of the Kingdom of Yugoslavia compiled registers of subversive, unreliable, and disloyal elements (as well as any others that were for any reason suspicious) for the needs of the regional administrations and the Ministry of Internal Affairs. According to one administrative circular, in the case of an enemy invasion such registers were to be destroyed. Unfortunately, many administrations and authorities did not comply with this instruction, and the Gestapo made extensive use of them in the organization of preventive police measures.

Note 7, page 64

The editor has established that Professor Wagner, allegedly because he was busy, never read these letters addressed to him. This is indeed a fortunate circumstance, if one considers the passages that concern him. Had Professor Wagner known about them, he would not have permitted the publication of the correspondence of his disloyal brother-in-law.

Note 8, page 102
Professors Schick and Holtmannhäuser considered the appearance of Adam's ghost to be a combined optical-accoustic hallucination, although the latter subsequently changed his mind in favor of a nightmare. Professor Birnbaum had a considerably more complicated explanation. He maintained that the whole episode had occurred in Konrad Rutkowski's mind, that it was a conversation prompted by his bad conscience, his sense of guilt for Adam's fate, projected into a psychopathological vision. He allowed that the whole tale of Adam Trpković's posthumous appearance had no basis in truth and that the letter of 17 September 1965 was a kind of *hieroglyph,* beneath which was hidden Konrad Rutkowski's conflict with himself. In brief, lacking the courage to confess this conflict—as he would do later—Rutkowski utilized literary symbolism and offered what was his mental reality in the guise of a story.

Note 9, page 130
Steinbrecher's remark was true for all services of the RSHA, especially the SD (Sicherheitsdienst). At the trials of the members of the Einsatzgruppen in 1947–48, which carried out the annihilation of racially inferior elements in German lebensraum, most of the twenty-one defendants had a university education, and more than half held doctorates. One of the most talented members of the service and a colleague of Rutkowski's at Heidelberg, Professor Dr. Franz Six, was an SS Brigadier-General (Oberführer) and achieved great success in the extermination squads throughout Russia. Another prominent intellectual, popular because of his mania for viewing everything as an object of scientific analysis (à la Steinbrecher), Otto Ohlendorf, was an SS Gruppenführer (i.e., Lieutenant General) and the commander of the mobile SS units in Russia. Without considering the remaining senior officers, the general corps of the SS offered an impressive picture of academic and intellectual prowess. The highly educated members of this elite caste included,

among others, the following SS generals: Bender, chief of the judicial department of the Waffen SS; Günther D'Alquen, the first publisher of the SS organ *Das schwarze Korps* and the chief of the propaganda section of the military forces in the war; Dietrich Otto, director of the press section in the Ministry of Propaganda; Wilhelm Keppler, Hitler's economic advisor; Professor Dr. Karl Gebhart, director of Hohenlychen Hospital and chief health consultant for the SS and the Gestapo; Paul Körner, the Prussian secretary of state; Hans Lammers, chief of the Reich Chancellery; Alfred Rosenberg, chief of the party foreign policy section and minister of the eastern territories; Günther Reinecke, chief justice of the Supreme Court of the SS and the police; Wilhelm Stuckart, state secretary of the Ministry of Internal Affairs and author of the immortal Nuremberg laws; Walter Schellenberg, Deputy Chief and subsequently Chief of the Foreign Intelligence Service of the SD and Himmler's personal adviser, then chief of the entire German intelligence service (after Canaris' fall); Oswald Pohl, director of the SS Economic and Administrative Central Office (WHVA), which included the inspection office of the concentration camps; Arthur Nöbe, who as the commander of the criminal police from 1933 to 1945 was the commander of the extermination squads; Joachim Mugrowski, professor of bacteriology and director of the SS health office; Otto Meissner, chief of the presidential office under both Hindenburg and Hitler; Ernst Grawitz, president of the German Red Cross; Dr. Karl Clauberg, main chief of the sterilization of Jewish women in Ravensbrück and Auschwitz; Walter Buch, presiding judge of the party tribunal; Philipp Bouhler, chief of the Office of Euthanasia; Dr. Karl Brandt, Reich Commissar for the People's Health; Werner Best, legal adviser of the SD and the Gestapo, etc., etc. . . .

Note 10, page 154
Space limitations make it impossible to offer a coherent picture of the SS Empire, or Civitates SS, which in the austere and unnatural conditions of the war symbolized the future organization of the new Europe. However, so the reader can become familiar with the spiritual environment in which Professor Rutkowski had to struggle with his own conscience and the rationalistic intellectual tradition, a few characteristics deserve brief mention. Let's begin with some citations

from the speeches of Adolf Hitler, which provided the ideological basis for the Black SS Empire, just as Christ's teachings were the foundations of Christianity. In *Mein Kampf,* Hitler wrote: "Whoever views national socialism only as a political movement has hardly understood anything. National socialism is even more than religion. It is the will to create a new human being. Without a biological basis and a biological goal, a political platform is meaningless today." Thus, the biological type of the SS-man arose. But Hitler also said: "I free men from the restraints of reason that inhibit them, the unclean and humiliating poisons of their so-called conscience and morals, their desire for freedom and personal independence." Thus arose the historical creation of the SS State. And finally, Hitler said: "After centuries of whining about the defense of the poor and humiliated, the moment has come for us to decide to defend the strong from the weak. Natural instinct commands all living beings not only to defeat their enemies, but to exterminate them. The victor has always had the right to exterminate whole nations and races." Thus arose the philosophy and methods of the new state. Until the death of Röhm and "The Night of the Long Knives" in 1934, the history of the SS evolved slowly. Date of birth—1922. Origin—the need for a bodyguard to protect the leader of the party. Original name—*Stosstruppe Adolf Hitler.* Numerical strength in 1929—280 men. From 1929 onward, its commander was Heinrich Himmler (about whom his own racial specialist, Gottlob Berger, stated at Nuremberg that he was "of unassimilated, mixed race, completely unsuitable for the SS"). In April 1932, its numerical strength was barely 30,000; but later, at the end of the war, it would number more than 600,000 in the Waffen SS (the armed military units) alone, not including the other three branches of the SS—the Totenkopf Verbände in the concentration camps, the members of the RSHA (the police-intelligence service), and honorary members of the SS in all parts of the government apparatus. During the very last phase of its history, the SS showed signs of metastasis, and to a certain extent, contrary to its own racial codices, it included a French contingent in the SS Division "Charlemagne," a Dutch contingent in the SS Division "Niederland," Belgian contingents in the "Flandern" and "Wallonia" divisions, and a Scandinavian contingent in the "Nordland" Division. The population of the SS empire also ended up including

Slavic subhumans in the 14th Ukrainian SS Division, and Bosnian Muslims in the "Handžar" and "Kama" divisions. The process of transforming the racially unsuitable into higher beings, which was dictated by historical necessity, reached its apex with the declaration that Mongolians were honorary Aryans. Blacks were the only ones to whom the possibility of becoming thousand-year rulers had not yet been extended, and that was certainly because the war had not yet been waged on their racial territory. In the beginning, however, prior to the inevitable degeneration that befalls all great historical creations, the demands placed on a candidate for the SS were extremely high. They are most evident in SS Oberstgruppenführer Paul Hausser's program for the SS officer corps training school, in addition to the extremely complex and difficult racial prerequisites that had to be fulfilled by every candidate prior to acceptance. An hour of intense physical training preceded breakfast, which would have been reduced to Himmler's mineral water and porridge, had not the SS economic administration acquired a monopoly on the food industry, taking over the firms "Appolonaris" and "Mattoni." The period following breakfast was devoted to exercises in weapons training, which three times a week were substituted by ideological education in national socialist philosophy and practice, utilizing texts such as *Mein Kampf,* Walther Darré's *Um Blut und Boden,* and Alfred Rosenberg's *Mythus.* After lunch, the drill continued with new training exercises, which ended in late afternoon with an orgy of cleaning, scrubbing, polishing, and shining for a final inspection. The hygienic and aesthetic requirements were so strict—a fresh, Teutonic appearance had to be maintained at all times—that every third recruit failed to pass the weekly inspection at the gates of the barracks. The psychological and physical tests, by means of which a recruit became a regular member of the SS brotherhood, thereby receiving a cultic dagger, are described in the handbook entitled *The Soldier's Friend* and repeated in Gerald Reitlinger's book *The SS— Alibi of a Nation, 1922–1945,* of which we shall give only two examples. The candidate had to dig into the ground in a certain period of time, after which a tank would drive over that spot—regardless of whether he had succeeded or not. A candidate for the officer corps could be requested to stand calmly until a grenade was detonated on his helmet. Such training exercises, in addition to tried and tested racial prerequisites, created the biological and psychological basis on which all the remaining components of the SS Empire could be constructed: the legal component by the police services of the SS (the Gestapo, the Kripo, etc.); the diplomatic component by the SD; the economic component by the WVHA (Wirtschafts- und Verwaltungshauptamt, or the SS Economic Administration Central Office), which managed slave labor, property, and the useful body parts of the enemy and racially inferior persons, and even the initial scientific preparations for the euthanasia program and the medical experiments in the camps. The defeat in 1945, for which the members of the SS were certainly not to blame, prevented the successful conclusion of one of the most daring mass experiments in the history of an—in any case—already fairly *experimental human race.*

Note 11, page 175

To all appearances, Rutkowski was a rare exception among those who joined the police after 1933. On writing down this observation and following its logic, the editor himself fell into a common misconception—that prior to 1933 the police possessed other qualities, more humane and kinder—in any case more legal. And again that meant that a radical change occurred in the German police apparatus in 1933 and that after Hitler consolidated power the entire police force of the Weimar Republic was replaced by a gang of moral monsters spawned by the National Socialist revolution. The truth is astonishing. Statistics prove that in 1938 the majority of the police officials had been inherited from the *social democratic* regime. (In 1938, out of every 100 members of the police in Koblenz, only 10–15 had joined the service *after* 1933.) Their methods, of course, had changed radically and had been brought into line with the brutal nature of the regime. It nevertheless remains a fact that such methods, seen through the lens of unbiased statistics, were applied by those whom democracy must have taught a different attitude toward citizens and their rights. Gerald Reitlinger writes: "Although it was not centralized, the pre-Nazi police was militarized. It was armed and organized according to a military system of ranks. It operated in military formations, and many demobilized officers joined it." The explanation makes sense, though it is hardly comforting.

Note 12, page 206

We do not know how far back human memory reaches. In any case, it is not shallow enough to confirm Steinbrecher's impossible time of events. For me, as the editor of these letters, who (though not responsible for their factuality) cannot reduce his role to that of a blind mediator, the Standartenführer's statements were the first alarm signal and reason to doubt the reliability of Konrad Rutkowski's confession, especially with regard to the episode involving Adam Trpković. Namely, the Standartenführer's statements were untenable precisely from the point of view of the logic that he so swore by. It follows from his statements that he questioned Adam from 3:35 to 3:45, that is to say *ten minutes*. By 3:45 he was already holding the fateful List in his hands. If someone tried to tell me now that at 3:35 in the morning an elderly man, with poor eyesight, overcome with anxiety and fear as well as the indefatigable need to uphold the standard of his profession under all circumstances and *write in calligraphic script,* and after seventy hours of almost uninterrupted interrogation (even if it really was just like the professor presents it to us), could compile in only *ten* minutes a three-year-old list of thirty-nine persons, including their names, addresses, personal descriptions, and other information necessary for a model, impeccably organized Steinbrecheresque raid, I would think him a lunatic or a liar. The Standartenführer was not crazy, at least not in this sense. Therefore, he was lying. He was protecting someone or torturing Rutkowski. Most probably both. And the fact that Rutkowski did not realize this then can only be blamed on the shock he experienced instead of triumph. The reason why he did not later consider this rationally will be his advanced state in the mental degeneration he undergoes in these letters. I had to reject the assumption that Rutkowski was lying to us, and that Steinbrecher told him that morning WHO gave him the names on the list. It was illogical. People do not lie to their own detriment—at least not when they are justifying themselves before history.

Note 13, page 208

Local sources describe this raid as the worst of the entire war. None of those arrested survived. But the editor could not establish with certainty that they were all executed by Standartenführer

Steinbrecher. There is mention of a transport to Germany a month later, so that it's possible that some of them were sent north. As no one returned from there either, the question is entirely academic.

Note 14, page 208

Steinbrecher is referring to one of the most brilliant victories scored by the Gestapo against the French section of the British intelligence service in 1942, in which he apparently finds the prototype for his victory over Rutkowski. In the action known as DONAR, all the radio-telegraphers of the secret reception and transmitter stations in the areas of Lyons, Marseilles, and Toulouse were arrested. The stations were taken over by the Germans under the command of Bömburg and Kiefer, in cooperation with the Abwehrgruppe III F. Fu. (Fahndung-Funk) and the Kripo. Then a so-called FUNKSPIEL, or RADIO-GAME, was undertaken, a procedure which resulted in the radio transmitter stations continuing to function without the enemy becoming aware of the change in ownership. An extraordinarily delicate affair, especially when one considers that over time certain habits had inevitably been established on all the secret lines, by which each radio-telegrapher could be recognized on the other side of the Channel. If one desired complete success, it was necessary to imitate all those habits. Kiefer managed to do this, and owing to their direct contact with London, the Germans uncovered the entire British intelligence network in France in early 1943. The deception was halted by the German side in May 1944. However, the Germans didn't know that the English had finally discovered the trick and that the very important messages for the preceding two months had been fabricated and calculated to deceive them until the intelligence network required for the invasion had been reestablished. The blow was paid back with interest. The editor, to be sure, doubts that the victims of Operation Donar benefited from the accumulated interest at all.

Note 15, page 249

The editor examined the protocol of the laboratory of the Bone Tuberculosis Clinic near D. and found the name Konrad Rutkowski recorded under the third entry for 26 September 1965. The result of the laboratory examination is clear: it was a case of water mixed with mineral particles. The consultation team was not informed of this finding and therefore made no comment on it.

Note 16, page 258

Dr. Schick considered "Adam's ascension by umbrella" to be a paranoid visual hallucination. Dr. Holtmannhäuser generally agreed with this diagnosis, but added to it his opinion that the hallucination was not merely a symptom of the professor's hereditary condition but was at the same time part of his war against Steinbrecher. Since according to Dr. Holtmannhäuser the mental disorder arose as a consequence of his conflict with the Standartenführer's demonic personality, "Adam's ascension" was an episode of that conflict: with this essentially reactive hallucination of Adam's *escape from death,* Rutkowski was taking revenge on *his own* tormentor, scoring a victory over the Standartenführer which he was constantly deprived of in reality. Dr. Birnbaum persisted in his view that this was a matter of a fairly radical degree of psychopathy complicated by a familiar mechanism—*rationalization.* Rutkowski was preparing to kill the Standartenführer. He was obviously completely incapable of performing the task his conscience had assigned to him. To desist without reason would have meant shattering the last remnants of his moral dignity, which had already been eroded by his work in the Gestapo. What he needed was an irresistible alibi. In the domain of the real and the natural, one couldn't be found that wouldn't sound like miserable intellectual excuses. All that remained was the domain of the supernatural, illogical, impossible. Rutkowski failed to kill Steinbrecher *only because* he had been paralyzed by "Adam's ascension," which his mind refused to accept.

Note 17, page 260

The letter of 26 September was apparently intended to be the end of the correspondence. In it Professor Rutkowski informs Professor Wagner explicitly: "This is the last letter." Why then was it followed not only by the letter of 28 September but also by the lengthy continuation of five letters and the postscripts? The editor has four possible explanations. Three of them concern Rutkowski's decision to end the correspondence unexpectedly; one concerns his decision to take it up again just as unexpectedly. Either Rutkowski had decided to go over any possible conclusions concerning his career face to face with his brother-in-law at some later time, thinking at that time—on the 26th of September—that they were not yet ripe for a written formulation; or he had not arrived at any definite conclusions at all; or he had finally changed his mind (which is the least likely possibility) and quit trying to draw from his confession some decisive conclusion, a turning point for his life. (Just as the Pythagoreans, out of superstition, carefully smoothed out the imprints left by their bodies wherever they had spent the night, Professor Rutkowski too, through the *catharsis* of his confession, smoothed out all the uneven parts of his past and eliminated the monstrous imprint that his misdeeds had left in it.) The mental crisis between the 26th and 28th of September forced him to resume the correspondence. The members of the consultation team, as usual, had diverging opinions. Dr. Schick thought that the cessation and continuation of the correspondence represented the acts of a compulsive maniacal disposition and saw no purpose in seeking any kind of rationality in the acts of a lunatic, a rationality which, even when present, has nothing of the logic of our world's common sense. Dr. Holtmannhäuser, on the other hand, maintained that both decisions, though contradictory and made with the logic of a mentally disturbed person, had their justifications in the subject of the professor's mania. Rutkowski broke off the correspondence when he came to "Adam's ascension," the cause of his mental breakdown in 1943, although at the time of his description of it, in 1965, he was in a more or less normal state. When the recurrence of his previous mental condition resulted in a repeat attack, between the 26th and 28th of September, he *naturally* continued to write, this time *in his maniacal state*. (This explanation is perhaps satisfactory with regard to Rutkowski's decision to stop writing, but fails to account for his subsequent decision to begin again.) Dr. Birnbaum's view was that in both of these cases we have a quite common psychopathic instability that characterizes, to varying degrees, even the most rational people. On 26 September, Rutkowski was in the grip of a depressive psychopathic cycle and his actions were controlled by mistrust, doubt, and suspicion as pseudosymptoms of a persecution complex; namely, he thought that he had already confided too much to Wagner, whom he hated, and that in this way he had put himself at a disadvantage in his relationship with his brother-in-law. It would not surprise Dr.

Birnbaum if at that time Rutkowski had completely altered reality in favor of his suspicions—for example, if he imagined that Wagner had coaxed him into this confession just as agents provocateurs do, most likely in collusion with his sister. As for his opposite decision of 28 September, to continue the correspondence, it was made in a manic cycle in which Rutkowski not only no longer cared about "Wagner's police and espionage tricks" and his "provocations," but also felt an irresistible need to incite them with continued confessions, as do arrestees when they abandon their defense and find their final mental satisfaction in an orgy of self- accusation and self-denigration.

Note 18, page 261
Sabina Rutkowski confirmed that at the time her husband complained of certain physical problems. But, because the majority of them occur in maniacs, paranoiacs, and psychopathic persons, the consultation team was unable to determine the nature of the professor's condition. In fact, they made three determinations. Dr. Schick maintained that it was a matter of hereditary circular psychosis (Psychosis maniaco-depressiva); Dr. Holtmannhäuser claimed it was a form of paranoia known as paraphrenia, combined with delusional ideas; Dr. Birnbaum thought that it was a case of cycloid psychopathy in a particularly severe and somewhat atypical form.

Note 19, page 263
Having a so-called "black eye" in Treblinka was a tacit death sentence. Every camp inmate who was struck by an SS man during the day, and who had a bruise around his eye at the next day's inspection, was selected for the gas chamber.

Note 20, page 264
Holding the view that this question has a broader meaning and delves more deeply into the eternal imbalance between the satisfaction of the survival instinct and the principles of intellectual morality, the editor, on the basis of eyewitness accounts, statistical data and the HANDBOOK OF THE NATIONAL SOCIALIST GERMAN WORKERS' PARTY, has attempted to verify Professor Rutkowski's statement and to determine what his real chances would have been of refusing to join or insisting on leaving the Gestapo and the SS. Some quotations from

the handbook concerning the purpose, nature, and organization of national socialism's elite corps may serve as an introduction: "The Schutzstaffel is an independent party unit which is led by the Reichsführer SS. The first and most important task of the SS is to provide security for the Führer. At the Führer's order, the task of the SS has been broadened to include ensuring the internal security of the country. In order to accomplish this task, fighting forces have been created, unified and bound by ideology, whose members were chosen from among the best members of the Aryan race. . . . Every member of the SS must be imbued with the spirit and essence of the National Socialist movement. Both physically and ideologically, he will be suitably trained, so that both as an individual and in the structure of his unit he may be sent into a successful action, into the tenacious battle for the National Socialist ideology. Only racially impeccable Germans are suitable for this struggle. . . . However, the selection does not concern only men, because the aim of the SS is also the preservation of a pure-blooded race. Thus, an SS man may only marry a racially worthy woman. . . . Loyalty, honor, obedience, and fearlessness predetermine the actions of every SS man. His weapon bears the Führer's motto, MY HONOR IS LOYALTY. . . . Unconditional obedience is demanded. It follows from the conviction that the National Socialist ideology must rule. . . . Because of this every SS man is ready to blindly execute any command from the Führer or his immediate superior, even if this demands the ultimate personal sacrifice. For an SS man, fearlessness in the battle for his ideology is the highest virtue. He fights openly and mercilessly against the most dangerous enemies of the Reich: Jews, Freemasons, Jesuits, and the political clergy. At the same time, they will by their example convince the weak and wavering, who are not yet capable of finding their own way through the National Socialist philosophy of life." From this it follows that the SS was considered the most narrow elite of the nation and the race, acquired by sifting the German race through progressively finer and finer sieves—the NSDAP, then the SA. Members of the RSHA, and to a still greater degree the Gestapo, could thus be considered fourfold hybrid flowers of national socialism. This in and of itself reduced one's chances of leaving the Corps and the Police. The handbook does not even mention this possibility for members of the SS, which allows us to conclude that it was not an option. But to gain at least a certain sense of the problem, let us see how the mother organization—the SA—regulated such cases. In this respect, the handbook says: "In principle, membership in the SA is voluntary. However, it is the will of the Führer"—not even his wish!—"that every German be continuously educated in the National Socialist spirit from early childhood to old age. . . . An SA man may leave the SA if he no longer believes himself capable of performing all duties placed on him by membership in the Organization. With such an honorable basis, a member of the SA may, at his own request, receive an honorable discharge from the Organization. If, however, a member of the SA exhibits a lack of interest or proves to be just someone along for the ride, who joined the SA out of capricious or opportunistic motives, discharge from the Organization shall be applied as an official measure." The editor doubts there was a single case of an honorable discharge, considering the meaning of expulsion from the Party, which in another place in the handbook is enunciated in the following manner: "In connection with expulsion from the NSDAP, extraordinary care and a high sense of responsibility must be demonstrated. Expulsion is the most extreme punishment the Party has at its disposal. *Today it means a loss of one's livelihood and the loss of one's entire personal position.*" Under such conditions, asking Professor Rutkowski to leave the SS—as if it were a tennis club—would mean having no sense of proportion at all. Even his request to be transferred from the Gestapo to the front did not mean leaving the SS, but rather a transfer to the Waffen SS, the combat units of the same organization.

Note 21, page 270
The change in method during the age of the Inquisition was imposed by the belief that occult crimes are not by their nature individual. From the thirteenth to the seventeenth centuries, sorcerers and witches were treated as conspiracies against Christian civilization (approximately the way the National Socialists treated the Communists), conspiracies organized and led by Satan in his eternal battle with God and man. At a time when the church was identified with the governmental, economic, and social order, and when religion was the pinnacle of the legal system, magnificent witches appeared on flying brooms as the first conscious rebels against Order, the System, and the Holy Dogma of societies in Europe after

Christ, as the forerunners of the great rebels of the future. (They also appeared as real people, made of flesh and blood, in an artificial, android world and its simulated history, which this editor described as our current experience in his novels *1999* and *Atlantis*. [*1999* and *Atlantis* are Pekić's two science fiction novels (published after *How to Quiet a Vampire*, in 1984 and 1988, respectively). Pekić, realizing that the traditional concepts of historical time and space prevented him from arriving at the "true reality of human condition," turned to science fiction in order to offer "a new, although poetical, explanation of the roots, development and end of our civilization"—Translators.])

Note 22, page 276
In Rutkowski's regaining of his composure, so visible in this letter, Dr. Schick saw evidence for the theory of a periodic mania in which mental breakdowns alternate with almost normal states. Dr. Holtmannhäuser considered this letter in particular to be the strongest piece of evidence for the hypothesis of paranoia because, in spite of Rutkowki's apparent control over his powers of reasoning, delusional ideas are clearly present. For his part, Dr. Birnbaum believed that this letter finally confirmed his diagnosis of psychopathy of varying intensity.

Note 23, page 285
The letter was not finished. A period of illness intervened again.

Note 24, page 291
It was determined that, at the time, the local police station investigated the damaged inflicted on the property of the pensione and its guests. As the culprits couldn't be found, a group of hippie campers was forced to leave the area.

Note 25, page 298
On account of this statement, the consultation team began to complicate the numerous deviations from its original diagnoses. Thus, Dr. Birnbaum began treating the Professor Rutkowski's dementia as *intentional* (his personal contribution to psychiatry), a

kind of disorder a subject consciously puts himself into so as to acquire complete freedom of action, a behavior similar to taking drugs or giving oneself over to some absolute idea.

Note 26, page 306

It was at this point that Dr. Holtmannhäuser decided to change his diagnosis. Now it is something varying acutely between paranoia and paranoid schizophrenia, because the systematic nature of the delusions still speaks for the former; it is not present in the latter. The depersonalization speaks for the latter; it is not present in the former. According to Dr. Holtmannhäuser, Rutkowski began gradually to turn into Steinbrecher, taking not only the content, but also the form of his ideas, as well as his arrogant manner of disseminating them. The fact that Rutkowski became what he deeply hated and what he was struggling against was another piece of evidence for the irrefutability of the hypothesis.

Note 27, page 310

The concept of "a drive in the last car" is linked to an anecdote from Hitler's life. The Führer concluded one of his anti-Semitic speeches with the promise that after all his measures against the Jews Europe's entire Hebrew population would fit into one automobile. (Some believe that the lack of any significant Jewish resistance to their extermination stemmed from every Jew's belief that HE would be in that automobile. A very human delusion, I might add.)

Note 28, page 317

If the part of the letter from the sentence "Thus, this is how I want man and woman to be . . ." to the slogan "In the beginning was the deed" is freed of its prophetic pathos and superfluous intellectual euphemisms and thus reduced to its bare content, it may just as successfully be reported in the earthly words of the *Handbook of the NSDAP*: "The leader created the Party realizing that our people, if they wish to live and proceed toward the Golden Age, must led by an ideology inherent in the German nature. That ideology demands an above-average person. Because of this, the Party will always represent a minority at the forefront of society. It is the national elite, comprised exclusively of fighters ready to do anything to further the realization of the National Socialist ideology. As an ideological instrument of education, the Party is the leading body of the German people, and is responsible for the total proliferation of the National Socialist spirit. The NSDAP must totally dominate public life . . . The criterion for acceptance into the Party must be not bourgeois but military in nature, and the decisive factor for assessing the character of every candidate is his conduct in the face of the enemy. The qualities of a member must be: integrity, sincerity, honor, orderliness, leadership ability, group spirit, reliability, fairness, independence, bravery, and decisiveness. A fighting spirit, devotion, and strength of character are qualities of a true National Socialist. A National Socialist is obligated to ask himself daily whether he can justify his conduct before the Führer. . . . Whoever does not know how to obey orders will never be any good at giving them. Never invoke your position. Only one position exists, and that is the position of Movement. . . . The basic principle of the Party is the principle of leadership. All senior officials are appointed by the Führer and responsible to him, but have unlimited authority over their subordinates. A leading member of the Party may not be weak and sensitive even for a moment. . . . The 'Führer principle' is a structure of pyramidal form, at the head of which is the Führer. The household is the lowest level of the National Socialist community. A household is the organizational community of citizens living in the same apartment, including their servants. A block consists of 40 to 60 households. The Blockleiter is the lowest leadership position in the NSDAP. Among other duties, he uncovers enemy elements and reports them. He must not only be a proponent of the National Socialist ideology, but must also gain the active cooperation of the members of his Block in implementing it."

Note 29, page 351
A contemporary Pythagorean would have no difficulty in proving that his teacher was correct. It would be sufficient to cite the role of numbers and counting in our lives. He could support his argument by citing the replacement of the names of concentration camp inmates with numbers, statistical analyses of human development, symbolic logic, computer operations, etc. Problems would arise only if he tried to convince us that the greatest misfortunes of the human

race stem from loving to eat beans, touching a white rooster, or sitting on a balance.

Note 30, page 351
A definition that could excite only a surveyor.

Note 31, page 351
A fairly heretical view for a saint, which verges on a denial of God's existence. For, if omnipotence is one of his essential qualities, the inability to make himself nonexistent disqualifies him as God. But the ability also disqualifies him. For, if he is omnipotent and can also not exist, he is not eternal and thus does not possess that other essential quality of God.

Note 32, page 351
According to Hobbes's definition, a man confined in a cell of two by three meters is also free.

Note 33, page 351
Nothing can be said against this; Leibnitz' definition is simply disarming.

Note 34, page 352
From this definition, it follows that the USSR was established exclusively for the purpose of protecting private property. Regardless of Locke's reputation, I doubt that Russian capitalists would concur with his view.

Note 35, page 353
The descendent of Hegel's convoluted definition was a law adopted on 15 September 1935 in Nuremberg that clarified it, in one area at least. Excerpts from the law read as follows: "A marriage between a Jew and a German or his blood relative is prohibited. Extra-marital relations between such persons are also prohibited. Jews are prohibited from employing women of German nationality. Jews are prohibited from displaying national flags and colors" (LAW ON THE PROTECTION OF GERMAN BLOOD AND GERMAN HONOR).

Note 36, page 353

Only a half a century after his notes on *The Will to Power,*
Nietzsche's compatriots borrowed from his discussion to compile
the training regulations of the SA, which read as follows: "National
Socialism is guided by two ideas, the idea of the community and
the idea of the individual. In the SA in particular, the mutual
relationship between the individual and the community must take
a form commensurate with its task of being the tool of the ethnic strengthening of the people. The goal of the training is to enable
the SA leaders and SA men to educate the broadest possible
group in the National Socialist ideology and the physical harden-
ing connected with it. To this end, three main programs of training
have been developed: (1) ideological, (2) general, (3) operative service. These programs cover the following areas: (1a) education and
training based on the goals and teachings of the Führer, as formulated for all aspects of our life and of National Socialist philosophy in *Mein Kampf* and the Party Program; (1b) instruction in
history of the German people and its values with regard to the tasks
of our day; and (1c) a practicum in the National Socialist doctrine of duty; (2a) unit duties; (2b) physical education; (2c) drill;
(2d) field training; (2e) weapons training; (2f) antigas and anti-
aircraft defense; and (2g) service in special units (navy, engineers,
cavalry, and the field of intelligence); and (3a) parades and demonstrations; (3b) competitions and qualifying tests; (3c) the security
service; and (3d) the emergency service." Who would believe that
on 3 January 1889, on the Carl Albert Square in Turin, Nietzsche—
that predecessor of Konrad Rutkowski—threw his arms around the
neck of a nag that had been beaten by its driver and went insane at
that very moment? And who would believe—if he did not know
about Rutkowski's case—that immediately afterward Nietzsche
conceived the idea of his missal to the Holy Father, in which he
announced to the Divine Representative on Earth and *Urbi et Orbi:*
"Nietzsche wants to unite and rule Europe as the Crucified. Let
the emperors of Europe and the Pope meet in Rome on January 8.
I'm coming on Tuesday!" (After which similar letters were also sent
to King Umberto, George Brandes, Strindberg, Burkhart, and so
on.)

Note 37, page 368

In part VI, section 2 of his *Tractatus Logico-Philosophicus,* in one of his lucid moments, Professor Rutkowski discusses the escalation of insanity in history. This is a significant and bitter confession for a man who openly agreed with Freud that "our greatest hope for the future lies in the Intellect (the scientific spirit, reason) over time attaining a *dictatorship* in the inner life of mankind." (It has already almost reached this state, but nothing in our lives is any better.) So why does he now radically reject the Intellect as a precondition for progress? Why the charge that it was the Intellect that, once it betrayed its calling, led to the individual, collective, and even historical insanity that Professor Rutkowski would so enthusiastically and wholeheartedly join company with in the next few pages of his correspondence, immediately after he packaged his *Tractatus* into the postscript? What were the *real* roots of his mental breakdown?

The doctors gave their opinions. The editor considers them conventional to a considerable extent, with the exception of Dr. Birnbaum's *temporary* hypothesis of *voluntary* insanity, which was rife with possibilities, and which was where the editor bid his final farewell to Konrad Rutkowski.

It has been known from the very beginnings of philosophical thought that man is made of clay and that, as such, he is subject to all forms of manipulation. At that time, the manipulators were the gods, of course. The Trojan War was the consequence of a vain quarrel on Mount Olympus, which men were dragged into as the executors of higher plans. All subsequent scientific interpretations reestablished this state of affairs in the area of interpersonal relationships as well as in the field of the individual's interaction with society. Thus, the problem was never to establish the fact of manipulation but to determine its extent, to define the limits within which men can be directed.

Investigations into the influence of advertising on a consumer society, of the mass media on our orientation, of various processes of indoctrination culminating with that of the "reform of ideas" (known in its final version by the name SZU—HSIANG KAO—TSAO) have indicated the sources, motives, and methods of manipulation, as well as the consequences for our lives.

It makes no difference whether manipulation occurs as an organic part of our education, for the purpose of the gradual assimilation of young individuals into the reigning social and spiritual system (of which the indoctrination in the traditional English public schools is an ideal example), whether it is carried out though advertising as an operational part of the free market, or finally whether it is practiced on fully formed individuals with the goal of reforming them and bringing them into accord with society's norms of thought and behavior. The purpose remains the same: the partial or complete alteration of the personality and its harmonization with some particular or general requirements of the community.

All the conditions required for manipulation are already present at birth. Manipulation is made possible first and foremost by the fact that our brain is a complex tool for adapting to the environment. A change in the surroundings in which we live provokes its vital action: a spontaneous process of adaptation begins.

Adaptation must not be understood as an acceptance out of necessity, however, though our being tends to behave in this way. Reality can be rejected. (What happens in that case is the subject of this note, inasmuch as it concerns Professor Rutkowski.) A change in the environment can be accepted, if it suits the personality *as* it exists already, but it can also be rejected if it clashes with that personality, whereby the rejection sometimes acquires psychopathic dimensions.

If the brain were predetermined by its adaptive functions to accept reality, we would reach the somber conclusion that one is valuable only to the extent that he succeeds in integrating his organism as comfortably as possible into the existing conditions, whatever they might be. This would mean that the most intelligent Jews were those who, not choosy about their means, best adapted to the inhuman conditions of the concentration camps and that those who offered resistance were the least valuable and by definition even insane.

Normality, in the practical meaning of the word, necessarily includes the ability to respond rationally to the demands of our physical and social environment. A person who attempts to swim on dry land is by all accounts abnormal. But what if that person is swimming against the main currents of the social and spiritual environment? Or let us ask a still more delicate question: If a man, in defense of his own person, agrees to renounce it temporarily, is he insane? If survival is the basic task of the mind, the answer must be negative. A man who acts like a lunatic among lunatics need not be insane. He is only a conformist. And conformism is the oldest form of mental adaptation to one's environment. If we view our mind first and foremost as the means to a *better* life, which in the final count is what it is, then we must reconcile ourselves to the amoral consequences of that definition, no matter how much they contradict our elevated intellectual principles, which Konrad Rutkowski discusses in his *Tractatus.*

There exists, however, a mode of manipulation that has not been the subject of much attention. The reason for this is to be found in our habit of accusing others for all our difficulties. The blame for our misfortunes always lies with someone else, never with ourselves. Others are also to blame for our shortcomings. We are always just victims. *We* are being manipulated. Someone else is manipulating us. We are the eternal and perpetual objects of manipulation, even when we are by some chance the agent, when we are the ones who are manipulating others. (There is not a single investigator who does not complain about his prisoners' tormenting, terrorizing, and trying to manipulate him!)

The idea that we could simultaneously be both the object and subject of manipulation, that we could *manipulate ourselves,* never crosses our minds. But in fact it is SELF-MANIPULATION that is the most frequent form of adaptation to the world.

The point of this note is to prove that the onetime SS Obersturmführer and later professor of history at Heidelberg University, Konrad Rutkowski, was the victim of one such kind of self-manipulation, self-indoctrination, and that it was the cause of his mental disorder.

Every mental disorder is a gradual transformation into *another* personality. Just as the task of the exorcist is to drive out of the possessed person an evil spirit that has taken over that person's life, the purpose of psychiatric treatment is to free an authentic personality of a dysfunctional usurper. But for that to be possible, a theory of the development of mental illnesses must be established, and it must be determined why and in which ways the *other* personality manifests itself. In addition, it is necessary to determine the limits of treatment, the fine line between returning the patient into his first, authentic personality and implanting a *third* personality in him.

On this subject Freud writes: "It is said that any education is biased and strives to incorporate a child into the reigning social order, regardless of the value and stability of that order. If we are convinced that our society is full of shortcomings, it is unjust to place a psychoanalytically oriented educational program in its service. Education must be assigned another, *higher* goal, free from the social demands of the moment." Leaving aside the obvious fact that science will be deprived of any influence on education if it states that it advocates an *antigovernment* agenda, Freud maintains that the active meddling of psychoanalysis in the freedom of human choice is completely unacceptable and that psychiatry is bound *solely* to return the individual into the community as healthy as possible.

(The issue is complicated, because such a limitation is opposed by the very method of the sole possible treatment. Neuroses offer the best example. They arise as the conflict between the EGO, a set of demands made by instinctual life, and the SUPER-EGO, the demands that result from education in accordance with the prevailing system of values in society. Treatment consists either of adapting the EGO to the SUPER-EGO, which is *immoral* if the social order represented by the SUPER-EGO is immoral, or of replacing the SUPER-EGO with another set of values, which again is immoral if society is moral. In the latter variant, the doctor would treat the patient only for the purpose of sending him to the gallows healthy.)

The ordinary psychoanalytical method proved to be rather impractical. Even the provincial general practitioner who examined Rutkowski in D. concluded that he did not have enough time for such an approach. In an age where time has become so expensive, long-term treatment is hard to market. But, nevertheless, we might note that Rutkowski, through his correspondence, submitted to it after a fashion.

Scientific progress has shortened treatment time. Logical analyses by medical doctors (not unlike those of Standartenführer Steinbrecher), drugs, and hypnosis have enabled all of us, even those of us who are completely healthy, to take equal advantage of the blessings of recent medical advances.

A patient is given an injection of pentothal (sodium thiopentone), sodium amytal, or scopolamine, which frees the memory of its dirty laundry.

On the basis of Jung's word-association tests, a secret conflict is uncovered in the patient's soul, and it simultaneously reveals the accused's secret.

Of all forms of therapy, posthypnotic suggestion seems to be the most suitable and most effective in the treatment of disorders of the psyche. (Its use for other purposes, however, does not seem likely at all. At first glance, it is very tempting to order someone to say or do something at some later time, while at the same time not knowing how the action was suggested to him. It is been claimed that some victims of Stalin's purges gave statements in such a state. Science has rejected that possibility. Posthypnosis has very uncertain effects. No conscientious investigator would rely on it if he already had family members as hostages or Rotkopf's pizzle whip at his disposal. Aside from that, to the great regret of the prosecutors everywhere, a hypnotized person will not commit acts contrary to his moral values and own personal interest.)

It would help to bring the reader's attention to the fact that Professor Rutkowski did not at any time, not even in his most acute state of deterioration, resort to drugs to free himself from the pressures of the past. It will be shown that his method was much more subtle. Rutkowski, from his Gestapo experience, knew that drugs *do not produce* either confessions of the truth or false confessions, as was suggested regarding the Great Moscow Trials, but rather that they only loosen the autocensorship as any anesthetic or even alcohol does, and that they do not change anyone's opinions but only their moods, thus creating a basis for the application of other methods. The one time he got drunk, drugging himself after learning that the monument had been erected to the "*wrong*" man, did not lead directly to his admission that HE WAS ONE WHO HAD KILLED THE RIGHT MAN, but to a hallucination, the posthumous appearance of Adam Trpković.

Let us review for a moment the history of psychiatry, because it helps us understand what is to follow. In 1933, Dr. Manfred Sakel discovered the positive therapeutic effects of an insulin shock on the early symptoms of schizophrenia. Dr. Cerletti added to them the successful effect of electrical shocks. Dr. Egaz Moniza finally introduced leucotomy: a surgical procedure that severs the links between the emotional centers of the thalamus and the cerebral cortex, where the sources of the illness are assumed to be located. The side effects can be considerable, occasionally even severe, but usually amount to an aggressive rebel being turned into a bland, conventional, ordinary personality.

Today, such operations have largely been abandoned. They have been replaced by a new generation of hallucinogenic drugs, stimulants, and sedatives: chlorpromazine (Largactil), isocarboxazid (Marplan), chlorprothixene (Teractan), amphetamine (Benzedrin), and especially lysergic acid diethylamide, or LSD. Nowadays they are used to return political madmen to normalcy, and the editor does not doubt that, had these drugs only been known at the time, the French Academy would have used them in the fight against the Impressionists, and bourgeois society against the first union leaders.

(To the above research one should add those experiments carried out with the goal of determining the reactions of the organism in conditions of space flight. A combination of sounds of different intensities can cause a nervous breakdown. Isolation in a sound-proof room causes hallucinations. The extraordinary difficulties of weightlessness, which can even include respiratory problems, have led many scientists to doubt man's ability to endure such conditions for prolonged periods of time without long-term consequences for his physical and mental health. Let us not lose sight of the fact that all those experiments were carried out *on earth* and that nothing except our conscience stands in the way of their being put to use for earthly purposes.)

One last thing we should mention is the crowning achievement of the unraveling of the secrets of the human soul. It lies without doubt in Pavlov's conditioned reflex, which Rutkowski discussed in one of his letters. In the process of self-manipulation, our professor passed through the three basic phases of the experiment. (I. THE EQUIVALENT PHASE: a dog secretes a certain amount of sputum regardless of the intensity of the stimulus. II. THE PARADOXICAL PHASE: the dog secretes more saliva in response to a weaker stimulus, whereas a stronger stimulus produces a protective inhibition and thus less salivation. III. THE ULTRA-PARADOXICAL PHASE: in this phase, positive stimuli produce a negative response and vice versa.)

Let us return to Konrad Rutkowski. We know wherein his problem lay. In trying to resolve his conflict with his own past, i.e., his conscience in relation to the past, he had three choices. Changing the situation that produced the stress was something he could not do. No one can change their past. Taking advantage of the effects of drugs that would influence the physiological processes that alleviate stress was not something he believed in. The only thing left was what he tried to do: to change his attitude toward the past. That would resolve the conflict. But it presupposed that he would come to agree with that past. To come to agree with it, he would have had to change his entire intellectual disposition, because his *old* attitude, as well as his current one, had rejected such a past while it was still the bloodstained present for Konrad Rutkowski.

The way this was done can be traced from letter to letter. In order to make the parallel between indoctrination or "thought reform" and self-indoctrination or self-reform clearer, the editor will give the table from Dr. Lifton's book *Thought Reform* and then transpose each phase to Rutkowski's mental life from 12 September to 5 October 1965.

Dr. Lifton distinguishes nine phases:

1. The destruction of identity.
2. The establishment of general guilt.
3. The self-betrayal.
4. Total conflict.
5. The desire for compromise.
6. The compulsion to confess (you can bet this will be satisfied)
7. The channeling of guilt
8. Reeducation
9. The state of complete harmony

1. *The destruction of identity.* The subject's profession, his academic title, rank, everything that makes him a *persona* is denied, and if any of that is acknowledged, its significance is denied. It is like accepting that someone studies history but at the same time claiming that studying history is beating a dead horse, the purpose of which is to cover up something much more sinister. The subject is prevented from having any contact with the outside world, except in the form of unpleasant facts; he is changed into a number and humiliated in every possible way. There are shocking descriptions in London's *The Confession* and in the interview with Dr. Vincent from Shanghai. Sleep deprivation is combined with the reduction of the subject to an animal that, bound in chains, must kneel down and eat food off a dirty floor. Rutkowski exhibits all these symptoms beginning with his first letter, in which he expresses doubts about

his scholarly endeavors and the sense of pursuing them. The process of disillusionment proceeds in several directions. He rejects history, which has led him astray. He begins to doubt whether anything like his "war on fascism" ever existed at all, except as an alibi for his evil activities. He suspects those in his immediate environment—his wife Sabina and his brother-in-law Hilmar (to whom in the meantime he confesses, just as a prisoner who constantly has suspicions about his investigator nevertheless continues to confide in him). Rutkowski is completely disoriented as to *where* he is, whether he is in a pensione in 1965 or the Gestapo headquarters in 1943. His contacts with the world are limited (to the "investigator" Hilmar, who really symbolizes his conscience and is thus all the more repulsive to him). In his confrontation with the past, he demeans himself at every turn. He suffers from chronic insomnia—he is not allowed to sleep because he must *write a confession.* And finally, that last link in the chain is present, which the editor thought was lacking in the letters. Sabina pointed out that when her husband arrived in D. he immediately began to feel some kind of physical inhibition, which made his movements seem slow and unnatural. W. James thinks that there are only two ways of freeing ourselves of hatred, worry, fear, and despair (feelings that characterized Rutkowski's state of mind on his arrival in D.): one is for us to be overcome with some stronger but *opposing* affectation, and the other is for our constant struggle against those feelings to exhaust us so much that we give up resistance. Resistance is exhausting. Conversions are built on this truth. In *The Devils of Loudin,* A. Huxley makes the cynical claim that even the most eminent philosophers of the best universities, if locked up for a certain time in a room with drums and Moroccan dervishes or entranced Haitian voodoo-dancers, would soon themselves begin to yell and dance in a frenzy around the fire. And the more consciously they resisted, the quicker they would do it. The first to fall from a cliff are those who try to keep from falling, not those who keep their minds on the climb. Rutkowski resisted; Rutkowski constantly found excuses for his actions during the war; he patiently tried to rationalize his treachery, seeking ever more complicated justifications for it. He tried wildly to resist the suggestions of Standartenführer Steinbrecher. All this is true. But the more he resisted, the more he thought about him. The first letters are almost entirely devoted to the Standartenführer and his satanic doctrines. One gets the impression that Rutkowski retells them with pleasure. The professor has already begun to dance—though not yet visibly— to the hypnotic music of the Nazi dervish. And all the while, his consciousness was echoing with a terrible, yet liberating, formula:

PRIZNAJ! (CONFESS!)

2. *The establishment of general guilt.* In this phase, a general state of guilt is established. (This theoretical phase is not particularly problematic for "researchers," and thus not for Rutkowski either, primarily because the sense of guilt is existential, and also because Rutkowski accepted his guilt to a certain extent from the very outset.) The meaning of this term is evident from an excerpt from the regulations governing work in Chinese prisons: "In dealing with criminals, one should regularly employ measures of corrective study classes, individual interviews, and organized discussions so the criminals will arrive at a realization of their guilt and a humility before the law, so the criminal nature of their offenses will be exposed, their criminal ideas completely eradicated and replaced by a new moral code." (This is the Eastern version of the Western psychodrama.) If we search for equivalents in the letters, we will find them in the studious manner in which they are written, in the constant return to the same problems, in Rutkowski's permanent state of *dialogue*—in which he found himself from the first line he wrote—with himself, Steinbrecher, Hilmar, Sabina, the philosophical ideas of the century, etc. In practice, the subject is released from solitary confinement, something always received with tremendous relief, and transferred to a joint cell, where he finds the *reconvalescents,* who are fairly advanced on the way to the reform of their ideas. In therapy groups, in continual sessions, they continue the investigator's work. Here it is not a matter of guilt being implanted into someone's conscience psychoanalytically, by collective suggestion, but rather of the conscience itself being excavated down to its deepest unconscious layers. False confessions are of no use. One must believe in his sin; confessing it is not enough. One must feel like a sinner. It is impossible to pretend you think $2 + 2 = 5$ when you will soon be assigned a task in which you will have to apply this math and where the mistaken result will show that you were lying and that $2 + 2$ is still only 4 for you. Sin in the abstract is never hard to find, no matter what condi-

tions have been stipulated. The Trotskyites thought badly of Stalin, stated this very often, and occasionally even undertook to act on this hatred. That was a real sin in which everyone had to believe, both the prisoner and the investigator. Who loved Stalin anyway? Here hatred seemed like the only possible sincere emotion and a confession seemed logical to the investigator, who was assumed to have worshipped that same Stalin. (Such a confession opens the door to all kinds of possibilities, which will be utilized in the phase of the channeling of guilt, when it becomes clear which ones most suit the current political needs. From that first compromise, the fall becomes inevitable and logical. When one accepts the idea that critical thinking represents a *legal* violation, capitulation is inevitable. Ideologies that assume the existence of objective truths, no matter what any of us might think of them, have the moral right to condemn those who do not accept such truths. Relativistic ideologies destroy men out of pragmatism, because they are in the way and not because they are in the wrong.) Let us return to our professor. Naturally, there are not any formal similarities with his case. The moment he accepted that he was guilty of something he could not have avoided, as otherwise he would have been destroyed (leaving the SS was impossible), his downfall was ensured. His attempt to lie about how for him $2 + 2 = 5$ (which is evident in his claim that he had to beat a man to a pulp in order to save his own life) proved to be futile as soon as he received the very next task: to tell how he questioned him. He needed to achieve a result that would show that, during the course of the operation, 2 added to 2 really equaled 5. In particular, that the worker was beaten and then somehow released from the Gestapo jail. However, the result revealed that for Rutkowski $2 + 2$ was still 4. The beating ended in death. And finally, what Rutkowski confessed to as a *sin* really was a sin. Killing people, under any pretext, despite all euphemisms, *is* a sin. Let us ask ourselves why Rutkowski broke. What kept him from breaking down when it would have been more natural, in 1943, rather than in 1965? Let the official report of the Defense Department of the United States of America, which contains data about the conduct of American soldiers held prisoner in China after the Korean War in 1953, assist us in this regard. Of 7,190 prisoners of war, 2,730 died; twenty-one decided to join the Chinese; of the remainder, every third soldier and officer was guilty of some degree of collaboration with the enemy: from anti-American propaganda to the brutal treatment of his compatriots in the name of new ideas. Of that third, seventy-five agreed to actively carry out espionage upon returning home. The only ones who saved themselves were those who showed no interest whatsoever in any kind of offer. After surviving a rather brief period of pressure, they were left alone. Everyone else broke. The more they relented, the more was requested of them. In comparison with the Americans, the conduct of the Turks from the Turkish contingent of UN forces is astonishing. Of 229 captured Turks, not a single one could be accused of collaborating with the enemy. In contrast to the individual conscience of the American soldier, which had been damaged by a lack of understanding of what he was really fighting for, the group conscience and authoritarian (i.e., patriarchal) order among the Turks provides evidence that a united group can resist more successfully than even a strong individual. (This, as an aside, leads to the gloomy conclusion that one system of restrictions is most successfully resisted if another such system has already been accepted.) And the reasons why the American soldiers broke were the exact same reasons why Rutkowski gave in as well. He lacked group morale, the possibility of joint resistance with his memories. He never attended a single postwar meeting of SS veterans, never met with anyone if he could help it, never spoke about his problem with anyone who might have been able to offer him a more sober explanation. He was alone, morally eroded, and desperate—just as alone, morally broken, and desperate as when he had attempted to wage an individual war against fascism and succeeded only in supporting it. He was alone, but his frightened soul resounded with the hellishly seductive echo:

T'AN PAI! (Confess!)

3. *The self-betrayal.* Paradoxically, it begins with the betrayal of *others*. In Rutkowski's case, it begins with tales of the sins and crimes of others, mainly Steinbrecher's, and continues with Adam's alleged sins and crimes. Then he gets trapped in a vicious circle of blaming everyone around him and even certain objects, which is when the first signs of his mental disorder becomes apparent. He thinks the guilt lies with Hilmar, Sabina, Adam's umbrella, etc. Rutkowski, indeed, realizes that someone must be guilty. Any possible attempt to betray an innocent person—which he described in the letter entitled "There Are No Minor Compromises"—would fail.

Thus, the victims of these betrayals must be guilty, by logic alone, because we as moral people would not have betrayed them were they not guilty. And once we admit that they are guilty of wrongdoing, we are automatically forced to confess our own guilt of the *same* cast. Because that voice is continually admonishing us:

GESTEHE! (Confess!)

4. *Total conflict.* As a consequence of the total mental confusion and the constant feelings of remorse—because a reasonable counterview of the matter has still been retained—there is mental disorder and a hysterical fear of complete destruction. A man feels helpless and abandoned, condemned without a hearing to be annihilated and leave no trace; just as a castaway feels when left to the mercy of the high sea and the elements. That is in fact fear of the ultimate punishment—hell, which is unavoidable because the law has not been obeyed. The Evangelists were famed proponents of hell. Reverend Taylor warns: "Hell has been at work for over 6,000 years! It grows fuller every day! And that goes on about 18 miles from here! In which direction? Straight down, 18 miles under us in the bowels of the earth!" So, is there any salvation for us? First of all, one must confess his sins and humble himself down to the level of the most wretched worm, in comparison to which even the worst cad is a genius of virtue, and then wait. What, even that won't save me? And what in the world must a man do to save himself? NOTHING. ABSOLUTELY NOTHING. NOTHING HE MIGHT DO CAN SAVE HIM. GOD DOES NOT SAVE MEN ACCORDING TO THEIR DEEDS, BUT ACCORDING TO HIS WILL, WHICH IS UNFATHOMABLE. Man can hope for salvation, but he cannot earn it. The Evangelical Church did not consider it sufficient for a believer to glorify God when he saves him, but also when he casts him into eternal torment. Especially then— His Name had to be praised especially then. This phase coincides with the first crisis, the first period of Rutkowski's mental delusion and lasts right up to his aborted suicide attempt. Suicide is in any case attempted most frequently in this phase. Later on, it is not considered at all. As for Rutkowski, at the same time, at the nadir of this phase, a decisive twist of fate occurs, which, through a path of insanity, leads to an acceptance of ideas contrary to his authentic personality. The voice, of course, keeps on repeating:

ПРИЗНАЙ! (Confess!)

5. *Seeking compromise.* In this phase, which borders on death, any sign of a peace offer or any kind of attention from the torturer, even the most wretched, is accepted with tremendous gratitude. The subject is prepared to pay any price for it. An extremely affective condition has made him vulnerable to any influence. Rutkowski enthusiastically accepts the offer to reject the past and all the torment connected to it in exchange for the recognition of a new doctrine (actually the old doctrine, against which he fought so unsuccessfully). The voice eggs him on:

CONFIESA! (Confess!)

6. *The compulsion to confess* is a natural continuation of the previous phase, and there is no boundary line between the two. In the continuation of his correspondence, Rutkowski finds more and more rational reasons for his wartime conduct, and fewer and fewer reasons for any concern at all in this regard. He is increasingly prepared to accept what he once unconditionally rejected, even a Steinbrecher! The voice keeps calling out:

AVOUE! (Confess!)

7. *The channeling of guilt* occurs with Konrad Rutkowski in a paradoxical way, corresponding to his state of insanity. Ordinarily it consists of a previously confessed guilt in the abstract (a crime against humanity in Rutkowski's case) being channeled into a materially tangible action (in Rutkowski's case, into the murder of the worker). This requires complete cooperation between the investigator and the interrogatee. The guilt must correspond to the possibilities of the accused and other circumstances in existence at that moment in time. It is not advisable to accuse a blind man of leading people across a border, or a deaf man of eavesdropping on confidential conversations. With Rutkowski, this channeling proceeds in a completely *opposite* direction. The magnetic pole of insanity disrupted all concepts in the investigation of himself that he was conducting. The abstract guilt of having worked in the Gestapo and having collaborated with a doctrine contradictory to his own convictions is *channeled* into a feeling of remorse that he was weak

enough to yield himself to such senseless thoughts of guilt at all. He is completely innocent, he has just been born, he has the right TO CHOOSE HIMSELF AGAIN. The voice still demands:

CONFESSERAI! (Confess!)

8. *Reeducation.* The subject studies the nature of his new ideas and how they differ from the old ones. In his final letters, Konrad Rutkowski, slowly but surely proceeds toward the Nazi doctrine and philosophy of life. The voice is persistent:

CONFESS!

9. *The state of complete harmony.* An acceptance of sinfulness means severing the link with the reality of God or something that, in its perfection, symbolizes God. This violates our natural desire to be a part of something greater, more stable, less mortal. With a public confession of sin, in the phase of rationalization and exploitation, the subject returns to the flock, though perhaps as a black sheep. But a black sheep is still a member of the flock; only a colorless one is a nonentity. The black sheep is accepted. It must bleat like a white one, but its black color never fades, and will always be its mark. True, by joining the flock we lose our personal freedom, but we also gain some communal ones: first and foremost, freedom from responsibility. Indoctrination, if it is successful, and conversion, if it is complete, assume not only unlimited and unconditional loyalty and submission to one line of thought, but also uncompromising and obligatory hatred toward everyone else: "When my heart was cold," Martin Luther writes, "and when it was impossible to pray, I tormented myself with thoughts of the Pope. My heart would be warmed by hatred and was again able to speak to God." Konrad Rutkowski's final letter entitled "How Professor Rutkowski Sold His Soul to the Devil, or *Beyond Good and Evil*" illustrates the stage of harmony. He is incredibly strong and happy, as if marching before his Führer in Nuremberg at the head of an SS regiment.

The conclusion is gloomy, but it would be unfair of us to blame it on Professor Rutkowski. No one can endure such a procedure without consequences. (Though they are most frequently contrary to one's intentions, as in his case.)

Dr. Brown correctly assumes that our illusions about the conclusiveness, perfection, and definitiveness of human thought and behavior stem from the fact that we always see people in the same conditions, which they have naturally adapted to; this does not allow us to conclude that in different conditions they would think and act the same way. We should add: if someone can briskly climb the stairs of a tall building, we cannot conclude that he could scale Mount Everest just as easily.

And do we know ourselves? Have any of us ever wondered how we would conduct ourselves if we were deprived of sleep, if we were spit on, if we were connected to the city electrical grid, if we were pierced with needles to discover the demonic zones on our skin, if we were thrown strappado onto stone floors, and so little was demanded of us in order to stop? What would we say in Rutkowski's place if we were offered to liberate ourselves from all the sins of the past in one fell swoop, and if the contract offered us an indulgence for all future sins?

We should bear in mind that there has never been a time when Power, outfitted with suitable prerogatives and means and un-encumbered by scruples, was incapable of inducing people to do what it wants. Lone heroes are the exception, not the rule. And let us hope we never have to join them in Valhalla. (The editor, however, thinks that no kind of subtle mental compulsory technique can replace the good old red-hot poker or its contemporary equivalent—electric shocks to the genitals—which were employed by French legionnaires and paratroops in Algeria.)

All we can do is hope that Mill's time will never come, when deviation from general opinions and nonconformism will no longer have any support, and that our great-great-grandchildren will not burn those who still believe the earth to be as flat as a pancake.

Note 38, page 368
The immediacy of our final farewell to Professor Konrad Rutkowski obligates me to report the results of my own research into "the case of Adam Trpković." The reason I did not present them earlier was my effort to keep from meddling in the story and not to take the suspense out of it. In a good detective story, the truth always arrives *late*—not too late to satisfy our curiosity, but too late to save the victims.

First I interviewed the inhabitants of D. First and foremost the

Trpković family and the current mayor, an active participant in the NOP. I also consulted the available Gestapo archives. In their defeat, the Germans proved not to be any more administratively conscientious than we are. During their withdrawal from the Balkans, the *entire* archive was not destroyed, contrary to what Rutkowski assumed. A few of their lists were saved, though in this case they could unfortunately also be called our lists. One of them was penned by the hand of the mayor of D. during the occupation. The date testifies that it was compiled before midnight on the day Obersturmführer Rutkowski was still wrestling with Adam Trpković, the day that would kill the future professor of Heidelberg University.

Those are the *facts* of the tragedy in D. But what of Adam? What are his *facts,* which make up his posthumous dust? Who was Adam? We will never know. While he was alive, we were not overly interested in him. When he died, we no longer knew how to learn anything about him. I myself succeeded in putting together a sketchy picture with the aid of various sources. It is not much, but it has one virtue: It was not reached exclusively by means of logic (if *x* then *y*). It is true that Adam was an insignificant cog in the municipal administration. It is true that he belonged to the People's Liberation Movement *only* as much as the entire local population did. It is even true that he was not expected to do what he did. But, no matter how insignificant, this "municipal file clerk and copyist in D., the official secretary and keeper of the Holy Protocol, *in summa* a state official of the former Kingdom of Yugoslavia, from the lowest and last gutter of the payroll" (Konrad Rutkowski: letter 1), he was not *ordinary.* On the contrary, he was very *unusual.* Some kind of eccentric, a Mediterranean "oddball." I, of course, don't know whether the story about the evil umbrella was one of his jokes. It would be logical if it were. Nevertheless, I would not make that claim. We at least know how things are with that "logic." What I do think, in light of all this information, is that he simply took in Obersturmführer Konrad Rutkowski—hook, line, and sinker. Rutkowski had been taken in by history, his own conscience, he had been taken in by the war and Steinbrecher, he was taken in by traditional philosophy, so why wouldn't Adam take him in as well? Whether Adam did this on a prankster's instinct, with premeditation, to protect his secret, or in some fit of equalizing premortal bravery, we will never know. I do not think that this is a bad end for any of them. What we do know is enough to compel us to bow down before the porphyry monument on the hill above D., saying:

ECCE HOMO—Now that was a Man.

Note 39, page 368

Konrad Adrian Rutkowski, Professor of Medieval History at Heidelberg University, died outside Vienna at dawn on 6 October 1965. His Mercedes hit an oak tree. The investigation determined that he bled to death. His abdomen had been pierced through by a men's umbrella, which he was holding in his hands instead of the steering wheel. There was a large pickax in the passenger's seat next to the corpse. The dust on it matched the stone of a damaged monument to Eugène Savoie in front of the Vienna Historical Museum. As no logical connection could be established between a German university professor, a pickax, Eugène Savoie, and an umbrella, the case was officially declared to be a highway accident and filed away. The editor's scientific consultation team diverged in their opinions one last time, very bitterly and arrogantly, it might be added. Dr. Holtmannhäuser concurred with the findings of the Vienna police: a highway accident caused by careless driving. Dr. Schick maintained that this was a case of murder, committed by one or more unknown persons. Neither version assumed any connection between the death and the professor's particular mental condition. Only Dr. Birnbaum's theory of suicide was based on that. As for the editor, he doesn't consider any of them correct, although Dr. Schick's view is the closest to the truth. He erred only in seeking the murderer among the living. The murderer was the umbrella. That was its way! Given all the circumstances, that was the only logical solution. Independent of the fact that it was found protruding from his abdomen—something suspicious in and of itself—the umbrella was cursed, from which it follows logically that it was the murderer, just as its evil nature inevitably and logically followed from that crime. But its demonic career has now come to an end as well. I have it, chained up and harmless, downstairs in the basement of my house here in London.

London
1971–72

GLOSSARY OF SELECTED
TERMS AND ABBREVIATIONS

Auslandsorganisation der NSDAP (AO) Foreign Organization of the NSDAP (for Germans living abroad)

Bund deutscher Mädel (BDM) League of German Girls (part of the Hitler Youth)

Deutsches Nachrichtenbüro (DNB) German News Office

Einsatzgruppen Extermination squads employed in Poland and Russia (tasked mainly with the killing of Jews)

Fernschreiben (FS) telex

Funk III (FU III) German counterintelligence radio monitoring

Geheime Feldpolizei (GFP) Secret Field Police

Hauptscharführer sergeant major

Hauptsturmführer captain

Hitler-Jugend (HJ) Hitler Youth

Kanzlei des Führers (KdF) Office of the Führer

Konzentrationslager (KZ) concentration camp

Kripo (Kriminalpolizei) Investigative police

Narodno-oslobodilački pokret (NOP) People's Liberation Movement (Yugoslav resistance organization during World War II)

Nationalsozialistische Deutsche Arbeiterpartei (NSDAP) National Socialist German Workers' (Nazi) Party.

Nationalsozialistischer Kraftfahrkorps (NSKK) National Socialist Drivers' Corps

Oberstgruppenführer general

Obersturmführer first lieutenant

Reichssicherheitshauptamt (RSHA) Reich Security Main Office

Rottenführer corporal

Schutzstaffel (SS) "Defense Staff" (Hitler's elite police and military units)

Sicherheitsdienst (SD) Security Service

Sonderkommando special detachment

SS-Wirtschafts- und Verwaltungshauptamt (WVHA) SS Economic and Administrative Central Office

Standartenführer colonel

Sturmabteilung (SA) "Storm Unit" (Nazi stormtroopers)

Sturmbannführer major

Untersturmführer second lieutenant

Volksdeutche Mittelstelle (VoMI) Ethnic German Central Office

Wehrmacht German armed forces (during World War II)

Wehrmacht-Nachrichtenverbindungen (WNV) Communications Channels of the Armed Forces (i.e, in the High Command)

■ □ ■ □ ■

ABOUT THE AUTHOR

Borislav Pekić was born in 1930 in Podgorica, Yugoslavia. A frequent political agitator and an occasional prisoner, Pekić worked as a screenwriter and an editor of a literary journal before publishing his first novel, at age thirty-five. In 1971 he began a self-imposed exile in London, where he died in 1992. His novels include *The Time of Miracles* and *The Houses of Belgrade*, both published by Northwestern University Press.

■ □ ■ □ ■

WRITINGS FROM AN UNBOUND EUROPE

For a complete list of titles, see the Writings from an Unbound Europe Web site at www.nupress.northwestern.edu/ue.